THE TESTAMENT

JOHN

GRISHAM

THE

TESTAMENT

DOUBLEDAY

New York   London   Toronto   Sydney   Auckland

PUBLISHED BY DOUBLEDAY
a division of Random House, Inc.
1540 Broadway, New York, New York 10036

DOUBLEDAY and the portrayal of an anchor with a dolphin are
trademarks of Doubleday, a division of Random House, Inc.

This novel is a work of fiction. Any references to real
events, businesses, organizations, and locales are intended
only to give the fiction a sense of reality and
authenticity. Any resemblance to actual persons,
living or dead, is entirely coincidental.

Book design by Paul Randall Mize

Library of Congress Cataloging-in-Publication Data applied for

ISBN 0-385-49380-0 (Hardcover)
ISBN 0-385-49381-9 (Large Print)
ISBN 0-385-49382-7 (Limited Edition)

THE TESTAMENT

ONE

DOWN TO THE LAST DAY, even the last hour now. I'm an old man, lonely and unloved, sick and hurting and tired of living. I am ready for the hereafter; it has to be better than this.

I own the tall glass building in which I sit, and 97 percent of the company housed in it, below me, and the land around it half a mile in three directions, and the two thousand people who work here and the other twenty thousand who do not, and I own the pipeline under the land that brings gas to the building from my fields in Texas, and I own the utility lines that deliver electricity, and I lease the satellite unseen miles above by which I once barked commands to my empire flung far around the world. My assets exceed eleven billion dollars. I own silver in Nevada and copper in Montana and coffee in Kenya and coal in Angola and rubber in Malaysia and natural gas in Texas and crude oil in Indonesia and steel in China. My company owns companies that produce electricity and make computers and build dams and print paperbacks and broadcast signals to my satellite. I have subsidiaries with divisions in more countries than anyone can find.

I once owned all the appropriate toys—the yachts and jets and blondes, the homes in Europe, farms in Argentina, an island in the Pacific, thoroughbreds, even a hockey team. But I've grown too old for toys.

The money is the root of my misery.

I had three families—three ex-wives who bore seven children, six of whom are still alive and doing all they can to torment me. To the best of my knowledge, I fathered all seven, and buried one. I should say his mother buried him. I was out of the country.

I am estranged from all the wives and all the children. They're gathering here today because I'm dying and it's time to divide the money.

I HAVE PLANNED this day for a long time. My building has fourteen floors, all long and wide and squared around a shaded courtyard in the rear where I once held lunches in the sunshine. I live and work on the top floor—twelve thousand square feet of opulence that would seem obscene to many but doesn't bother me in the least. By sweat and brains and luck I built every dime of my fortune. Spending it is my prerogative. Giving it away should be my choice too, but I'm being hounded.

Why should I care who gets the money? I've done everything imaginable with it. As I sit here in my wheelchair, alone and waiting, I cannot think of a single thing I want to buy, or see, or a single place I want to go, or another adventure I want to pursue.

I've done it all, and I'm very tired.

I don't care who gets the money. But I do care very much who does not get it.

Every square foot of this building was designed by me, and so I know exactly where to place everyone for this little ceremony. They're all here, waiting and waiting, though they don't mind. They'd stand naked in a blizzard for what I'm about to do.

The first family is Lillian and her brood—four of my offspring born to a woman who rarely let me touch her. We married young—I was twenty-four and she was eighteen—and so Lillian is old too. I haven't seen her in years, and I won't see her today. I'm sure she's still playing the role of the grieving, abandoned yet dutiful first wife who got traded in for a trophy. She has never remarried, and I'm sure she hasn't had sex in fifty years. I don't know how we reproduced.

Her oldest is now forty-seven, Troy Junior, a worthless idiot who is cursed with my name. As a boy he adopted the nickname of TJ, and still prefers it to Troy. Of the six children gathered here now, TJ is the dumbest, though it's close. He was tossed from college when he was nineteen for selling drugs.

TJ, like the rest, was given five million dollars on his twenty-first birthday. And like the rest, it ran like water through his fingers.

I cannot bear to recount the miserable histories of Lillian's children. Suffice to say they're all heavily in debt and virtually unemployable, with little hope of changing, so my signing of this will is the most critical event in their lives.

Back to the ex-wives. From the frigidity of Lillian, I ran to the steamy passion of Janie, a beautiful young thing hired as a secretary in Accounting but promoted rapidly when I decided I needed her on business trips. I divorced Lillian and married Janie, who was twenty-two years younger than I was and determined to keep me satisfied. She had two children as fast as she could. She used them as anchors to keep me close. Rocky, the younger, was killed in a sports car with two of his buddies, in a wreck that cost me six million to settle out of court.

I married Tira when I was sixty-four. She was twenty-three and pregnant by me with a little monster she named Ramble, for some reason that was never clear to me. Ramble is now fourteen, and already has one arrest for shoplifting and one arrest for possession of marijuana. His oily hair sticks to his neck and falls way down his back, and he adorns himself with rings in his ears, eyebrows, and nose. I'm told he goes to school when he feels like it.

Ramble is ashamed that his father is almost eighty, and his father is ashamed that his son has silver beads pierced through his tongue.

And he, along with the rest of them, expects me to sign my name on this will and make his life better. As large as my fortune is, the money won't last long among these fools.

A dying old man should not hate, but I cannot help it. They are a miserable bunch, all of them. Their mothers hate me, so the children in turn have been taught to hate me too.

They are vultures circling with clawed feet, sharp teeth, and hungry eyes, giddy with the anticipation of unlimited cash.

THE SOUNDNESS of my mind is of great issue now. They think I have a tumor because I say weird things. I babble on incoherently in meetings and on the phone, and my aides behind my back whisper and nod and think to themselves, Yes, it's true. It's the tumor.

I made a will two years ago and left everything to the last live-in, who at the time paraded around my apartment in leopard print panties and nothing else and, yes, I guess I'm crazy about twenty-year-old blondes with all the curves. But she later got the boot. The shredder got the will. I simply got tired.

Three years ago I made a will, just for the hell of it, and left everything to charities, over a hundred of them. I was cursing TJ one day, and he was cursing me, and I told him about this new will. He and his mother and his siblings hired a bunch of crooked lawyers and ran to court in an attempt to have me committed to an institution for treatment and evaluation. This was actually smart on the part of their lawyers because if I'd been judged mentally incompetent my will would have been void.

But I have many lawyers, and I pay them a thousand dollars an hour to manipulate the legal system in my favor. I was not committed, though at the time I was probably a bit off my rocker.

And I have my own shredder, one I've used for all the old wills. They're all gone, eaten by a little machine.

I wear long white robes made of Thai silk, and I shave my head like a monk, and I eat little, so that my body is small and shriveled. They think I'm a Buddhist but in reality I study Zoroaster. They don't know the difference. I can almost understand why they think my mental capacity has diminished.

Lillian and the first family are in the executive conference room on the thirteenth floor, just below me. It's a large room, marble and mahogany, with rich rugs and a long oval table down the center, and it's now filled with very nervous people. Not surprisingly, there are more lawyers than family members. Lillian has a lawyer, and so does each of her four children, except for TJ, who has brought along three to show his importance and make certain all scenarios are properly counseled. TJ has more legal problems than most death row inmates. At one end of the table is a large digital screen which will broadcast the proceedings.

TJ's brother is Rex, age forty-four, my second son, currently married to a stripper. Amber is her name, a poor creature without a brain but with a large fake chest, who, I think, is his third wife. Second or third, but who am I to condemn? She's here, along with the rest of the current spouses and/or live-ins, fidgeting nervously as eleven billion is about to be divided.

Lillian's first daughter, my oldest, is Libbigail, a child I loved desperately until she left for college and forgot about me. Then she married an African and I erased her name from my wills.

Mary Ross was the last child born to Lillian. She's married to a doctor who aspires to be super-rich, but they are heavily in debt.

Janie and the second family wait in a room on the tenth floor. Janie has had two husbands since our divorce many years ago. I'm almost certain she is living alone at the moment. I hire investigators to keep me posted, but not even the FBI could keep track of her bed-hopping. As I mentioned, Rocky, her son, was killed. Her daughter Geena is here with her second husband, a moron with an MBA who is just dangerous enough to take a half a billion or so and masterfully lose it in three years.

And then there's Ramble, slouching in a chair on the fifth floor, licking the gold ring in the corner of his lip, fingering his sticky green hair, scowling at his mother, who had the gall to appear here today with a hairy little gigolo. Ramble expects to get rich today, to be handed a fortune simply because he was sired by me. And Ramble has a lawyer too, a hippie radical sort Tira saw on television and hired right after she laid him. They're waiting, along with the rest.

I know these people. I watch them.

SNEAD APPEARS from the rear of my apartment. He's been my gofer for almost thirty years now, a round homely little man in a white waistcoat, meek and humble, perpetually bent at the waist as if bowing to the king. Snead stops before me, hands clasped at the belly, as always, head cocked to one side, drippy smile, and says, "How are you, sir?" in an affected lilt he acquired years back when we were staying in Ireland.

I say nothing, because I'm neither required nor expected to respond to Snead.

"Some coffee, sir?"

"Lunch."

Snead winks with both eyes and bows even deeper, then waddles from the room, his trouser cuffs dragging the floor. He too expects to be made rich when I die, and I suppose he's counting the days like the rest of them.

The trouble with having money is that everybody wants a little of it. Just a slice, a small sliver. What's a million dollars to a man with billions? Give me a million, old boy, and you'll never know the difference. Float me a loan, and we'll both forget about it. Wedge my name in the will somewhere; there's room for it.

Snead's nosy as hell and years ago I caught him picking through my desk, looking, I think, for the current will. He wants me to die because he expects a few million.

What right does he have to expect anything? I should've fired him years ago.

His name is not mentioned in my new will.

He sets a tray before me: an unopened tube of Ritz crackers, a small jar of honey with the plastic seal around the lid, and a twelve-ounce can of Fresca, room temperature. Any variation and Snead would be fired on the spot.

I dismiss him, and dip the crackers in the honey. The final meal.

7

TWO

I SIT AND STARE through the tinted glass walls. On a clear day, I can see the top of the Washington Monument six miles away, but not today. Today is raw and cold, windy and overcast, not a bad day to die. The wind blows the last of the leaves from their branches and scatters them through the parking lot below.

Why I am worried about the pain? What's wrong with a little suffering? I've caused more misery than any ten people.

I push a button and Snead appears. He bows and pushes my wheelchair through the door of my apartment, into the marble foyer, down the marble hall, through another door. We're getting closer, but I feel no anxiety.

I've kept the shrinks waiting for over two hours.

We pass my office and I nod at Nicolette, my latest secretary, a darling young thing I'm quite fond of. Given some time, she might become number four.

But there is no time. Only minutes.

A mob is waiting—packs of lawyers and some psychiatrists who'll determine if I'm in my right mind. They are crowded around a long table in my conference room, and when I enter, their conversation

8

stops immediately and everybody stares. Snead situates me on one side of the table, next to my lawyer, Stafford.

There are cameras pointing in all directions, and the technicians scramble to get them focused. Every whisper, every move, every breath will be recorded because a fortune is at stake.

The last will I signed gave little to my children. Josh Stafford prepared it, as always. I shredded it this morning.

I'm sitting here to prove to the world that I am of sufficient mental capacity to make a new will. Once it is proved, the disposition of my assets cannot be questioned.

Directly across from me are three shrinks—one hired by each family. On folded index cards before them someone has printed their names—Dr. Zadel, Dr. Flowe, Dr. Theishen. I study their eyes and faces. Since I am supposed to appear sane, I must make eye contact.

They expect me to be somewhat loony, but I'm about to eat them for lunch.

Stafford will run the show. When everyone is settled and the cameras are ready, he says, "My name is Josh Stafford, and I'm the attorney for Mr. Troy Phelan, seated here to my right."

I take on the shrinks, one at a time, eye to eye, glare to glare, until each blinks or looks away. All three wear dark suits. Zadel and Flowe have scraggly beards. Theishen has a bow tie and looks no more than thirty. The families were given the right to hire anyone they wanted.

Stafford is talking. "The purpose of this meeting is to have Mr. Phelan examined by a panel of psychiatrists to determine his testamentary capacity. Assuming the panel finds him to be of sound mind, then he intends to sign a will which will dispose of his assets upon his death."

Stafford taps his pencil on a one-inch-thick will lying before us. I'm sure the cameras zoom in for a close-up, and I'm sure the very sight of the document sends shivers up and down the spines of my children and their mothers scattered throughout my building.

They haven't seen the will, nor do they have the right to. A will is a private document revealed only after death. The heirs can only speculate as to what it might contain. My heirs have received hints, little lies I've carefully planted.

They've been led to believe that the bulk of my estate will somehow be divided fairly among the children, with generous gifts to the ex-wives. They know this; they can feel it. They've been praying fervently for this for weeks, even months. This is life and death for them because they're all in debt. The will lying before me is supposed to make them rich and stop the bickering. Stafford prepared it, and in conversations with their lawyers he has, with my permission, painted in broad strokes the supposed contents of the will. Each child will receive something in the range of three hundred to five hundred million, with another fifty million going to each of the three ex-wives. These women were well provided for in the divorces, but that, of course, has been forgotten.

Total gifts to the families of approximately three billion dollars. After the government rakes off several billion the rest will go to charity.

So you can see why they're here, shined, groomed, sober (for the most part), and eagerly watching the monitors and waiting and hoping that I, the old man, can pull this off. I'm sure they've told their shrinks, "Don't be too hard on the old boy. We want him sane."

If everyone is so happy, then why bother with this psychiatric examination? Because I'm gonna screw 'em one last time, and I want to do it right.

The shrinks are my idea, but my children and their lawyers are too slow to realize it.

Zadel goes first. "Mr. Phelan, can you tell us the date, time, and place?"

I feel like a first-grader. I drop my chin to my chest like an imbecile and ponder the question long enough to make them ease to the edge of their seats and whisper, "Come on, you crazy old bastard. Surely you know what day it is."

"Monday," I say softly. "Monday, December 9, 1996. The place is my office."

"The time?"

"About two-thirty in the afternoon," I say. I don't wear a watch.

"And where is your office?"

"McLean, Virginia."

Flowe leans into his microphone. "Can you state the names and birthdates of your children?"

"No. The names, maybe, but not the birthdates."

"Okay, give us the names."

I take my time. It's too early to be sharp. I want them to sweat. "Troy Phelan, Jr., Rex, Libbigail, Mary Ross, Geena, and Ramble." I utter these as if they're painful to even think about.

Flowe is allowed a follow-up. "And there was a seventh child, right?"

"Right."

"Do you remember his name?"

"Rocky."

"And what happened to him?"

"He was killed in an auto accident." I sit straight in my wheelchair, head high, eyes darting from one shrink to the next, projecting pure sanity for the cameras. I'm sure my children and my ex-wives are proud of me, watching the monitors in their little groups, squeezing the hands of their current spouses, and smiling at their hungry lawyers because old Troy so far has handled the preliminaries.

My voice may be low and hollow, and I may look like a nut with my white silk robe, shriveled face, and green turban, but I've answered their questions.

Come on, old boy, they're pleading.

Theishen asks, "What is your current physical condition?"

"I've felt better."

"It's rumored you have a cancerous tumor."

Get right to the point, don't you?

"I thought this was a mental exam," I say, glancing at Stafford, who can't suppress a smile. But the rules allow any question. This is not a courtroom.

"It is," Theishen says politely. "But every question is relevant."

"I see."

"Will you answer the question?"

"About what?"

"About the tumor."

"Sure. It's in my head, the size of a golf ball, growing every day, inoperable, and my doctor says I won't last three months."

I can almost hear the champagne corks popping below me. The tumor has been confirmed!

"Are you, at this moment, under the influence of any medication, drug, or alcohol?"

"No."

"Do you have in your possession any type of medication to relieve pain?"

"Not yet."

Back to Zadel: "Mr. Phelan, three months ago *Forbes* magazine listed your net worth at eight billion dollars. Is that a close estimate?"

"Since when is *Forbes* known for its accuracy?"

"So it's not accurate?"

"It's between eleven and eleven and a half, depending on the markets." I say this very slowly, but my words are sharp, my voice carries authority. No one doubts the size of my fortune.

Flowe decides to pursue the money. "Mr. Phelan, can you describe, in general, the organization of your corporate holdings?"

"I can, yes."

"Will you?"

"I suppose." I pause and let them sweat. Stafford assured me I do not have to divulge private information here. Just give them an overall picture, he said.

"The Phelan Group is a private corporation which owns seventy different companies, a few of which are publicly traded."

"How much of The Phelan Group do you own?"

"About ninety-seven percent. The rest is held by a handful of employees."

Theishen joins in the hunt. It didn't take long to focus on the gold. "Mr. Phelan, does your company hold an interest in Spin Computer?"

"Yes," I answer slowly, trying to place Spin Computer in my corporate jungle.

"How much do you own?"

"Eighty percent."

"And Spin Computer is a public company?"

"That's right."

Theishen fiddles with a pile of official-looking documents, and I can see from here that he has the company's annual report and quarterly statements, things any semiliterate college student could obtain. "When did you purchase Spin?" he asks.

"About four years ago."

"How much did you pay?"

"Twenty bucks a share, a total of three hundred million." I want to answer these questions more slowly, but I can't help myself. I stare holes through Theishen, anxious for the next one.

"And what's it worth now?" he asks.

"Well, it closed yesterday at forty-three and a half, down a point. The stock has split twice since I bought it, so the investment is now worth around eight-fifty."

"Eight hundred and fifty million?"

"That's correct."

The examination is basically over at this point. If my mental capacity can comprehend yesterday's closing stock prices, then my adversaries are certainly satisfied. I can almost see their goofy smiles. I can almost hear their muted hoorahs. Atta boy, Troy. Give 'em hell.

Zadel wants history. It's an effort to test the bounds of my memory. "Mr. Phelan, where were you born?"

"Montclair, New Jersey."

"When?"

"May 12, 1918."

"What was your mother's maiden name?"

"Shaw."

"When did she die?"

"Two days before Pearl Harbor."

"And your father?"

"What about him?"

"When did he die?"

"I don't know. He disappeared when I was a kid."

Zadel looks at Flowe, who's got questions packed together on a notepad. Flowe asks, "Who is your youngest daughter?"

"Which family?"

"Uh, the first one."

"That would be Mary Ross."

"Right—"

"Of course it's right."

"Where did she go to college?"

"Tulane, in New Orleans."

"What did she study?"

"Something medieval. Then she married badly, like the rest of them. I guess they inherited that talent from me." I can see them stiffen and bristle. And I can almost see the lawyers and the current live-ins and/or spouses hide little smiles because no one can argue the fact that I did indeed marry badly.

And I reproduced even more miserably.

Flowe is suddenly finished for this round. Theishen is enamored with the money. He asks, "Do you own a controlling interest in MountainCom?"

"Yes, I'm sure it's right there in your stack of paperwork. It's a public company."

"What was your initial investment?"

"Around eighteen a share, for ten million shares."

"And now it—"

"It closed yesterday at twenty-one a share. A swap and a split in the past six years and the holding is now worth about four hundred million. Does that answer your question?"

"Yes, I believe it does. How many public companies do you control?"

"Five."

Flowe glances at Zadel, and I'm wondering how much longer this will take. I'm suddenly tired.

"Any more questions?" Stafford asks. We are not going to press them because we want them completely satisfied.

Zadel asks, "Do you intend to sign a new will today?"

"Yes, that is my intent."

"Is that the will lying on the table there before you?"

"It is."

"Does that will give a substantial portion of your assets to your children?"

"It does."

"Are you prepared to sign the will at this time?"

"I am."

Zadel carefully places his pen on the table, folds his hands thoughtfully, and looks at Stafford. "In my opinion, Mr. Phelan has sufficient testamentary capacity at this time to dispose of his assets." He pronounces this with great weight, as if my performance had them hanging in limbo.

The other two are quick to rush in. "I have no doubt as to the soundness of his mind," Flowe says to Stafford. "He seems incredibly sharp to me."

"No doubt?" Stafford asks.

"None whatsoever."

"Dr. Theishen?"

"Let's not kid ourselves. Mr. Phelan knows exactly what he's doing. His mind is much quicker than ours."

Oh, thank you. That means so much to me. You're a bunch of shrinks struggling to make a hundred thousand a year. I've made billions, yet you pat me on the head and tell me how smart I am.

"So it's unanimous?" Stafford says.

"Yes. Absolutely." They can't nod their heads fast enough.

Stafford slides the will to me and hands me a pen. I say, "This is the last will and testament of Troy L. Phelan, revoking all former wills and codicils." It's ninety pages long, prepared by Stafford and someone in his firm. I understand the concept, but the actual print eludes me. I haven't read it, nor shall I. I flip to the back, scrawl a name no one can read, then place my hands on top of it for the time being.

It'll never be seen by the vultures.

"Meeting's adjourned," Stafford says, and everyone quickly packs. Per my instructions, the three families are hurried from their respective rooms and asked to leave the building.

One camera remains focused on me, its images going nowhere but the archives. The lawyers and psychiatrists leave in a rush. I tell Snead to take a seat at the table. Stafford and one of his partners, Durban, remain in the room, also seated. When we are alone, I reach under the edge of my robe and produce an envelope, which I open. I remove from it three pages of yellow legal paper and place them before me on the table.

Only seconds away now, and a faint ripple of fear goes through me. This will take more strength than I've mustered in weeks.

Stafford, Durban, and Snead stare at the sheets of yellow paper, thoroughly bewildered.

"This is my testament," I announce, taking a pen. "A holographic will, every word written by me, just a few hours ago. Dated today, and now signed today." I scrawl my name again. Stafford is too stunned to react.

"It revokes all former wills, including the one I signed less than five minutes ago." I refold the papers and place them in the envelope.

I grit my teeth and remind myself of how badly I want to die.

I slide the envelope across the table to Stafford, and at the same instant I rise from my wheelchair. My legs are shaking. My heart is pounding. Just seconds now. Surely I'll be dead before I land.

"Hey!" someone shouts, Snead I think. But I'm moving away from them.

The lame man walks, almost runs, past the row of leather chairs, past one of my portraits, a bad one commissioned by a wife, past everything, to the sliding doors, which are unlocked. I know because I rehearsed this just hours ago.

"Stop!" someone yells, and they're moving behind me. No one has seen me walk in a year. I grab the handle and open the door. The air is bitterly cold. I step barefoot onto the narrow terrace which borders my top floor. Without looking below, I lunge over the railing.

THREE

SNEAD WAS TWO STEPS behind Mr. Phelan, and thought for a second that he might catch him. The shock of seeing the old man not only rise and walk but also practically sprint to the door froze Snead. Mr. Phelan hadn't moved that fast in years.

Snead reached the railing just in time to scream in horror, then watched helplessly as Mr. Phelan fell silently, twisting and flailing and growing smaller and smaller until he struck the ground. Snead clenched the railing and stared in disbelief, then he began to cry.

Josh Stafford arrived on the terrace a step behind Snead, and witnessed most of the fall. It happened so quickly, at least the jump; the fall itself seemed to last for an hour. A man weighing a hundred and fifty pounds will drop three hundred feet in less than five seconds, but Stafford later told people the old man floated for an eternity, like a feather whirling in the wind.

Tip Durban got to the railing just behind Stafford, and saw only the body's impact on the brick patio between the front entrance and a circular drive. For some reason Durban held the envelope, which he had absently picked up during the rush to catch old Troy. It felt a lot heavier as he stood in the frigid air, looking down at a scene from a horror film, watching the first onlookers move up to the casualty.

TROY PHELAN'S DESCENT did not reach the level of high drama he had dreamed of. Instead of drifting to the earth like an angel, a perfect swan dive with the silk robe trailing behind, and landing in death before his terror-stricken families, who he'd imagined would be leaving the building at just the right moment, his fall was witnessed only by a lowly payroll clerk, hustling through the parking lot after a very long lunch in a bar. The clerk heard a voice, looked up at the top floor, and watched in horror as a pale naked body tumbled and flapped with what appeared to be a bedsheet gathered at the neck. It landed on its back, on brick, with the dull thud one would expect from such an impact.

The clerk ran to the spot just as a security guard noticed something wrong and bolted from his perch near the front entrance of Phelan Tower. Neither the clerk nor the guard had ever met Mr. Troy Phelan, so neither knew at first upon whose remains they were gazing. The body was bleeding, barefoot, twisted, and naked, and exposed with a sheet bunched at the arms. And it was quite dead.

Another thirty seconds, and Troy would have had his wish. Because they were stationed in a room on the fifth floor, Tira and Ramble and Dr. Theishen and their entourage of lawyers were the first to leave the building. And, therefore, the first to happen upon the suicide. Tira screamed, not from pain nor love nor loss, but from the sheer shock of seeing old Troy splattered on the brick. It was a wretched piercing scream that was heard clearly by Snead, Stafford, and Durban, fourteen floors up.

Ramble thought the scene was rather cool. A child of TV and an addict of video games, he found the gore a magnet. He moved away from his shrieking mother and knelt beside his dead father. The security guard placed a firm hand on his shoulder.

"That's Troy Phelan," one of the lawyers said as he hovered above the corpse.

"You don't say," said the guard.

"Wow," said the clerk.

More people ran from the building.

Janie, Geena, and Cody, with their shrink Dr. Flowe and their lawyers, were next. But there were no screams, no breakdowns. They stuck together in a tight bunch, well away from Tira and her group, and gawked like everyone else at poor Troy.

Radios crackled as another guard arrived and took control of the scene. He called for an ambulance.

"What good will that do?" asked the payroll clerk, who, by virtue of being the first on the scene, assumed a more important role in the aftermath.

"You want to take him away in your car?" asked the guard.

Ramble watched the blood fill in the mortar cracks and run in perfect angles down a gentle slope, toward a frozen fountain and a flagpole nearby.

In the atrium, a packed elevator stopped and opened and Lillian and the first family and their entourage emerged. Because TJ and Rex had once been allowed offices in the building, they had parked in the rear. The entire group turned left for an exit, then someone near the front of the building yelled, "Mr. Phelan's jumped!" They switched directions and raced through the front door, onto the brick patio near the fountain, where they found him.

They wouldn't have to wait for the tumor after all.

IT TOOK Joshua Stafford a minute or so to recover from the shock and start thinking like a lawyer again. He waited until the third and last family was visible below, then asked Snead and Durban to step inside.

The camera was still on. Snead faced it, raised his right hand, and swore to tell the truth, then, fighting tears, explained what he had just witnessed. Stafford opened the envelope and held the yellow sheets of paper close enough for the camera to see.

"Yes, I saw him sign that," Snead said. "Just seconds ago."

"And is that his signature?" Stafford asked.

"Yes, yes it is."

"Did he declare this to be his last will and testament?"

"He called it his testament."

Stafford withdrew the papers before Snead could read them. He repeated the same testimony with Durban, then placed himself before the camera and gave his version of events. The camera was turned off, and the three of them rode to the ground to pay their respects to Mr. Phelan. The elevator was packed with Phelan employees, stunned but anxious to have a rare and last glimpse of the old man. The building was emptying. Snead's quiet sobs were muffled in a corner.

Guards had backed the crowd away, leaving Troy alone in his puddle. A siren was approaching. Someone took photographs to memorialize the image of his death, then a black blanket was placed over his body.

For the families, slight twinges of grief soon overcame the shock of death. They stood with their heads low, their eyes staring sadly at the blanket, organizing their thoughts for the issues to come. It was impossible to look at Troy and not think about the money. Grief for an estranged relative, even a father, cannot stand in the way of a half a billion dollars.

For the employees, shock gave way to confusion. Troy was rumored to live up there above them, but very few had ever seen him. He was eccentric, crazy, sick—the rumors covered everything. He didn't like people. There were important vice presidents in the building who saw him once a year. If the company ran so well without him, surely their jobs were secure.

For the psychiatrists—Zadel, Flowe, and Theishen—the moment was filled with tension. You declare a man to be of sound mind, and minutes later he jumps to his death. Yet even a crazy man can have a lucid interval—that's the legal term they repeated to themselves as they shivered in the crowd. Crazy as a bat, but one clear, lucid interval in the midst of the madness, and a person can execute a valid will. They would stand firm with their opinions. Thank God everything was on tape. Old Troy was sharp. And lucid.

And for the lawyers, the shock passed quickly and there was no grief. They stood grim-faced next to their clients and watched the pitiful sight. The fees would be enormous.

An ambulance drove onto the bricks and stopped near Troy. Stafford walked under the barricade and whispered something to the guards.

Troy was quickly loaded onto a stretcher and taken away.

TROY PHELAN had moved his corporate headquarters to northern Virginia twenty-two years earlier to escape taxation in New York. He spent forty million on his Tower and grounds, money he saved many times over by being domiciled in Virginia.

He met Joshua Stafford, a rising D.C. lawyer, in the midst of a nasty lawsuit that Troy lost and Stafford won. Troy admired his style and tenacity, and so he hired him. In the past decade, Stafford had doubled the size of his firm and become rich with the money he earned fighting Troy's battles.

In the last years of his life, no one had been closer to Mr. Phelan than Josh Stafford. He and Durban returned to the conference room on the fourteenth floor and locked the door. Snead was sent away with instructions to lie down.

With the camera running, Stafford opened the envelope and removed the three sheets of yellow paper. The first sheet was a letter to him from Troy. He spoke to the camera: "This letter is dated today, Monday, December 9, 1996. It is handwritten, addressed to me, from Troy Phelan. It has five paragraphs. I will read it in full:

" 'Dear Josh: I am dead now. These are my instructions, and I want you to follow them closely. Use litigation if you have to, but I want my wishes carried out.

" 'First, I want a quick autopsy, for reasons that will become important later.

" 'Second, there will be no funeral, no service of any type. I want to be cremated, with my ashes scattered from the air over my ranch in Wyoming.

" 'Third, I want my will kept confidential until January 15, 1997.

The law does not require you to immediately produce it. Sit on it for a month.

" 'So long. Troy.' "

Stafford slowly placed the first sheet on the table, and carefully picked up the second. He studied it for a moment, then said for the camera, "This is a one-page document purporting to be the last testament of Troy L. Phelan. I will read it in its entirety:

" 'The last testament of Troy L. Phelan. I, Troy L. Phelan, being of sound and disposing mind and memory, do hereby expressly revoke all former wills and codicils executed by me, and dispose of my estate as follows:

" 'To my children, Troy Phelan, Jr., Rex Phelan, Libbigail Jeter, Mary Ross Jackman, Geena Strong, and Ramble Phelan, I give each a sum of money necessary to pay off all of the debts of each as of today. Any debts incurred after today will not be covered by this gift. If any of these children attempt to contest this will, then this gift shall be nullified as to that child.

" 'To my ex-wives, Lillian, Janie, and Tira, I give nothing. They were adequately provided for in the divorces.

" 'The remainder of my estate I give to my daughter Rachel Lane, born on November 2, 1954, at Catholic Hospital in New Orleans, Louisiana, to a woman named Evelyn Cunningham, now deceased.' "

Stafford had never heard of these people. He had to catch his breath before plowing ahead.

" 'I appoint my trusted lawyer, Joshua Stafford, as executor of this will, and grant unto him broad discretionary powers in its administration.

" 'This document is intended to be a holographic will. Every word has been written by my hand, and I hereby sign it.

" 'Signed, December 9, 1996, three P.M., by Troy L. Phelan.' "

Stafford placed it on the table and blinked his eyes at the camera. He needed a walk around the building, perhaps a blast of frigid air, but he pressed on. He picked up the third sheet, and said, "This is a one-paragraph note addressed to me again. I will read it: 'Josh: Rachel Lane is a World Tribes missionary on the Brazil–Bolivia border. She works with a remote Indian tribe in a region known as the Pantanal. The nearest town is Corumbá. I couldn't find her. I've had no contact with her in the last twenty years. Signed, Troy Phelan.' "

Durban turned the camera off, and paced around the table twice as Stafford read the document again and again.

"Did you know he had an illegitimate daughter?"

Stafford was staring absently at a wall. "No. I drafted eleven wills for Troy, and he never mentioned her."

"I guess we shouldn't be surprised."

Stafford had declared many times that he had become incapable of being surprised by Troy Phelan. In business and in private, the man was whimsical and chaotic. Stafford had made millions running behind his client, putting out fires.

But he was, in fact, stunned. He had just witnessed a rather dramatic suicide, during which a man confined to a wheelchair suddenly sprang forth and ran. Now he was holding a valid will that, in a few hasty paragraphs, transferred one of the world's great fortunes to an unknown heiress, without the slightest hint of estate planning. The inheritance taxes would be brutal.

"I need a drink, Tip," he said.

"It's a bit early."

They walked next door to Mr. Phelan's office, and found everything unlocked. The current secretary and everybody else who worked on the fourteenth floor were still on the ground.

They locked the door behind themselves, and hurriedly went through the desk drawers and file cabinets. Troy had expected them to. He would never have left his private spaces unlocked. He knew Josh would step in immediately. In the center drawer of his desk, they found a contract with a crematorium in Alexandria, dated five weeks earlier. Under it was a file on World Tribes Missions.

They gathered what they could carry, then found Snead and made him lock the office. "What's in the testament, that last one?"

he asked. He was pale and his eyes were swollen. Mr. Phelan couldn't just die like that without leaving him something, some means to survive on. He'd been a loyal servant for thirty years.

"Can't say," Stafford said. "I'll be back tomorrow to inventory everything. Do not allow anyone in."

"Of course not," Snead whispered, then began weeping again.

Stafford and Durban spent half an hour with a cop on a routine call. They showed him where Troy went over the railing, gave him the names of witnesses, described with no detail the last letter and last will. It was a suicide, plain and simple. They promised a copy of the autopsy report, and the cop closed the case before he left the building.

They caught up with the corpse at the medical examiner's office, and made arrangements for the autopsy.

"Why an autopsy?" Durban asked in a whisper as they waited for paperwork.

"To prove there were no drugs, no alcohol. Nothing to impair his judgment. He thought of everything."

It was almost six before they made it to a bar in the Willard Hotel, near the White House, two blocks from their office. And it was only after a stiff drink that Stafford managed his first smile. "He thought of everything, didn't he?"

"He's a very cruel man," Durban said, deep in thought. The shock was wearing off, but the reality was settling in.

"He *was,* you mean."

"No. He's still here. Troy's still calling the shots."

"Can you imagine the money those fools will spend in the next month?"

"It seems a crime not to tell them."

"We can't. We have our orders."

FOR LAWYERS whose clients seldom spoke to each other, the meeting was a rare moment of cooperation. The largest ego in the room belonged to Hark Gettys, a brawling litigator who'd represented Rex Phelan for a number of years. Hark had insisted on the meeting not long after he returned to his office on Massachusetts Avenue. He had actually whispered an idea to the attorneys for TJ and Libbigail as they watched the old man being loaded into the ambulance.

It was such a good idea that the other lawyers couldn't argue. They arrived, along with Flowe, Zadel, and Theishen, at Gettys' office after five. A court reporter and two video cameras were waiting.

For obvious reasons, the suicide made them nervous. Each psychiatrist was taken separately, and quizzed at length about his observations of Mr. Phelan just before he jumped.

There was not a scintilla of doubt among the three that Mr. Phelan knew precisely what he was doing, that he was of sound mind, and had more than sufficient testamentary capacity. You don't have to be insane to commit suicide, they emphasized carefully.

When the lawyers, all thirteen of them, had extracted every opinion possible, Gettys broke up the meeting. It was almost 8 P.M.

FOUR

ACCORDING TO *Forbes*, Troy Phelan was the tenth richest man in America. His death was a newsworthy event; the manner he chose made it downright sensational.

Outside Lillian's mansion in Falls Church, a cluster of reporters waited on the street for a family spokesman to come forth. They filmed friends and neighbors as they came and went, tossing out banal questions about how the family was doing.

Inside, Phelan's four eldest children gathered with their spouses and their children to receive condolences. The mood was somber when the guests were present. When the guests were gone, the tone changed dramatically. The presence of Troy's grandchildren—eleven of them—forced TJ, Rex, Libbigail, and Mary Ross to at least try and suppress their festive feelings. It was difficult. Fine wine and champagne were served, lots of it. Old Troy wouldn't want them grieving, now would he? The older grandchildren drank more than their parents.

A TV set in the den was kept on CNN, and every half hour they would gather for the latest announcement of Troy's dramatic death.

A financial correspondent pieced together a ten-minute segment on the vastness of the Phelan fortune, and everyone smiled.

Lillian kept a stiff upper lip and did a credible job of being the grieving widow. Tomorrow she would work on the arrangements.

Hark Gettys arrived around ten, and explained to the family that he had spoken to Josh Stafford. There would be no funeral, no service of any type; just an autopsy, a cremation, and a scattering of ashes. It was in writing, and Stafford was prepared to do battle in court to protect his client's wishes.

Lillian didn't give a damn what they did with Troy, nor did her children. But they had to protest and argue with Gettys. It just wasn't right to send him off with no service. Libbigail even managed a small tear and a breaking voice.

"I wouldn't fight this," Gettys advised gravely. "Mr. Phelan put it in writing just before his death, and the courts will honor his wishes."

They came around quickly. No sense wasting a lot of time and money on legal fees. No sense prolonging the grieving. Why make matters worse? Troy always got what he wanted anyway. And they had learned the hard way not to tangle with Josh Stafford.

"We will abide by his wishes," Lillian said, and the other four nodded sadly behind their mother.

There was no mention of the will and when they might actually see it, though the question was just below the surface. Best to be properly grim for a few more hours, then they could get down to business. Since there would be no wake, no funeral or service, perhaps they might meet as early as tomorrow and discuss the estate.

"Why the autopsy?" asked Rex.

"I have no idea," Gettys answered. "Stafford said it was in writing, but even he is not sure."

Gettys left and they drank some more. The guests stopped coming, so Lillian went to bed. Libbigail and Mary Ross left with their families. TJ and Rex went to the billiards room in the basement, where they locked the door and switched to whiskey. At midnight, they were slapping balls around the table, drunk as sailors, celebrating their fabulous new wealth.

AT 8 A.M., the day after the death of Mr. Phelan, Josh Stafford addressed the anxious directors of The Phelan Group. Two years earlier, Josh himself had been placed on the board by Mr. Phelan, but it was not a role he enjoyed.

For the past six years, The Phelan Group had operated quite profitably without much assistance from its founder. For some reason, probably depression, Troy had lost interest in the day-to-day managing of his empire. He became content to simply monitor the markets and the earnings reports.

The current CEO was Pat Solomon, a company man Troy had hired almost twenty years earlier. He was as nervous as the other seven when Stafford entered the room.

There was ample cause for anxiety. Within the company's culture there was a rich body of lore surrounding Troy's wives and his offspring. The vaguest hint that the ownership of The Phelan Group might somehow fall into the hands of those people would terrorize any board.

Josh began by stating Mr. Phelan's desires regarding burial. "There will be no funeral," he said somberly. "Frankly, there is no way to pay your last respects."

They absorbed this without comment. With the passing of a normal person, such non-arrangements would seem bizarre. But with Troy, it was difficult to be surprised.

"Who will own the company?" Solomon asked.

"I can't say now," Stafford said, well aware of how evasive and unsatisfactory his answer was. "Troy signed a will moments before he jumped, and he instructed me to keep it private for a period of time. I cannot, under any circumstances, divulge its contents. At least, not for now."

"When?"

"Soon. But not now."

"So it's business as usual?"

"Exactly. This board remains intact; everybody keeps his job. The company does tomorrow what it did last week."

This sounded fine, but no one believed it. Ownership of the company was about to change hands. Troy had never believed in sharing stock in The Phelan Group. He paid his people well, but he did not buy into the trend of allowing them to own a piece of the company. About 3 percent of the stock was held by a few of his favored employees.

They spent an hour haggling over the wording of a press release, then adjourned for a month.

Stafford met Tip Durban in the lobby, and together they drove to the medical examiner's office in McLean. The autopsy was finished.

The cause of death was obvious. There was no trace of alcohol or drugs of any kind.

And there was no tumor. No sign of cancer. Troy was in good physical health at the time of his death, though slightly malnourished.

TIP BROKE THE SILENCE as they were crossing the Potomac, on the Roosevelt Bridge. "Did he tell you he had a brain tumor?"

"Yes. Several times." Stafford drove, though he was oblivious to roads, bridges, streets, cars. How many more surprises did Troy have?

"Why did he lie?"

"Who knows? You're trying to analyze a man who just jumped from a building. The brain tumor made everything urgent. Everybody, including me, thought he was dying. The wackiness made the panel of shrinks seem like a great idea. He set the trap, they rushed in, and now their own psychiatrists are swearing that Troy was perfectly sound. Plus, he wanted sympathy."

"But he was crazy, wasn't he? He did, after all, take a leap."

"Troy was weird in a lot of ways, but he knew exactly what he was doing."

"Why did he jump?"

"Depression. He was a very lonely old man."

They were on Constitution Avenue, sitting in heavy traffic, both staring at the taillights in front of them and trying to think it through.

"It seems fraudulent," Durban said. "He lures them in with the promise of money; he satisfies their psychiatrists, then at the last second he signs a will that completely guts them."

"It was fraudulent, but this is a will, not a contract. A will is a gift. Under Virginia law, a person is not required to leave a dime to his children."

"But they'll attack, won't they?"

"Probably. They have lots of lawyers. There's too much money at stake."

"Why did he hate them so much?"

"He thought they were leeches. They embarrassed him. They fought with him. They never earned an honest dime and went through many of his millions. Troy never planned to leave them anything. He figured that if they could squander millions, then they could waste billions as well. And he was right."

"How much of the family fighting was his fault?"

"A lot. Troy was a hard man to love. He told me once that he'd been a bad father and a terrible husband. He couldn't keep his hands off women, especially ones who worked for him. He thought he owned them."

"I remember some claims for sexual harassment."

"We settled them quietly. And for big bucks. Troy didn't want the embarrassment."

"Any chance of more unknown heirs out there?"

"I doubt it. But what do I know? I never dreamed he had another heir, and the idea of leaving her everything is something I cannot comprehend. Troy and I spent hours talking about his estate and how to divide it."

"How do we find her?"

"I don't know. I haven't thought about her yet."

□ □ □ □

THE STAFFORD LAW FIRM was in a frenzy when Josh returned. By Washington standards, it was considered small—sixty lawyers. Josh was the founder and principal partner. Tip Durban and four others were called partners, which meant Josh listened to them occasionally and shared some of the profits. For thirty years it had been a rough-and-tumble litigation firm, but as Josh approached sixty he spent less time in the courtroom and more time behind his cluttered desk. He could've had a hundred lawyers if he wanted ex-Senators, lobbyists, and regulatory analysts, the usual D.C. lineup. But Josh loved trials and courtrooms, and he hired only young associates who had tried at least ten jury cases.

The average career of a litigator is twenty-five years. The first heart attack usually slows them down enough to delay a second. Josh had avoided burnout by tending to Mr. Phelan's maze of legal needs—securities, antitrust, employment, mergers, and dozens of personal matters.

Three sets of associates waited in the reception room of his large office. Two secretaries shoved memos and phone messages in his direction as he removed his overcoat and settled behind his desk. "Which is most urgent?" he asked.

"This, I think," answered a secretary.

It was from Hark Gettys, a man Josh had talked to at least three times a week for the past month. He dialed the number and Hark was immediately on the line. They quickly went through the pleasantries, and Hark got right to the point.

"Listen, Josh, you can imagine how the family is breathing down my neck."

"I'm sure."

"They want to see the damned will, Josh. Or at least they want to know what's in it."

The next few sentences would be crucial, and Josh had plotted them carefully. "Not so fast, Hark."

A very slight pause, then, "Why? Is something the matter?"

"The suicide bothers me."

"What! What do you mean?"

"Look, Hark, how can a man be of sound mind seconds before he jumps to his death?"

Hark's edgy voice rose an octave, and the words carried even more anxiety. "But you heard our psychiatrists. Hell, they're on tape."

"Are they sticking by their opinions, in light of the suicide?"

"Damned right they are!"

"Can you prove this? I'm looking for help here, Hark."

"Josh, last night we examined our three shrinks again. We drilled them, and they're sticking like glue. Each signed an affidavit eight pages long swearing to the sound mental capacity of Mr. Phelan."

"Can I see the affidavits?"

"I'll courier them over right now."

"Please do." Josh hung up and smiled to no one in particular. The associates were marched in, three sets of bright and fearless young lawyers. They sat around a mahogany table in one corner of the office.

Josh began by summarizing the contents of Troy's handwritten will, and the legal problems it was likely to create. To the first team he assigned the weighty issue of testamentary capacity. Josh was concerned about time, the gap between lucidity and insanity. He wanted an analysis of every case even remotely involving the signing of a will by a person considered crazy.

The second team was dispatched to research holographic wills; specifically, the best ways to attack and defend them.

When he was alone with the third team, he relaxed and sat down. They were the lucky ones, because they would not spend the next three days in the library. "You have to find a person who, I suspect, does not want to be found."

He told them what he knew about Rachel Lane. There wasn't much. The file from Troy's desk provided little information.

"First, research World Tribes Missions. Who are they? How do they operate? How do they pick their people? Where do they send them? Everything. Second, there are some excellent private locators

in D.C. They're usually ex-FBI and government types who special-
ize in finding missing people. Select the top two, and we'll make a
decision tomorrow. Third, Rachel's mother's name was Evelyn
Cunningham, now deceased. Let's put together a bio on her.
We're assuming she and Mr. Phelan had a fling that produced a
child."

"Assuming?" asked one of the associates.

"Yes. We take nothing for granted."

He dismissed them and walked to a room where a small press
conference had been arranged by Tip Durban. No cameras, just
print media. A dozen reporters sat eagerly around a table, tape
recorders and microphones scattered about. They were from large
newspapers and well-known financial publications.

The questions began. Yes, there was a last-minute will, but he
could not reveal its contents. Yes, there'd been an autopsy, but
he couldn't discuss it. The company would continue operating
with no changes. He couldn't talk about who the new owners
would be.

To no one's surprise, it became obvious that the families had
spent the day chatting privately with reporters.

"There's a strong rumor that Mr. Phelan's last will divides his
fortune among his six children. Can you confirm or deny this?"

"I cannot. It's just a rumor."

"Wasn't he dying of cancer?"

"That would go to the autopsy, and I can't comment on that."

"We've heard that a panel of psychiatrists examined him shortly
before his death, and pronounced him mentally sound. Can you
confirm this?"

"Yes," Stafford said, "this is true." So they spent the next twenty
minutes picking and prying into the mental exam. Josh held his
ground, allowing only that Mr. Phelan "appeared" to be of sound
mind.

The financial reporters wanted numbers. Because The Phelan
Group was a private company, very tightly held, information had

always been hard to come by. This was an opportunity to crack the door, or so they thought. But Josh gave them little.

He excused himself after an hour, and returned to his office, where a secretary informed him that the crematorium had called. Mr. Phelan's remains were ready to be picked up.

FIVE

TJ NURSED his hangover until noon, then drank a beer and decided it was time to flex his muscle. He called his principal lawyer to check on the current state of things, and the lawyer cautioned him to be patient. "This will take a little time, TJ," the lawyer said.

"Maybe I'm not in the mood to wait," TJ shot back, his head splitting.

"Give it a few days."

TJ slammed the phone down and walked to rear of his dirty condo, where, thankfully, he couldn't find his wife. They had been through three fights already, and it was barely noon. Perhaps she was out shopping, spending a fraction of his new fortune. The shopping didn't bother him now.

"The old goat's dead," he said out loud. There was no one else around.

His two children were away at college, their tuition paid for by Lillian, who still had some of the money she'd taken from Troy in the divorce decades earlier. So TJ lived alone with Biff, a thirty-year-old divorcée whose two kids lived with their father. Biff had a real estate license and sold darling little starters to newlyweds.

He opened another beer and stared at himself in a full-length mirror in the hall. "Troy Phelan, Jr.," he proclaimed. "Son of Troy Phelan, tenth richest man in America, net worth of eleven billion, now deceased, survived by his loving wives and loving children, all of whom will love him even more after probate. Yes!"

He decided right then and there that from that day forward, TJ would be ditched and he would go through life as Troy Phelan, Jr. The name was magic.

The condo had a certain smell to it because Biff refused to do housework. She was too busy with her cell phones. The floors were covered with debris but the walls were bare. The furniture was rented from a company that had hired lawyers to recover everything. He kicked a sofa, and yelled, "Come get this crap! I'll be hiring designers before long."

He could almost torch the place. Another beer or two, and he might start playing with matches.

He dressed in his best suit, a gray one he'd worn yesterday when Dear Old Dad faced the psychiatrists and performed so wonderfully. Since there would be no funeral, he wouldn't be forced to rush out and buy a new black one. "Armani, here I come," he whistled joyfully as he zipped up his pants.

At least he had a BMW. He might live in a dump, but the world would never see it. The world, however, noticed his car, and so he struggled every month to scratch together $680 for the lease. He cursed his condo as he backed away in the parking lot. It was one of eighty new ones wrapped around a shallow pool in an overflow section of Manassas.

He'd been raised better. Life had been soft and luxurious for the first twenty years, and then he received his inheritance. But his five million had disappeared before he reached thirty, and his father despised him for it.

They fought with vigor and regularity. Junior had held various jobs within The Phelan Group, and each ended in disaster. Senior fired him numerous times. Senior had an idea for a venture, and two years later the idea was worth millions. Junior's ideas ended in bankruptcy and litigation.

In recent years the fighting had almost stopped. Neither could change, so they simply ignored each other. But when the tumor appeared, TJ reached out again.

Oh what a mansion he would build! And he knew just the architect, a Japanese woman in Manhattan he'd read about in a magazine. Within a year he'd probably move to Malibu or Aspen or Palm Beach, where he could show the money and be taken seriously.

"What does one do with half a billion dollars?" he asked himself as he sped along the interstate. "Five hundred million tax-free dollars." He began to laugh.

An acquaintance managed the BMW-Porsche dealership where he'd leased his car. Junior walked into the showroom like the king of the world, strutting and smiling smugly. He could buy the whole damned place if he wanted. On a salesman's desk he saw the morning paper; a nice bold headline about the death of his father. Not a twinge of grief.

The manager, Dickie, bounded from his office and said, "TJ, I'm very sorry."

"Thanks," Troy Junior said with a brief frown. "He's better off, you know."

"My sympathies anyway."

"Forget it." They stepped into the office and closed the door.

Dickie said, "The paper says he signed a will just before he died. Is that true?"

Troy Junior was already looking at the slick brochures for the latest models. "Yes. I was there. He divided his estate into six pieces, one for each of us." He said this without looking up, quite casually, as if the money were already in hand, and already becoming a burden.

Dickie's mouth slipped open and he lowered himself into his chair. Was he suddenly in the presence of serious wealth? This guy, the worthless TJ Phelan, now a billionaire? Like everyone else who knew TJ, Dickie assumed the old man had cut him off for good.

"Biff would like a Porsche," Troy Junior said, still studying the charts. "A red 911 Carrera Turbo, with both tops."

"When?"

Troy Junior glared at him. "Now."

"Sure, TJ. What about payment?"

"I'll pay for it the same time I pay for my black one, also a 911. How much are they?"

"About ninety thousand each."

"No problem. When can we take delivery?"

"I'll have to find them first. That should take a day or two. Cash?"

"Of course."

"When will you get the cash?"

"A month or so. But I want the cars now."

Dickie caught his breath and did a squirm. "Look, TJ, I can't turn loose two new cars without some type of payment."

"Fine. Then we'll look at Jaguars. Biff's always wanted a Jaguar."

"Come on, TJ."

"I could buy this entire dealership, you know. I could walk into any bank right now and ask for ten million or twenty million or whatever it would take to buy this place, and they would happily give it to me for sixty days. Do you understand that?"

Dickie's head rocked up and down, his eyes narrow. Yes, he understood. "How much did he leave you?"

"Enough to buy the bank too. Are you giving me the cars, or shall I go down the street?"

"Let me find them."

"Smart man," TJ said. "Hurry. I'll check back this afternoon. Get on the phone." He tossed the brochures on Dickie's desk, and strutted from the office.

RAMBLE'S IDEA of mourning was to spend the day locked in the basement den smoking pot, listening to rap, ignoring those who knocked or called. His mother granted him an absence from school because of the tragedy; in fact, she excused him for the rest of the week. If she'd had a clue, she would've known he hadn't been to school in a month.

Driving away from Phelan Tower yesterday, his lawyer had told him the money would go into a trust until he was either eighteen or twenty-one, depending on the terms of the will. And though he couldn't touch the money now, he was certainly entitled to a generous allowance.

He would form a band, and with his money they would make albums. He had friends in bands going nowhere because they couldn't afford to rent studio time, but his would be different. His band would be called Ramble, he decided, and he would play bass and sing lead and be chased by the girls. Alternative rock with strong rap influences, something new. Something he was already inventing.

Two floors up, in the study of their spacious home, Tira, his mother, spent the day on the phone chatting with friends who called with their halfhearted condolences. Most of the friends gossiped long enough to ask how much she might be getting from the estate, but she was afraid to guess. She had married Troy in 1982, at the age of twenty-three, and before doing so she signed a thick prenuptial which gave her only ten million and a house in the event of a divorce.

They had split six years earlier. She was down to her last two million.

Her needs were so great. Her friends had beach houses nestled in quiet coves in the Bahamas; she was relegated to luxury hotels. They bought their designer clothes in New York; she picked them up locally. Their children were away in boarding schools, out of the way; Ramble was in the basement and wouldn't come out.

Surely Troy had left her fifty million or so. One percent of his estate would be around a hundred million. One lousy percent. She did the math on a paper napkin as she talked on the phone to her lawyer.

□ □ □ □

GEENA PHELAN STRONG was thirty and surviving what had evolved into a tumultuous marriage with Cody, husband number two. His family was old money from up East, but so far the money had only been a rumor. She certainly hadn't seen any of it. Cody was beautifully educated—Taft and Dartmouth and an MBA from Columbia—and he considered himself a visionary in the world of commerce. No job could hold him. His talents could not be constricted by the walls of an office. His dreams would not be cramped by the orders and whims of bosses. Cody would be a billionaire, self-made of course, and probably the youngest in history.

But after six years together, Cody had yet to find his niche. In fact, his losses were staggering. There had been a bad gamble on copper futures in 1992 that had taken over a million of Geena's money. And two years later, he was scalded by naked options when the stock market dipped dramatically. Geena left him for four months, but returned after counseling. An idea for "Snow-Packed Chickens" turned sour, and Cody escaped with a loss of only a half a million.

They spent a lot. Their counselor recommended traveling as a means of therapy, so they'd seen the world. Being young and rich soothed many of their problems, but the money was drying up. The five million Troy gave her on her twenty-first birthday had shrunk to less than a million, and their debts were mounting. The pressure on their marriage had reached the breaking point when Troy leaped from his terrace.

And so they spent a busy morning looking for homes in Swinks Mill, the place of their grandest dreams. Their dreams grew as the day progressed, and by lunch they were making inquiries into homes worth over two million. At two they met an anxious real estate agent, a woman named Lee, with teased hair, gold rings, two cell phones, and a shiny Cadillac. Geena introduced herself as "Geena Phelan," with the last name pronounced heavy and uncheated. Evidently, Lee did not read financial publications because the name missed its mark, and well into the third showing Cody was forced to pull her aside and whisper the truth about his father-in-law.

"That rich guy who jumped?" Lee said, hand over mouth. Geena was inspecting a hallway closet with a small sauna tucked into it.

Cody nodded sadly.

By dusk they were looking at an empty home priced at four million five, and the prospective buyers were seriously considering making an offer. Lee rarely saw such wealthy clients, and they'd worked her into a frenzy.

REX, AGE FORTY-FOUR, brother to TJ, was, at the time of Troy's death, the only one of his children under criminal investigation. His troubles stemmed from a bank that failed, with various lawsuits and investigations spinning wildly from it. Bank examiners and the FBI had been making rather fierce inquiries for three years.

To fund his defense, and his expensive lifestyle, Rex had purchased from the estate of a man killed in a gunfight a string of topless bars and strip clubs in the Fort Lauderdale area. The skin business was lucrative; traffic was always good and cash was easy to skim. Without being overly greedy, he pocketed around twenty-four thousand a month in tax-free dollars, roughly four thousand from each of his six clubs.

The clubs were held in the name of Amber Rockwell, his wife and a former stripper he'd first noticed lurching on a bar one night. In fact, all of his assets were in her name, and this caused him no small amount of anxiety. With the addition of clothing and minus the makeup and kinky shoes, Amber passed herself off as respectable in their Washington circles. Few people knew her past. But she was a whore at heart, and the fact that she owned everything caused poor Rex many sleepless nights.

At the time of his father's death, Rex had lodged against him in excess of seven million dollars' worth of liens and judgments from creditors, business partners, and investors in the bank. And the total was growing. The judgments, though, remained unsatisfied because there was nothing for the creditors to attach. Rex was asset-free; he owned nothing, not even his car. He and Amber leased a condo and matching Corvettes, with all the paperwork in her name. The clubs and bars were owned by an offshore corporation organized by her without a trace of him. Rex so far had proved too slippery to catch.

The marriage was as stable as could be expected from two people with histories of instability; they partied a lot and had wild friends, clingers drawn to the Phelan name. Life was fun, in spite of the financial pressures. But Rex worried fanatically about Amber and her assets. A nasty argument, and she could vanish.

The worrying stopped with Troy's death. The seesaw tilted, and suddenly Rex was on top, his last name finally worth a fortune. He'd sell the bars and clubs, pay off his debts with a wicked swipe, then play with his money. One false move, and she'd be dancing on tables again with wet dollar bills stuck in her G-string.

Rex spent the day with Hark Gettys, his lawyer. He wanted the money quickly, desperately, and he pressured Gettys to call Josh Stafford and ask for a look at the will. Rex made plans, large and ambitious plans for how to handle the money, and Hark would be with him every step of the way. He wanted control of The Phelan Group. His portion of the stock, whatever it might be, added to TJ's and both sisters', would surely give them a majority of voting shares. But was the stock placed in trust, or given outright, or tied up in any one of a hundred devious ways that Troy would certainly enjoy from the grave?

"We have to see that damned will!" he yelled at Hark throughout the day. Hark calmed him with a long lunch and good wine, then they switched to Scotch in the early afternoon. Amber dropped by and found them both drunk, but she wasn't angry. There was no way Rex could anger her now. She loved him more than ever.

SIX

THE TRIP WEST would be a pleasant respite from the chaos
Mr. Phelan created with his leap. His ranch was near Jackson
Hole, in the Tetons, where a foot of snow was already on the
ground and more was expected. What would Miss Manners say
about the scattering of ashes over land covered with snow? Should
one wait until the thaw? Or sprinkle them anyway? Josh didn't give
a damn. He'd toss them in the face of any natural disaster.

He was being hounded by the lawyers for the Phelan heirs. His
cautious comments to Hark Gettys about the old man's testamentary capacity had sent shockwaves through the families, and they
were reacting with predictable hysteria. And threats. The trip would
be a short vacation. He and Durban could sort through the preliminary research and make their plans.

They left National Airport on Mr. Phelan's Gulfstream IV, a
plane Josh had been privileged to fly on only once before. It was the
newest of the fleet, and at a price of thirty-five million had been
Mr. Phelan's fanciest toy. The summer before they had flown it to
Nice, where the old man walked naked on the beach and gawked at

young French girls. Josh and his wife had kept their clothes on with the rest of the Americans and sunned by the pool.

A stewardess served them breakfast, then disappeared into the rear galley as they spread their papers on a round table. The flight would take four hours.

The affidavits signed by Drs. Flowe, Zadel, and Theishen were long and verbose, laden with opinions and redundancies that ran on for paragraphs and left not a scintilla of doubt that Troy was of sound and disposing mind and memory. He was downright brilliant, and knew exactly what he was doing in the moments before his death.

Stafford and Durban read the affidavits and enjoyed the humor. When the new will was read, those three experts would be fired, of course, and a half dozen more would be brought in to deliver all sorts of dark and dire suppositions about poor Troy's mental illnesses.

On the subject of Rachel Lane—little had been learned about the world's richest missionary. The investigators hired by the firm were digging furiously.

According to the early research pulled from the Internet, World Tribes Missions was headquartered in Houston, Texas. Founded in 1920, the organization had four thousand missionaries spread around the world working exclusively with native peoples. Its sole purpose and goal was to spread the Christian Gospel to every remote tribe in the world. Obviously, Rachel did not inherit her religious beliefs from her father.

No less than twenty-eight Indian tribes in Brazil were currently being ministered to by World Tribes missionaries, and at least ten in Bolivia. Another three hundred in the rest of the world. Because their target tribes were secluded and detached from modern civilization, the missionaries received exhaustive training in survival, wilderness living, languages, and medical skills.

Josh read with great interest a story written by a missionary who had spent seven years living in a lean-to, in a jungle, trying to learn enough of the primitive tribe's language to communicate. The Indians had had little to do with him. He was, after all, a white man from Missouri who'd backpacked into their village with a vocabulary limited to "Hello" and "Thank you." If he needed a table, he built one. If he needed food, he killed it. Five years passed before the Indians began to trust him. He was well into his sixth year before he told his first Bible story. He was trained to be patient, to build relationships, learn language and culture, and slowly, very slowly, begin to teach the Bible.

The tribe had little contact with the outside world. Life had hardly changed in a thousand years.

What kind of person could possess enough faith and commitment to forsake modern society and enter such a prehistoric world? The missionary wrote that the Indians did not accept him until they realized he wasn't leaving. He had chosen to live with them, forever. He loved them and wanted to be one of them.

So Rachel lived in a hut or a lean-to, and slept on a bed she'd built herself, and cooked over a fire, and ate food she'd grown or trapped and killed, and taught Bible stories to the children and the Gospel to the adults, and knew nothing and certainly cared nothing for the events and worries and pressures of the world. She was very content. Her faith sustained her.

It seemed almost cruel to bother her.

Durban read the same materials and said, "We may never find her. No phones, no electricity; hell, you have to hike through the mountains to get to these people."

"We have no choice," Josh said.

"Have we contacted World Tribes?"

"Later today."

"What do you tell them?"

"I don't know. But you don't tell them you're looking for one of their missionaries because she's just inherited eleven billion dollars."

"Eleven billion before taxes."

"There will be a nice sum left over."

"So what do you tell them?"

"We tell them there's a pressing legal matter. It's quite urgent, and we must speak to Rachel face to face."

One of the fax machines on board began humming, and the memos started. The first was from Josh's secretary with a list of the morning's calls—almost all from attorneys for the Phelan heirs. Two were from reporters.

The associates were reporting in, with preliminary research on various aspects of applicable Virginia law. With each page that Josh and Durban read, old Troy's hastily scrawled testament got stronger and stronger.

Lunch was light sandwiches and fruit, again served by the stewardess, who kept to the rear of the cabin and managed to appear only when their coffee cups were empty.

They landed in Jackson Hole in clear weather, with heavy snow plowed to the sides of the runway. They stepped off the plane, walked eighty feet, and climbed onto a Sikorsky S-76C, Troy's favorite helicopter. Ten minutes later they were hovering over his beloved ranch. A stiff wind bounced the chopper, and Durban turned pale. Josh slid open a door, slowly and quite nervously, and a sharp wind blasted him in the face.

The pilot circled at two thousand feet while Josh emptied the ashes from a small black urn. The wind instantly blew them in all directions so that Troy's remains vanished long before they hit the snow. When the urn was empty, Josh retracted his frozen arm and hand and shut the door.

The house was technically a log cabin, with enough massive timbers to give the appearance of something rustic. But at eleven thousand square feet, it was anything but a cabin. Troy had bought it from an actor whose career went south.

A butler in corduroy took their bags and a maid fixed their coffee. Durban admired the stuffed game hanging from the walls while Josh called the office. A fire roared in the fireplace, and the cook asked what they wanted for dinner.

□ □ □ □

THE ASSOCIATE'S NAME was Montgomery, a four-year man who'd been handpicked by Mr. Stafford. He got lost three times in the sprawl of Houston before he found the offices of World Tribes Missions tucked away on the ground floor of a five-story building. He parked his rented car and straightened his tie.

He had talked to Mr. Trill twice on the phone, and though he was an hour late for the appointment it didn't seem to matter. Mr. Trill was polite and soft-spoken but not eager to help. They exchanged the required preliminaries. "Now, what can I do for you?" Trill asked.

"I need some information about one of your missionaries," Montgomery said.

Trill nodded but said nothing.

"A Rachel Lane."

The eyes drifted as if he was trying to place her. "Name doesn't ring a bell. But then, we have four thousand people in the field."

"She's working near the border of Brazil and Bolivia."

"How much do you know about her?"

"Not much. But we need to find her."

"For what purpose?"

"It's a legal matter," Montgomery said, with just enough hesitation to sound suspicious.

Trill frowned and pulled his elbows close to his chest. His small smile disappeared. "Is there trouble?" he asked.

"No. But the matter is quite urgent. We need to see her."

"Can't you send a letter or a package?"

"Afraid not. Her cooperation is needed, along with her signature."

"I assume it's confidential."

"Extremely."

Something clicked and Trill's frown softened. "Excuse me for a minute." He disappeared from the office, and left Montgomery to inspect the spartan furnishings. The only decoration was a collection of enlarged photos of Indian children on the walls.

Trill was a different person when he returned, stiff and unsmiling and uncooperative. "I'm sorry, Mr. Montgomery," he said without sitting. "We will not be able to help you."

"Is she in Brazil?"

"I'm sorry."

"Bolivia?"

"I'm sorry."

"Does she even exist?"

"I can't answer your questions."

"Nothing?"

"Nothing."

"Could I speak to your boss or supervisor?"

"Sure."

"Where is he?"

"In heaven."

AFTER A DINNER of thick steaks in mushroom sauce, Josh Stafford and Tip Durban retired to the den, where a fire roared. A different butler, a Mexican in a white jacket and starched jeans, served them very old single-malt Scotch from Mr. Phelan's cabinet. Cuban cigars were ordered. Pavarotti sang Christmas songs on a distant stereo.

"I have an idea," Josh said as he watched the fire. "We have to send someone to find Rachel Lane, right?"

Tip was in the midst of a lengthy draw from his cigar, so he only nodded.

"And we can't just send anyone. It has to be a lawyer; someone who can explain the legal issues. And it has to be someone from our firm because of confidentiality."

His jaws filled with smoke, Tip kept nodding.

"So who do we send?"

Tip exhaled slowly, through both his mouth and his nose, and smoke boiled across his face and drifted upward. "How long will it take?" he finally asked.

"I don't know, but it's not a quick trip. Brazil's a big country, almost as big as the lower forty-eight. And we're talking jungles and mountains. These people are so remote they've never seen a car."

"I'm not going."

"We can hire local guides and such, but it still might take a week or so."

"Don't they have cannibals down there?"

"No."

"Anacondas?"

"Relax, Tip. You're not going."

"Thanks."

"But you see the problem, don't you? We have sixty lawyers, all busy as hell and swamped with more work than we can possibly do. None of us can suddenly drop everything and go find this woman."

"Send a paralegal."

Josh didn't like that idea. He sipped his Scotch and puffed his cigar and listened to the flames pop in the fireplace. "It has to be a lawyer," he said, almost to himself.

The butler returned with fresh drinks. He inquired about dessert and coffee, but the guests already had what they wanted.

"What about Nate?" Josh asked when they were alone again.

It was obvious Josh had been thinking about Nate all along, and this slightly irritated Tip. "You kidding?" he said.

"No."

They pondered the idea of sending Nate for a while, each working past their initial objections and fears. Nate O'Riley was a partner, a twenty-three-year man who was, at the moment, locked away in a rehab unit in the Blue Ridge Mountains west of D.C. In the past ten years, he had been a frequent visitor to rehab facilities, each time drying out, breaking habits, growing closer to a higher power, working on his tan and tennis game, and vowing to kick his addictions once and for all. And while he swore that each crash was the last one, the final descent to rock bottom, each was always followed by an even harder fall. Now, at the age of forty-eight, he was broke, twice divorced, and freshly indicted for income tax evasion. His future was anything but bright.

"He used to be an outdoor type, didn't he?" Tip asked.

"Oh yeah. Scuba diving, rock climbing, all that crazy stuff. Then the slide began and he did nothing but work."

The slide had begun in his mid-thirties, at about the time he put together an impressive string of large verdicts against negligent doctors. Nate O'Riley became a star in the medical malpractice game, and also began drinking heavily and using coke. He neglected his family and became obsessive about his addictions—big verdicts, booze, and drugs. He somehow balanced both, but was always on the edge of disaster. Then he lost a case, and fell off the cliff for the first time. The firm hid him in a designer spa until he was sufficiently dried out, and he made an impressive comeback. The first of several.

"When does he get out?" Tip asked, no longer surprised by the idea and liking it more and more.

"Soon."

But Nate had become a serious addict. He could stay clean for months, even years, but he always crashed. The chemicals ravaged his mind and body. His behavior became quite bizarre, and the rumors of his craziness crept through the firm and ultimately spread through the lawyers' network of gossip.

Almost four months earlier, he had locked himself in a motel room with a bottle of rum and a sack of pills in what many of his colleagues viewed as a suicide attempt.

Josh committed him for the fourth time in ten years.

"It might be good for him," Tip said. "You know, to get away for a while."

SEVEN

O N THE THIRD DAY after Mr. Phelan's suicide, Hark
    Gettys arrived at his office before dawn, already tired but
anxious for the day to begin. He'd had a late dinner with Rex
Phelan, followed by a couple of hours in a bar, where they fretted
over the will and plotted strategy. So his eyes were red and puffy
and his head ached, but he was nonetheless moving quickly around
the coffeepot.

Hark's hourly rates varied. In the past year, he'd handled a nasty
divorce for as little as two hundred dollars an hour. He quoted
three-fifty to every prospective client, which was a bit low for such
an ambitious D.C. lawyer, but if he got them in the door at three-
fifty, he could certainly pad the billing and earn what he deserved.
An Indonesian cement company had paid him four hundred and
fifty an hour for a small matter, then tried to stiff him when the bill
came. He had settled a wrongful death case in which he earned a
third of three hundred and fifty thousand. So he was all over the
board when it came to fees.

Hark was a litigator in a forty-lawyer firm, a second-tier outfit
with a history of infighting and bickering which had hampered its

growth, and he longed to open his own shop. Almost half of his annual billings went for the overhead; the way he figured it, the money belonged in his pocket.

At some point during the sleepless night, he'd made the decision to raise his rate to five hundred an hour, and to make it retroactive a week. He'd worked on nothing but the Phelan matter for the past six days, and now that the old man was dead his crazy family was a lawyer's dream.

What Hark desperately wanted was a will contest—a long vicious fight with packs of lawyers filing tons of legal crap. A trial would be wonderful, a high-profile battle over one of the largest estates in America, with Hark in the center. Winning it would be nice, but winning wasn't crucial. He'd make a fortune, and he'd become famous, and that's what modern lawyering was all about.

At five hundred dollars an hour, sixty hours a week, fifty weeks a year, Hark's gross annual billings would be one and a half million. The overhead for a new office—rent, secretaries, paralegals—would be half a million at most, and so Hark could clear a million bucks if he left his miserable firm and opened a new one down the street.

Done. He gulped coffee and mentally said good-bye to his cluttered office. He'd bolt with the Phelan file and maybe one or two others. He'd take his secretary and his paralegal, and he'd do it quickly, before the firm laid claim to any of the Phelan fees.

He sat at his desk, his pulse racing with the anticipation of his spanking new venture, and he thought of all the ways he could start a war with Josh Stafford. There was reason to worry. Stafford had been unwilling to reveal the contents of the new will. He had questioned its validity, in light of the suicide. Hark had been rattled by the change in Stafford's tone immediately after the suicide. Now, Stafford had left town and refused to return calls.

Oh, how he longed for a fight.

At nine, he met with Libbigail Phelan Jeter and Mary Ross Phelan Jackman, the two daughters from Troy's first marriage. Rex had arranged the meeting, at Hark's insistence. Though both women had lawyers at the moment, Hark wanted them as clients. More clients meant more clout at the bargaining table and in the court-room, and it also meant he could bill each one of them five hundred an hour for the same work.

The meeting was awkward; neither woman trusted Hark because they didn't trust their brother Rex. TJ had three lawyers of his own, and their mother had another. Why should they join forces when no one else was doing so? With so much money at stake, shouldn't they keep their own lawyers?

Hark pressed but gained little ground. He was disappointed, but later charged ahead with plans to leave his firm immediately. He could smell the money.

LIBBIGAIL PHELAN JETER had been a rebellious child who disliked Lillian, her mother, and craved the attention of her father, who was seldom at home. She was nine when her parents divorced.

When she was fourteen, Lillian shipped her away to boarding school. Troy disapproved of boarding schools, as if he knew some-thing about child-rearing, and throughout high school he made an uncharacteristic effort to keep in touch with her. He often told her she was his favorite. She was certainly the brightest.

But he missed her graduation and forgot to send a gift. In the summer before college, she dreamed of ways to hurt him. She fled to Berkeley, ostensibly to study medieval Irish poetry, but in fact she planned to study very little, if at all. Troy hated the idea of her attending college anywhere in California, especially on such a radi-cal campus. Vietnam was ending. The students had won and it was time to celebrate.

She slipped easily into the culture of drugs and casual sex. She lived in a three-story house with a group of students of all races, sexes, and sexual preferences. The combinations changed weekly, as did the numbers. They called themselves a commune, but there was no structure or rules. Money was no problem because most came from wealthy families. Libbigail was known simply as a rich kid from Connecticut. At the time, Troy was worth only a hundred million or so.

With a sense of adventure, she moved along the drug chain until heroin seized her. Her supplier was a jazz drummer named Tino, who had somehow taken up residence in the commune. Tino was in his late thirties, a high school dropout from Memphis, and no one knew exactly how or when he became a member of their group. No one cared.

Libbigail cleaned herself up enough to travel East for her twenty-first birthday, a glorious day for all Phelan children because that was when the old man bestowed The Gift. Troy didn't believe in trusts for his children. If they weren't stable by the age of twenty-one, then why string them along? Trusts required trustees and lawyers and constant fights with the beneficiaries, who resented having their money doled out by accountants. Give them the money, Troy reasoned, let 'em sink or swim.

Most Phelans drowned quickly.

Troy skipped her birthday. He was somewhere in Asia on business. By then he was well into his second marriage, with Janie. Rocky and Geena were little kids, and he'd lost whatever interest he had in his first family.

Libbigail didn't miss him. The lawyers completed the arrangements for The Gift, and she laid up with Tino in a swanky Manhattan hotel for a week, stoned.

Her money lasted for almost five years, a stretch of time that included two husbands, numerous live-ins, two arrests, three lengthy lockdowns in detox units, and a car wreck that almost took her left leg.

Her current husband was an ex-biker she'd met in rehab. He weighed 320 pounds and had a gray frizzy beard that fell to his chest. He went by the name of Spike, and he had actually evolved into a decent sort. He built cabinets in a shop behind their modest home in the Baltimore suburb of Lutherville.

LIBBIGAIL'S LAWYER was a rumpled fellow named Wally Bright, and she went straight to his office after leaving Hark's. She made a full report of everything Hark had said. Wally was a small-timer who advertised quickie divorces on bus benches in the Bethesda area. He'd handled one of Libbigail's divorces and waited a year before he was paid for it. But he'd been patient with her. She was, after all, a Phelan. She would be his ticket to the fat fees he'd never quite been able to command.

In her presence, Wally called Hark Gettys and started a vicious phone fight that raged for fifteen minutes. He stomped around behind his desk, arms flailing, screaming obscenities into the phone. "I will kill for my client!" he raged at one point, and Libbigail was most impressed.

When he finished, he walked her gently to the door and kissed her on the cheek. He stroked her and patted her and fussed over her. He gave her the attention she had craved all her life. She was not a bad-looking woman; a bit heavy and showing the effects of a hard life, but Wally had seen much worse. Wally had slept with much worse. Given the right moment, Wally might make a move.

EIGHT

NATE'S LITTLE MOUNTAIN was covered with six inches of new snow when he was awakened by the stirring sounds of Chopin piped through his walls. Last week it had been Mozart. The week before, he couldn't remember. Vivaldi had been in his recent past, but so much of it was a haze.

As he had done every morning for almost four months, Nate walked to his window and gazed at the Shenandoah Valley spread before him, three thousand feet below. It too was covered with white, and he remembered that it was almost Christmas.

He would be out in time for Christmas. They—his doctors and Josh Stafford—had promised him that much. He thought about Christmas and became saddened by it. There had been some pleasant ones in the not too distant past, when the kids were small and life was stable. But the kids were gone now, either grown or taken away by their mothers, and the last thing Nate wanted was another Christmas in a bar with other miserable drunks singing carols and pretending all was merry.

The valley was white and still, a few cars moving like ants far away.

He was supposed to meditate for ten minutes, either in prayer or with the yoga they'd tried to teach him at Walnut Hill. Instead he did sit-ups, then went for a swim.

Breakfast was black coffee and a muffin, which he took with Sergio, his counselor/therapist/guru. And for the past four months, Sergio had also been his best friend. He knew everything about the miserable life of Nate O'Riley.

"You have a guest today," Sergio said.

"Who?"

"Mr. Stafford."

"Wonderful."

Any contact with the outside was welcome, primarily because it was so restricted. Josh had visited once a month. Two other friends from the firm had made the three-hour drive from D.C., but they were busy and Nate understood.

Television was prohibited at Walnut Hill because of the beer ads and because so many of the shows and movies glorified drinking, even drugs. Most popular magazines were kept away for the same reasons. It didn't matter to Nate. After four months, he didn't care what was happening at the Capitol or on Wall Street or in the Middle East.

"When?" he asked.

"Late morning."

"After my workout?"

"Of course."

Nothing interfered with the workout, a two-hour orgy of sweat and grunting and yelling with a sadistic personal trainer, a sharply toned female Nate secretly adored.

He was resting in his suite, eating a blood orange and watching the valley again, when Josh arrived.

"You look great," Josh said. "How much weight have you lost?"

"Fourteen pounds," Nate said, patting his flat stomach.

"Very lean. Maybe I should spend some time here."

"I highly recommend it. The food is completely fat-free, taste-free, prepared by a chef with an accent. The portions cover half a saucer, couple of bites and you're done. Lunch and dinner take about seven minutes if you chew slowly."

"For a thousand bucks a day you expect great food."

"Did you bring me some cookies or something, Josh? Some Chips Ahoy or Oreos? Surely you hid something in your briefcase."

"Sorry, Nate. I'm clean."

"Some Doritos or M&M's?"

"Sorry."

Nate took a bite of his orange. They were sitting next to each other, enjoying the view. Minutes passed.

"How you doing?" Josh asked.

"I need to get out of here, Josh. I'm becoming a robot."

"Your doc says another week or so."

"Great. Then what?"

"We'll see."

"What does that mean?"

"It means we'll see."

"Come on, Josh."

"We'll take our time, and see what happens."

"Can I come back to the firm, Josh? Talk to me."

"Not so fast, Nate. You have enemies."

"Who doesn't? But hell, it's your firm. Those guys will go along with whatever you say."

"You have a couple of problems."

"I have a thousand problems. But you can't kick me out."

"The bankruptcy we can work through. The indictment is not so easy."

No, it was not so easy, and Nate couldn't simply dismiss it. From 1992 to 1995, he had failed to report about sixty thousand dollars in other income.

He tossed the orange peel in a wastebasket, and said, "So what am I supposed to do? Sit around the house all day?"

"If you're lucky."

"What's that supposed to mean?"

Josh had to be delicate. His friend was emerging from a black hole. Shocks and surprises had to be avoided.

"Do you think I'm going to prison?" Nate asked.

"Troy Phelan died," Josh said, and it took Nate a second to change course.

"Oh, Mr. Phelan," he said.

Nate had had his own little wing in the firm. It was at the end of a long hallway, on the sixth floor, and he and another lawyer and three paralegals and a half-dozen secretaries worked on suing doctors and cared little about the rest of the firm. He certainly knew who Troy Phelan was, but he'd never touched his legal work. "I'm sorry," he said.

"So you haven't heard?"

"I hear nothing here. When did he die?"

"Four days ago. Jumped from a window."

"Without a parachute?"

"Bingo."

"Couldn't fly."

"No. He didn't try. I saw it happen. He had just signed two wills—the first prepared by me; the second, and last, handwritten by himself. Then he bolted and jumped."

"You saw it?"

"Yes."

"Wow. Musta been a crazy bastard."

There was a trace of humor in Nate's voice. Nearly four months earlier, he'd been found by a maid in a motel room, his stomach full of pills and rum.

"He left everything to an illegitimate daughter I'd never heard of."

"Is she married? What does she look like?"

"I want you to go find her."

"Me?"

"Yes."

"She's lost?"

"We don't know where she is."

"How much did he—"

"Somewhere around eleven billion, before taxes."

"Does she know it?"

"No. She doesn't even know he's dead."

"Does she know Troy's her father?"

"I don't know what she knows."

"Where is she?"

"Brazil, we think. She's a missionary working with a remote tribe of Indians."

Nate stood and walked around the room. "I spent a week there once," he said. "I was in college, or maybe law school. It was Carnaval, naked girls dancing in the streets of Rio, the samba bands, a million people partying all night." His voice trailed away as the nice little memory surfaced and quickly faded.

"This is not Carnaval."

"No. I'm sure it's not. Would you like some coffee?"

"Yes. Black."

Nate pressed a button on the wall and announced his order into the intercom. A thousand bucks a day also covered room service.

"How long will I be gone?" he asked, sitting again by the window.

"It's a wild guess, but I'd say ten days. There's no hurry, and she might be hard to find."

"What part of the country?"

"Western, near Bolivia. This outfit she works for specializes in sending its people into the jungles, where they minister to Indians from the Stone Age. We've done some research, and they seem to take pride in finding the most remote people on the face of the earth."

"You want me to first find the right jungle, then hike into it in search of the right tribe of Indians, then somehow convince them that I'm a friendly lawyer from the States and they should help me find a woman who probably doesn't want to be found to begin with."

"Something like that."

"Might be fun."

"Think of it as an adventure."

"Plus, it'll keep me out of the office, right, Josh? Is that it? A diversion while you sort things out."

"Someone has to go, Nate. A lawyer from our firm has to meet this woman face to face, show her a copy of the will, explain it to her, and find out what she wants to do next. It cannot be done by a paralegal or a Brazilian lawyer."

"Why me?"

"Because everybody else is busy. You know the routine. You've lived it for more than twenty years. Life at the office, lunch at the courthouse, sleep on the train. Plus, it might be good for you."

"Are you trying to keep me away from the streets, Josh? Because if you are, then you're wasting your time. I'm clean. Clean and sober. No more bars, no more parties, no more dealers. I'm clean, Josh. Forever."

Josh nodded along because he was certainly expected to. But he'd been there before. "I believe you," he said, wanting to very badly.

The porter knocked and brought their coffee on a silver tray.

After a while, Nate asked, "What about the indictment? I'm not supposed to leave the country until it's wrapped up."

"I've talked to the Judge, told him it was pressing business. He wants to see you in ninety days."

"Is he nice?"

"He's Santa Claus."

"So if I'm convicted, do you think he'll give me a break?"

"That's a year away. Let's worry about it later."

Nate was sitting at a small table, hunched over his coffee, staring into the cup as he thought of questions. Josh was on the other side, still gazing into the distance.

"What if I say no?" Nate asked.

Josh shrugged as if it didn't matter. "No big deal. We'll find someone else. Think of it as a vacation. You're not afraid of the jungle, are you?"

"Of course not."

"Then go have some fun."

"When would I leave?"

"In a week. Brazil requires a visa, and we'll have to pull some strings. Plus there are some loose ends around here."

Walnut Hill required at least a week of PreRelease, a period of conditioning before it fed its clients back to the wolves. They had been pampered, sobered, brainwashed, and nudged into emotional, mental, and physical shape. PreRelease braced them for the reentry.

"A week," Nate repeated to himself.

"About a week, yes."

"And it'll take ten days."

"I'm just guessing."

"So I'll be down there during the holidays."

"I guess it looks that way."

"That's a great idea."

"You want to skip Christmas?"

"Yes."

"What about your kids?"

There were four of them, two by each wife. One in grad school and one in college, two in middle school.

He stirred his coffee with a small spoon, and said, "Not a word, Josh. Almost four months here, and not a word from any of them." His voice ached and his shoulders sagged. He looked quite frail, for a second.

"I'm sorry," Josh said.

Josh had certainly heard from the families. Both wives had lawyers who'd called to sniff around for money. Nate's oldest child was a grad student at Northwestern who needed tuition money, and he personally had called Josh to inquire not about his father's well-being or whereabouts but, more important, his father's share of the firm's profits last year. He was cocky and rude, and Josh had finally cursed him.

"I'd like to avoid all the parties and holiday cheer," Nate said, rallying as he got to his bare feet and walked around the room.

"So you'll go?"

"Is it the Amazon?"

"No. It's the Pantanal, the largest wetlands in the world."

"Piranhas, anacondas, alligators?"

"Sure."

"Cannibals?"

"No more than D.C."

"Seriously."

"I don't think so. They haven't lost a missionary in eleven years."

"What about a lawyer?"

"I'm sure they would enjoy filleting one. Come on, Nate. This is not heavy lifting. If I weren't so busy, I'd love to go. The Pantanal is a great ecological reserve."

"I've never heard of it."

"That's because you stopped traveling years ago. You went into your office and didn't come out."

"Except for rehab."

"Take a vacation. See another part of the world."

Nate sipped coffee long enough to redirect the conversation. "And what happens when I get back? Do I have my office? Am I still a partner?"

"Is that what you want?"

"Of course," Nate said, but with a slight hesitation.

"Are you sure?"

"What else would I do?"

"I don't know, Nate, but this is your fourth rehab in ten years. The crashes are getting worse. If you walked out now, you'd go straight to the office and be the world's greatest malpractice litigator for six months. You'd ignore the old friends, the old bars, the old neighborhoods. Nothing but work, work, work. Before long you'd have a couple of big verdicts, big trials, big pressure. You'd step it up a notch. After a year, there would be a crack somewhere. An old friend might find you. A girl from another life. Maybe a bad jury gives you a bad verdict. I'd be watching every move, but I can never tell when the slide begins."

"No more slides, Josh. I swear."

"I've heard it before, and I want to believe you. But what if your demons come out again, Nate? You came within minutes of killing yourself last time."

"No more crashes."

"The next one will be the last, Nate. We'll have a funeral and say good-bye and watch them lower you into the ground. I don't want that to happen."

"It won't, I swear."

"Then forget about the office. There's too much pressure there."

The thing Nate hated about rehab was the long periods of silence, or meditation, as Sergio called them. The patients were expected to squat like monks in the semidarkness, close their eyes, and find inner peace. Nate could do the squatting and all that, but behind the closed eyes he was retrying lawsuits, and fighting the IRS, and plotting against his ex-wives, and, most important, worrying about the future. This conversation with Josh was one he'd played out many times.

But his smart retorts and quick comebacks failed him under pressure. Almost four months of virtual solitude had dulled his reflexes. He could manage to look pitiful, and that was all. "Come on, Josh. You can't just kick me out."

"You've litigated for over twenty years, Nate. That's about average. It's time to move on to something else."

"So I'll become a lobbyist, and do lunch with the press secretaries for a thousand little congressmen."

"We'll find a place for you. But it won't be in the courtroom."

"I'm not good at doing lunch. I want to litigate."

"The answer is no. You can stay with the firm, make a lot of money, stay healthy, take up golf, and life will be good, assuming the IRS doesn't send you away."

For a few pleasant moments the IRS had been forgotten. Now it was back, and Nate sat down again. He squeezed a small pack of honey into his lukewarm coffee; sugar and artificial sweeteners couldn't be allowed in a place as healthy as Walnut Hill.

"A couple of weeks in the Brazilian wetlands is beginning to sound good," he said.

"So you'll go?"

"Yes."

SINCE NATE HAD plenty of time to read, Josh left him a thick file on the Phelan estate and its mysterious new heir. And there were two books on remote Indians of South America.

Nate read nonstop for eight hours, even neglecting dinner. He was suddenly anxious to leave, to begin his adventure. When Sergio checked on him at ten, he was sitting like a monk in the middle of his bed, papers sprawled around him, lost in another world.

"It's time for me to leave," Nate said.

"Yes, it is," Sergio replied. "I'll start the paperwork tomorrow."

NINE

THE INFIGHTING grew worse as the Phelan heirs spent less time talking to each other and more time in their lawyers' offices. A week passed with no will, and no plans to probate. With their fortunes within sight but just out of reach, the heirs became even more agitated. Several lawyers were fired, with more brought in to replace them.

Mary Ross Phelan Jackman fired hers because he wasn't charging enough per hour. Her husband was a successful orthopedic surgeon with lots of business interests. He dealt with lawyers every day. Their new one was a fireball named Grit, who made a noisy entrance into the fray at six hundred dollars per hour.

While the heirs waited, they also incurred massive debt. Contracts were signed for mansions. New cars were delivered. Consultants were hired to do such varied things as design pool houses, locate just the right private jet, and give advice on which thoroughbred to purchase. If the heirs weren't fighting, then they were shopping. Ramble was the exception, but only because he was a minor. He hung out with his lawyer, who was certainly incurring debt on behalf of his client.

Snowball litigation is often commenced with a race to the court-house. With Josh Stafford refusing to reveal the will, and at the same time dropping mysterious hints about Troy's lack of testamentary capacity, the lawyers for the Phelan heirs finally panicked.

Ten days after the suicide, Hark Gettys went to the Circuit Court of Fairfax County, Virginia, and filed a Petition to Compel the Last Will and Testament of Troy L. Phelan. With all the finesse of an ambitious lawyer to be reckoned with, he tipped a reporter from the *Post*. They chatted for an hour after the filing, some comments off the record, others offered for the glory of the lawyer. A photographer took some pictures.

Oddly, Hark filed his petition on behalf of all Phelan heirs. And he listed their names and addresses as if they were his clients. He faxed them copies when he returned to his office. Within minutes his phone lines were burning.

The *Post*'s story the next morning was complemented by a large photo of Hark frowning and rubbing his beard. The story covered even more space than he'd dreamed of. He read it at sunrise in a coffee shop in Chevy Chase, then hurriedly drove to his new office.

A couple of hours later, just after nine, the circuit court clerk's office in Fairfax County was crawling with lawyers, more so than normal. They arrived in tight little packs, spoke in terse sentences to the clerks, and worked hard at ignoring each other. Their petitions were varied but they all wanted the same things—recognition in the Phelan matter, and a look at the will.

Probate matters in Fairfax County were randomly assigned to one of a dozen judges. The Phelan matter landed on the desk of the Honorable F. Parr Wycliff, age thirty-six, a jurist with little experience but lots of ambition. He was thrilled to get such a high-profile case.

Wycliff's office was in the Fairfax County Courthouse, and throughout the morning he monitored the filings in the clerk's office. His secretary hauled in the petitions, and he read them immediately.

When the dust settled below him, he called Josh Stafford to introduce himself. They chatted politely for a few minutes, the usual lawyerly preliminaries, stiff and cautious because weightier matters were coming. Josh had never heard of Judge Wycliff.

"Is there a will?" Wycliff finally asked.

"Yes, Your Honor. There is a will." Josh chose his words carefully. It was a felony in Virginia to hide a will. If the Judge wanted to know, then Josh would certainly cooperate.

"Where is it?"

"Here in my office."

"Who is the executor?"

"Me."

"When do you plan to probate it?"

"My client asked me to wait until January fifteenth."

"Hmmmm. Any particular reason?"

There was a simple reason. Troy wanted his greedy children to enjoy one last spending spree before he jerked the rug from under them. It was mean and cruel, vintage Troy.

"I have no idea," Josh said. "The will is holographic. Mr. Phelan signed it just seconds before he jumped."

"A holographic will?"

"Yes."

"Weren't you with him?"

"Yes. It's a long story."

"Perhaps I should hear it."

"Perhaps you should."

Josh had a busy day. Wycliff did not, but he made it sound as though every minute were planned. They agreed to meet for lunch, a quick sandwich in Wycliff's office.

SERGIO DID NOT LIKE the idea of Nate's trip to South America. After almost four months in a highly structured place like Walnut Hill, where the doors and gates were locked and an unseen guard with a gun watched the road a mile down the mountain, and where TV, movies, games, magazines, and phones were heavily monitored, the reentry into a familiar society was often traumatizing. The notion of a reentry by way of Brazil was more than troubling.

Nate didn't care. He was not at Walnut Hill by court order. Josh had put him there, and if Josh asked him to play hide-and-seek in the jungles, so be it. Sergio could bitch and moan all he wanted.

PreRelease turned into a week from hell. The diet changed from no-fat to low-fat, with such inevitable ingredients as salt, pepper, cheese, and a little butter added to prepare his system for the evils out there. Nate's stomach rebelled, and he lost three more pounds.

"Just an inkling of what's waiting for you down there," Sergio said smugly.

They fought during therapy, which was common at Walnut Hill. Skin had to be thickened, edges sharpened. Sergio began to distance himself from his patient. It was usually difficult to say good-bye, and Sergio shortened the sessions and became aloof.

With the end in sight, Nate began counting the hours.

JUDGE WYCLIFF inquired as to the contents of the will, and Josh politely declined to tell him. They were eating deli sandwiches at a small table in His Honor's small office. The law did not require Josh to reveal what was in the will, at least not now. And Wycliff was slightly out of bounds to ask, but his curiosity was understandable.

"I'm somewhat sympathetic to the petitioners," he said. "They have a right to know what's in the will. Why delay it?"

"I'm just following my client's wishes," Josh replied.

"You have to probate the will sooner or later."

"Of course."

Wycliff slid his appointment book up to his plastic plate, and gazed down with a squint over his reading glasses. "Today is December twentieth. There's no way to assemble everyone before Christmas. How does the twenty-seventh look to you?"

"What do you have in mind?"

"A reading of the will."

The idea struck Josh, and he almost choked on a dill spear. Gather them all together, the Phelans and their entourages and new friends and hangers-on, and all their merry lawyers, and pack them into Wycliff's courtroom. Make sure the press knows about it. As he crunched on another bite of pickle, and looked at his little black book, he worked hard to suppress a grin. He could hear the gasps and groans, the shockwaves, the utter, bitter disbelief, then the muted cursing. Then, perhaps a sniffle and maybe a sob or two as the Phelans tried to absorb what their beloved father had done to them.

It would be a vicious, glorious, thoroughly unique moment in the history of American law, and Josh suddenly couldn't wait. "The twenty-seventh is fine with me," he said.

"Good. I'll notify the parties as soon as I can identify all of them. There are lots of lawyers."

"It helps if you remember that there are six kids and three ex-wives, so there are nine principal sets of lawyers."

"I hope my courtroom is big enough."

Standing room only, Josh almost said. People packed together, with not a sound as the envelope is opened, the will unfolded, the unbelievable words read. "I suggest you read the will," Josh said.

Wycliff certainly intended to. He was seeing the same scene as Josh. It would be one of his finest moments, reading a will that disposed of eleven billion dollars.

"I assume the will is somewhat controversial," the Judge said.

"It's wicked."

His Honor actually smiled.

TEN

BEFORE HIS most recent crash, Nate had lived in an aging condo in Georgetown, one he'd leased after his last divorce. But it was gone now, a victim of the bankruptcy. So, literally, there was no place for Nate to spend his first night of freedom.

As usual, Josh had carefully planned the release. He arrived at Walnut Hill on the appointed day with a duffel bag filled with new and neatly pressed J. Crew shorts and shirts for the trip south. He had the passport and the visa, plenty of cash, lots of directions and tickets, a game plan. Even a first-aid kit.

Nate never had the chance to be anxious. He said good-bye to a few members of the staff, but most were busy elsewhere because they avoided departures. He walked proudly through the front door after 140 days of wonderful sobriety; clean, tanned, fit, down 17 pounds to 174, a weight he hadn't known in twenty years.

Josh drove, and for the first five minutes nothing was said. The snow blanketed the pastures, but thinned quickly as they left the Blue Ridge. It was December 22. At a very low volume, the radio played carols.

"Could you turn that off?" Nate finally said.

"What?"

"The radio."

Josh punched a button, and the music he hadn't heard disappeared.

"How do you feel?" Josh asked.

"Could you pull over at the nearest quick shop?"

"Sure. Why?"

"I'd like to get a six-pack."

"Very funny."

"I'd kill for a tall Coca-Cola."

They bought soft drinks and peanuts at a country store. The lady at the cash register said a cheery "Merry Christmas," and Nate could not respond. Back in the car, Josh headed for Dulles, two hours away.

"Your flight goes to São Paulo, where you'll lay over three hours before catching one to a city called Campo Grande."

"Do these people speak English?"

"No. They're Brazilian. They speak Portuguese."

"Of course they do."

"But you'll find English at the airport."

"How big is Campo Grande?"

"Half a million, but it's not your destination. From there, you'll catch a commuter flight to a place called Corumbá. The towns get smaller."

"And so do the airplanes."

"Yes, same as here."

"For some reason, the idea of a Brazilian commuter flight is not appealing. Help me here, Josh. I'm nervous."

"Either that or a six-hour bus ride."

"Keep talking."

"In Corumbá, you'll meet a lawyer named Valdir Ruiz. He speaks English."

"Have you talked to him?"

"Yes."

"Could you understand him?"

"Yes, for the most part. A very nice man. Works for about fifty bucks an hour, if you can believe that."

"How big is Corumbá?"

"Ninety thousand."

"So they'll have food and water, and a place to sleep."

"Yes, Nate, you'll have a room. That's more than you can say for here."

"Ouch."

"Sorry. Do you want to back out?"

"Yes, but I'm not going to. My goal at this point is to flee this country before I hear 'Jingle Bells' again. I'd sleep in a ditch for the next two weeks to avoid 'Frosty the Snowman.' "

"Forget the ditch. It's a nice hotel."

"What am I supposed to do with Valdir?"

"He's looking for a guide to take you into the Pantanal."

"How? Plane? Helicopter?"

"Boat, probably. As I understand the area, it's nothing but swamps and rivers."

"And snakes, alligators, piranhas."

"What a little coward you are. I thought you wanted to go."

"I do. Drive faster."

"Relax." Josh pointed to a briefcase behind the passenger's seat. "Open that," he said. "It's your carry-on bag."

Nate pulled and grunted. "It weighs a ton. What's in here?"

"Good stuff."

It was made of brown leather, new but built to look well used, and large enough to hold a small legal library. Nate sat it on his knees and popped it open. "Toys," he said.

"That tiny gray instrument there is the latest high-tech digital phone," Josh said, proud of the things he'd collected. "Valdir will have local service for you when you get to Corumbá."

"So they have phones in Brazil."

"Lots of them. In fact, telecommunications are booming down there. Everybody has a cell phone."

"Those poor people. What's this?"

"A computer."

"What the hell for?"

"It's the latest thing. Look how small."

"I can't even read the keyboard."

"You can hook it to the phone and actually get your e-mail."

"Wow. And I'm supposed to do this in the middle of a swamp with snakes and alligators watching?"

"It's up to you."

"Josh, I don't even use e-mail at the office."

"It's not for you. It's for me. I want to keep up with you. When you find her, I want to know immediately."

"What's this?"

"The best toy in the box. It's a satellite phone. You can use it anywhere on the face of the earth. Keep the batteries charged, and you can always find me."

"You just said they had a great phone system."

"Not in the Pantanal. It's a hundred thousand square miles of wetlands, with no towns and very few people. That SatFone will be your only means of communication once you leave Corumbá."

Nate opened the hard plastic case and examined the glossy little phone. "How much did this cost you?" he asked.

"Me, not a dime."

"Okay, how much did it cost the Phelan estate?"

"Forty-four hundred bucks. Worth every penny of it."

"Do my Indians have electricity?" Nate was flipping through the owner's manual.

"Of course not."

"Then how am I supposed to keep the batteries charged?"

"There's an extra battery. You'll think of something."

"So much for a quiet getaway."

"It's going to be very quiet. You'll thank me for the toys when you get there."

"Can I thank you now?"

"No."

"Thanks, Josh. For everything."

"Don't mention it."

IN THE CROWDED TERMINAL, at a small table across from a busy bar, they sipped weak espresso and read newspapers. Josh was very conscious of the bar; Nate didn't seem to be. The neon Heineken logo was hard to miss.

A tired and skinny Santa Claus ambled by, looking for children to take cheap gifts from his bag. Elvis sang "Blue Christmas" from a jukebox in the bar. The foot traffic was thick, the noise unnerving, everyone flying home for the holidays.

"Are you okay?" Josh asked.

"Yes, I'm fine. Why don't you leave? I'm sure you have better things to do."

"I'll stay."

"Look, Josh, I'm fine. If you think I'm waiting for you to leave so I can dash over there to the bar and guzzle vodka, you're wrong. I have no desire for booze. I'm clean, and very proud of it."

Josh looked a bit sheepish, primarily because Nate had read his mind. Nate's binges were legendary. If he cracked, there wasn't enough booze in the airport to satisfy him. "I'm not worried about that," he said, lying.

"Then go. I'm a big boy."

They said good-bye at the gate, a warm embrace and promises to call almost on the hour. Nate was anxious to settle into his nest in first class. Josh had a thousand things to do at the office.

Two small, secret precautionary steps had been taken by Josh. First, adjacent seats had been booked for the flight. Nate would have the window; the aisle would remain vacant. No sense having some thirsty executive sitting next to Nate, swilling Scotch and wine. The seats cost over seven thousand dollars each for the round trip, but money was of no concern.

Second, Josh had talked at length with an airline official about Nate's rehab. No alcohol was to be served, under any circumstances. A letter from Josh to the airline was on board, just in case it had to be produced to convince Nate.

A flight attendant served him orange juice and coffee. He wrapped himself in a thin blanket, and watched the sprawl of D.C. disappear below him as the Varig airplane climbed through the clouds.

There was relief in the escape, from Walnut Hill and Sergio, from the city and its grind, from the past troubles with the last wife and the bankruptcy, and from the current mess with the IRS. At thirty thousand feet, Nate had almost decided he would never return.

But every reentry was nerve-racking. The fear of another slide was always there, just beneath the surface. The frightening part now was that there had been so many reentries he felt like a veteran. Like wives and big verdicts, he could now compare them. Would there always be another one?

During dinner, he realized Josh had been working behind the scenes. Wine was never offered. He picked through the food with the caution of one who'd just spent nearly four months enjoying the great lettuces of the world; until a few days ago, no fat, butter, grease, or sugar. The last thing he wanted was a queasy stomach.

He napped briefly, but he was tired of sleeping. As a busy lawyer and late-night prowler, he'd learned to live with little sleep. The first month at Walnut Hill they'd drugged him with pills and he'd slept ten hours a day. He couldn't fight them if he were in a coma.

He assembled his toys in the empty seat next to him, and began reading his collection of owner's manuals. The satellite phone intrigued him, though it was difficult to believe he would actually be forced to use it.

Another phone caught his attention. It was the latest technical gadget in air travel, a sleek little device practically hidden in the wall next to his seat. He grabbed it and called Sergio at home. Sergio was having a late dinner, but happy to hear from him nonetheless.

"Where are you?" he asked.

"In a bar," Nate replied, his voice low because the lights in the cabin were down.

"Very funny."

"I'm probably over Miami, with eight hours to go. Just found this phone on board and wanted to check in."

"So you're okay."

"I'm fine. Do you miss me?"

"Not yet. You miss me?"

"Are you kidding? I'm a free man, flying off to the jungle for a marvelous adventure. I'll miss you later, okay?"

"Okay. And you'll call if you get in trouble."

"No trouble, Serge. Not this time."

"Atta boy, Nate."

"Thanks, Serge."

"Don't mention it. Just call me."

A movie started, but no one was watching. The flight attendant brought more coffee. Nate's secretary was a long-suffering woman named Alice, who'd cleaned up after him for almost ten years. She lived with her sister in an old house in Arlington. He called her next. They'd spoken once in the past four months.

The conversation lasted for half an hour. She was delighted to hear his voice, and learn that he'd been released. She knew nothing about his trip to South America, which was a bit odd because she normally knew everything. But she was reserved on the phone, even cautious. Nate, the trial lawyer, smelled a rat, and attacked as if on cross-examination.

She was still in litigation, still at the same desk, doing pretty much the same thing but for a different lawyer. "Who?" Nate demanded.

A new guy. A new litigator. Her words were deliberate, and Nate knew that she had been fully briefed by Josh himself. Of course Nate would call her as soon as he was released.

Which office was the new guy in? Who was his paralegal? Where did he come from? How much medical malpractice had he done? Was her assignment with him just temporary?

Alice was sufficiently vague.

"Who's in my office?" he asked.

"No one. It hasn't been touched. Still has little stacks of files in every corner."

"What's Kerry doing?"

"Staying busy. Waiting for you." Kerry was Nate's favorite paralegal.

Alice had all the right answers, while revealing little. She was especially mum about the new litigator.

"Get ready," he said as the conversation ran out of steam. "It's time for a comeback."

"It's been dull, Nate."

He hung up slowly, and played back her words. Something was different. Josh was quietly rearranging his firm. Would Nate get lost in the shuffle? Probably not, but his courtroom days were over.

He would worry about it later, he decided. There were so many people to call, and so many phones to do it with. He knew a judge who'd kicked booze ten years earlier, and he wanted to check in with his wonderful report from rehab. His first ex-wife deserved a blistering call, but he wasn't in the mood. And he wanted to phone all four of his children and ask why they'd hadn't called or written.

Instead he took a folder from his case and began reading about Mr. Troy Phelan and the business at hand. At midnight, somewhere over the Caribbean, Nate drifted away.

ELEVEN

A N HOUR before dawn, the plane began its descent. He had
slept through breakfast, and when he awoke a flight attendant hurriedly brought coffee.

The city of São Paulo appeared, an enormous sprawl that covered
almost eight hundred square miles. Nate watched the sea of lights
below and wondered how one city could hold twenty million people.

In a rush of Portuguese, the pilot said good morning and then
several paragraphs of greetings that Nate missed entirely. The English translation that followed was not much better. Surely he
wouldn't be forced to point and grunt his way across the country.
The language barrier caused a short bout of anxiety, but it ended
when a pretty Brazilian flight attendant asked him to buckle his seat
belt.

The airport was hot and swarming with people. He collected his
new duffel bag, walked it through customs without so much as a
glance from anyone, and rechecked it on Varig to Campo Grande.
Then he found a coffee bar with the menu on the wall. He pointed
and said, "Espresso," and the cashier rang him up. She frowned at

his American money, but changed it anyway. One Brazilian real equaled one American dollar. Nate now owned a few reais.

He sipped the coffee while standing shoulder to shoulder with some rowdy Japanese tourists. Other languages flew around him; German and Spanish mixing with the Portuguese coming over the loudspeakers. He wished he'd bought a phrase book so he could at least understand a word or two.

Isolation settled in, slowly at first. In the midst of multitudes, he was a lonely man. He didn't know a soul. Almost no one knew where he was at that moment, and damned few people cared. Cigarette smoke from the tourists boiled around him, and he walked quickly away, into the main concourse, where he could see the ceiling two levels above and the ground floor below. He began walking through the crowds, aimlessly, carrying the heavy briefcase, cursing Josh for filling it with so much junk.

He heard loud English, and drifted toward it. Some businessmen were waiting near the United counter, and he found a seat near them. It was snowing in Detroit, and they were anxious to get home for Christmas. A pipeline had brought them to Brazil, and before long Nate tired of their drivel. They cured whatever homesickness he felt.

He missed Sergio. After the last rehab, the clinic had placed Nate in a halfway house for a week to ease the reentry. He hated the place and the routine, but with hindsight the idea had merit. You needed a few days to get reoriented. Maybe Sergio was right. He called him from a pay phone, and woke him up. It was six-thirty in São Paulo, but only four-thirty in Virginia.

Sergio didn't mind. It went with the territory.

THERE WERE no first-class seats on the flight to Campo Grande, nor any empty ones. Nate was pleasantly surprised to observe that every face was behind the morning news, and a wide variety of papers at that. The dailies were as slick and modern as any in the States, and they were being read by people who had a thirst for the news. Perhaps Brazil wasn't as backward as he thought. These people could read! The airliner, a 727, was clean and newly refurbished. Coca-Cola and Sprite were on the drink cart; he almost felt at home.

Sitting by the window twenty rows back, he ignored the memo on Indians in his lap, and admired the countryside below. It was vast and lush and green, rolling with hills, dotted with cattle farms and crisscrossed with red dirt roads. The soil was a vivid burnt orange, and the roads ran haphazardly from one small settlement to the next. Highways were virtually nonexistent.

A paved road appeared, and there was traffic. The plane descended and the pilot welcomed them to Campo Grande. There were tall buildings, a crowded downtown, the obligatory soccer field, lots of streets and cars, and every residence had a red-tiled roof. Thanks to the typical big-firm efficiency, he possessed a memo, one no doubt prepared by the greenest of associates working at three hundred dollars an hour, in which Campo Grande was analyzed as if its presence were crucial to the matters at hand. Six hundred thousand people. A center for cattle trade. Lots of cowboys. Rapid growth. Modern conveniences. Nice to know, but why bother? Nate would not sleep there.

The airport seemed remarkably small for a city its size, and he realized he was comparing everything to the United States. This had to stop. When he stepped from the plane, he was hit with the heat. It was at least ninety degrees. Two days before Christmas, and it was sweltering in the southern hemisphere. He squinted in the brilliance of the sun, and descended the steps with a firm hand on the guardrail.

He managed to order lunch in the airport restaurant, and when it was brought to his table he was pleased to see that it was something he could eat. A grilled chicken sandwich in a bun he'd never seen before, with fries as crisp as those in any fast food joint in the States. He ate slowly while watching the runway in the distance. Halfway through lunch, a twin-engine turbo-prop of Air Pantanal landed and taxied to the terminal. Six people got off.

He stopped chewing as he wrestled with a sudden attack of fear. Commuter flights were the ones you read about and saw on CNN, except that no one back home would ever hear about this one if it went down.

But the plane looked sturdy and clean, even somewhat modern, and the pilots were well-dressed professionals. Nate continued eating. Think positive, he told himself.

He roamed the small terminal for an hour. In a news shop he bought a Portuguese phrase book and began memorizing words. He read travel ads for adventures into the Pantanal—ecotourism, it was called in English. There were cars for rent. A money exchange booth, a bar with beer signs and whiskey bottles lined on a shelf. And near the front entrance was a slender, artificial Christmas tree with a solitary string of lights. He watched them blink to the tune of some Brazilian carol, and despite his efforts not to, Nate thought of his children.

It was the day before Christmas Eve. Not all memories were painful.

He boarded the plane with teeth clenched and spine stiffened, then slept for most of the hour it took to reach Corumbá. The small airport there was humid and packed with Bolivians waiting for a flight to Santa Cruz. They were laden with boxes and bags of Christmas gifts.

He found a cabdriver who spoke not a word of English, but it didn't matter. Nate showed him the words "Palace Hotel" on his travel itinerary, and they sped away in an old, dirty Mazda.

Corumbá had ninety thousand people, according to yet another memo prepared by Josh's staff. Situated on the Paraguay River, on the Bolivian border, it had long since declared itself to be the capital of the Pantanal. River traffic and trade had built the city, and kept it going.

Through the heat and swelter of the back of the taxi, Corumbá appeared to be a lazy, pleasant little town. The streets were paved and wide and lined with trees. Merchants sat in the shade of their storefronts, waiting for customers and chatting with each other. Teenagers darted through traffic on scooters. Barefoot children ate ice cream at sidewalk tables.

As they approached the business district, cars bunched together and stopped in the heat. The driver mumbled something, but was not particularly disturbed. The same driver in New York or D.C. would've been near the point of violence.

But it was Brazil, and Brazil was in South America. The clocks ran slower. Nothing was urgent. Time was not as crucial. Take off your watch, Nate told himself. Instead, he closed his eyes and breathed the heavy air.

The Palace Hotel was in the center of downtown, on a street that descended slightly toward the Paraguay River sitting majestically in the distance. He gave the cabbie a handful of reais, and waited patiently for his change. He thanked him in Portuguese, a feeble *"Obrigado."* The cabbie smiled and said something he didn't understand. The doors to the lobby were open, as were all doors facing the sidewalks of Corumbá.

The first words he heard upon entering were being yelled by someone from Texas. A band of roughnecks was in the process of checking out. They had been drinking and were in a festive mood, anxious to get home for the holidays. Nate took a seat near a television and waited for them to clear.

His room was on the eighth floor. For eighteen dollars a day he got a twelve-by-twelve with a narrow bed very close to the floor. If it had a mattress, it was quite thin. No box spring to speak of. There were a desk with a chair, a window unit of AC, a small refrigerator with bottled water, colas, and beer, and a clean bathroom with soap and plenty of towels. Not bad, he told himself. This was an adventure. Not the Four Seasons, but certainly livable.

For half an hour, he tried to call Josh. But the language barrier stopped him. The clerk at the front desk knew enough English to find an outside operator, but from there the Portuguese took over. He tried his new cell phone, but the local service had not been activated.

Nate stretched his tired body the length of his flimsy little bed, and went to sleep.

VALDIR RUIZ was a short man with a tiny waist, light brown skin, a small slick head missing most of the hair except for a few strands he kept oiled and combed back. His eyes were black and bunched with wrinkles, the result of thirty years of heavy smoking. He was fifty-two, and at the age of seventeen he'd left home to spend a year with a family in Iowa as a Rotary exchange student. He was proud of his English, though he didn't use it much in Corumbá. He watched CNN and American television most nights in an effort to stay sharp.

After the year in Iowa, he went to college in Campo Grande, then law school in Rio. He reluctantly returned to Corumbá to work in his uncle's small law firm, and to care for his aging parents. For more years than he cared to count, Valdir had endured the languid pace of advocacy in Corumbá, while dreaming of what might have been in the big city.

But he was a pleasant man, happy with life in the way most Brazilians tend to be. He worked efficiently in his small office, just himself and a secretary who answered the phone and did the typing. Valdir liked real estate, the deeds and contracts and such. He never went to court, primarily because courtrooms were not an integral part of practicing law in Brazil. Trials were rare. American-style litigation had not found its way south; in fact, it was still confined to the fifty states. Valdir marveled at the things lawyers did and said on CNN. Why do they clamor for the attention? he often asked himself. Lawyers staging press conferences, and hustling from one talk show to the next chatting about their clients. It was unheard of in Brazil.

His office was three blocks from the Palace Hotel, on a wide shaded lot his uncle had bought decades earlier. Thick trees covered the roof, so regardless of the heat, Valdir kept his windows open. He liked the gentle noise from the street. At three-fifteen, he saw a man he'd never seen before stop and examine his office. The man was obviously a stranger, and an American. Valdir knew it was Mr. O'Riley.

THE SECRETARY brought them *cafezinho*, the strong sugary black coffee Brazilians drink all day in tiny cups, and Nate was instantly addicted to it. He sat in Valdir's office, already on a first-name basis, and admired the surroundings: the squeaky ceiling fan above them, the open windows with the muted sounds of the street drifting in, the neat rows of dusty files on the shelves behind Valdir, the scuffed and worn plank floor under them. The office was quite warm, but not uncomfortable. Nate was sitting in a movie, one shot fifty years ago.

Valdir phoned D.C., and got Josh. They talked for a moment, then he handed the phone across the desk. "Hello, Josh," Nate said. Josh was obviously relieved to hear his voice. Nate recounted his journey to Corumbá, with emphasis on the fact that he was doing well, still sober, and looking forward to the rest of his adventure.

Valdir busied himself with a file in a corner, trying to appear as if he had no interest in the conversation, but absorbing every word. Why was Nate O'Riley so proud of being sober?

When the phone call was over, Valdir produced and unfolded a large air navigational map of the state of Mato Grosso do Sul, roughly the same size as Texas, and pointed to the Pantanal. It covered the entire northwestern portion of the state, and continued into Mato Grosso to the north and Bolivia to the west. Hundreds of rivers and streams spread like veins through the swampland. It was shaded yellow, and there were no towns or cities in the Pantanal. No roads or highways. A hundred thousand square miles of swamp, Nate recalled from the innumerable memos Josh had packed for him.

Valdir lit a cigarette as they studied the map. He had done some homework. There were four red X's along the western edge of the map, near Bolivia.

"There are tribes here," he said, pointing to the red marks. "Guató and Ipicas."

"How large are they?" Nate asked, leaning close, his first real glimpse at the terrain he was expected to comb in search of Rachel Lane.

"We don't really know," Valdir replied, his words very slow and precise. He was trying hard to impress the American with his English. "A hundred years ago, there were many more. But the tribes grow smaller with each generation."

"How much contact do they have with the outside world?" Nate asked.

"Very little. Their culture hasn't changed in a thousand years. They trade some with the riverboats, but they have no desire to change."

"Do we know where the missionaries are?"

"It's difficult to say. I talked with the Minister of Health for the state of Mato Grosso do Sul. I know him personally, and his office has a general idea of where the missionaries are working. I also spoke with a representative from FUNAI—it's our Bureau of Indian Affairs." Valdir pointed to two of the X's. "These are Guató. There are probably missionaries around here."

"Do you know their names?" Nate asked, but it was a throwaway question. According to a memo from Josh, Valdir had not been given the name of Rachel Lane. He had been told that the woman worked for World Tribes, but that was it.

Valdir smiled and shook his head. "That would be too easy. You must understand that there are at least twenty different American and Canadian organizations with missionaries in Brazil. It's easy to get into our country, and it's easy to move around. Especially in the undeveloped areas. No one really cares who's out there and what they're doing. We figure if they're missionaries, then they are good people."

Nate pointed at Corumbá, then to the nearest red X. "How long does it take to get from here to there?"

"Depends. By plane, about an hour. By boat, from three to five days."

"Then where's my plane?"

"It's not that easy," Valdir said, reaching for another map. He unrolled it and pressed it on top of the first one. "This is a topographical map of the Pantanal. These are the *fazendas*."

"The what?"

"*Fazendas*. Large farms."

"I thought it was all swamp."

"No. Many areas are elevated just enough to raise cattle. The *fazendas* were built two hundred years ago, and are still worked by the *pantaneiros*. Only a few of the *fazendas* are accessible by boat, so they use small airplanes. The airstrips are marked in blue."

Nate noticed that there were very few airstrips near the Indian settlements.

Valdir continued, "Even if you flew into the area, you would then have to use a boat to get to the Indians."

"How are the airstrips?"

"They're all grass. Sometimes they cut the grass, sometimes they don't. The biggest problem is cows."

"Cows?"

"Yes, cows like grass. Sometimes it's hard to land because the cows are eating the runway." Valdir said this with no effort at humor.

"Can't they move the cows?"

"Yes, if they know you're coming. But there are no phones."

"No phones in the *fazendas*?"

"None. They are very isolated."

"So I couldn't fly into the Pantanal, then rent a boat to find the Indians?"

"No. The boats are here in Corumbá. As are the guides."

Nate stared at the map, especially the Paraguay River as it wound and looped its way northward in the direction of the Indian settlements. Somewhere along the river, hopefully in proximity to it, in the midst of this vast wetlands, was a simple servant of God, living each day in peace and tranquillity, thinking little of the future, quietly ministering to her flock.

And he had to find her.

"I'd like to at least fly over the area," Nate said.

Valdir rerolled the last map. "I can arrange an airplane and a pilot."

"What about a boat?"

"I'm working on that. This is the flood season, and most of the boats are in use. The rivers are up. There's more river traffic this time of the year."

How nice of Troy to kill himself during the flood season. According to the firm's research, the rains came in November and lasted until February, and all of the lowest areas and many of the *fazendas* were under water.

"I must warn you, though," Valdir said, lighting another cigarette as he refolded the first map, "air travel is not without risk. The planes are small, and if there's engine trouble, well . . ." His voice trailed away as he rolled his eyes and shrugged as if all hope was lost.

"Well what?"

"There's no place for an emergency landing, no place to put it down. A plane went down a month ago. They found it near a riverbank, surrounded by alligators."

"What happened to the passengers?" Nate asked, terrified of the answer.

"Ask the alligators."

"Let's change the subject."

"More coffee?"

"Yes, please."

Valdir yelled at his secretary. They walked to a window and watched the traffic. "I think I have found a guide," he said.

"Good. Does he speak English?"

"Yes, very well. He's a young man, just out of the army. A fine boy. His father was a river pilot."

"That's nice."

Valdir walked to his desk and picked up the phone. The secretary brought Nate another small cup of *cafezinho*, and he sipped it standing in the window. Across the street was a small bar with three tables on the sidewalk under a canopy. A red sign advertised Antartica beer. Two men in shirtsleeves and ties shared a table with a large bottle of Antartica between them. It was a perfect setting—a hot day, a festive mood, a cold drink enjoyed by two friends in the shade.

Nate was suddenly dizzy. The beer sign blurred, the scene came and went, then came back as his heart pounded and his breathing stopped. He touched the windowsill to steady himself. His hands shook, so he placed the *cafezinho* on a table. Valdir was behind him, oblivious, rattling away in Portuguese.

Sweat popped out in neat rows above his eyebrows. He could taste the beer. The slide was beginning. A chink in the armor. A crack in the dam. A rumbling in the mountain of resolve he'd built the last four months with Sergio. Nate took a deep breath, and collected himself. The moment would pass; he knew it would. He'd been here before, many times now.

He picked up the coffee and sipped it furiously as Valdir was hanging up and announcing that the pilot was hesitant to fly anywhere on Christmas Eve. Nate returned to his seat under the squeaking fan. "Offer him some more money," he said.

Valdir had been informed by Mr. Josh Stafford that money was no object during this mission. "He'll call me back in an hour," he said.

Nate was ready to leave. He produced his brand-new cell phone, and Valdir walked him through the procedure of finding an AT&T operator who spoke English. As a test, he dialed Sergio and got his answering machine. Then he dialed Alice, his secretary, and wished her a Merry Christmas.

The phone worked fine; he was very proud of it. He thanked Valdir and made his way out of the office. They would talk again before the day was over.

He walked toward the river, down just a few blocks from Valdir's, and found a small park where workers were busy arranging chairs for a concert. The late afternoon was humid; his shirt was stained with sweat and stuck to his chest. The little episode back at Valdir's scared him more than he cared to admit. He sat on the edge of a picnic table, and gazed at the great Pantanal lying before him. A mangy teenager appeared from nowhere and offered to sell him marijuana. It was in tiny bags, in a small wooden box. Nate waved him off. Maybe in another life.

A musician began tuning his guitar, and a crowd slowly gathered as the sun sank over the Bolivian mountains not far away.

TWELVE

THE MONEY WORKED. The pilot reluctantly agreed to fly, but insisted that they leave early and be back in Corumbá by noon. He had small children, an angry wife, and it was, after all, Christmas Eve. Valdir promised and soothed, and paid a nice deposit in cash.

A deposit was also paid to Jevy, the guide Valdir had been negotiating with for a week. Jevy was twenty-four, single, a weightlifter with thick arms, and when he bounced into the lobby of the Palace Hotel, he wore a bush hat, denim shorts, black army boots, a tee shirt with no sleeves, and a shiny bowie knife tucked into his belt just in case he might need to skin something. He crushed Nate's hand as he shook it. *"Bom dia,"* he said through a large, wide smile.

"Bom dia," Nate said, gritting his teeth as his fingers cracked. The knife could not be ignored; its blade was eight inches long.

"You speak Portuguese?" Jevy asked.

"No. Just English."

"No problem," he said, finally releasing his death grip. "I speak English." The accent was thick, but so far Nate had caught every word. "Learned it in the army," Jevy said proudly.

Jevy was instantly likable. He took Nate's briefcase and said something smart to the girl behind the desk. She blushed and wanted more.

His truck was a 1978 Ford three-quarter-ton pickup, the largest vehicle Nate had seen so far in Corumbá. It appeared to be jungle-ready, with large tires, a winch on the front bumper, thick grates over the headlights, a black shade tree paint job, no fenders. And no air conditioning.

They roared through the streets of Corumbá, slowing only slightly at red lights, completely ignoring stop signs, and in general bullying cars and motorcycles, all anxious to avoid Jevy's tank. Either by design or by neglect, the muffler worked badly. The engine was loud, and Jevy felt compelled to talk as he clutched the wheel like a race driver. Nate didn't hear a word. He smiled and nodded like an idiot while holding his position—feet planted on the floor, one hand clenching the window frame, the other holding his brief-case. His heart stopped with each new intersection.

Evidently the drivers understood a traffic system where the rules of the road, if any, were ignored. There were no accidents, no carnage. Everyone, including Jevy, managed to stop or yield or swerve just in the nick of time.

The airport was deserted. They parked by the small terminal and walked to one end of the tarmac, where four small airplanes were tied down. One was being prepped by the pilot, a man Jevy did not know. Introductions were made in Portuguese. The pilot's name sounded like Milton. He was friendly enough, but it was obvious he'd rather not be flying or working on the day before Christmas.

As the Brazilians talked, Nate examined the aircraft. The first thing he noticed was the need for a paint job, and this in itself concerned him greatly. If the outside was peeling, could the inside be much better? The tires were slick. There were oil stains around the engine compartment. It was an old Cessna 206, single engine.

The fueling took fifteen minutes, and the bright and early start dragged on, with 10 A.M. approaching. Nate withdrew his fancy cell phone from the deep pocket of his khaki shorts, and called Sergio.

He was having coffee with his wife, making plans for last-minute shopping, and Nate was again grateful that he was out of the country, away from the holiday frenzy. It was cold and sleeting along the mid-Atlantic. Nate assured him he was still together; no problems.

He had stopped the slide, he thought. He had awakened with fresh resolve and strength; it had only been a passing moment of weakness. So he didn't mention it to Sergio. He should have, but why worry him now?

As they talked, the sun slipped behind a dark cloud, and a few scattered raindrops fell around Nate. He hardly noticed. He hung up after the standard "Merry Christmas."

The pilot announced he was ready. "Do you feel safe?" Nate asked Jevy as they loaded the briefcase and a backpack.

Jevy laughed, and said, "No problem. This man has four small children, and a pretty wife, so he says. Why would he risk his life?"

Jevy wanted to take flying lessons, so he volunteered to take the right seat, next to Milton. It was fine with Nate. He sat behind them in a small cramped seat, his belt and shoulder straps fastened as snug as possible. The engine started with some reluctance, too much in Nate's opinion, and the small cabin was an oven until Milton opened his window. The backdraft from the propeller helped them breathe. They taxied and bounced across the tarmac to the end of the runway. Clearance was not a problem because there was no other traffic. When they lifted off, Nate's shirt was stuck to his chest and sweat ran down his neck.

Corumbá was instantly beneath them. It looked prettier from the air, with its neat rows of small houses on streets that all appeared to be smooth and orderly. Downtown was busy now, with cars waiting in traffic and pedestrians darting across the streets. The city was on a bluff with the river below it. They followed the river north, climbing slowly as Corumbá faded behind. There were scattered clouds and light turbulence.

At four thousand feet, the majesty of the Pantanal suddenly appeared as they passed through a large, ominous cloud. To the east and north, a dozen small rivers spun circles around and through each other, going nowhere, linking each marsh to a hundred others. Because of the floods, the rivers were full and in many places ran together. The water had differing shades. The stagnant marshes were dark blue, almost black in some places where the weeds were thick. The deeper ponds were green. The smaller tributaries carried a reddish dirt, and the great Paraguay was full and as brown as malted chocolate. On the horizon, as far as the eye could see, all water was blue and all earth was green.

While Nate looked to the east and north, his two companions were looking to the west, to the distant mountains of Bolivia. Jevy pointed, catching Nate's attention. The sky was darker beyond the mountains.

Fifteen minutes into the flight, Nate saw the first dwelling of any type. It was a farm on the banks of the Paraguay. The house was small and neat, with the mandatory red-tiled roof. White cows grazed in a pasture and drank at the edge of the river. The daily wash hung from a clothesline near the house. No sign of human activity—no vehicles, no TV antenna, no electrical lines. A small square garden with a fence around it was a short walk from the house, down a dirt path. The plane passed through a cloud, and the farm disappeared.

More clouds. They thickened, and Milton dropped to three thousand feet to stay below them. Jevy told him that it was a sight-seeing mission, so stay as low as possible. The first Guató settlement was about an hour from Corumbá.

They veered away from the river for a few minutes, and in doing so flew over a *fazenda*. Jevy folded his map, drew a circle around something, and thrust it back to Nate. "Fazenda da Prata," he said, then pointed below. On the map, the *fazendas* were all named, as if they were grand estates. On the ground, Fazenda da Prata was not much bigger than the first farm Nate had seen. There were more cows, a couple of small outbuildings, a slightly larger house, and a long straight belt of land that Nate finally realized was the airstrip. There was no river close by, and certainly no roads. Access was only by air.

Milton was increasingly worried about the dark sky to the west. It was moving east, they were moving north, a meeting seemed inevitable. Jevy leaned back and shouted, "He doesn't like that sky over there."

Nor did Nate, but he wasn't the pilot. He shrugged because he could think of no other response.

"We'll watch it for a few minutes," Jevy said. Milton wanted to go home. Nate wanted to at least see the Indian villages. He still held the faint hope that he could somehow fly in to meet Rachel, and perhaps whisk her away to Corumbá, where they could have lunch in a nice café and discuss her father's estate. Faint hopes, and rapidly fading.

A helicopter was not out of the question. The estate could certainly afford it. If Jevy could find the right village, and the right spot to make a landing, Nate would rent a chopper in an instant.

He was dreaming.

Another small *fazenda*, this one a short distance from the Paraguay River. Raindrops began hitting the windows of the plane, and Milton dropped to two thousand feet. An impressive row of mountains was to the left, much nearer, with the river snaking its way through the dense forests at their base.

From over the mountaintops, the storm rushed at them with a fury. The sky was suddenly much darker; the winds jolted the Cessna. It dipped sharply, causing Nate's head to hit the top of the cabin. He was instantly terrified.

"We're turning around," Jevy shouted back. His voice lacked the calmness Nate would've preferred. Milton was stonefaced, but the cool aviator's sunshades were gone, and sweat covered his forehead. The plane veered hard to the right, east then southeast, and as it completed its southward turn, a sickening sight awaited them. The sky toward Corumbá was black.

Milton wanted no part of it. He quickly turned east, and said something to Jevy.

"We can't go to Corumbá," Jevy yelled to the rear seat. "He

wants to look for a *fazenda*. We'll land and wait for the storm to pass." His voice was high and anxious, his accent much thicker.

Nate nodded as best he could. His head was bobbing and bouncing, and aching from the first crack into the ceiling. And his stomach was beginning to rumble.

For a few minutes it seemed as though the race would be won by the Cessna. Surely, Nate thought, an airplane of any size can outrun a storm. He rubbed the crown of his head, and decided against looking behind them. But the dark clouds were coming from the sides now.

What kind of backward, half-ass pilot takes off without checking the radar? On the other hand, the radar, if they even had it, was probably twenty years old and unplugged for the holidays.

The rain peppered the aircraft. The winds howled around it. The clouds boiled past it. The storm caught and overtook them, and the small plane was yanked and thrust up and down and pushed from side to side. For a very long two minutes Milton was unable to fly it because of the turbulence. He was riding a bronco, not flying an airplane.

Nate was looking out his window, and seeing nothing, no water or marshes or nice little *fazendas* with long airstrips. He slumped even lower. He locked his teeth and vowed that he would not vomit.

An air pocket dropped the plane a hundred feet in less than two seconds, and all three men yelled something. Nate's was a very loud "Oh shit!" His Brazilian buddies cursed in Portuguese. The exclamations were wrapped in heavy layers of fear.

There was a break, a very quick one in which the air was still. Milton pushed the control yoke forward and began a nosedive. Nate braced himself with both hands on the back of Milton's seat, and for the first and hopefully only time in his life he felt like a kamikaze pilot. His heart was racing and his stomach was in his throat. He closed his eyes and thought of Sergio, and of the yoga instructor at Walnut Hill who'd taught him prayer and meditation. He tried to meditate and he tried to pray, but it was impossible trapped in a falling airplane. Death was only seconds away.

A thunderclap just above the Cessna stunned them, like a shotgun in a dark room, and it shook them to their bones. Nate's eardrums practically burst.

The dive ended at five hundred feet as Milton fought the winds and leveled off. "Look for a *fazenda!*" Jevy yelled from the front, and Nate, reluctantly, peeked out the window. The earth below was being pelted by rain and wind. The trees swayed and the small ponds had whitecaps. Jevy scanned a map, but they were hopelessly lost.

The rain came in white sheets that cut visibility to only a few hundred feet. At times, Nate could barely see the ground. They were surrounded by torrents of rain, all being blown sideways by a brutal wind. Their little plane was being tossed about like a kite. Milton fought the controls while Jevy looked desperately in all directions. They were not going down without a fight.

But Nate gave up. If they couldn't see the ground, how could they expect to land safely? The worst of the storm had yet to catch them. It was over.

He would not plea bargain with God. This was what he deserved for the life he had led. Hundreds of people die in plane crashes every year; he was no better.

He caught a glimpse of a river, just under them, and he suddenly remembered the alligators and anacondas. He was horrified by the thought of crash landing in a swamp. He saw himself badly injured but not dead, clinging to life, fighting for survival, trying to get the damned satellite phone to work while at the same time fending off hungry reptiles.

Another thunderclap shook the cabin, and Nate decided to fight after all. He searched the ground in a vain attempt to find a *fazenda*. A flash of lightning blinded them for a second. The engine sputtered and almost stalled, then caught itself and rattled away. Milton dropped to four hundred feet, a safe altitude under normal circumstances. At least there were no hills or mountains to worry about in the Pantanal.

Nate pulled his shoulder harness even tighter, then vomited between his legs. He felt no disgrace in doing so. He felt nothing but utter terror.

Darkness engulfed them. Milton and Jevy yelled back and forth as they bounced and fought to control the airplane. Their shoulders hit and rubbed together. The map was stuck between Jevy's legs, totally useless.

The storm moved under them. Milton descended to two hundred feet, where the ground could be seen in patches. A gust blew them sideways, literally yanking the Cessna to one side, and Nate realized how helpless they were. He saw a white object below, and yelled and pointed, "A cow! A cow!" Jevy screamed the translation to Milton.

They dropped through the clouds at eighty feet, in a blinding rain, and flew directly over the red roof of a house. Jevy yelled again, and pointed to something on his side of the plane. The airstrip looked to be the length of a nice suburban driveway, dangerous even in good weather. It didn't matter. They had no choice. If they crashed, at least there were people nearby.

They had spotted the strip too late to land with the wind, so Milton muscled the plane around for a landing into the face of the storm. The wind slapped the Cessna around and practically stalled it. The rain reduced visibility to almost nothing. Nate leaned over for a look at the runway, and saw only the water drenching the windshield.

At fifty feet, the Cessna was blown sideways. Milton fought it back into position. Jevy yelled, *"Vaca! Vaca!"* Nate immediately understood that *vaca* meant cow. Nate saw it too. They missed the first one.

In the flash of images before they hit, Nate saw a boy with a stick running through tall grass, soaking wet and frightened. And he saw a cow running away from the airstrip. He saw Jevy brace himself while staring through the windshield, eyes wild, mouth open but no words coming out.

They slammed into the grass, but kept moving forward. It was a landing, not a crash, and in that split second Nate hoped they would not die. Another gust lifted them ten feet into the air, then they hit again.

"Vaca! Vaca!"

The propeller ripped into a large, curious, stationary cow. The plane flipped violently, all windows bursting outward, all three men screaming their last words.

NATE WOKE UP sideways, covered in blood, scared beyond words, but very much alive and suddenly aware that it was still raining. The wind howled through the plane. Milton and Jevy were tangled on top of each other, but moving too and trying to get themselves unbuckled.

Nate found a window and stuck his head out. The Cessna was on its side, with a wing cracked and folded under the cabin. Blood was everywhere, but it was from the cow, not the passengers. The rain, still coming down in sheets, was quickly washing it away.

The boy with the stick led them to a small stable near the airstrip. Out of the storm, Milton dropped to his knees and mumbled an earnest little prayer to the Virgin Mary. Nate watched, and sort of prayed along with him.

There were no serious injuries. Milton had a slight cut on his forehead. Jevy's right wrist was swelling. More soreness would come later.

They sat in the dirt for a long time, watching the rain, hearing the wind, thinking of what could've been, saying nothing.

THIRTEEN

THE OWNER of the cow appeared an hour or so later, as the storm began to subside and the rain stopped for a moment. He was barefoot, clad in faded denim shorts and a threadbare Chicago Bulls tee shirt. Marco was his name, and Marco was not filled with holiday cheer.

He sent the boy away, then began a heated discussion with Jevy and Milton about the value of the cow. Milton was more concerned about his airplane, Jevy with his swollen wrist. Nate stood by the window and wondered exactly how it came to be that he was presently in the middle of the Brazilian outback on Christmas Eve in a smelly manger, sore and bruised, covered with the blood of a cow, listening to three men argue in a foreign tongue, and lucky to be alive. There were no clear answers.

Judging by the other cows grazing nearby, they couldn't be worth much. "I'll pay for the damned thing," Nate said to Jevy.

Jevy asked the man how much, then said, "A hundred reais."

"Does he take American Express?" Nate asked, but the humor missed its mark. "I'll pay it." A hundred bucks. He'd pay that much just for Marco to stop griping.

The deal was sealed, and the man became their host. He led them to his house, where lunch was being prepared by a short barefoot woman who smiled and welcomed them profusely. For obvious reasons, guests were unheard of in the Pantanal, and when they realized Nate was from the States they sent for the kids. The boy with the stick had two brothers, and their mother told them to examine Nate because he was an American.

She took the men's shirts and soaked them in a basin filled with soap and rainwater. They ate rice and black beans around a small table, bare-chested and unconcerned about it. Nate was proud of his toned biceps and flat stomach. Jevy had the cut look of a serious weightlifter. Poor Milton showed the signs of rapidly approaching middle age, but clearly didn't care.

The three said little over lunch. The horror of the crash was still fresh. The children sat on the floor beside the table, eating flat bread and rice, watching every move Nate made.

There was a small river a quarter of a mile down the trail, and Marco had a boat with a motor. The Paraguay River was five hours away. Maybe he had enough gasoline, maybe he didn't. But it would be impossible with all three men in the boat.

When the sky cleared, Nate and the children walked to the wrecked plane and removed his briefcase. Along the way he taught them to count to ten in English. And they taught him in Portuguese. They were sweet boys, terribly shy at first but warming to Nate by the minute. It was Christmas Eve, he reminded himself. Did Santa visit the Pantanal? No one seemed to be expecting him.

On a smooth flat stump in the front yard, Nate carefully unpacked and arranged the satellite phone. The receiving dish was a square foot in size, and the phone itself was no larger than a compact laptop. A cord connected the two. Nate turned on the power, punched in his ID and PIN numbers, then slowly turned the dish until it picked up the signal from the Astar-East Satellite, a hundred miles above the Atlantic, hovering somewhere near the equator. The signal was strong, a steady beep confirmed it, and Marco and the rest of his family huddled even closer around Nate. He wondered if they'd ever seen a phone.

Jevy called out the numbers to Milton's home in Corumbá. Nate pressed them slowly, then held his breath and waited. If the call did not work, they were simply stuck with Marco and family for Christmas. The house was small; Nate was assuming he'd sleep in the stable. Perfect.

Plan B was to send Jevy and Marco in the boat. It was almost 1 P.M. Five hours to the Paraguay would put them there just before dark, assuming there was enough gas. Once on the big river, they would then be faced with the task of finding help, and this could take hours. If there wasn't enough gas, they would be stranded deep in the Pantanal. Jevy had not vetoed this plan outright, but no one was pushing it.

There were other factors. Marco was reluctant to leave this late in the day. Normally, when he went to the Paraguay to trade, he left at sunrise. And while there was a chance he could find extra gas from a neighbor an hour away, this was far from certain.

"Oi," came a female voice over the speaker, and everyone smiled. Nate handed the phone to Milton, who said hello to his wife, then slid into a sad narrative about their plight. Jevy whispered a translation to Nate. The children marveled at the English.

The conversation grew tense, then suddenly stopped. "She's looking for a phone number," Jevy explained. The number came across, that of a pilot Milton knew. He promised to be home for dinner and hung up.

The pilot wasn't home. His wife said he was in Campo Grande on business, and should return by dark. Milton explained where he was, and she found more phone numbers where her husband might be reached.

"Ask him to talk fast," Nate said as he punched in another number. "This battery doesn't last forever."

No answer to the next number. To the next, the pilot came to the phone and was explaining that his airplane was being repaired when the signal was interrupted.

The clouds were back.

Nate looked at the darkening sky in disbelief. Milton was on the verge of tears.

IT WAS A QUICK SHOWER, a cool rain the children played in while the adults sat on the porch and watched them in silence.

Jevy had another plan. There was an army base on the edge of Corumbá. He had not been stationed there, but he lifted weights with several of the officers. When the sky was clear again, they returned to the stump and huddled around the phone. Jevy called a friend who found phone numbers.

The army had helicopters. It was, after all, a plane crash. When the second officer answered the phone, Jevy rapidly explained what had happened and asked for help.

Watching Jevy's end of the conversation was torture for Nate. He understood not a word, but the body language told the story. Smiles and frowns, urgings and pleas, frustrating pauses, then the repetition of things already said.

When Jevy finished, he said to Nate, "He will call his commandant. He wants me to call back in an hour."

An hour seemed like a week. The sun returned and baked the wet grass. The humidity was thick. Still shirtless, Nate began to feel the stinging of a sunburn.

They retired to the shade of a tree to escape the sun. The madam checked on their shirts, which had been left hanging during the last shower and were still wet.

Jevy and Milton had skin several shades darker than Nate's, and they were unconcerned about the sun. It didn't bother Marco either, and the three of them walked to the airplane to inspect the damage. Nate stayed behind, under the tree, where it was safe. The heat of the afternoon was stifling. His chest and shoulders were beginning to stiffen, and the idea of a nap crossed his mind. But the boys had other plans. He finally got their names—Luis was the oldest, the one who'd chased a cow from the airstrip seconds before they landed, Oli was the middle one, and the smallest was Tomas. Using the phrase book he kept in his briefcase, Nate slowly broke the language barrier. Hello. How are you? What is your name? How old are you? Good afternoon. The boys repeated the phrases in Portuguese so Nate could learn the pronunciation, then he made them do it in English.

Jevy returned with maps, and they made the phone call. There appeared to be some interest on the part of the army. Milton pointed to a map and said, "Fazenda Esperança," which Jevy repeated with great enthusiasm. It waned, though, seconds later, then he hung up. "He can't find the commandant," he said in English, trying to appear hopeful. "It is, you know, Christmas."

Christmas in the Pantanal. Ninety-five degrees with humidity even higher. A scorching sun with no sunblock. Bugs and insects with no repellent. Cheerful little kids with no hope of getting toys. No music because there was no electricity. No Christmas tree. No Christmas food, or wine, or champagne.

This is an adventure, he kept telling himself. Where's your sense of humor?

Nate returned the phone to its case and clamped it shut. Milton and Jevy walked to the airplane. Madam went into the house. Marco had something to do in the backyard. Nate went for the shade again, thinking how nice it would be to hear just one verse of "White Christmas" while sipping a glass of bubbly.

Luis appeared with three of the scrawniest horses Nate had ever seen. One had a saddle, a cruel-looking device made of leather and wood and resting on a bright orange pad, which appeared to be old shag carpet. The saddle was for Nate. Luis and Oli hopped on their bareback horses without the slightest effort; just a skip and a jump and they were mounted, perfectly balanced.

Nate studied his horse. *"Onde?"* he asked. Where?

Luis pointed to a trail. Nate knew from the pointing over lunch and afterward that the trail led to the river where Marco kept his boat.

Why not? It was an adventure. What else was there to do as the hours dragged on? He retrieved his shirt from the clothesline, then managed to mount the poor horse without falling off or hurting himself.

In late October, Nate and some of the other addicts at Walnut Hill had spent a pleasant Sunday on horseback, trailing through the Blue Ridge, taking in the glories of fall. His butt and thighs had ached for a week, but his fear of the beasts had been overcome. Somewhat.

He fought the stirrups until his feet were stuck through them, then clutched the bridle so tight the animal wouldn't move. The boys watched with great amusement, then began trotting away. Nate's horse finally trotted too, a slow rough trot that slapped him in the crotch and bounced him from side to side. Preferring to simply walk, he yanked the bridle and the horse slowed. The boys circled back and walked beside him.

The trail led through a small pasture and around a bend, so the house was soon out of sight. There was water ahead—a swamp, just like the countless ones Nate had seen from the air. It did not deter the boys, because the trail ran through the middle of it and the horses had crossed it many times before. They never slowed. The water was at first only inches deep, then a foot, then it touched the stirrups. Of course, the boys were barefoot and leather-skinned and completely unconcerned about the water or what might be in it. Nate was wearing his favorite pair of Nikes, which were soon wet.

Piranhas, vicious little fish with razor-sharp teeth, were all over the Pantanal.

He preferred to turn around, but had no idea how to communicate this. "Luis," he said, his voice betraying his fears. The boys looked at him without the slightest trace of concern.

When the water was chest-deep on the horses, they slowed a little. A few more steps and Nate saw his feet again. The horses emerged on the other side where the trail resumed.

They passed the remnants of a fence to their left. Then, a dilapidated dwelling. The trail widened into an old roadbed. Many years earlier, the *fazenda* had been more substantial, no doubt with a large cattle operation and many employees.

The Pantanal had been settled over two hundred years earlier, Nate knew from his collection of reading materials, and little had changed. The isolation of the people was astounding. There was no sign of neighbors, or other children, and Nate kept thinking about schools and education. Do the kids flee when they're old enough, to Corumbá to find jobs and spouses? Or do they tend the small farms and raise the next generation of *pantaneiros*? Could Marco and his wife read and write, and if so did they teach their children?

He would ask Jevy these questions. There was more water ahead, a larger swamp with rotted trees bunched together on both sides. And of course the trail ran through the middle of it. It was the flood season, the water was high everywhere. In the dry months, the swamp was a patch of mud, and a novice could follow the trail without fear of being eaten. Come back then, Nate told himself. Small chance.

The horses plodded along like machines, unconcerned about the swamp and the water splashing to their knees. The boys were half-asleep. The pace slowed a bit as the water rose. When Nate's knees were wet, and he was ready to yell something desperate at Luis, Oli pointed very nonchalantly to the right, to a spot where two decayed stumps rose ten feet in the air. Between them lying low in the water was a large black reptile.

"*Jacaré*," Oli said, sort of over his shoulder as if Nate might want to know. Alligator.

The eyes protruded above the rest of the body, and Nate was certain they were following him specifically. His heart raced and he wanted to cry out, to scream for help. Then Luis turned around and grinned because he knew his guest was terrified. His guest tried to smile as if he were thrilled to finally see one this close.

The horses raised their heads as the water rose. Nate kicked his, under the water, but nothing happened. The alligator slowly lowered himself until nothing could be seen but the eyes, then he pushed forward, in their direction, and disappeared into the black water. Nate yanked his feet from the stirrups and pulled his knees to his chest, so that he teetered on the saddle. The boys said something and began giggling, but Nate didn't care.

Past the middle of the swamp, the water fell to the horses' legs, then their feet. Safely on the other side, Nate relaxed. Then he laughed at himself. He could sell this back home. He had friends who were into extreme vacations—backpackers and whitewater rafters, gorilla trekkers, safari types always trying to outdo the rest with tales of near-death experiences on the other side of the world. Throw in the ecological angle of the Pantanal, and for ten thousand dollars they would gladly hop on a pony and wade through swamps, photographing snakes and alligators along the way.

With no river in sight, Nate decided it was time to turn back. He pointed at his watch, and Luis led them home.

THE COMMANDANT himself was brought to the phone. He and Jevy traded army talk for five minutes—places they'd been stationed, people they knew—while the battery indicator light blinked faster and the SatFone slowly ran out of gas. Nate pointed; Jevy responded by explaining to the commandant that this was their last chance.

No problem. A chopper was ready; a crew was being scrambled. How bad were the injuries?

Internal, Jevy said, glancing at Milton.

The *fazenda* was forty minutes away by helicopter, according to the army pilots. Give us an hour, the commandant said. Milton smiled for the first time that day.

An hour passed and the optimism faded. The sun was dropping quickly in the west; dusk was approaching. A nighttime rescue was out of the question.

They gravitated to the broken airplane, where Milton and Jevy had worked steadily throughout the afternoon. The fractured wing had been removed, as had the propeller. It was in the grass near the plane, still stained with blood. The right landing brace was bent, but would not require replacement.

The dead cow had been butchered by Marco and his wife. Its carcass was barely visible in the brush next to the airstrip.

According to Jevy, Milton planned to return by boat as soon as he could find a new wing and propeller. To Nate, this seemed virtually impossible. How could he haul something as bulky as an airplane wing on a boat small enough to navigate the tributaries of the Pantanal, then carry it through the same swamps Nate had seen on horseback?

That was his problem. Nate had other things to worry about.

Madam brought warm coffee and brittle cookies, and they sat in the grass next to the stable and chattered away. Nate's three little shadows sat close to him, afraid he might leave them. Another hour passed.

It was Tomas, the youngest, who heard the humming sound first. He said something, then stood and pointed and the rest of them froze. The sound grew louder, and became the unmistakable whir of a helicopter. They ran to the center of the airstrip and watched the sky.

When it landed, four soldiers jumped from the open bay and ran to the group. Nate knelt among the boys, and gave them each ten reais. *"Feliz Natal,"* he said. Merry Christmas. Then he hugged them quickly, picked up his briefcase, and ran to the helicopter.

Jevy and Nate waved at the little family as they lifted off. Milton was too busy thanking the pilots and soldiers. At five hundred feet, the Pantanal began to stretch to the horizon. It was dark to the east.

And it was dark in Corumbá when they flew over the city a half hour later. It was a beautiful sight—the buildings and houses, the Christmas lights, the traffic. They landed at the army base west of town, on a bluff above the Paraguay River. The commandant met them and received the profuse thanks he so richly deserved. He was surprised at the lack of serious injuries, but happy nonetheless at the success of the mission. He sent them away in an open jeep driven by a young private.

As they entered the city, the jeep made a sudden turn and stopped in front of a small grocery. Jevy walked inside, and returned with three bottles of Brahma beer. He gave one to Milton, and one to Nate.

After a slight hesitation, Nate unscrewed the cap and turned the bottle up. It was very wet, and cold, and thoroughly delicious. And it was Christmas, and what the hell. He could handle it.

Riding in the back of the jeep through the dusty streets, the humid air rushing against his face, cold beer in hand, Nate reminded himself of how lucky he was to be alive.

Nearly four months earlier he had tried to kill himself. Seven hours earlier he had survived a crash landing.

But the day had accomplished nothing. He was no closer to Rachel Lane than he'd been the day before.

The first stop was the hotel. Nate wished them all a Merry Christmas, then went to his room, where he undressed and stood in the shower for twenty minutes.

There were four cans of beer in the refrigerator. He drank them all in an hour, assuring himself with each can that this was not a slide. It would not lead to a crash. Things were under control. He'd cheated death, so why not celebrate with a little Christmas cheer? No one would ever know. He could handle it.

Besides, sobriety had never worked for him. He would prove to himself that he could handle a little alcohol. No problem. A few beers here and there. What was the harm?

FOURTEEN

THE PHONE woke him, but it took a while to get to it. The beer had no lingering effect, other than guilt, but the little adventure in the Cessna was taking its toll. His neck, shoulders, and waist were already dark blue—neat rows of bruises where the harnesses had held him in place as the plane slammed into the ground. There were at least two knots on his skull, the first from a lick he could remember, the second from one he could not. His knees had cracked the backs of the pilots' seats—slight injuries at first, he'd thought, but their severity had increased during the night. His arms and neck were sunburned.

"Merry Christmas," the voice greeted him. It was Valdir, and it was almost nine.

"Thank you," Nate said. "Same to you."

"Yes. How are you feeling?"

"Fine. Thanks."

"Yes, well, Jevy called me last night and told me about the airplane. Milton must be a crazy man to fly into a storm. I'll never use him again."

"Neither will I."

"Are you okay?"

"Yes."

"Do you need a doctor?"

"No."

"Jevy said he thought you were okay."

"I'm fine, just a little sore."

There was a slight pause as Valdir changed speeds. "We're having a small Christmas party in my home this afternoon. Just my family and a few friends. Would you like to join us?"

There was a stiffness to the invitation. Nate couldn't tell if Valdir was only trying to be polite, or if it was a matter of language and accent.

"That's very kind of you," he said. "But I have a lot of reading to do."

"Are you sure?"

"Yes, thanks."

"Very well. I have some good news. I rented a boat yesterday, finally." It didn't take long to leave the party and get to the boat.

"Good. When do I go?"

"Perhaps tomorrow. They're getting it ready. Jevy knows the boat."

"I'm anxious to get on the river. Especially after yesterday."

Valdir then launched into a windy narrative of how he'd played hardball with the owner of the boat, a notorious tightwad who had initially demanded a thousand reais per week. They had settled on six hundred. Nate listened but didn't care. The Phelan estate could handle it.

Valdir said good-bye with another Merry Christmas.

His Nikes were still wet, but he put them on anyway, along with running shorts and a tee shirt. He would try to jog, but if the parts wouldn't work then he'd simply walk. He needed fresh air and exercise. Moving slowly around the room, he saw the empty beer cans in the wastebasket.

He would deal with it later. This was not a slide, and it would not lead to a crash. His life had flashed before him yesterday, and that changed things. He could have died. Every day was a gift now, every moment was to be savored. Why not enjoy a few of life's pleasures? Just a little beer and wine, nothing stronger and certainly no narcotics.

This was familiar turf; lies he'd lived before.

He took two Tylenol and covered his exposed skin with sunblock. In the lobby, a Christmas show was on the television but no one was watching, no one was there. The young lady behind the counter smiled and said good morning. The heavy, sticky heat wafted in through the open glass doors. Nate stopped for a quick shot of sweet coffee. The thermos was on the counter, the tiny paper cups stacked neatly beside it, waiting for anyone to pause and enjoy an ounce of *cafezinho*.

Two shots, and he was sweating before he left the lobby. On the sidewalk, he tried to stretch but his muscles were screaming and his joints were locked. The challenge was not running; rather, it was walking without an obvious limp.

But no one was watching. The shops were locked and the streets were empty, as he'd expected them to be. After two blocks, his shirt was already sticking to his back. He was exercising in a sauna.

Avenida Rondon was the last paved street along the bluff above the river. He followed the sidewalk next to it for a long way, limping slightly as the muscles reluctantly loosened a little and the joints stopped grinding. He found the same small park he'd stopped at two days earlier, on the twenty-third, when the crowd gathered for music and carols. Some of the folding chairs were still there. His legs needed rest. He sat on the same picnic table, and glanced about for the mangy teenager who'd tried to sell him drugs.

But there wasn't a soul. He gently rubbed his knees and looked at the great Pantanal, expanding for miles, disappearing on the horizon. Magnificent desolation. He thought of the boys—Luis, Oli, and Tomas—his little buddies with ten reais in their pockets and no way to spend it. Christmas meant nothing to them; every day was the same.

Somewhere in the vast wetlands before him was one Rachel

Lane, now just a humble servant of God but about to become one of the richest women in the world. If he actually found her, how would she react to the news of her great fortune? How would she react when she met him, an American lawyer who'd managed to track her down?

The possible answers made him uncomfortable.

For the first time, it occurred to Nate that maybe Troy had been crazy after all. Would a rational, lucid mind give eleven billion dollars to a person who had no interest in wealth? A person practically unknown to everyone, including the one signing the hand-scrawled will? The act seemed insane, much more so now that Nate was sitting above the Pantanal, looking at its wilderness, three thousand miles from home.

Little had been learned about Rachel. Evelyn Cunningham, her mother, was from the small town of Delhi, Louisiana. At the age of nineteen, she moved to Baton Rouge and found a job as a secretary with a company involved in the exploration of natural gas. Troy Phelan owned the company, and during one of his routine visits from New York, he spotted Evelyn. Evidently she had been a beautiful woman, and naive in her small-town upbringing. Ever the vulture, Troy struck quickly, and within a few months Evelyn found herself pregnant. This was in the spring of 1954.

In November of that year, Troy's people at the home office quietly arranged for Evelyn to be admitted to the Catholic Hospital in New Orleans, where Rachel was born on the second. Evelyn never saw her child.

With plenty of lawyers and lots of pressure, Troy arranged for the quick, private adoption of Rachel by a minister and his wife in Kalispell, Montana. He was buying copper and zinc mines in the state, and had contacts through his companies there. The adoptive parents did not know the identities of the biological ones.

Evelyn didn't want the child, nor did she want anything further to do with Troy Phelan. She took ten thousand dollars and returned to Delhi, where, typically, rumors of her sins were waiting for her.

She moved in with her parents, and they waited patiently for the storm to pass. It did not. With the cruelty that is peculiar to small towns, Evelyn found herself an outcast among the people she most needed. She rarely left the house, and with time retreated even farther, to the darkness of her bedroom. It was there, in the hidden gloom of her own little world, that Evelyn began to miss her daughter.

She wrote letters to Troy, none of which were answered. A secretary hid them and filed them away. Two weeks after his suicide one of Josh's investigators found them buried in Troy's personal archives in his apartment.

As the years passed Evelyn sank deeper into her own abyss. The rumors became sporadic but never went away. The appearance of her parents at church or at the grocery always prompted stares and whispers, and they eventually withdrew too.

Evelyn killed herself on November 2, 1959, on Rachel's fifth birthday. She drove her parents' car to the edge of town, and jumped off a bridge.

The obituary and the story of her death in the local paper found their way to Troy's office in New Jersey, where they were also filed away and hidden.

Very little had been learned about Rachel's childhood. The Reverend and Mrs. Lane moved twice, from Kalispell to Butte, then from Butte to Helena. He died of cancer when Rachel was seventeen. She was an only child.

For reasons no one but Troy could explain, he decided to reenter her life as she was finishing high school. Perhaps he felt some measure of guilt. Perhaps he was worried about her college education and how she would afford it. Rachel knew she was adopted, but had never expressed an interest in knowing her real parents.

The specifics were unknown, but Troy met Rachel sometime in the summer of 1972. Four years later, she graduated from the University of Montana. Gaps appeared thereafter, huge voids in her history that no investigation had been able to fill.

Nate suspected that only two people could properly document the relationship. One was dead; the other was living like an Indian somewhere out there, on the banks of one of a thousand rivers.

He tried to jog for a block, but quit in pain. Walking was difficult enough. Two cars passed, people were stirring. The roar approached quickly from behind and was upon him before he could react. Jevy slammed on the brakes next to the sidewalk. *"Bom dia,"* he yelled above the engine.

Nate nodded. *"Bom dia."*

Jevy turned the switch and the engine died. "How do you feel?"

"Sore. And you?"

"No problem. The girl at the desk said you were running. Let's go for a ride."

Nate preferred jogging in pain to riding with Jevy, but the traffic was light and the streets were safer.

They drove through downtown, with his chauffeur still thoroughly ignoring all lights and stop signs. Jevy never looked around as they sped through intersections.

"I want you to see the boat," Jevy said at one point. If he was sore and stiff from the crash landing, he didn't show it. Nate only nodded.

There was a boatyard of sorts on the east end of town, at the foot of the bluff, on a small inlet where the water was murky and oil-stained. A sad collection of boats rocked gently in the river—some had been scrapped decades earlier, others were rarely used. Two were obviously cattle boats, with their decks sectioned into muddy wooden pens.

"There it is," Jevy said as he pointed in the general direction of the river. They parked on the street and walked down the bank. There were several fishing boats, small and low in the water, and their owners were either coming or going. Nate couldn't tell. Jevy yelled at two of them, and they retorted with something humorous.

"My father was a boat captain," Jevy explained. "I was here every day."

"Where is he now?" Nate asked.

"He drowned in a storm."

Wonderful, thought Nate. The storms get you both in the air and on the water.

A sagging sheet of plywood bridged the dirty water and led to their boat. They stopped at the edge of the bank to admire the vessel, the *Santa Loura*. "How do you like it?" Jevy asked.

"I don't know," Nate replied. It was certainly nicer than the cattle boats. Someone was hammering in the back of it.

A coat of paint would help tremendously. The boat was at least sixty feet long, with two decks and a bridge at the top of the steps. It was larger than Nate had expected.

"It's just me, right?" he asked.

"Right."

"No other passengers?"

"No. Just you, me, and a deckhand who can also cook."

"What's his name?"

"Welly."

The plywood creaked but didn't break. The boat dipped a little as they jumped on board. Barrels of diesel fuel and water lined the bow. Through a door and two steps down, and they were in the cabin, which had four bunks, each with white sheets and a thin layer of foam rubber as a mattress. Nate's sore muscles flinched at the thought of a week on one of those. The ceiling was low, the windows shut, and the first major problem was the fact that there was no air conditioning. The cabin was an oven.

"We'll get a fan," Jevy said, reading his mind. "It's not so bad when the boat is moving." This was impossible to believe. Shuffling sideways, they moved along the narrow walkway toward the rear of the boat, passing along the way a kitchen with a sink and a propane stove, the engine room, and finally a small bathroom. In the engine room a grimy, shirtless man was sweating profusely and staring at a wrench in his hand as if it had offended him.

Jevy knew the man, and managed to say the wrong thing, be-cause sharp words suddenly filled the air. Nate retreated to the rear walkway, where he found a small aluminum boat tied to the *Santa*

Loura. It had paddles and an outboard motor, and Nate suddenly had a vision of himself and Jevy scooting across shallow water, darting through weeds and trunks, dodging alligators, chasing another dead end. The adventure was growing.

Jevy laughed and the tension eased. He walked to the rear of the boat and said, "He needs an oil pump. The store is closed today."

"What about tomorrow?" Nate asked.

"No problem."

"What's this little boat for?"

"Lots of things."

They climbed the grated steps to the bridge, where Jevy inspected the wheel and engine switches. Behind the bridge was a small open room with two bunks; Jevy and the deckhand would take turns sleeping there. And farther behind was a deck, about fifteen square feet in size and shaded with a bright green canopy. Stretched the length of the deck was a comfortable-looking hammock, which immediately caught Nate's attention.

"This is yours," Jevy said with a smile. "You will have lots of time to read and sleep."

"How nice," Nate said.

"This boat is sometimes used for tourists, usually Germans, who want to see the Pantanal."

"Have you worked as the captain on this boat?"

"Yes, a couple of times. Several years ago. The owner is not a pleasant man."

Nate carefully sat on the hammock, then swung his damaged legs around until he was fully fitted into it. Jevy gave him a push, then left to have another chat with the mechanic.

FIFTEEN

L ILLIAN PHELAN'S DREAMS of a cozy Christmas dinner were shattered when Troy Junior arrived late and drunk and in the midst of a nasty fight with Biff. They came in separate cars, each driving new Porsches of different colors. The shouting spread as Rex, who'd also had a few drinks, chastised his older brother for ruining their mother's Christmas. The house was full. Lillian's four children—Troy Junior, Rex, Libbigail, and Mary Ross—were there, as well as all eleven grandchildren, along with an assortment of their friends, most of whom had not been specifically invited by Lillian.

The Phelan grandchildren, like their parents, had attracted new pals and confidants since Troy's passing.

Until Troy Junior's arrival, it had been a delightful celebration of Christmas. Never had so many fabulous gifts been exchanged. The Phelan heirs bought for each other and for Lillian without regard to cost—designer clothing, jewelry, electronic gadgets, even art. For a few hours, the money brought out the best in them. Their generosity knew no bounds.

In only two days the will would be read.

Libbigail's husband Spike, the ex-biker she'd met in rehab, attempted to intervene in the rift between Troy Junior and Rex, and in the process got himself cursed by Troy Junior, who reminded him that he was a "fat hippie whose brain had been fried by LSD." This offended Libbigail, who called Biff a slut. Lillian ran to her bedroom and locked the door. The grandchildren and their entourages drifted to the basement, where someone had stashed a cooler of beer.

Mary Ross, arguably the most reasonable and certainly the least volatile of the four, convinced her brothers and Libbigail to stop yelling and find separate corners between rounds. They drifted off into little groups; some in the den, some in the living room. An uneasy ceasefire settled in.

The lawyers hadn't helped matters. They now worked in teams as they represented what they claimed to be the best interests of each Phelan heir. And they also spent hours conniving and figuring ways to get a larger piece of the pie. Four very distinct little armies of lawyers—six if you counted Geena's and Ramble's—all working feverishly. The more time the Phelan heirs spent with their lawyers, the more they distrusted each other.

After an hour of peace, Lillian emerged and surveyed the truce. Saying nothing, she went to the kitchen and finished preparing dinner. A buffet now made sense. They could eat in shifts, come in groups and fill their plates and retire to the safety of their corners.

And so the first Phelan family enjoyed a quiet Christmas dinner after all. Troy Junior ate ham and sweet potatoes by himself at the bar near the rear patio. Biff ate with Lillian in the kitchen. Rex and his wife Amber, the stripper, enjoyed turkey in the bedroom with a football game on. Libbigail, Mary Ross, and their husbands ate on TV trays in the den.

And the grandchildren and their groupies took frozen pizza to the basement, where the beer was flowing.

THE SECOND FAMILY had no Christmas at all, at least not together. Janie had never been fond of the holiday, and so she fled the country, to Klosters in Switzerland, where the pretty people from Europe gathered to be seen and ski. She took with her a bodybuilder named Lance, who at twenty-eight was half her age, but happy to be along for the ride.

Her daughter Geena was forced to spend Christmas with in-laws in Connecticut, normally a bleak and gloomy prospect, but things had changed dramatically. For Geena's husband Cody, it was a triumphant return to the family's aging country estate near Waterbury.

The Strong family once had a fortune built in shipping, but after centuries of mismanagement and inbreeding the money had practically dried up. The name and the pedigree still guaranteed acceptance to the right schools and the proper clubs, and a Strong wedding still received a lengthy announcement. But the trough was only so wide and long, and too many generations had been eating from it.

They were an arrogant bunch, proud of their name and accent and bloodlines, and on the surface unconcerned about the dwindling family money. They had careers in New York and Boston. They spent what they earned because the family fortune had always been their safety net.

The last Strong with any vision had evidently seen the end and established trusts for education, thick trusts written by squads of lawyers, impenetrable trusts clad with iron and able to withstand the desperate assaults from future Strongs. The assaults came; the trusts held firm, and any young Strong was still guaranteed a fine education. Cody boarded at Taft, was an average student at Dartmouth, then received an MBA from Columbia.

His marriage to Geena Phelan had not been well received by the family, primarily because it was her second. The fact that her estranged father was worth, at the time of the wedding, six billion dollars helped ease her entry into the clan. But she would always be looked down on because she was a divorcée and poorly educated at non–Ivy League schools, and also because Cody was a bit odd.

But they were all there to greet her on Christmas Day. She had never seen so many smiles from people she detested; so many stiff little hugs and awkward pecks on the cheeks and pats on the shoulder. She hated them even more for their phoniness.

A couple of drinks, and Cody began talking. The men grouped around him in the den and it wasn't long before someone asked, "How much?"

He frowned as if the money was already a burden. "Probably half a billion," he said, the perfect delivery of a line he'd rehearsed in front of his bathroom mirror.

Some of the men gasped. Others grimaced because they knew Cody, and they were all Strongs, and they knew they would never see a dime of it. They all quietly seethed with envy. Word filtered out from the group and before long the women scattered around the house were whispering about the half a billion. Cody's mother, a prim and shriveled little woman whose wrinkles cracked when she smiled, was appalled by the obscenity of the fortune. "It's new money," she said to a daughter. New money earned by a scandalous old goat with three wives and a string of bad children, not a one of whom had attended an Ivy League school.

New or old, the money was much envied by the younger women. They could see the jets and beach houses and fabulous family gatherings on distant islands, and trust funds for nieces and nephews, and perhaps even outright gifts of cash.

The money thawed the Strongs, thawed them to a warmness they had never shown to an outsider, thawed them to the point of melting. It taught them openness and love, and made for a warm, cozy Christmas.

Late in the afternoon, as the family gathered around the table for the traditional dinner, it began to snow. What a perfect Christmas, all the Strongs said. Geena hated them more than ever.

RAMBLE SPENT the holiday with his lawyer, at six hundred dollars an hour, though the billing would be hidden as only lawyers can hide such things.

Tira likewise had left the country with a young gigolo. She was on a beach somewhere, topless and probably bottomless too, and completely unconcerned with what her fourteen-year-old son might be doing.

The lawyer, Yancy, was single, twice divorced, and had twin eleven-year-old sons from his second marriage. The boys were exceptionally bright for their age; Ramble was painfully slow for his, so they had a great time playing video games in the bedroom while Yancy watched football alone.

His client was set to receive the obligatory five million dollars on his twenty-first birthday, and given the client's level of maturity and direction at home, the money wouldn't even last as long as it had for the other Phelan offspring. But Yancy wasn't concerned with a meager five million; hell, he'd make that much in fees off Ramble's cut from the will.

Yancy had other worries. Tira had hired a new law firm, an aggressive one near the Capitol, one with all the right connections. She was only an ex-wife, not an offspring, and her portion would be much smaller than anything Ramble received. The new lawyers of course realized this. They were pressuring Tira to ditch Yancy and steer young Ramble into their corner. Fortunately, the mother didn't care much for the child, and Yancy was doing a splendid job of manipulating child away from mother.

The laughter of the boys was music to his ears.

SIXTEEN

LATE IN the afternoon, he stopped at a small deli a few blocks from the hotel. He was roaming the sidewalks, saw that the deli was open, and walked into it with the hope of finding a beer. Nothing but a beer, maybe two. He was alone on the far side of the world. It was Christmas and he had no one to share it with. A wave of loneliness and depression fell hard upon Nate, and he began to slide. Self-pity seized him.

He saw the rows of bottles of liquor, all full and unopened, whiskeys and gins and vodkas, lined up like pretty little soldiers in bright uniforms. His mouth was instantly dry, even parched. His jaw dropped and his eyes closed. He grabbed the counter so he wouldn't waver, and his entire face contorted with pain as he thought about Sergio back at Walnut Hill and Josh and the ex-wives and the ones he'd hurt so many times when he crashed. Thoughts spun wildly and he was about to faint when the little man said something. Nate glowered at him, bit his lip, and pointed at the vodka. Two bottles, eight reais.

Every crash had been different. Some were slow in building, a drink here, a snort there, a crack in the dam followed by more.

Once he'd actually driven himself to a detox center. Another time he'd awakened strapped to a bed with an IV in his wrist. With the last crash, a maid had found him in a cheap motel room, thirty bucks a day, comatose.

He clutched the paper sack and walked with a purpose to his hotel, stepping around a group of sweaty little boys dribbling a soccer ball on the sidewalk. So lucky are the children, he thought. No burdens, no baggage. Tomorrow's just another game.

It would be dark in an hour, and Corumbá was gently coming to life. The sidewalk cafés and bars were opening, a few cars moved about. At the hotel, live music from the pool drifted through the lobby, and for a second Nate was tempted to get a table for one last song.

But he didn't. He went to his room, where he locked the door and filled a tall plastic cup with ice. He placed the bottles side by side, opened one, slowly poured the vodka over the ice, and vowed not to stop until both were empty.

JEVY WAS WAITING for the parts merchant when he arrived at eight. The sun was up and unfiltered by clouds. The sidewalks were hot to the touch.

There was no oil pump, at least not one for a diesel engine. The merchant made two calls, and Jevy roared away in his pickup. He drove to the edge of Corumbá where a boat dealer ran a salvage yard cluttered with the remains of dozens of scrapped vessels. In the engine shop a parts boy produced a well-used oil pump, covered with oil and grease and wrapped in a dirty shop rag. Jevy gladly paid twenty reais for it.

He drove to the river and parked near the water's edge. The *Santa Loura* hadn't moved. He was pleased to see that Welly had arrived. Welly was a novice deckhand, not yet eighteen, who claimed he could cook, pilot, guide, clean, navigate, and perform any and all other services required. Jevy knew he was lying, but such bravado was not uncommon among boys looking for work on the river.

"Have you seen Mr. O'Riley?" Jevy asked.

"The American?" asked Welly.

"Yes, the American."

"No. No sign of him."

A fisherman in a wooden boat yelled something at Jevy, but he was preoccupied with other matters. He bounced across the plywood onto the boat, where the banging had started again in the rear. The same grimy mechanic was wrestling with the engine. He hovered over it in a half-crouch, shirtless and dripping with sweat. The engine room was suffocating. Jevy handed him the oil pump and he inspected it with his short stubby fingers.

The engine was a five-cylinder in-line diesel, with the pump at the bottom of the crankcase, just below the edge of the grated floor. The mechanic shrugged as if Jevy's purchase might indeed do the trick, then he maneuvered his belly around the manifold, dropped slowly to his knees, and bent low with the top of his head resting on the exhaust.

He grunted something, and Jevy handed him a wrench. The replacement pump was slowly fitted into place. Jevy's shirt and shorts were soaked within minutes.

With both men wedged tightly into the engine room, Welly decided to appear and ask if he was needed. No, in fact he was not. "Just watch for the American," Jevy said, wiping sweat from his forehead.

The mechanic cursed and flung wrenches for half an hour, then declared the pump ready for use. He started the engine, and spent a few minutes monitoring the oil pressure. He finally smiled, then gathered his tools.

Jevy drove downtown to the hotel to find Nate.

The shy girl at the front desk had not seen Mr. O'Riley. She phoned his room and no one answered. A maid walked by the desk and got herself quizzed. No, to her knowledge, he had not left the room. Reluctantly, the girl gave Jevy a key.

The door was locked but unchained, and Jevy entered slowly. The first odd thing he noticed was the empty bed with its disheveled sheets. Then he saw the bottles. One was empty and lying on its side on the floor; the other was half-filled. The room was very cool, the air conditioner running at full speed. He saw a bare foot, then stepped closer to see Nate, lying naked, wedged between the bed and the wall with a sheet pulled down and wrapped around his knees. Jevy gently kicked his foot, and the leg jerked.

At least he wasn't dead.

Jevy spoke to him and jabbed his shoulder, and after a few seconds a grunt was heard. A low, painful emission. Squatting on the bed, Jevy carefully clasped his hands under the nearest armpit and pulled Nate up from the floor, away from the wall, and managed to roll him onto the bed, where he quickly covered his privates with a sheet.

Another painful groan. Nate was on his back with one foot hanging off the bed, eyes swollen and still closed, hair wild, his breathing slow and labored. Jevy stood at the end of the bed and stared at him.

The maid and the girl from the front desk appeared at the crack in the door, and Jevy waved them away. He locked it, and picked up the empty bottle.

"It's time to go," he said, and received no response whatsoever. Perhaps he should call Valdir, who in turn would report to the Americans who'd sent this poor drunk to Brazil. Maybe later.

"Nate!" he said loudly. "Speak to me!"

No response. If he didn't rally soon, Jevy would call a doctor. A bottle and a half of vodka in one night could kill a man. Maybe his system was poisoned and he needed a hospital.

In the bathroom he soaked a towel with cold water, then wrapped it around Nate's neck. Nate began to squirm, and he opened his mouth in an effort to speak. "Where am I?" he grunted, his tongue thick and sticky.

"In Brazil. In your hotel room."

"I'm alive."

"More or less."

Jevy took an edge of the towel and wiped Nate's face and eyes. "How do you feel?" he asked.

"I want to die," Nate said, reaching for the towel. He took it, eased it into his mouth, and began sucking on it.

"I'll get some water," Jevy said. He opened the refrigerator and removed a bottle of water. "Can you lift your head?" he asked.

"No," Nate grunted.

Jevy dripped water onto Nate's lips and tongue. Some of it rolled down his cheeks and into the towel. He didn't care. His head was splitting and pounding and his first thought was exactly how in hell did he wake up.

An eye opened, the right one, barely. The lids on the left were still matted together. Light scalded his brain and a wave of nausea rolled from his knees to his throat. With surprising suddenness, he flipped to one side, then rocked on all fours as the vomit shot forth.

Jevy jumped back, then went for another towel. He lingered in the bathroom, listening to the gagging and coughing. The sight of a naked man on his hands and knees in the middle of a bed puking his guts out was something he could do without. He turned on the shower and adjusted the water.

His deal with Valdir paid him a thousand reais to take Mr. O'Riley into the Pantanal, find the person he was searching for, then deliver him back to Corumbá. It was good money, but he wasn't a nurse and he wasn't a baby-sitter. The boat was ready. If Nate couldn't answer the bell without an escort, then Jevy would move along to the next job.

There was a break in the nausea, and Jevy manhandled Nate into the bathroom, into the shower, where he crumpled onto the plastic floor. "I'm sorry," he said over and over. Jevy left him there, to drown for all he cared. He folded the sheets and tried to clean the mess, then he went downstairs for a pot of strong coffee.

IT WAS ALMOST TWO when Welly heard them coming. Jevy parked on the bank, his huge truck scattering rocks and waking fishermen as it roared to a stop. There was no sign of the American.

Then a head slowly lifted itself from somewhere in the cab. The eyes were covered with thick shades, and a cap was pulled as low as possible. Jevy opened the passenger door and helped Mr. O'Riley onto the rocks. Welly walked to the truck and grabbed Nate's bag and briefcase from the back. He wanted to meet Mr. O'Riley, but the timing was bad. He was quite ill, with bleached skin that was soaked with sweat, and he was too weak to walk on his own. Welly followed them to the edge of the water and helped guide them along the rickety plywood walkway onto the boat. Jevy practically carried Mr. O'Riley up the steps to the bridge, then along the catwalk to the small deck, where the hammock was waiting. He shoveled him into it.

When they returned to the deck, Jevy started the engine and Welly pulled the ropes. "What's wrong with him?" Welly asked.

"He's drunk."

"But it's only two o'clock."

"He's been drunk for a long time."

The *Santa Loura* eased away from the shore, and, moving upriver, slowly made its way past Corumbá.

NATE WATCHED the city go by. The roof above him was a thick, green worn canvas stretched over a metal frame anchored to the deck by four poles. Two of these supported his hammock, which had rocked a bit just after the launch. The nausea crept back. He tried not to move. He wanted everything to be perfectly still. The boat moved gently upstream. The river was smooth. There was no wind at the moment, so Nate was able to lie deep in his hammock and stare at the dark green canvas above him and try to ponder things. The pondering was difficult, though, because his head spun and ached. Concentration was a challenge.

He had called Josh from his room just before checking out. With ice packs on his neck and a wastebasket between his feet he had dialed the number and tried mightily to sound normal. Jevy hadn't told Valdir. Valdir hadn't told Josh. No one knew but Nate and Jevy, and they had agreed to keep it that way. There was no alcohol on the boat, and Nate had promised sobriety until they returned. How was he supposed to find a drink in the Pantanal?

If Josh was worried, his voice didn't convey it. The firm was still closed for Christmas, et cetera, but he was busy as hell. The usual.

Nate said that he was doing just fine. The boat was adequate and now properly repaired. They were anxious to set sail. When he hung up he vomited again. And then he showered again. Then Jevy helped him to the elevator and through the lobby.

The river bent slightly and turned again, and Corumbá disappeared. The boat traffic around the city thinned as their journey gained momentum. Nate's vantage point gave him a view of the wake and of the muddy brown water bubbling behind them. The Paraguay was less than a hundred yards wide and narrowed quickly around the bends. They passed a rickety boat laden with green bananas, and two small boys waved.

The steady knock of the diesel failed to stop, as Nate had hoped, but it became a low hum, a constant vibration throughout the entire vessel. There was no choice but to accept it. He tried swinging in the hammock, a gentle swing as a breeze crept through. The nausea was gone.

Don't think about Christmas, and home and children and broken memories, and don't think about your addictions. The crash is over, he told himself. The boat was his treatment center. Jevy was his counselor. Welly was his nurse. He'd dry out in the Pantanal, then never drink again.

How many times could he lie to himself?

The aspirin Jevy had given him wore off, and his head pounded again. He lapsed into a near-sleep, and awoke when Welly appeared with a bottle of water and a bowl of rice. He ate it with a spoon, his hands shaking so badly he spilled the rice on his shirt and in the hammock. It was warm and salty, and he ate every grain.

"*Mais?*" Welly asked.

Nate shook his head no, then sipped the water. He sank into the hammock and tried to nap.

SEVENTEEN

AFTER A FEW false starts, the jet lag and fatigue and the aftereffects of the vodka caught up with him. The rice helped too, and Nate fell into a hard deep sleep. Welly checked on him every hour. "He's snoring," he reported to Jevy in the wheel-house.

The sleep was dreamless. His nap lasted four hours as the *Santa Loura* inched ahead in the general direction of north, against the current and the wind. Nate awoke to the steady beat of the diesel and the sensation that the boat was not really moving. He rose gently in the hammock and peeked over the edge and studied the riverbank for signs of progress. The vegetation was dense. The river appeared completely uninhabited. There was a wake behind the boat and by staring at a tree he could tell that, yes, they were in fact going somewhere. But very slowly. The water was up because of the rains; navigation was easier but traffic upstream was not as fast.

The nausea and headaches were gone, but movements were still delicate. He began the challenge of removing himself from the hammock, primarily because he needed to urinate. He managed to safely place his feet on the deck without incident, and as he paused for a moment Welly appeared like a mouse and handed him a small cup of coffee.

Nate took the warm cup, cradled it and sniffed it. Nothing had ever smelled better. *"Obrigado,"* he said. Thanks.

"Sim," Welly said with an even brighter smile.

Nate sipped the precious sweet coffee and tried not to return Welly's stare. The kid was dressed in the standard river garb; old gym shorts, old tee shirt, and cheap rubber sandals that protected the soles of scarred and hardened feet. Like Jevy and Valdir, and most of the Brazilians he'd met so far, Welly had black hair and dark eyes, semi-Caucasian features, and a shade of brown skin that was lighter than some, darker than others, but a shade all his own.

I'm alive and sober, Nate thought, sipping. I have once again touched briefly the edge of hell and survived. I've bottomed, I've crashed, I've stared at the blurred image of my face and welcomed death, yet here I am sitting and breathing. Twice in three days I have uttered my last words. Maybe it's not my time.

"Mais?" Welly asked, nodding at the empty cup.

"Sim," Nate replied, and handed it to him. Two steps and he was gone.

Stiff from the plane wreck and shaky from the vodka, Nate pulled himself up and stood unaided in the center of the deck, wobbly and bent at the knees. But he was able to stand, and this alone meant everything. Recovery was nothing but a series of small steps, small victories. String them together with no stumbles and no defeats and you're treated. Never cured, just treated or rehabbed or sanitized for a while. He'd done the puzzle before; celebrate every little piece.

Then the flat bottom of the boat brushed a sandbar, jolting it, and Nate fell hard against the hammock. It flipped him onto the deck, where his head cracked on a wooden plank. He scrambled to his feet and clutched the railing with one hand while rubbing his skull with the other. No blood, just a small knot, just another little wound to the flesh. But the blow woke him, and when his eyes cleared, he moved slowly along the railing to the small cramped bridge, where Jevy sat on a stool, one hand draped over the wheel.

The quick Brazilian smile, then, "How do you feel?"

"Much better," Nate said, almost ashamed. But shame was an emotion Nate had abandoned years earlier. Addicts know no shame. You disgrace yourself so many times you become immune to it.

Welly bounced up the steps with coffee in both hands. He gave one to Nate and the other to Jevy, then took his perch on a narrow bench next to the captain.

The sun was beginning to fall behind the distant mountains of Bolivia, and clouds were forming to the north, directly in front of them. The air was light and much cooler. Jevy found his tee shirt and put it on. Nate feared another storm, but the river wasn't wide. Surely they could land the damned boat and tie it to a tree.

They approached a little square house, the first dwelling Nate had seen since Corumbá. There were signs of life: a horse and a cow, wash on the line, a canoe near the water. A man with a straw hat, a bona fide *pantaneiro,* stepped onto the porch and gave them a lazy wave.

Past the house, Welly pointed to a spot where thick undergrowth spilled into the river. *"Jacarés,"* he said. Jevy looked but seemed not to care. He'd seen a million alligators. Nate had seen only one, from the back of a horse, and as he gazed at the slimy reptiles watching them from the mud he was struck by how much smaller they appeared from the deck of a boat. He preferred the distance.

Something told him, though, that before his journey was over he would once again get too close for comfort. The johnboat trailing behind the *Santa Loura* would have to be used in their search for Rachel Lane. He and Jevy would navigate small rivers, dodge undergrowth, wade through dark and weedy waters. Surely there would be *jacarés* and other species of vicious reptiles waiting for lunch.

But, oddly, Nate didn't care at the moment. So far in Brazil he'd proved himself quite resistant. It was an adventure, and his guide seemed fearless.

Grasping the handrail, he managed the steps down with great care, then shuffled along the narrow walkway past the cabin and the kitchen, where Welly had a pot on the propane stove. The diesel roared in the engine room. The last stop was the rest room, a small closet with a toilet, a dirty sink in a corner, and a flimsy showerhead swinging back and forth inches above his head. He relieved himself while studying the cord for the shower. He backed away and pulled it. Warm water with a slight brownish tint came down with sufficient force. It was obviously river water, scooped from an unlimited supply and presumably unfiltered. There was a wire basket above the door for a towel and a change of clothes, so you had to strip and somehow straddle the toilet while pulling the shower rope with one hand and bathing with the other.

What the hell, thought Nate. There simply wouldn't be many showers.

He looked in the pot on the stove and found it filled with rice and black beans and wondered if every meal would be the same. But he didn't really care. Food was not an issue with him. At Walnut Hill they dried you out while gently starving you. His appetite had shrunk months earlier.

He sat on the steps to the bridge, his back to the captain and Welly, and watched the river grow dark. In the dusk the wildlife prepared itself for the night. Birds flew low over the water, moving from tree to tree, looking for one last minnow or fish for the night. They called to each other as the boat passed, their chants and shrieks rising well above the steady drone of the diesel. Water splashed along the banks as alligators moved about. Perhaps there were snakes in there too, large anacondas bedding down, but Nate preferred not to think about them. He felt quite safe on the *Santa Loura*. The breeze was slight and warmer now, and blowing at them. The storm had not materialized.

Time was racing somewhere else, but in the Pantanal time was of no consequence. He was slowly adjusting to it. He thought of Rachel Lane. What would the money do to her? No one, regardless of his level of faith and commitment, could remain the same. Would she leave with him, and go to the States to tend to her father's estate? She could always return to her Indians. How would she greet the news? How would she react to the sight of an American lawyer who'd tracked her down?

Welly strummed an old guitar and Jevy added some low and unrefined vocals. Their duet was pleasant, almost soothing; the song of simple men who lived by the day and not by the minute. Men who gave little thought to tomorrow and none for what may or may not happen next year. He envied them, at least while they were singing.

It was quite a comeback for a man who'd tried to drink himself to death a day earlier. He was enjoying the moment, happy to be alive, looking forward to the rest of his adventure. His past was truly in another world, light years away, in the cold wet streets of Washington.

Nothing good could happen there. He'd proved clearly that he could not stay clean living there, knowing the same people, doing the same work, ignoring the same old habits until he crashed. He would always crash.

Welly started a solo that snapped Nate away from his past. It was a slow mournful ballad that lasted until the river was completely dark. Jevy switched on two small floodlights, one on each side of the bow. The river was easy to navigate. It rose and fell with the seasons and never attained much depth. The boats were shallow and flat on the bottom, and built to take sandbars that sometimes got in the way. Jevy hit one just after dark, and the *Santa Loura* stopped moving. He reversed the engine, then thrust it forward, and after five minutes of this maneuvering they were free again. The boat was unsinkable.

In a corner of the cabin, not far from the four bunks, Nate ate alone at a table that was bolted to the floor. Welly served him the beans and rice, along with boiled chicken and an orange. He drank cold water from a bottle. A bulb on a light cord swung above his food. The cabin was hot and unventilated. Welly had suggested sleeping in the hammock.

Jevy arrived with a navigational map of the Pantanal. He wanted to plot their progress, and so far there had been little. They were indeed inching up the Paraguay, with only a tiny gap between their current position and Corumbá.

"The water is high," Jevy explained. "We'll go much faster on the return."

The return was not something Nate had thought much about. "No problem," he said. Jevy pointed in various directions and made some more calculations. "The first Indian village is in this area," he said, pointing to a spot that looked weeks away, given their current pace.

"Guató?"

"*Sim.* Yes. I think we should go there first. If she is not there, then maybe someone knows where she is."

"How long before we get there?"

"Two, maybe three days."

Nate shrugged. Time had stopped. His wristwatch was in his pocket. His collection of hourly, daily, weekly, monthly planners was long forgotten. His trial calendar, the one great inviolate map of his life, had been tucked away in some secretary's drawer. He had cheated death, and so every day now was a gift.

"I have lots of reading," he said.

Jevy carefully refolded the map. "Are you okay?" he asked.

"I'm fine. I feel good."

There was a lot more Jevy wanted to ask. Nate was not ready for a confessional. "I'm fine," he said again. "This little trip will be good for me."

He read for an hour at the table, under the swaying light, until he realized he was soaked with sweat. From his bunk he gathered insect repellent, a flashlight, and a stack of Josh's memos, and carefully made his way to the bow, then up the steps to the wheelhouse, where Welly was in command and Jevy was catching a nap. He

sprayed his arms and legs, then crawled into the hammock, squirming and adjusting until his head was properly elevated above his butt.
When things were perfectly balanced, and the hammock swung
gently with the flow of the river, Nate clicked on his flashlight and
began reading again.

EIGHTEEN

I T WAS A SIMPLE HEARING, a reading of a will, but the details were crucial. F. Parr Wycliff had thought of little else during his Christmas holiday. Every seat in his courtroom would be filled, with more spectators packed three deep against the walls. He'd worried so much that the day after Christmas he had walked around his empty courtroom pondering where to seat everyone.

And, typically, the press was out of control. They wanted cameras inside, and he had vehemently refused. They wanted cameras in the hallway peering in through the small square windows in the doors, and he said no. They wanted preferred seating; again, no. They wanted interviews with him, and he was stiff-arming them at the moment.

The lawyers too were showing their asses. Some wanted the entire hearing closed to the world, others wanted it televised, for obvious reasons. Some wanted the file sealed, others wanted copies of the will faxed over for their perusal. There were motions for this and that, requests to have seating here and there, concerns about who would be allowed inside the courtroom and who would not.

Several of the lawyers went so far as to suggest that they be allowed to open and read the will. It was quite thick, you know, and they might be forced to explain some of the more intricate provisions as they read along.

Wycliff arrived early and met with the extra deputies he'd requested. They followed him, along with his secretary and his law clerk, around the courtroom as he made seat assignments and tested the sound system and counted chairs. He was very concerned with the details. Someone said a television news crew was attempting to set up camp down the hall, and he quickly dispatched a deputy to retake the area.

With the courtroom secure and organized, he retired to his office to tend to other matters. Concentration was difficult. Never again would his daily calendar promise such excitement. Quite selfishly, he hoped that the will of Troy Phelan was scandalously controversial; that it stripped money from one ex-family and awarded it to another. Or perhaps it screwed all of his crazy children and made someone else rich. A long nasty will contest would certainly liven up Wycliff's rather mundane career in probate. He'd be the center of the storm, one that would no doubt rage for years, with eleven billion at stake.

He was certain this would happen. Alone, with his door locked, he spent fifteen minutes ironing his robe.

The first spectator was a reporter who arrived just after eight, and because he was the first he received the full treatment from the jumpy security detail blocking the double doors to the courtroom. He was greeted gruffly, asked to produce a picture ID and sign a sheet for journalists, got his steno pad inspected as if it were a grenade, then was directed through the metal detector, where two thick guards were obviously disappointed when no sirens erupted as he passed through. He was grateful he did not get strip-searched. Once inside, he was led down the center aisle by yet another uniformed officer to a spot two rows from the front. He was relieved to get a seat. The courtroom was empty.

The hearing was set for ten, and by nine a nice crowd had assembled in the foyer outside the courtroom. Security was taking its time with the paperwork and the searches. A line formed down the hall.

Some of the lawyers for the Phelan heirs arrived in a rush and became instantly irritated with the delay in getting into the courtroom. Harsh words were exchanged; threats were made and received by the lawyers and by the deputies. Someone sent for Wycliff, but he was polishing his boots and didn't want to be disturbed. And, like a bride before the wedding, he didn't want to be seen by the guests. The heirs and the lawyers were given priority, and this eased the tense situation.

The courtroom slowly filled. Tables were placed in a U-shape, with the Judge's bench at the open end, so that His Honor could look down from his perch and see everyone: lawyers, heirs, spectators. To the left of the bench, in front of the jury box, was a long table where the Phelans were being placed. Troy Junior was first, with Biff in tow. They were directed to a spot nearest the bench, where they sat and huddled with three lawyers from their legal team while working desperately to appear somber and at the same time ignore everyone else in the courtroom. Biff was furious because the security detail had confiscated her cell phone. She couldn't make real estate calls.

Ramble was next. For the occasion he had neglected his hair, which still bore streaks of lime green and hadn't been washed in two weeks. His rings were in full glory—ear, nose, eyebrow. Black leather jacket with no sleeves, temporary tattoos on his skinny arms. Ragged jeans; old boots. Surly attitude. He caught the attention of the journalists when he walked down the aisle. He was coddled and fussed over every step of the way by Yancy, his aging hippie lawyer, who had somehow managed to hang on to his prized client.

Yancy took a quick look at the seating scheme, and asked to sit as far away from Troy Junior as possible. The deputy complied and put them at the end of a temporary table facing the bench. Ramble sank into his chair, green hair hanging over the back of it. The spectators watched him in horror—this thing was about to inherit a half a billion dollars? The potential for mayhem seemed limitless.

Geena Phelan Strong was next with her husband Cody and two of their lawyers. They gauged the distance between Troy Junior and Ramble, then split the difference and sat as far away from both as possible. Cody was particularly burdened and earnest and immediately began reviewing some important papers with one of his lawyers. Geena just gawked at Ramble; she couldn't believe they were half-brother and -sister.

Amber the stripper made a grand entrance in a short skirt and low-cut blouse that gave away most of her expensive breasts. The deputy escorting her down the aisle couldn't believe his good fortune. He chatted her up along the way, eyes glued to the edge of her blouse. Rex followed behind in a dark suit, carrying a bulky briefcase as if he had serious work today. Behind him was Hark Gettys, still the noisiest advocate of the bunch. Hark brought with him two of his new associates; his firm was growing by the week. Since Amber and Biff weren't speaking, Rex quickly intervened and pointed to a spot between Ramble and Geena.

The tables were filling; the gaps were closing. Before long some of the Phelans would be sitting close to each other.

Ramble's mother Tira brought two young men of about the same age. One had tight jeans and a hairy chest; the other was well groomed in dark pinstripes. She was sleeping with the gigolo. The lawyer would get his on the back-end.

Another gap was filled. On the other side of the bar, the courtroom was alive with the hum of gossip and speculation. "No wonder the old man jumped," one reporter said to another as they examined the Phelans.

The Phelan grandchildren were forced to sit with the spectators and common folk. They huddled with their small entourages and support groups and giggled nervously as fate was about to swing their way.

Libbigail Jeter arrived with her husband Spike, the three-hun-

dred-twenty-pound ex-biker, and they waddled down the aisle, as
out of place as anyone, though they'd seen their share of courtrooms. They followed Wally Bright, their yellow page lawyer. Wally
wore a spotted raincoat that dragged the floor, scuffed wing tips,
and a polyester tie that was twenty years old, and if the spectators
had voted right then he would've easily won the award for the
worst-dressed lawyer. He carried his papers in an expandable file,
one that had been used for countless divorces and other matters. For
some reason, Bright had never purchased a briefcase. He'd finished
tenth in his class in night school.

They went straight for the widest gap, and as they were taking
their seats Bright began the noisy process of removing his raincoat.
The ragged hem of it brushed against the neck of one of Hark's
nameless associates, an earnest young man already bothered by
Bright's body odor.

"If you don't mind!" he said sharply, swinging a backhand
toward Bright, and missing. The words cracked through the tense
and edgy air. Heads jerked around the tables as important documents were instantly ignored. Everybody hated everybody.

"Sorry!" Bright responded with great sarcasm. Two deputies
moved forward to intervene if necessary. But the raincoat found a
place under the table without further incident, and Bright finally
managed to seat himself, next to Libbigail, with Spike sitting on the
other side stroking his beard and staring at Troy Junior as if he'd
love to slap him.

Few people in the courtroom expected the brief skirmish to be
the last among the Phelans.

You die with eleven billion, and people care about your last will
and testament. Especially if there's a chance that one of the world's
great fortunes is about to be fed to the vultures. The tabloids were
there, along with the local papers and all the important financial
magazines. The three rows Wycliff had designated for the press were
full by nine-thirty. The journalists had a delightful time watching
the Phelans gather in front of them. Three artists worked feverishly;

the panorama before them was rich with inspiration. The punk with the green hair received more than his share of sketches.

Josh Stafford made his appearance at nine-fifty. Tip Durban was with him, along with two other members of the firm and a couple of paralegals to round out the team. Stern and somber-faced, they took seats at their table, a rather spacious one compared to the cramped quarters holding all the Phelans and all their lawyers. Josh placed a single thick file in front of him, and all eyes were immediately upon it. Inside was what appeared to be a document, almost two inches thick and very similar to what old Troy had signed on video just nineteen days earlier.

They couldn't help staring at it. Everyone but Ramble. Virginia law allowed heirs to receive early distributions if the estate was liquid and there was no concern about the payment of debts and taxes. Estimates from the Phelan lawyers ranged from a low of ten million per heir, all the way to Bright's guess of fifty million. Bright in his entire life had never seen fifty thousand.

At ten the deputies locked the doors, and upon some unseen cue Judge Wycliff emerged from an opening behind the bench, and the room was silent. He eased into the chair, his crisp robe settling around him, and smiled. "Good morning," he said into the microphone.

Everyone smiled back. To his great satisfaction, the room was filled to capacity. A quick deputy count revealed eight armed and ready. He studied the Phelans; there were no gaps left. Some of their lawyers were practically touching one another.

"Are all of the parties present?" he asked. Heads shook from around the tables.

"I need to identify everyone," he said, reaching for papers. "The first petition was filed by Rex Phelan." Before the words settled, Hark Gettys was on his feet, clearing his throat.

"Your Honor, I'm Hark Gettys," he boomed toward the bench. "And I represent Mr. Rex Phelan."

"Thank you. You may keep your seat."

He went around the tables, methodically taking names of the heirs and the lawyers. All the lawyers. The reporters scribbled them as fast as the Judge. Six heirs in all, three ex-wives. Everyone was present.

"Twenty-two lawyers," Wycliff mumbled to himself.

"Do you have the will, Mr. Stafford?" he asked.

Josh stood, holding a different file. "I do."

"Would you please take the witness stand?"

Josh made his way around the tables and past the court reporter to the witness stand, where he raised his right hand and swore to tell the truth.

"You represented Troy Phelan?" Wycliff asked.

"I did. For a number of years."

"Did you prepare a will for him?"

"I prepared several."

"Did you prepare his last will?"

There was a pause, and as it grew longer the Phelans inched closer.

"No, I did not," Josh said slowly, looking at the vultures. The words were soft, but they cut through the air like thunder. The Phelan lawyers reacted much more quickly than the Phelan heirs, several of whom weren't sure what to make of it. But it was serious, and unexpected. Another layer of tension settled around the tables. The courtroom grew even quieter.

"Who prepared his last will and testament?" Wycliff asked, like a bad actor reading a script.

"Mr. Phelan himself."

It wasn't so. They had seen the old man sit at the table with lawyers all around him, and the three shrinks—Zadel, Flowe, and Theishen—directly across the table. He'd been declared sane on the spot, and seconds later had taken a thick will prepared by Stafford and one of his associates, declared it to be his, and signed it.

There was no dispute about this.

"Oh my God," Hark Gettys said, under his breath but loud enough for everyone to hear.

"When did he sign it?" Wycliff asked.

"Moments before he jumped to his death."

"Is it handwritten?"

"It is."

"Did he sign it in your presence?"

"He did. There were other witnesses. The signing was also videotaped."

"Please hand me the will."

Josh deliberately withdrew a single envelope from the file and passed it up to His Honor. It looked awfully small. There was no way it contained enough language to convey to the Phelans what was rightfully theirs.

"What the hell is this?" Troy Junior hissed at the nearest lawyer. But the lawyer couldn't respond.

The envelope held only one sheet of yellow paper. Wycliff removed it slowly for all to see, unfolded it carefully, then studied it for a moment.

Panic seized the Phelans, but there was nothing they could do. Had the old man screwed them one last time? Was the money slipping away? Maybe he had changed his mind and given them even more. Around the tables they nudged and elbowed their lawyers, all of whom were remarkably quiet.

Wycliff cleared his throat and leaned a bit closer to the microphone. "I'm holding here a one-page document purporting to be a will handwritten by Troy Phelan. I will read it straight through:

" 'The last testament of Troy L. Phelan. I, Troy L. Phelan, being of sound and disposing mind and memory, do hereby expressly revoke all former wills and codicils executed by me, and dispose of my estate as follows:

" 'To my children, Troy Phelan, Jr., Rex Phelan, Libbigail Jeter, Mary Ross Jackman, Geena Strong, and Ramble Phelan, I give each a sum of money necessary to pay off all the debts of each as of today. Any debts incurred after today will not be covered by this gift. If any of these children attempt to contest this will, then this gift shall be nullified as to that child.' "

Even Ramble heard the words, and understood them. Geena and Cody started crying softly. Rex leaned forward, elbows on the table, face buried in his hands, his mind numb. Libbigail looked past Bright to Spike and said, "That son of a bitch." Spike concurred. Mary Ross covered her eyes as her lawyer rubbed her knee. Her husband rubbed the other one. Only Troy Junior managed a poker face, but not for much longer.

There was more damage yet to come. Wycliff wasn't finished. " 'To my ex-wives, Lillian, Janie, and Tira, I give nothing. They were adequately provided for in the divorces.' "

At that moment, Lillian, Janie, and Tira were wondering what the hell they were doing in the courtroom. Had they really expected to receive more cash from a man they hated? They felt the stares and tried to hide among their lawyers.

The reporters and journalists were downright giddy. They wanted to take notes, but they were afraid of missing a single word. Some couldn't help but grin.

" 'The remainder of my estate I give to my daughter Rachel Lane, born on November, 2, 1954, at Catholic Hospital in New Orleans, Louisiana, to a woman named Evelyn Cunningham, now deceased.' "

Wycliff paused, though not for dramatic effect. With only two small paragraphs left, the damage was done. The eleven billion had been given to an illegitimate heir he'd not read about. The Phelans sitting before him had been stripped. He couldn't help but look at them.

" 'I appoint my trusted lawyer, Joshua Stafford, as executor of this will, and grant unto him broad discretionary powers in its administration.' "

For the moment they had forgotten about Josh. But there he sat, in the box like the innocent witness of a car wreck, and they glared at him with as much hatred as possible. How much had he known? Was he a conspirator? No doubt he could've done something to prevent this.

Josh fought to keep a straight face.

" 'This document is intended to be a holographic will. Every word has been written by my hand, and I hereby sign it.' " Wycliff lowered it and said, "The testament was signed by Troy L. Phelan at three P.M. on December 9, 1996."

He laid it down, and looked around the courtroom, the epicenter. The quake was ending and now it was time for the aftershocks. The Phelans sat low in their seats, some rubbing eyes and foreheads, others staring wildly at the walls. For the moment, all twenty-two lawyers were incapable of speech.

The shocks rippled through the rows of spectators, where, oddly, a few smiles could be seen. Ah, it was the media, suddenly anxious to race from the room and start reporting.

Amber sobbed loudly, then caught herself. She'd met Troy only once, and he'd made a crude advance. Her grief was not for the loss of a loved one. Geena cried quietly, as did Mary Ross. Libbigail and Spike chose to curse instead. "Don't worry," Bright said, waving them off as if he could remedy this injustice in a matter of days.

Biff glared at Troy Junior, and the seeds of a divorce were planted. Since the suicide, he'd been especially arrogant and condescending to her. She'd tolerated it for obvious reasons, but no longer. She relished the first fight, one that would no doubt begin just a few feet outside the courtroom doors.

Other seeds were planted. For the thick-skinned lawyers, the surprise was received, absorbed, then shaken off as instinctively as a duck shakes off water. They were about to get rich. Their clients were heavily in debt with no relief in sight. They had no choice but to contest the will. Litigation would rage for years.

"When do you anticipate probating the will?" Wycliff asked Josh.

"Within a week."

"Very well. You may step down."

Josh returned to his seat, triumphant, as the lawyers began shuffling papers and pretending everything was fine.

"We are adjourned."

NINETEEN

THERE WERE three fights in the hallway after adjournment. Fortunately, none involved Phelans fighting Phelans. Those would come later.

A mob of reporters waited outside the courtroom doors as the Phelans were consoled inside by their lawyers. Troy Junior was the first to exit, and he was immediately surrounded by a pack of wolves, several with microphones in the attack position. He was hungover to begin with, and now that he was half a billion dollars poorer he was in no mood to talk about his father.

"Are you surprised?" some idiot asked, from behind a microphone.

"Damned right," he said, trying to walk through the group.

"Who is Rachel Lane?" asked another.

"I guess she's my sister," he snapped.

A skinny little boy with stupid eyes and a bad complexion stopped directly in front of him, thrust a tape recorder in his face, and asked, "How many illegitimate children did your father have?"

Troy Junior instinctively shoved the tape recorder back at him. It landed sharply just above his nose, and as he fell back Troy Junior launched a wild left hook that popped him in the ear and knocked him down. In the commotion, a deputy pushed Troy Junior in another direction and they made a quick escape.

Ramble spit on another reporter, who had to be restrained by a colleague who reminded him the kid was underage.

The third skirmish happened when Libbigail and Spike lumbered out of the courtroom behind Wally Bright. "No comment!" Bright yelled at the horde closing ranks around them. "No comment! Please get out of the way!"

Libbigail, who was crying, tripped over a TV cable and tumbled into a reporter, who also fell. There were shouts and curses, and as the reporter was on all fours and getting to his feet, Spike kicked him in the ribs. He squealed and fell flat again, and as he was thrashing about trying to get up, his foot caught the edge of Libbigail's dress, and she slapped him for good measure. Spike was about to slaughter him when a deputy intervened.

Deputies broke up each fight, always siding with the Phelans over the reporters. They helped rush the beleaguered heirs and their lawyers down the stairs, through the lobby, and out of the building.

Lawyer Grit, who represented Mary Ross Phelan Jackman, was overcome by the sight of so many reporters. The First Amendment seized him, or at least his own rudimentary understanding of it, and he felt compelled to speak freely. With his arm around his distraught client, he grimly offered their reaction to the surprise will. It was obviously the work of a demented man. How else could you explain the passing of such a great fortune to an unknown heir? His client adored her father, loved him deeply, worshiped him, and as Grit babbled on and on about the incredible love between father and daughter, Mary Ross finally took the hint and began crying. Grit himself appeared on the verge of tears. Yes, they would fight. They would battle this grave injustice to the U.S. Supreme Court. Why? Because this was not the work of the Troy Phelan they knew. Bless his heart. He loved his children, and they loved him. Theirs was an incredible bond, forged through tragedy and hardship. They would fight because their beloved father was not himself when he scribbled this ghastly document.

Josh Stafford was in no hurry to leave. He spoke quietly to Hark Gettys and some of the attorneys from the other tables. He promised to send them copies of the hideous will. Things were initially cordial but hostilities were growing by the minute. A reporter he knew from the *Post* was waiting in the hall, and Josh spent ten minutes with him while saying nothing. Of particular interest was Rachel Lane; her history and whereabouts. There were lots of questions, but Josh had no answers.

Surely Nate would find her before anyone else.

THE STORY GREW. It shot from the courthouse on the waves of the latest telecommunications gadgets and hi-tech hardware. The reporters scrambled with cell phones and laptops and pagers, talking without thinking.

The major wires began running the news twenty minutes after adjournment, and an hour later the first round-the-clock news-gab-a-thon broke into its running series of repetitive stories to go live to a reporter in front of a camera outside the courthouse. "Stunning news here . . ." she began and then told the story, getting most of it right.

Seated in the rear of the courtroom was Pat Solomon, the last person selected by Troy to run The Phelan Group. He'd been CEO for six years, six very uneventful and very profitable years.

He left the courthouse without being recognized by any reporter. As he rode away, in the back of his limo, Solomon attempted to analyze Troy's last bombshell. He was not shocked by it. After working for Troy for twenty years nothing surprised him. The reaction of his idiot children and their lawyers was comforting. Solomon had once been assigned the impossible task of finding within the company a job that Troy Junior could perform without causing a dip in quarterly profits. It had been a nightmare. Spoiled, immature, badly educated, and lacking basic management skills, Troy

Junior had run roughshod through an entire division in Minerals before Solomon was given the green light from above to sack him.

A few years later, a similar episode involved Rex and his pursuit of his father's approval and money. In the end, Rex had gone to Troy in an effort to remove Solomon.

The wives and other children had butted in for years, but Troy had held fast. His private life was a fiasco, but nothing hampered his beloved company.

Solomon and Troy had never been close. In fact, no one, perhaps with the exception of Josh Stafford, had ever managed to become a confidant. The parade of blondes had shared the obvious intimacies, but Troy had no friends. And as he withdrew and declined both physically and mentally, those who ran the company sometimes whispered about its ownership. Surely Troy would not leave it to his children.

He hadn't, at least not the usual suspects.

The board was waiting, on the fourteenth floor, in the same conference room where Troy had produced his testament, then taken flight. Solomon described the scene in the courtroom, and his colorful narrative became humorous. Thoughts of the heirs gaining control had caused great discomfort among the board. Troy Junior had let it be known that he and his siblings had the votes to seize a majority, and that he planned to clean house and show some real profits.

They wanted to know about Janie, wife number two. She'd worked for the company as a secretary until her promotion to mistress, then to wife, and after reaching the top she had been particularly abusive to many of the employees. Troy banned her from the corporate headquarters.

"When she left she was crying," Solomon said happily.

"And Rex?" asked a director, the chief financial officer who had once been fired by Rex in an elevator.

"Not a happy boy. He's under investigation, you know."

They talked about most of the children and all of the wives, and the meeting grew festive.

"I counted twenty-two lawyers," Solomon said with a smile. "Talk about a sad bunch."

Since it was an informal board meeting, Josh's absence was of no consequence. The head of Legal declared the will to be a stroke of great luck after all. They had to worry about only one, unknown heir, as opposed to six idiots.

"Any idea where this woman is?"

"None," answered Solomon. "Maybe Josh knows."

BY LATE AFTERNOON, Josh had been forced from his office and had retreated to a small library in the basement of his building. His secretary stopped counting phone messages at a hundred and twenty. The lobby off the main entrance had been crammed with reporters since late morning. He'd left behind strict instructions with his secretaries that no one should disturb him for an hour. So the knock on the door was especially aggravating.

"Who is it?" he shot at the door.

"It's an emergency, sir," answered a secretary.

"Come in."

Her head entered just far enough to look him in the face and say, "It's Mr. O'Riley." Josh stopped rubbing his temples and actually smiled. He glanced around the room and remembered there were no phones. She took two steps and placed a portable on the table, then disappeared.

"Nate," he said into the receiver.

"That you, Josh?" came the reply. The volume was fine but the words were a little scratchy. The reception was better than most car phones.

"Yes, can you hear me, Nate?"

"Yes."

"Where are you?"

"I'm on the satellite, on the back of my little yacht, floating down the Paraguay River. Can you hear me?"

"Yes, fine. Are you okay, Nate?"

"I'm wonderful, having a ball, just a little boat trouble."

"What kind of trouble?"

"Well, the propeller snagged a line of old rope, and the engine choked down. My crew is attempting to unravel it. I'm supervising."

"You sound great."

"It's an adventure, right, Josh?"

"Of course. Any sign of the girl?"

"Not a chance. We're a couple of days away at best, and now we're floating backward. I'm not sure we'll ever get there."

"You have to, Nate. We read the will this morning in open court. The whole world will soon be looking for Rachel Lane."

"I wouldn't worry about that. She's safe."

"I wish I were with you."

The edge of a cloud nipped the signal. "What did you say?" Nate asked, louder.

"Nothing. So you'll see her in a couple of days, huh."

"If we're lucky. The boat runs around the clock, but we're going upriver, and it's the rainy season so the rivers are full and the currents are strong. Plus, we're not exactly sure where we're going. Two days is very optimistic, assuming we get the damned propeller fixed."

"So the weather's bad," Josh said, almost at random. There wasn't much to discuss. Nate was alive and well and moving in the general direction of the target.

"It's hot as hell and it rains five times a day. Other than that it's lovely."

"Any snakes?"

"A couple. Anacondas longer than the boat. Lots of alligators. Rats as big as dogs. They call them *capivaras*. They live at the edge of the rivers among the alligators, and when these people get hungry enough they kill them and eat them."

"But you have plenty of food?"

"Oh yes. Our cargo is black beans and rice. Welly cooks them for me three times a day."

Nate's voice was sharp and filled with adventure.

"Who's Welly?"

"My deckhand. Right now he's under the boat in twelve feet of water, holding his breath and cutting rope from the prop. Like I said, I'm supervising."

"Stay out of the water, Nate."

"Are you kidding? I'm on the upper deck. Look, I gotta run. I'm using juice and I haven't found a way to recharge these batteries."

"When will you call again?"

"I'll try and wait until after I find Rachel Lane."

"Good idea. But call if you have trouble."

"Trouble? Why would I call you, Josh? There's not a damned thing in the world you can do."

"You're right. Don't call."

TWENTY

THE STORM HIT at dusk, as Welly was boiling rice in the kitchen and Jevy was watching the river grow dark. The wind woke Nate, a sudden howling blast that shook the hammock and snapped him to his feet. Thunder and lightning followed. He walked to Jevy's side and looked north into a vast blackness. "A big storm," Jevy said, seemingly indifferent.

Shouldn't we park this thing? Nate thought. At least find shallow water? Jevy didn't appear concerned; his nonchalance was somewhat comforting. When the rain started, Nate went below for his rice and beans. He ate in silence with Welly in the corner of the cabin. The bulb above them swayed as the wind rocked the boat. Heavy raindrops battered the windows.

On the bridge, Jevy put on a yellow poncho stained with grease and fought the rain hitting him sharply in the face. The tiny wheelhouse had no windows. The two floodlights attempted to show the way through the darkness, but revealed no more than fifty feet of churning water in front of them. Jevy knew the river well, and he'd been through worse storms.

Reading was difficult with the boat swaying and rolling. After a few minutes of it, Nate felt sick. In his bag he found a knee-length poncho with a hood. Josh had thought of everything. Clutching the railings, he slowly made his way up the stairs where Welly sat hud-dled next to the wheelhouse, drenched.

The river bent to the east, toward the heart of the Pantanal, and when they turned, the wind caught them broadside. The boat rocked and threw Nate and Welly hard into the railings. Jevy braced himself with the door of the wheelhouse, his thick arms holding himself in place and maintaining control.

The gusts became relentless, one after the other, only seconds apart, and the *Santa Loura* stopped moving upstream. The storm shoved it toward shore. The rain pellets were hard and cold now, and poured down upon them in sheets. Jevy found a long flashlight in a box beside the wheel, and gave it to Welly.

"Find the bank!" he yelled, his voice struggling over the howling wind and heavy rain.

Nate grappled along the railings to a spot next to Welly because he too wanted to see where they might be headed. But the beam caught nothing but rain, rain so thick it looked like fog swirling above the water.

Then lightning came to their aid. A flash, and they saw the dense black growth of the riverbank not far away. The wind was pushing them toward it. Welly shouted and Jevy yelled something back just as another gust slammed into the boat and tipped it violently to its starboard side. The sudden jolt knocked the flashlight out of Welly's hand and they watched it disappear into the water.

Crouched on the walkway, clutching the railing, soaked and shivering, it occurred to Nate that one of two things was about to happen. And neither was within their control. First, the boat was going to capsize. If it didn't, then they were about to be shoved into the side of the river, into the quagmire where the reptiles lived. He was only slightly scared until he thought about the papers.

Under no circumstances could the papers be lost. He suddenly stood, just as the boat tipped again, and he almost went over the rail.

"I have to go below!" he yelled to Jevy, who was gripping the wheel. The captain was scared too.

With his back to the wind, Nate crept down the grated steps. The deck was slick with diesel fuel. A drum had tipped over and was leaking. He tried to lift it, but it would take two men. He ducked into the cabin, flung his poncho in a corner, and went for his briefcase under the cot. The wind slammed into the boat. It pitched and caught Nate with his hands free. He landed hard against the wall with his feet above his head.

There were two things he couldn't lose, he decided. First, the papers; second, the SatFone. Both were in the briefcase, which was new and nice but certainly not waterproof. He clutched it across his chest and lay on his bunk while the *Santa Loura* rode out the storm.

The knocking stopped. He hoped Jevy had killed the engine with a switch. He could hear their footsteps directly above him. We're about to hit the bank, he thought, and it's best for the prop to be disengaged. Surely it wasn't engine trouble.

The lights went out. Complete darkness.

Lying there in the dark, swaying with the pitch and roll, waiting for the *Santa Loura* to crash into the riverbank, Nate had a horrible thought. If she refused to sign the acknowledgment and/or the waiver, a return trip might be necessary. Months down the road, or maybe years, someone, probably Nate himself, would be forced to trek back up the Paraguay and inform the world's richest missionary that things were finalized and the money was hers.

He'd read that missionaries took furloughs—long breaks in their work when they returned to the States and recharged their batteries. Why couldn't Rachel take a furlough, maybe even fly home with him, and hang around long enough for Daddy's mess to get cleaned up? For eleven billion, that seemed the least she could do. He'd suggest it to her, if he ever got the chance to meet her.

There was a crash, and Nate was tossed to the floor. They were in the brush.

□ □ □ □

THE *SANTA LOURA* was flat-bottomed, built, like all the boats in the Pantanal, to scrape across sandbars and take the hits of river debris. After the storm, Jevy started the engine and for half an hour worked the boat back and forth, slowly dislodging it from the sand and mud. When they were free, Welly and Nate cleared the deck of limbs and brush. Their search of the boat found no new passengers, no snakes or *jacarés*. During a quick coffee break, Jevy told the story of an anaconda that had found its way on board, years ago. Attacked a sleeping deckhand.

Nate said he didn't particularly care for snake stories. His search was slow and deliberate.

The clouds went away and a beautiful half-moon appeared above the river. Welly brewed a pot of coffee. After the violence of the storm, the Pantanal seemed determined to be perfectly still. The river was as smooth as glass. The moon guided them, disappearing when they turned with the river, but always there when they headed north again.

Because Nate was half-Brazilian now, he wore no wristwatch. Time mattered little. It was late, probably midnight. The rain had battered them for four hours.

NATE SLEPT a few hours in the hammock, and awakened just after dawn. He found Jevy snoring on his bunk in the tiny cabin behind the wheelhouse. Welly was at the wheel, himself half-asleep. Nate sent him for coffee and took the helm of the *Santa Loura*.

The clouds were back, but no rain was in sight. The river was littered with limbs and leaves, the rubble and remains from last night's storm. It was wide and there was no traffic, so Nate the skipper sent Welly to the hammock for a nap while he commanded the vessel.

It beat the hell out of a courtroom. Shirtless, shoeless, sipping sweet coffee while leading an expedition into the heart of the world's largest swamp. In the glory days, he would've been racing to a trial somewhere, juggling ten things at once, phones stuck in every pocket. He didn't really miss it; no lawyer in his right mind really missed the courtroom. But he would never admit that.

The boat practically guided itself. With Jevy's binoculars, he watched the shoreline for *jacarés*, snakes, and *capivaras*. And he counted tuiuius, the tall, white, long-necked bird with a red head that had become the symbol of the Pantanal. There were twelve in one flock on a sandbar. They stood still and watched the boat go by.

The captain and his sleepy crew steamed northward, as the sky turned orange and the day began. Deeper and deeper into the Pantanal, uncertain where their journey would lead them.

TWENTY-ONE

THE COORDINATOR of South American Missions was a woman named Neva Collier. She was born in an igloo in Newfoundland, where her parents had worked for twenty years among the Inuit natives. She herself had spent eleven years working in the mountains of New Guinea, so she knew firsthand the trials and challenges of the nine hundred or so people whose activities she coordinated.

And she was the only person who knew that Rachel Porter had once been Rachel Lane, illegitimate daughter of Troy Phelan. After med school, Rachel had changed names in an effort to erase as much of her past as possible. She had no family; both adoptive parents had died. No siblings. No aunts, uncles, or cousins. At least none that she knew. She had only Troy, and she was desperate to remove him from her life. After completing the World Tribes seminary, Rachel had confided her secrets to Neva Collier.

The higher-ups at World Tribes knew Rachel had secrets, but not a history that would impede her yearning to serve God. She was a doctor, a graduate of their seminary, a dedicated and humble servant of Christ who was eager to enter the mission field. They promised never to divulge anything about Rachel, including her exact location in South America.

Sitting in her small neat office in Houston, Neva read the extraordinary account of the reading of Mr. Phelan's will. She had been following the story since the suicide.

Communication with Rachel was a slow process. They exchanged mail twice a year, in March and in August, and Rachel usually called once a year from a pay phone in Corumbá when she went there for supplies. Neva had spoken to her the year before. Her last furlough had been in 1992. After six weeks she'd abandoned it and returned to the Pantanal. She had no interest in being in the United States, she had confided in Neva. It was not her home. She belonged with her people.

Judging from the lawyers' comments in the article, the issue was far from settled. Neva put the file away and decided to wait. At the appropriate time, whenever that might be, she would inform her governing board of Rachel's old identity.

She hoped that moment would never come. But how, exactly, does one hide eleven billion dollars?

NO ONE really expected the lawyers to agree on where to meet. Each firm insisted on choosing the site of the summit. The fact that they agreed to actually get together, on such short notice, was monumental.

So they met at a hotel, the Ritz in Tysons Corner, in a banquet room where tables had been hastily wedged together in a perfect square. When the door was finally closed, there were close to fifty people in the room, for every firm felt obliged to bring along extra associates and paralegals and even secretaries to impress.

The tension was almost visible. No Phelans were present, only their legal teams.

Hark Gettys called the meeting to order, and did the wise thing of cracking a very funny joke. Like humor in the courtroom, where people were anxious and not expecting comedy, the laughter was loud and healthy. He suggested they go around the table and let one lawyer per Phelan heir say what was on his or her mind. He would go last.

An objection was lodged. "Who exactly are the heirs?"

"The six Phelan children," Hark responded.

"What about the three wives?"

"They're not heirs. They're ex-wives."

This upset the attorneys for the wives, and after a heated battle they threatened to walk out. Someone suggested allowing them to speak anyway, and this solved the problem.

Grit, the feisty litigator hired by Mary Ross Phelan Jackman and her husband, stood and made a plea for war. "We have no choice but to challenge the will," he said. "There was no undue influence, so we have to prove the old buzzard was crazy. Hell, he jumped to his death. And he gave one of the world's great fortunes to some unknown heir. Sounds crazy to me. We can find psychiatrists who'll testify."

"What about the three who examined him before he jumped?" someone shot from across the table.

"That was stupid," Grit snarled back. "It was a setup, and you guys fell for it."

This upset Hark and the other lawyers who had agreed on the mental exam. "Perfect hindsight," Yancy said, and that stalled Grit for the moment.

The legal team for Geena and Cody Strong was headed by a woman named Langhorne, who was tall and thick and wore an Armani dress. She had once been a professor at Georgetown Law and when she addressed the group she did so with the air of one who knew everything. Point one: There were only two grounds for contesting a will in Virginia—undue influence and lack of mental capacity. Since no one knew Rachel Lane, it was safe to assume she had little or no contact with Troy. Therefore, it would be difficult if not impossible to prove she somehow unduly influenced him when he made his last will. Point two: Lack of testamentary capacity was their only hope. Point three: Forget fraud. Sure he lured them into the mental exam under false pretenses, but a will cannot be attacked on the grounds of fraud. A contract yes, a will no. They had already done the research and she had the cases, if anyone cared.

She worked from a brief of some sort, and was impeccably prepared. No less than six others from her firm huddled behind her in support.

Point four: The mental exam would be very difficult to crack. She'd seen the video. They would probably lose the war, but they could get paid for the battle. Her conclusion: Challenge the will with a fury, and hope for a lucrative out-of-court settlement.

Her lecture lasted for ten minutes, and covered little new ground. She was tolerated without interruption because she was female and the chip was almost visible.

Wally Bright, he of the night school, was next, and in sharp contrast to Ms. Langhorne, he raged and railed at injustice in general. Nothing was prepared—no brief, no notes, no thoughts about what he would say next, just a lot of hot air by a brawler who perpetually flew by the seat of his pants.

Two of Lillian's lawyers stood at the same time, and appeared to be joined at the hip. Both wore black suits, and had the pale faces of estate lawyers who rarely saw the sun. One would start a sentence and the other would finish it. One would ask a rhetorical question, the other had the answer. One mentioned a file, the other pulled it from a briefcase. The tag team was efficient, to the point, and repeated in succinct fashion what had already been said.

A consensus was quickly emerging. Fight, for (a) there was little to lose, (b) there was nothing else to do, and (c) it was the only way to force a settlement. Not to mention (d), wherein they would get paid handsomely by the hour for fighting.

Yancy was particularly forceful in urging the use of litigation. And rightly so. Ramble was the only minor among the heirs, and had no debts to speak of. The trust that would pay him five million on his twenty-first had been established decades earlier, and could not be revoked. With five million guaranteed, Ramble was in far better shape financially than any of his siblings. With nothing to lose, why not sue for more?

An hour passed before someone mentioned the contest clause in the will. The heirs, excluding Ramble, ran the risk of losing what little Troy left them if they contested the will. This issue was given slight treatment by the lawyers. They had already decided to fight the will, and they knew their greedy clients would follow their advice.

A lot was not being said. The litigation would be cumbersome to begin with. The wisest and most cost-efficient course would be to select one firm with experience to act as chief trial counsel. The others could take a step back, still protect their clients, and be kept abreast of every development. Such a strategy would require two things: (1) cooperation, and (2) the voluntary downsizing of most of the egos in the room.

It was never mentioned during the three-hour meeting.

Through no grand scheme of their own—schemes require cooperation—the lawyers had managed to divide the heirs so that no two shared the same firm. Through skillful manipulation that is not taught in law school but acquired naturally thereafter, the lawyers had convinced the clients to spend more time talking to them than to their fellow heirs. Trust was not a virtue known to the Phelans, nor to their attorneys.

It was shaping up to be one long chaotic lawsuit.

Not one brave voice suggested the will be left alone. There was not the slightest interest in following the wishes of the man who'd actually made the fortune they now conspired to carve up.

During the third or fourth trip around the tables, an effort was made to determine the level of debt held by each of the six heirs at the time of Mr. Phelan's death. But the effort fizzled under a barrage of legal nitpicking.

"Are the debts of spouses included?" asked Hark, attorney for Rex, whose wife Amber the stripper owned the skin clubs and had her name on most of the debts.

"What about obligations to the IRS?" asked the attorney for Troy Junior, who'd been having tax trouble for fifteen years.

"My clients have not authorized me to divulge financial information," said Langhorne, who with that dire declaration effectively iced the issue.

The reluctance confirmed what everybody knew—the Phelan heirs were up to their ears in loans and mortgages.

All the lawyers, being lawyers, were deeply concerned about publicity, and how their fight would be portrayed by the media. Their clients were not simply a bunch of spoiled, greedy children who'd been cut out by their father. But they feared the press might take this posture. Perceptions were crucial.

"I suggest we hire a public relations firm," Hark announced. It was a wonderful idea, one that several others immediately seized as their own. Hire a pro to paint the Phelan heirs as the brokenhearted children who'd loved a man who had little time for them. An eccentric, philandering, half-crazy . . . Yes! That was it! Make Troy the bad guy. And make their clients the victims!

The idea bloomed and the fiction spread happily around the tables until someone asked just exactly how they would pay for such services.

"They're horribly expensive," said a lawyer, who happened to be charging six hundred dollars an hour for himself and four hundred an hour for each of his three useless associates.

The idea lost steam quickly until Hark offered the lame suggestion that each firm could front some expense money. The meeting grew incredibly quiet. Those who'd had so much to say about everything were now captivated by the magical language of briefs and old cases.

"We can talk about this later," Hark said, attempting to save face. No doubt the idea would never be mentioned again.

They then discussed Rachel, and where she might be. Should they retain a top-notch security firm to locate her? Almost every lawyer happened to know one. The idea was quite appealing and received more attention than it should have. What lawyer wouldn't want to represent the chosen heir?

But they decided against looking for Rachel, primarily because they couldn't agree on what they would do if they found her. She would surface soon enough, no doubt with her own entourage of lawyers.

The meeting ended on a pleasant note. The lawyers gave themselves the outcome they wanted. They left with plans to immediately call their clients and proudly report how much progress was made. They could say unequivocally that it was the combined wisdom of all the Phelan lawyers that the will should be attacked with a vengeance.

TWENTY-TWO

THE RIVER ROSE throughout the day, slowly leaving its banks in some places, swallowing sandbars, rising into the thick brush, flooding the small muddy yards of houses they passed once every three hours. The river carried more and more debris—weeds and grass, limbs and saplings. As it grew wider it grew stronger, and the currents running against the boat slowed them even more.

But no one was watching the clock. Nate had been politely relieved of his captain's duties after the *Santa Loura* was struck by a wayward tree trunk, one he never saw. No damage, but the jolt sent Jevy and Welly scurrying to the wheelhouse. He returned to his own little deck with the hammock stretched through the center, and there he spent the morning reading and watching wildlife.

Jevy joined him for coffee. "So what do you think of the Pantanal?" he asked. They sat next to each other on a bench with their arms through the railing and their bare feet dangling over the side of the boat.

"It's pretty magnificent."

"Do you know Colorado?"

"I've been there, yes."

"During the rainy season, the rivers in the Pantanal overflow. The flooded area is the size of Colorado."

"Have you been to Colorado?"

"Yes. I have a cousin there."

"Where else have you been?"

"Three years ago, my cousin and I rode a big bus, a Greyhound, across the country. We were in every state but six."

Jevy was a poor Brazilian boy of twenty-four. Nate was twice his age and for most of his career had had plenty of money. Yet Jevy had seen much more of the United States than Nate.

When the money was good, though, Nate had always traveled to Europe. His favorite restaurants were in Rome and Paris.

"When the floods stop," Jevy continued, "we have the dry season. Grasslands, marshes, more lagoons and swamps than anyone can count. The cycle—the flooding and the dry season—produces more wildlife than any place in the world. We have six hundred and fifty species of birds here, more than Canada and the U.S. combined. At least two hundred and sixty species of fish. Snakes, caiman, alligators, even giant otters live in the water."

As if on cue, he pointed to a thicket at the edge of a small forest. "Look, it's a deer," he said. "We have lots of deer. And lots of jaguars, giant anteaters, *capivaras*, tapirs, and macaws. The Pantanal is filled with wildlife."

"You were born here?"

"I took my first breath in the hospital in Corumbá, but I was born on these rivers. This is my home."

"You told me your father was a river pilot."

"Yes. When I was a small boy I began going with him. Early in the morning, when everybody was asleep, he would allow me to take the wheel. I knew all the main rivers by the time I was ten."

"And he died on the river."

"Not this, but the Taquiri, to the east. He was guiding a boat of German tourists when a storm hit them. The only survivor was a deckhand."

"When was this?"

"Five years ago."

Forever the trial lawyer, Nate had a dozen more questions about the accident. He wanted the details—details win lawsuits. But he said, "I'm sorry," and let it go.

"They want to destroy the Pantanal," Jevy said.

"Who?"

"Lots of people. Big companies that own big farms. To the north and east of the Pantanal they are clearing large sections of land for farms. The main crop is *soja*, which you call soybeans. They want to export it. The more forests they clear, the more runoff collects in the Pantanal. Sediment rises each year in our rivers. Their farm soil is not good, so the companies use many sprays and fertilizers to grow crops. We get the chemicals. Many of the big farms dam up rivers to create new pastures. This upsets the flooding cycle. And mercury is killing our fish."

"How does mercury get here?"

"Mining. To the north, they mine gold, and they do it with mercury. It runs into the rivers, the rivers eventually run into the Pantanal. Our fish swallow it and die. Everything gets dumped into the Pantanal. Cuiabá is a city of a million people to the east. It has no waste treatment. Guess where its sewage goes."

"Doesn't the government help?"

Jevy managed a bitter laugh. "Have you heard of Hidrovia?"

"No."

"It's a big ditch, to be cut through the Pantanal. It is supposed to link Brazil, Bolivia, Paraguay, Argentina, and Uruguay. It is supposed to save South America. But it will drain the Pantanal. And our government is supporting it."

Nate almost said something pious about environmental responsibility, then remembered that his countrymen were the biggest energy hogs the world had ever seen. "It's still beautiful," he said.

"It is." Jevy finished his coffee. "Sometimes I think it's too big for them to destroy."

They passed a narrow inlet where more water entered the Paraguay. A small herd of deer waded through the floodwaters, nibbling at green vines, oblivious to the noise from the river. Seven deer, two of which were spotted fawns.

"There is a small trading post a few hours away," Jevy said, getting to his feet. "We should be there before dark."

"What are we shopping for?"

"Nothing, I guess. Fernando is the owner, and he hears everything on the river. Maybe he will know something about missionaries."

Jevy emptied his cup into the river and stretched his arms. "Sometimes he has beer for sale. *Cerveja.*"

Nate kept his eyes on the water.

"I think we should not buy any," Jevy said, and walked away.

Fine with me, thought Nate. He drained his cup, sucking down the grounds and grains of sugar.

A cold brown bottle, perhaps Antartica or Brahma, the two brands he'd already sampled in Brazil. Excellent beer. A favorite haunt had been a college bar near Georgetown with 120 foreign beers on the menu. He'd tried them all. They served roasted peanuts by the basket and expected you to throw the hulls on the floor. When his pals from law school were in town they always met at the bar and reminisced about the old days. The beer was ice cold, the peanuts hot and salty, the floor cracked with hulls when you walked, and the girls were young and loose. The place had been there forever, and during each trip through rehab and sobriety it was the bar Nate missed most.

He began to sweat, though the sun was hidden and there was a cool breeze. He buried himself in the hammock and prayed for sleep, a deep hard coma that would take him past their little stop and into the night. The sweating worsened until his shirt was soaked. He started a book about the demise of the Brazilian Indians, then tried to sleep again.

He was wide awake when the engine was throttled down and the boat moved close to the bank. There were voices, then a gentle bump as they docked at the trading post. Nate slowly removed himself from the hammock and returned to the bench, where he sat.

It was a country store of sorts, built on stilts—a tiny building, made of unpainted boards with a tin roof and a narrow porch where, not surprisingly, a couple of locals were lounging with cigarettes and tea. A smaller river circled behind it and disappeared into the Pantanal. A large fuel tank was braced to the side of the building.

A flimsy pier jutted into the river to dock the boats. Jevy and Welly eased along the pier, carefully, because the currents were strong. They chatted with the *pantaneiros* on the porch, then went through the open door.

Nate had vowed to remain on the boat. He went to the other side of the deck, sat on the opposite bench, stuck his arms and legs through the rail, and watched the full width of the river go by. He would stay up on the deck, on the bench, with his arms and legs locked in the rail. The coldest beer in the world couldn't pull him away.

As he had learned, there was no such thing as a short visit in Brazil. Especially on the river, where visits were rare. Jevy bought thirty gallons of diesel fuel to replace what had been lost in the storm. The engine started.

"Fernando says there is a woman missionary. She works with the Indians." Jevy handed him a bottle of cold water. They were moving again.

"Where?"

"He's not sure. There are some settlements to the north, near Bolivia. But the Indians don't move on the river, so he doesn't know much about them."

"How far is the nearest settlement?"

"We should be close by morning. But we can't take this boat. We must use the little one."

"Sounds like fun."

"You remember Marco, the farmer whose cow was killed by our plane?"

"Sure I do. He had three little boys."

"Yes. He was there yesterday," Jevy said, pointing to the store, which was disappearing around a bend. "He comes once a month."

"Were the boys with him?"

"No. It's too dangerous."

What a small world. Nate hoped the boys had spent the money he'd given them for Christmas. He watched the store until it was out of sight.

Perhaps on the return leg he'd be well enough to stop and have a cool one. Just a couple, to celebrate their successful journey. He crawled back into the safety of his hammock, and cursed himself for his weakness. In the wilderness of a gigantic swamp he had had a near brush with alcohol, and for hours his thoughts had been consumed with nothing else. The anticipation, the fear, the sweating, and the scheming of ways to get a drink. Then the near miss, the escape through no strength of his own, and now in the aftermath the fantasy of renewing his romance with alcohol. A few drinks would be fine because then he could stop. That was his favorite lie.

He was just a drunk. Run him through a designer rehab clinic at a thousand bucks a day, and he was still an addict. Run him through AA in the basement of a church on Tuesday nights, and he was still a drunk.

His addictions gripped him, and desperation settled around Nate. He was paying for the damned boat; Jevy worked for him. If he insisted that they turn around and go straight to the store, they would do so. He could buy all the beer Fernando owned, load it on ice below the deck, and sip Brahma all the way to Bolivia. And there wasn't a damned thing anyone could do about it.

Like a mirage, Welly appeared with a smile and a cup of fresh coffee. "*Vou cozinhar*," he said. I'm going to cook.

Food would help, Nate thought. Even another platter of beans, rice, and boiled chicken. Food would satisfy his tastes, or least divert his attention from other cravings.

He ate slowly, on the upper deck, alone and in the dark, swatting thick mosquitoes away from his face. When he was finished, he sprayed repellent from his neck to his bare feet. The seizure was over, only slight aftershocks gripped him. He could no longer taste beer or smell the peanuts from his favorite bar.

He retreated to his sanctuary. It was raining again, a quiet rain with no wind or thunder. Josh had sent along four books for his reading pleasure. All the briefs and memos had been read and re-read. Nothing remained but the books. He'd already read half of the thinnest one.

He burrowed deep in the hammock and went back to reading the sad history of the native people of Brazil.

WHEN THE PORTUGUESE explorer Pedro Alvares Cabral first stepped on Brazilian soil, on the coast of Bahia, in April of 1500, the country had five million Indians, scattered among nine hundred tribes. They spoke 1,175 languages, and except for the usual tribal skirmish they were peaceful people.

After five centuries of getting themselves "civilized" by Europeans, the Indian population had been decimated. Only 270,000 survived, in 206 tribes using 170 languages. War, murder, slavery, territorial losses, diseases—no method of exterminating Indians had been neglected by those from civilized cultures.

It was a sick and violent history. If the Indians were peaceful and tried to cooperate with the colonists, they were subject to strange diseases—smallpox, measles, yellow fever, influenza, tuberculosis— for which they had no natural defenses. If they did not cooperate, they were slaughtered by men using weapons more sophisticated than arrows and poison darts. When they fought back and killed their attackers, they were branded as savages.

They were enslaved by miners, ranchers, and rubber barons. They were driven from their ancestral homes by any group with enough guns. They were burned at the stake by priests, hunted by armies and gangs of bandits, raped at will by any able-bodied man with the desire, and slaughtered with impunity. At every point in history, whether crucial or insignificant, when the interests of native Brazilians conflicted with those of white people, the Indians had lost.

You lose for five hundred years, and you expect little from life. The biggest problem facing some modern-day tribes was the suicide of its young people.

After centuries of genocide, the Brazilian government finally decided it was time to protect its "noble savages." Modern-day massacres had brought international condemnation, so bureaucracies were established and laws were passed. With self-righteous fanfare, some tribal lands were returned to the natives and lines were drawn on government maps declaring them to be safe zones.

But the government was also the enemy. In 1967, an investigation into the agency in charge of Indian affairs shocked most Brazilians. The report revealed that agents, land speculators, and ranchers—thugs who either worked for the agency or had the agency working for them—had been systematically using chemical and bacteriological weapons to wipe out Indians. They issued clothing to the Indians that was infected with smallpox and tuberculosis germs. With airplanes and helicopters, they bombed Indian villages and land with deadly bacteria.

And in the Amazon Basin and other frontiers, ranchers and miners cared little for lines on maps.

In 1986, a rancher in Rondônia used crop dusters to spray nearby Indian land with deadly chemicals. He wanted to farm the land, but first had to eliminate the inhabitants. Thirty Indians died, and the rancher was never prosecuted. In 1989, a rancher in Mato Grosso offered rewards to bounty hunters for the ears of murdered Indians. In 1993, gold miners in Manaus attacked a peaceful tribe because they would not leave their land. Thirteen Indians were murdered, and no one was ever arrested.

In the 1990s, the government had aggressively sought to open up the Amazon Basin, a land of vast natural resources to the north of the Pantanal. But the Indians were still in the way. The majority of those surviving inhabited the Basin; in fact, it was estimated that as many as fifty jungle tribes had been lucky enough to escape contact with civilization.

Now civilization was on the attack again. The abuse of Indians was growing as miners and loggers and ranchers pushed deep into the Amazon, with the support of the government.

THE HISTORY was fascinating, if depressing. Nate read for four hours nonstop and finished the book.

He walked to the wheelhouse and drank coffee with Jevy. The rain had stopped.

"Will we be there by morning?" he asked.

"I think so."

The lights from the boat rocked gently up and down with the current. It seemed as though they were hardly moving.

"Do you have any Indian blood?" Nate asked, after some hesitation. It was a personal matter, one that in the United States no one would dare ask.

Jevy smiled without taking his gaze from the river. "All of us have Indian blood. Why do you ask?"

"I've been reading the history of Indians in Brazil."

"So what do you think?"

"It's pretty tragic."

"It is. Do you think the Indians have been treated badly here?"

"Of course they have."

"What about in your country?"

For some reason, General Custer was the first thought. At least the Indians had won something. And we didn't burn them at the stake, or spray them with chemicals, or sell them into slavery. Did we? What about all those reservations? Land everywhere.

"Not much better, I'm afraid," he said in defeat. It was not a discussion he wanted.

After a long silence, Nate eased down to the toilet. When he finished his work there, he pulled the chain above it and left the small room. Light brown river water ran into the toilet bowl and flushed the waste through a tube and sent it directly into the river.

TWENTY-THREE

I T WAS STILL DARK when the engine stopped and woke Nate. He touched his left wrist and remembered he wasn't wearing a watch. He listened as Welly and Jevy moved below him. They were at the rear of the boat, talking quietly.

He was proud of himself for another sober morning, another clean day for the books. Six months earlier, every wake-up had been a blur of swollen eyes, cobwebbed thoughts, seared mouth, arid tongue, bitter breath, and the great daily question of "Why did I do it?" He often vomited in the shower, sometimes inducing it himself to get it over with. After the shower, there was always the dilemma of what to have for breakfast. Something warm and oily to settle the stomach, or perhaps a bloody mary to settle the nerves? Then he was off to work, always at his desk by eight to begin another brutal day as a litigator.

Every morning. No exceptions. In the final days of his last crash he had gone weeks without a clear morning. Out of desperation he'd seen a counselor, and when asked if he could recall the last day he'd stayed sober, he admitted he could not.

He missed the drinking, but not the hangovers.

Welly pulled the johnboat to the port side of the *Santa Loura*, and tied it closely. They were loading it when Nate crept down the steps. The adventure was moving into a new phase. Nate was ready for a change of scenery.

It was overcast and threatening more rain. The sun finally broke through at about six. Nate knew because he'd rearmed himself with a watch.

A rooster crowed. They were docked near a small farmhouse, their bow tied to a timber that once held a pier. Westward, to their left, a much smaller river met the Paraguay.

The challenge was to pack the boat without overloading it. The smaller tributaries they were about to encounter were flooded; banks would not always be visible. If the boat sat too low in the water, they might run aground, or worse, damage the prop of the outboard. There was only one motor on the johnboat, no backup, just a couple of paddles that Nate studied from the deck as he drank his coffee. The paddles would work, he decided, especially if wild Indians or hungry animals were in pursuit.

Three five-gallon gas tanks were arranged neatly in the center of the boat. "These should give us fifteen hours," Jevy explained.

"That's a long time."

"I'd rather be safe."

"How far away is the settlement?"

"I'm not sure." He pointed to the house. "The farmer there said four hours."

"Does he know the Indians?"

"No. He doesn't like Indians. Says he never sees them on the river."

Jevy packed a small tent, two blankets, two mosquito nets, a rain fly for the tent, two buckets to dip out rainfall, and his poncho. Welly added a box of food and a case of bottled water.

Seated on his bunk in the cabin, Nate took the copy of the will, the acknowledgment, and the waiver from his briefcase, folded them together, and placed them in a letter-sized envelope. An official Stafford Law Firm envelope. Since there were no Ziploc bags or garbage liners on board, he wrapped the envelope in a twelve-inch square section he cut from the hem of his poncho. He taped the seams with duct tape, and after examining his handiwork declared his package to be waterproof. Then he taped it to his tee shirt, across his chest, and covered it with a light denim pullover.

There were copies of the papers in his briefcase, which he would leave behind. And since the *Santa Loura* seemed much more secure than the johnboat, he decided to leave the SatFone too. He double-checked the papers and the phone, then locked the briefcase and left it on his bunk. Today could be the day, he thought to himself. There was a nervous excitement in finally meeting Rachel Lane.

Breakfast was a quick roll with butter on the deck, standing above the johnboat and watching the clouds. Four hours meant six or eight in Brazil, and Nate was anxious to cast off. The last item Jevy loaded into the boat was a clean shiny machete with a long handle. "This is for the anacondas," he said, laughing. Nate tried to ignore it. He waved good-bye to Welly, then huddled over his last cup of coffee as they floated with the river until Jevy started the outboard.

Mist settled just above the water, and it was cool. Since leaving Corumbá Nate had observed the river from the safety of the top deck; now he was practically sitting on it. He glanced around and saw no life jackets. The river slapped the hull. Nate kept a wary eye on the mist, watching for debris; a nice fat tree trunk with a jagged end and the johnboat was history.

They went crosscurrent until they entered the mouth of the tributary that would take them to the Indians. The water there was much calmer. The outboard whined and left a boiling wake. The Paraguay disappeared quickly.

On Jevy's river map the tributary was officially labeled as the Cabixa. Jevy had never navigated it before, because there had been no need. It coiled like string out of Brazil and into Bolivia, and apparently went nowhere. At its mouth it was eighty feet wide at most, and narrowed to about fifty as they followed it. It had flooded in some places; in others the brush along the banks was thicker than the Paraguay.

Fifteen minutes in, Nate checked his watch. He would time everything. Jevy slowed the boat as they approached the first fork, the first of a thousand. A river of the same size branched to the left, and the captain was faced with the decision of which route would keep them on the Cabixa. They kept to the right, but somewhat slower, and soon entered a lake. Jevy stopped the motor. "Hold on," he said, and stood on the gas tanks, gazing at the floodwaters that encircled them. The boat was perfectly still. A ragged row of scrub trees caught his attention. He pointed and said something to himself.

Exactly how much guesswork was involved Nate couldn't tell. Jevy had studied his maps and had lived on these rivers. They all led back to the Paraguay. If they took a wrong turn and got lost, surely the currents would eventually lead them back to Welly.

They followed the scrub trees and flooded thickets that, in the dry season, made up the riverbank, and soon they were in the middle of a shallow stream with limbs overhead. It didn't look like the Cabixa, but a quick glance at the captain's face revealed nothing but confidence.

An hour into the journey they approached the first dwelling—a mud-splattered little hut with a red-tiled roof. Three feet of water covered the bottom of it, and there was no sign of humans or animals. Jevy slowed so they could talk.

"In the flood season, many people in the Pantanal move to higher ground. They load up their cows and kids and leave for three months."

"I haven't seen higher ground."

"There's not much of it. But every *pantaneiro* has a place to go this time of the year."

"What about the Indians?"

"They move around too."

"Wonderful. We don't know where they are, and they like to move around."

Jevy chuckled and said, "We'll find them."

They floated by the hut. It had no doors or windows. Not much to come home to.

Ninety minutes, and Nate had completely forgotten about being eaten when they rounded a bend and came close to a pack of alligators sleeping in a pile in six inches of water. The boat startled them and upset their nap. Tails slapped and water splashed. Nate glanced at the machete, just in case, then laughed at his own foolishness.

The reptiles did not attack. They watched the boat ease past.

No animals for the next twenty minutes. The river narrowed again. The banks squeezed together so close that trees from both sides touched each other above the water. It was suddenly dark. They were floating through a tunnel. Nate checked his watch. The *Santa Loura* was two hours away.

As they zigzagged through the marshes, they caught glimpses of the horizon. The mountains of Bolivia were looming, getting closer, it seemed. The water widened, the trees cleared, and they entered a large lake with more than a dozen little rivers twisting into it. They circled slowly the first time, then even slower the second. All the tributaries looked the same. The Cabixa was one of a dozen, and the captain had not a clue.

Jevy stood on the gas tanks and surveyed the flood while Nate sat motionless. A fisherman was in the weeds on the other side of the lake. Finding him would be their only luck of the day.

He was sitting patiently in a small, handmade canoe, one carved from a tree a very long time ago. He wore a ragged straw hat that hid most of his face. When they were only a few feet away, close enough to inspect him, Nate noticed that he was fishing without the benefit of a pole or a rod. No stick of any sort. The line was wrapped around his hand.

Jevy said all the right things in Portuguese, and handed him a bottle of water. Nate just smiled and listened to the soft slurring sounds of the strange language. It was slower than Spanish, almost as nasal as French.

If the fisherman was happy to see another human in the middle of nowhere, he certainly didn't show it. Where could the poor man live?

Then they started pointing, in the general direction of the mountains, though by the time they finished the little man had encompassed the entire lake with his bearings. They chatted some more, and Nate got the impression Jevy was extracting every scrap of information. It could be hours before they saw another face. With the swamps and rivers swollen, navigation was proving difficult. Two and a half hours in, and they were already lost.

A cloud of small black mosquitoes swept over them, and Nate scrambled for the repellent. The fisherman watched him with curiosity.

They said good-bye and paddled away, drifting with the slight wind. "His mother was an Indian," Jevy said.

"That's nice," Nate replied, hammering mosquitoes.

"There's a settlement a few hours from here."

"A few hours?"

"Three maybe."

They had fifteen hours of fuel, and Nate planned to count every minute of it. The Cabixa began again near an inlet where another, very identical river also left the lake. It widened, and they were off, at full throttle.

Nate moved lower in the boat, and found a spot on the bottom between the box of food and the buckets, with his back to the bench. From there the mist couldn't spray his head. He was contemplating a nap when the motor sputtered. The boat lurched and slowed. He kept his eyes on the river, afraid to turn around and look at Jevy.

Engine trouble was not something he had spent time worrying about, yet. Their journey had enough little perils already. It would take days of backbreaking labor to paddle back to Welly. They would be forced to sleep in the boat, eat what they'd brought until the food ran out, dip water from it during the rains, and hope like hell they could find their little fishing buddy to point them to safety.

Suddenly Nate was terrified.

Then they were off again, the motor howling as if nothing had happened. It became a routine; every twenty minutes or so, just as Nate was about to doze off, the steady strain of the motor would break. The bow would dip. Nate would quickly look at the edges of the river to inspect the wildlife. Jevy would curse in Portuguese, fiddle with the choke and the throttle, and then things would be fine for another twenty minutes or so.

They had lunch—cheese, saltines, and cookies—under a tree in a small fork as rain fell around them.

"That little fisherman back there," Nate said. "Does he know the Indians?"

"Yes. About once a month they go to the Paraguay to trade with a boat. He sees them."

"Did you ask him if he'd ever seen a female missionary?"

"I did. He has not. You are the first American he's ever seen."

"Lucky guy."

THE FIRST SIGN of the settlement came at almost seven hours. Nate saw a thin line of blue smoke rising above the trees, near the foot of a hill. Jevy was certain they were in Bolivia. The ground was higher and they were close to the mountains. The flooded areas were behind them.

They came to a gap in the trees and in a clearing were two canoes. Jevy guided the johnboat to the clearing. Nate quickly jumped ashore, anxious to stretch his legs and feel the earth.

"Stay close," Jevy warned as he switched gas tanks in the boat. Nate looked at him. Their eyes met, and Jevy nodded to the trees.

An Indian was watching them. A male, brown-skinned, bare-chested, with a straw skirt of some sort hanging from his waist, no visible weapon. The fact that he was unarmed helped immensely because Nate was at first terrified of him. The Indian had long black hair and red stripes on his forehead, and if he'd been holding a spear Nate would've surrendered without a word.

"Is he friendly?" he asked without taking his eyes off the man.

"I think so."

"Does he speak Portuguese?"

"I don't know."

"Why don't you go find out?"

"Relax."

Jevy stepped from the boat. "He looks like a cannibal," he whispered. The attempt at humor didn't work.

They took a few steps toward the Indian, and he took a few steps toward them. All three stopped with a nice gap in the center. Nate was tempted to raise the palm of his hand and say, "Howdy."

"*Fala português?*" Jevy said with a nice smile.

The Indian pondered the question for a long time, and it became painfully obvious that he did not speak Portuguese. He looked young, probably not yet twenty, and just happened to be near the river when he heard their outboard.

They examined each other from twenty feet as Jevy considered his options. There was a movement in the brush behind the Indian. Along the tree line, three of his tribesmen emerged, all mercifully weaponless. Outnumbered and trespassing, Nate was ready to bolt. They weren't particularly large, but they had the home-field advantage. And they weren't friendly folks, no smiles or hellos.

A young female suddenly appeared from the trees and stood next to the first Indian. She too was brown and bare-chested, and Nate tried not to stare. *"Falo,"* she said.

Speaking slowly, Jevy explained what they were up to, and asked to see their tribal leader. She translated his words and relayed them to the men, who huddled and talked grimly among themselves.

"Some want to eat us now," Jevy said under his breath. "Some want to wait until tomorrow."

"Very funny."

When the men finished their deliberations they reported to the woman. She then told the intruders that they must wait, by the river, while news of their arrival was duly reported to the higher-ups. This suited Nate just fine, but Jevy was a bit perturbed by it. He asked if a woman missionary lived with them.

You must wait, she said.

The Indians vanished into the woods.

"What do you think?" Nate asked when they were gone. Neither he nor Jevy had moved an inch. They stood in grass ankle-high and looked at the trees, thick woods from which Nate was certain they were being watched.

"They catch diseases from outsiders," Jevy explained. "That's why they are careful."

"I'm not touching anybody."

They retreated to the boat, where Jevy busied himself by cleaning the spark plugs. Nate removed both of his shirts and inspected the contents of his makeshift waterproof pouch. The papers were still dry.

"Those papers are for the woman?" Jevy asked.

"Yes."

"Why? What has happened to her?"

The rigid rules governing client confidentiality seemed less constricting at that moment. They were life and death in practice, but sitting in a boat deep in the Pantanal, with no other American even remotely near, the rules could be bent. And why not? Who could Jevy tell? What harm could come from a little gossip?

Per Josh's strict instructions to Valdir, Jevy had been told only that there was an important legal matter back home that required them to find Rachel Lane.

"Her father died a few weeks ago. He left her a lot of money."

"How much?"

"Several billion."

"Billion?"

"That's right."

"He was very wealthy."

"Yes, he was."

"Did he have other children?"

"Six, I think."

"Did he give them several billion?"

"No. He gave them very little."

"Why did he give her so much?"

"No one knows. It was a surprise."

"Does she know her father is dead?"

"No."

"Did she love her father?"

"I doubt it. She was illegitimate. It looks as though she tried to run away from him, and from everything else. Wouldn't you say so?" Nate waved his arm at the Pantanal as he said this.

"Yes. It's a very good place to hide. Did he know where she was when he died?"

"Not exactly. He knew she was a missionary working with the Indians somewhere around here."

Jevy ignored the spark plug in his hand and absorbed the news. He had many questions. The lawyer's breach of confidentiality was growing wider.

"Why would he leave such a fortune to a child who didn't love him?"

"Maybe he was crazy. He jumped out of a window."

This was more than Jevy could handle at one moment. He squinted his eyes and looked at the river, deep in thought.

TWENTY-FOUR

THE INDIANS were Guató, longtime residents who lived like their ancestors and preferred no contact with outsiders. They grew their food in small patches, fished the rivers, and hunted with bows and arrows.

Evidently, they were a deliberate people. After an hour, Jevy smelled smoke. He climbed a tree near the boat, and when he was forty feet up he saw the roofs of their huts. He asked Nate to join him.

Nate had not been in a tree in forty years, but at the moment there was nothing else to do. He made the climb with less ease than Jevy, and finally came to rest on a frail branch. He hugged the trunk with one arm.

They could see the tops of three huts—thick straw laid in neat rows. The blue smoke rose between two of the huts, from a point they couldn't see.

Could he be that close to Rachel Lane? Was she there now, listening to her people and deciding what to do? Would she send a warrior to fetch them, or would she herself simply walk through the woods and say hello?

"It's a small settlement," Nate said, trying not to move.

"There could be more huts."

"What do you think they're doing?"

"Talking. Just talking."

"Well I hate to bring this up, but we need to make a move. We left the boat eight and a half hours ago. I'd like to see Welly before dark."

"No problem. We'll go back with the current. Plus I know the way. It will be much faster."

"You're not worried?"

Jevy shook his head as if he hadn't given a thought to shooting down the Cabixa in the dark. Nate certainly had. Of particular concern were the two large lakes they had encountered, each with various tributaries, all of which appeared identical in the daylight.

His plan was to simply say hello to Ms. Lane, give her a bit of history, cover the required legalities, show her the paperwork, answer the basic questions, get her signature, thank her, and complete the meeting as soon as possible. He was worried about the time of day, and the sputtering motor, and the trip back to the *Santa Loura.* She would probably want to talk, or maybe she wouldn't. Maybe she would say very little and want them to leave and never come back.

Back on the ground, he had settled into the boat for a nap when Jevy saw the Indians. He said something and pointed, and Nate looked at the woods.

They slowly approached the river, in a line behind their leader, the oldest Guató they'd seen so far. He was stocky with an ample belly, and he carried a long stick of some sort. It didn't appear to be sharp or dangerous. It had pretty feathers near the tip, and Nate surmised that it was probably just a ceremonial spear.

The leader quickly sized up the two intruders, and directed his comments at Jevy.

Why are you here? he asked in Portuguese. His face wasn't friendly, but there was no aggression in his presence. Nate studied the spear.

We are looking for an American missionary, a woman, Jevy explained.

Where are you from? The chief asked this while glancing at Nate.

Corumbá.

And him? All eyes were on Nate.

He's an American. He needs to find the woman.

Why does he need to find the woman?

It was the first hint that the Indians might know of Rachel Lane. Was she hiding back there somewhere, in the village or maybe in the woods, listening?

Jevy went through a windy narrative explaining how Nate had traveled great distances and almost lost his life. It was an important matter among the Americans, nothing he, Jevy, or the Indians would ever understand.

Is she in danger?

No. None.

She is not here.

"He says she's not here," Jevy said to Nate.

"Tell him I think he's a lying bastard," Nate said, softly.

"I don't think so."

Have you ever seen a woman missionary around here? Jevy asked.

The leader shook his head. No.

Have you ever heard of one?

At first, there was no response. His eyes narrowed as he stared at Jevy, sizing him up, as if to say, Can this man be trusted? Then, a slight nod.

Where is she? Jevy asked.

With another tribe.

Where?

He said he wasn't sure, but he began pointing anyway. Somewhere off to the north and west, he said, with his spear waving across half the Pantanal.

"Guató?" Jevy asked.

He frowned and shook his head, as if she lived among undesirables. "Ipicas," he said with scorn.

How far away?

A day.

Jevy attempted to pin him down on the time, but soon learned that hours meant nothing to the Indians. A day wasn't twenty-four hours and it wasn't twelve. It was simply a day. He tried the concept of half a day, and made progress.

"Twelve to fifteen hours," he said to Nate.

"But that's in one of those little canoes, right?" Nate whispered.

"Yes."

"So how fast can we get there?"

"Three or four hours. If we can find it."

Jevy retrieved two maps and spread them on the grass. The Indians were very curious. They squatted close to their leader.

To find out where they were going, they first had to determine where they were. And this took a bad turn when the leader informed Jevy that the river that brought them in was not, in fact, the Cabixa. They had taken a wrong turn at some point after meeting the fisherman, and stumbled onto the Guató. Jevy took the news hard, and whispered it to Nate.

Nate took it even harder. He was trusting Jevy with his life.

Fancy-colored navigational maps meant little to the Indians. They were soon ignored as Jevy began drawing his own. He started with the unnamed river lying before them, and, chatting constantly with the chief, slowly made his way to the north. The chief received input from two young men. The two, he explained to Jevy, were excellent fishermen and traveled occasionally to the Paraguay.

"Hire them," Nate whispered.

Jevy tried, but in the course of negotiations learned that the two had never seen the Ipicas, didn't particularly want to, didn't know exactly where they were, and didn't understand the concept of working and getting paid for it. Plus the chief didn't want them to leave.

The route went from one river to the next, twisting northward, until the chief and his fishermen could no longer agree on where to go next. Jevy compared his drawing to his maps.

"We've found her," he said to Nate.

"Where?"

"There is a settlement of Ipicas here," he said, pointing to a map. "South of Porto Indio, at the edge of the mountains. Their directions take us close to it."

Nate leaned lower and examined the markings. "How do we get there?"

"I think we go back to the boat, and go north a half a day on the Paraguay. Then we use the little boat again to get to the settlement."

The Paraguay looped relatively close to their target, and traveling to it on the *Santa Loura* struck Nate as a splendid idea. "How many hours in the little boat?" Nate asked.

"Four, more or less."

"More or less" covered everything in Brazil. The distance, though, looked less than what they had covered since early morning.

"Then what are we waiting for?" Nate asked, standing and smiling at the Indians.

Jevy began saying thanks to their hosts, while folding his maps. Now that they were leaving, the Indians loosened up and wanted to be hospitable. They offered food, which Jevy declined. He explained that they were suddenly in a hurry, since they planned to return to the big river before dark.

Nate grinned at them as he backtracked to the river. They wanted to see the boat. They stood at the edge of the water, watching with great curiosity as Jevy adjusted the motor. When he started it, they took a step back.

The river, whatever it was named, looked entirely different going in the other direction. As they approached the first bend, Nate glanced over his shoulder and saw the Guató, still standing in the water.

The time was almost 4 P.M. With luck, they could make it past the large lakes before dark, then onto the Cabixa. Welly would be waiting, with beans and rice. As Nate did these quick calculations, he felt the first raindrops.

THE FLAW in the motor was not dirty spark plugs. It shut down completely fifty minutes into the return leg. The boat drifted with the current while Jevy removed the cover and attacked the carburetor with a screwdriver. Nate asked if he could help, and was quickly informed that he could not. At least not with the engine. He could, however, take a bucket and begin dipping out the rainwater. And he could take a paddle and keep them in the center of the river, whatever it was named.

He did both. The current kept them moving, although at a much slower pace than Nate preferred. The rain was intermittent. The river grew shallow as they approached a sharp curve, but Jevy was too busy to notice. The boat gained speed, and the rapids shoved it toward a thicket of dense brush.

"I need some help here," Nate said.

Jevy grabbed a paddle. He turned the boat so the bow would hit and it wouldn't flip. "Hold on!" he said as they rammed into the thicket. Vines and branches flew around Nate and he fought them with his paddle.

A small snake dropped into the boat just over Nate's shoulder. He didn't see it. Jevy scooped it up with his paddle and flung it into the river. It was best not to mention it.

They battled the current for a few minutes, as well as battling each other. Nate somehow managed to push water in all the wrong directions. His enthusiasm for paddling kept the boat precariously close to rolling.

When they were free again, away from the brush and the wildlife, Jevy confiscated both paddles and found a new job for Nate. He asked him to stand over the motor, holding his poncho wide to keep the rain off the carburetor. So Nate hovered, sort of like an angel with his arms spread, one foot on a gas tank, one foot on the side of the boat, frozen with fear.

Twenty minutes dragged by, as they drifted aimlessly down the narrow river. The Phelan estate could purchase every shiny new outboard motor in Brazil, and here Nate was watching an amateur mechanic try to patch one that was older than he was.

Jevy bolted the top on it, then worked with the throttle for an eternity. He yanked the starter rope, as Nate found himself saying a prayer. On the fourth pull, the miracle happened. The engine howled, though not as smoothly as before. It missed and sputtered, and Jevy adjusted throttle cables without much luck.

"We'll have to go slower," he reported, without looking at Nate.

"Fine. As long as we know where we are."

"No problem."

The storm crept over the mountains of Bolivia, then roared into the Pantanal, much like the one that had almost killed them in the airplane. Nate was sitting low in the boat, under the safety of his poncho, watching the river to the east, searching for something familiar, when he felt the first gust of wind. And the rain suddenly fell harder. He slowly turned and looked behind him. Jevy had already seen it, but said nothing.

The sky was dark gray, almost black. Clouds boiled low to the ground so that the mountains could not be seen. The rain began to drench them. Nate felt completely exposed and helpless.

There was nowhere to hide, no safe harbor to dock at and ride out the storm. There was nothing but water around them, water for miles in all directions. They were in the middle of a flood, with only the tops of the brush and a few trees to guide them through the rivers and swamps. They would stay in the boat because they had no choice.

A gale swept in behind them, driving the boat forward as the rain pelted their backs. The sky darkened. Nate wanted to curl up under his aluminum bench, clutch his floatable cushion, and hide as much as possible under his poncho. But the water was accumulating around his feet. The supplies were getting wet. He took his bucket and began shoveling rainwater.

They came to a fork that Nate was certain they had not passed earlier, then to a junction of rivers they could barely see through the rain. Jevy reduced the throttle to survey the waters, then hit the gas and took a sharp right as if he knew precisely where he was going. Nate was convinced they were lost.

After a few minutes, the river disappeared into a thicket of rotted trees—a memorable sight they had not seen earlier. Jevy quickly turned the boat around. Now they raced into the storm, and it was a terrifying sight. The sky was black. The current was churning with whitecaps.

Back at the junction, they talked for a moment, shouting through the wind and rain, then selected another river.

JUST BEFORE DARK they passed through a large flooded plain, a temporary lake that looked vaguely similar to the place where they'd found the fisherman in the weeds. He wasn't around.

Jevy selected a tributary, one of several, and proceeded as if he navigated this corner of the Pantanal every day. Then lightning came and for a while they could almost see where they were going. The rain slackened. The storm was slowly leaving them.

Jevy stopped the motor and studied the edges of the river.

"What are you thinking?" Nate asked. There had been very little conversation during the storm. They were lost, that much was certain. But Nate would not force Jevy to admit it.

"We should make camp," Jevy said. It was more of a suggestion than a plan.

"Why?"

"Because we have to sleep somewhere."

"We can take turns napping in the boat," Nate said. "It's safer here." He said this with the confidence of a seasoned river guide.

"Maybe. But I think we should stop here. We might get lost if we keep going in the dark."

We've been lost for three hours, Nate wanted to say.

Jevy guided the boat to a bank with some growth. They drifted downriver, staying close to the shore and watching the shallow waters with their flashlights. Two little red dots glowing just above the surface meant an alligator was watching too, but thankfully they saw none. They anchored by tying a guide rope to a limb ten feet from the bank.

Dinner was semidry saltines, canned little fish that Nate had never experienced, bananas and cheese.

When the winds stopped, the mosquitoes arrived. Repellent was passed back and forth. Nate rubbed it on his neck and face, even his eyelids and his hair. The tiny bugs were quick and vicious and moved in small black clouds from one end of the boat to the other. Though the rain had stopped, neither man removed his poncho. The mosquitoes tried fiercely, but they could not penetrate the plastic.

Around 11 P.M. the sky cleared somewhat, but there was no moon. The current gently rocked the boat. Jevy offered to hold the first watch, and Nate tried his best to get comfortable enough to doze. He propped his head on the tent, and stretched his legs. A gap opened in his poncho and a dozen mosquitoes rushed forth, chewing him at the waist. Something splashed, perhaps a reptile. The aluminum boat was not designed for reclining.

Sleep was out of the question.

TWENTY-FIVE

F LOWE, ZADEL, AND THEISHEN, the three psychiatrists
who had examined Troy Phelan only weeks earlier and had
presented the unified opinion, both on video and later in long
affidavits, that he was of sound mind, were fired. Not only were
they fired, they were rebuked by the Phelan lawyers as nuts, even
crackpots.

New psychiatrists were found. Hark bought the first one, at three
hundred bucks an hour. He found him in a magazine for trial
lawyers, in the classifieds, among the ads for everything from accident reconstructionists to X-ray analysts. He was Dr. Sabo, retired
from active practice and now willing to sell his testimony. One brief
look at the behavior of Mr. Phelan and he ventured the preliminary
opinion that he clearly lacked testamentary capacity. Jumping from
a window was not the act of a clear and lucid mind. And leaving an
eleven-billion-dollar fortune to an unknown heir was evidence of a
deeply disturbed person.

Sabo relished the idea of working on the Phelan case. Refuting
the opinions of the first three psychiatrists would be challenging.

The publicity was seductive—he'd never had a famous case. And the money would pay for a trip to the Orient.

All of the Phelan lawyers were scrambling to undo the testimony of Flowe, Zadel, and Theishen. The only way to discredit them was to find new experts with new opinions.

Fat hourly rates yielded to contingencies. The heirs wouldn't be able to pay the hefty monthly fees they were about to incur, so their lawyers graciously agreed to simplify matters by taking percentages. The range was staggering, though no firm would ever divulge its cut. Hark wanted 40 percent, but Rex berated him for his greediness. They finally agreed on 25 percent. Grit squeezed 25 percent out of Mary Ross Phelan Jackman.

The clear victor was Wally Bright, the street fighter, who insisted on an even deal with Libbigail and Spike. He would get half of their settlement.

In the mad scramble before they filed their suits, not a single Phelan heir asked if they were doing the right thing. They trusted their lawyers, and besides, everybody else was contesting the will. No one could afford to be left out. There was so much at stake.

BECAUSE HARK had been the loudest of the Phelan lawyers, he caught the attention of Snead, Troy's longtime gofer. No one had noticed Snead in the aftermath of the suicide. He'd been forgotten in the stampede to the courthouse. His employment had been terminated. And when the will was read, Snead himself was sitting in the courtroom, his face disguised with sunglasses and a hat, recognized by no one. He had left in tears.

He hated the Phelan children because Troy hated them. Over the years, Snead had been forced to do all sorts of unpleasant things to protect Troy from his families. Snead had arranged abortions, and had bribed cops when the boys were caught with drugs. He had lied to the wives to protect the mistresses, and when the mistresses became wives, then poor Snead lied to them too, to protect the girlfriends.

In return for his good work, the children and wives had called him a fag.

And in return for a career of faithful service, Mr. Phelan left him nothing. Not a cent. He'd been paid well over the years, and had some money in mutuals, but not enough to survive on. He had sacrificed everything for his job and his master. He'd been denied a normal life because Mr. Phelan expected him to be on duty every hour of the day. A family had been out of the question. He had no real friends to speak of.

Mr. Phelan had been his friend, his confidant, the only person Snead could trust.

Over the years, there had been many promises made by the old man about taking care of Snead. He knew for a fact that he'd been named in one will. He'd seen the document himself. He would inherit a million bucks upon Mr. Phelan's death. At the time, Troy had a net worth of three billion, and Snead remembered thinking how small a million seemed. As the old man got richer, Snead imagined his own bequest growing with each will.

He'd occasionally asked about the matter, subtle, gentle inquiries made at just the right moments, he thought. But Mr. Phelan had cursed him and threatened to cut him out completely. "You're as bad as my children," he had said, crushing poor Snead.

Somehow he'd gone from a million to zero, and he was bitter about it. He would be forced to join the enemies simply because he had no choice.

He found the new office of Hark Gettys & Associates near Dupont Circle. The receptionist explained that Mr. Gettys was very busy. "So am I," Snead replied rudely. Because he'd been so close to Troy, he had spent most of his life around lawyers. They were always busy.

"Give him this," he said, handing her an envelope. "It's quite urgent. I'll wait over there for ten minutes, then I'll walk down the street to the next law office."

Snead took a seat and stared at the floor. Cheap new carpet. The receptionist hesitated for a moment, then disappeared through a door. The envelope held a small handwritten note that read: "I worked for Troy Phelan for thirty years. I know everything. Malcolm Snead."

Hark appeared in a flash, holding the note, smiling goofily as if friendliness would impress Snead. They practically ran down the hall to a large office, the receptionist behind them. No, Snead did not want coffee, tea, water, or a cola. Hark slammed the door and locked it.

The office smelled of fresh paint. The desk and shelves were new and the woods didn't match. Boxes of files and junk were stacked along the walls. Snead took his time examining the details. "Just move in?" he said.

"Couple of weeks ago."

Snead hated the place, and he wasn't sure about the lawyer either. He wore a cheap wool suit, much less expensive than the one Snead was wearing.

"Thirty years, huh?" Hark said, still holding the note.

"That's right."

"Were you with him when he jumped?"

"No. He jumped alone."

A fake laugh, then the smile returned. "I mean, were you in the room?"

"Yes. I almost caught him."

"Must've been terrible."

"It was. Still is."

"Did you see him sign the will, the last one?"

"I did."

"Did you see him write the damned thing?"

Snead was perfectly prepared to lie. The truth meant nothing because the old man had lied to him. What was there to lose?

"I saw a lot of things," he said. "And I know a lot more. This visit is about nothing but money. Mr. Phelan promised that he would take care of me in his will. There were many promises, all broken."

"So you're in the same boat as my client," Hark said.

"I hope not. I despise your client and his miserable siblings. Let's get that straight on the front end."

"I think it's straight."

"No one was closer to Troy Phelan than I. I saw and heard things no one else can testify to."

"So you wanna be a witness?"

"I am a witness, an expert. And I'm very expensive."

Their eyes locked for a second. The message was delivered and received.

"The law says that laymen cannot render opinions as to the mental capacity of one executing a will, but you can certainly testify as to specific acts and deeds that prove an unsound mind."

"I know all this," Snead said rudely.

"Was he crazy?"

"He was or he wasn't. Doesn't matter to me. I can go either way."

Hark had to stop and contemplate this. He scratched his face and studied the wall.

Snead decided to help him. "This is the way I see it. Your boy got screwed, along with his brother and sisters. They each got five million bucks when they turned twenty-one, and we know what they did with the money. Since they're all heavily in debt, they have no choice but to contest the will. No jury's gonna feel sorry for them, though. They're a bunch of greedy losers. It'll be a tough case to win. But you and the other legal eagles will attack the will, and you'll create this huge mess of a lawsuit that quickly gets in the tabloids because there's eleven billion at stake. Since you don't have much of a case, you hope for a settlement before you go to trial."

"You catch on quick."

"No. I watched Mr. Phelan for thirty years. Anyway, the size of your settlement depends on me. If my recall is clear and detailed, then perhaps my old boss lacked testamentary capacity when he wrote the will."

"Then your memory comes and goes."

"My memory is whatever I want it to be. There's no one to question it."

"What do you want?"

"Money."

"How much?"

"Five million."

"That's a lot."

"It's nothing. I'll take it from this side, or the other. It doesn't matter."

"How am I supposed to get five million bucks to you?"

"Don't know. I'm not a lawyer. I figure you and your cronies can conjure up some dirty little plan."

There was a long pause as Hark began the conjuring. He had a lot of questions, but suspected he wouldn't get a lot of answers. At least not now.

"Any more witnesses?" he asked.

"Only one. Her name is Nicolette. She was Mr. Phelan's last secretary."

"How much does she know?"

"Depends. She can be bought."

"You've already talked to her."

"Every day. We're a package."

"How much for her?"

"She'll be covered in the five million."

"A real bargain. Anybody else?"

"No one of consequence."

Hark closed his eyes and massaged both temples. "I don't object to your five million," he said, pinching his nose. "I just don't know how we can funnel it to you."

"I'm sure you'll think of something."

"Give me some time, okay? I need to think about this."

"I'm in no hurry. I'll give you a week. If you say no, then I'll go to the other side."

"There is no other side."

"Don't be so certain."

"You know something about Rachel Lane?"

"I know everything," Snead said, then left the office.

TWENTY-SIX

THE FIRST STREAKS of dawn brought no surprises. They were tied to a tree at the edge of a small river that looked like all the others they'd seen. The clouds were heavy again; the light of day came slowly.

Breakfast was a small box of cookies, the last of the rations Welly had packed for them. Nate ate slowly, wondering with each bite when he might eat again.

The current was strong, so they drifted with it as the sun rose. The only sound was the rush of the water. They were conserving gas and delaying the moment when Jevy would be forced to try and start the motor.

They drifted into a flooded area where three streams met, and for a few moments sat in the stillness.

"I guess we're lost, aren't we?" Nate said.

"I know exactly where we are."

"Where?"

"We're in the Pantanal. And all rivers run to the Paraguay."

"Eventually."

"Yes, eventually." Jevy removed the top cover of the motor and wiped the moisture from the carburetor. He adjusted the throttle, checked the oil, then tried to start the motor. On the fifth pull, the motor caught and sputtered, then quit.

I will die here, Nate said to himself. I'll either drown, starve, or be eaten, but it is here, in this immense swamp, that I will breathe my last.

To their surprise, they heard a shout. The voice was high, like that of a young girl. The sputtering of the motor had attracted the attention of another human. The voice came from a weedy marsh along the bank of a converging stream. Jevy yelled and a few seconds later the voice yelled back.

A kid of no more than fifteen came through the weeds in a tiny canoe, hand-carved from the trunk of a tree. With a homemade paddle he cut through the water with amazing ease and speed. *"Bom dia,"* he said with a wide smile. The little face was brown and square, and probably the most beautiful Nate had seen in years. He threw a rope and the two boats were attached.

A long lazy conversation ensued, and after a while Nate was agitated. "What's he saying?" he snapped at Jevy.

The kid looked at Nate, and Jevy said, *"Americano."*

"He says we're a great distance from the Cabixa River," Jevy said.

"I could've told you that."

"He says the Paraguay is a half a day to the east."

"By canoe, right?"

"No, by plane."

"Funny. How long will it take us?"

"Four hours, more or less."

Five, maybe six hours. And that was with a properly running motor. It would take a week if they were forced to paddle.

The Portuguese resumed, in no particular hurry. The canoe was empty except for a roll of fishing line wrapped around a tin can, and a jar of mud which Nate assumed contained worms or some type of bait. What did he know about fishing? He scratched his mosquito bites.

A year ago he'd been skiing in Utah with the boys. The drink of the day had been some type of tequila concoction, which, typically, Nate consumed with gusto until he passed out. The hangover had lasted for two days.

There was a flourish in the chatter, and suddenly they were pointing. Jevy looked at him as he spoke.

"What is it?" Nate asked.

"The Indians are not far away."

"How far?"

"One hour, maybe two."

"Can he take us there?"

"I know the way."

"I'm sure you do. But I'd feel better if he'd tag along."

It was a slight affront to Jevy's pride, but under the circumstances he could not argue. "He may want a little money."

"Whatever." If the kid only knew. The Phelan estate on one side of the table, and this skinny little *pantaneiro* on the other. Nate smiled at the mental picture. How about a fleet of canoes, with rods and reels and depth finders? Just name it, son, and it's yours.

"Ten reais," Jevy said, after brief negotiations.

"Fine." For about ten bucks, they would be delivered to Rachel Lane.

A plan was devised. Jevy tilted the outboard so that the prop was out of the water, and they began paddling. They followed the boy in the canoe for twenty minutes until they entered a small shallow stream with rapid currents. Nate withdrew his paddle, caught his breath, and wiped sweat from his face. His heart was pounding and his muscles were already tired. The clouds were breaking up, so the sun was bearing down.

Jevy went to work on the motor. Luckily it started, and kept running, and they followed the boy, his canoe easily outpacing them and their sputtering outboard.

IT WAS ALMOST ONE when they found the higher ground. The floodwaters gradually disappeared, so that the rivers were lined with thick brush and the trees were dense. The kid was somber and, oddly, concerned with the position of the sun.

Just up there, he told Jevy. Just around the bend. He seemed afraid to go further.

I'll stop here, he said. I need to return home.

Nate handed him the money, and they thanked him. He headed back with the current and disappeared quickly. They plowed ahead, the outboard halting and struggling at half-speed, but getting them there nonetheless.

The river ran into a forest where the trees hung low over the water, so low that they weaved together above and formed a tunnel that blocked out light. It was dark, and the uneven hum of their motor resounded from the banks. Nate had the eerie suspicion that they were being watched. He could almost feel the arrows being aimed at him. He braced for an attack of deadly blow darts by savages dressed in war paint and trained to kill anyone with a white face.

But they saw children first, happy little brown bodies splashing in the water. The tunnel ended near a settlement.

The mothers were bathing too, just as completely naked as their children, and thoroughly unconcerned about it. At first, they retreated to the bank when they saw the johnboat. Jevy killed the engine and began talking and smiling as they drifted in. An older girl ran away, in the direction of the settlement.

"Fala português?" Jevy asked the crowd of four women and seven children. They just stared. The smaller ones hid behind their mothers. The women were short, with thick bodies and small breasts.

"Are they friendly?" Nate asked.

"The men will tell us."

The men arrived within minutes, three of them, also short, thick, and muscular. Thankfully, their privates were covered with small leather pouches.

The oldest one claimed to speak Jevy's language, but his Portuguese was rudimentary at best. Nate stayed in the boat, where things appeared to be safe, while Jevy leaned on a tree near the water and tried to make himself understood. The Indians crowded around Jevy, who was a foot taller than the men.

After a few minutes of repetition and hand gestures, Nate said, "Translation please."

The Indians looked at Nate.

"*Americano*," Jevy explained, and another conversation ensued.

"What about the woman?" Nate asked.

"We haven't got that far yet. I'm still trying to convince them not to burn you alive."

"Try harder."

More Indians arrived. Their huts were visible a hundred yards away, near the edge of a forest. Upriver, a half-dozen canoes were tied to the bank. The children became bored. They slowly left their mothers and waded close to the boat to inspect it. They were also intrigued by the man with the white face. Nate smiled and winked and before long got a grin. If Welly hadn't been so damned cheap with the cookies, Nate would've had something to share with them.

The conversation poked along. The Indian doing the talking would periodically turn to his pals and make a report, and inevitably his words caused great concern. Their language was a series of primal grunts and strains, all delivered with as little lip movement as possible.

"What's he saying?" Nate growled.

"I don't know," Jevy replied.

A little boy placed his hand on the edge of the boat, and studied Nate with black pupils as big as quarters. Very softly he said, "Hello." Nate knew they were in the right place.

No one heard the boy but Nate. He leaned forward, and softly said, "Hello."

"Good-bye," the boy said, without moving. Rachel had taught him at least two English words.

"What is your name?" Nate asked, his voice a whisper.

"Hello," he repeated.

Under the tree, the translating was making the same progress.

The male Indians were huddling in animated conversation while the women said nothing.

"What about the woman?" Nate repeated.

"I asked. They have no answer."

"What does that mean?"

"I'm not sure. I think she's here, but they are reluctant for some reason."

"Why would they be reluctant?"

Jevy frowned and looked away. How was he supposed to know? They talked some more, then the Indians left en masse—men first, then the women, then the children. They trooped single file to the settlement, disappearing from view.

"Did you make them mad?"

"No. They want to have a meeting of some kind."

"Do you think she's here?"

"I think so." Jevy took his seat in the boat and prepared himself for a nap. It was almost one, in whatever time zone they happened to be in. Lunch was over and done with without so much as a soggy saltine.

THE HIKE BEGAN around three. They were led by a small group of young men away from the river, along the dirt path to the village, through the huts where everyone stood still and watched, then away again, along another path into the woods.

It's a death march, thought Nate. They're taking us into the jungle for some Stone Age blood ritual. He followed Jevy, who loped along in a confident gait. "Where the hell are we going?" he hissed, like a prisoner of war afraid to offend his captors.

"Relax."

The woods opened to a clearing, and they were near the river again. The leader suddenly stopped, and pointed. At the edge of the water, an anaconda stretched in the sun. He was black with yellow markings on his underside. His girth was at least a foot at its widest. "How long is he?" Nate asked.

"Six or seven meters. Finally, you see an anaconda," Jevy said.

Nate's knees buckled and his mouth was dry. He had been joking about the snakes. The sight of a real one, long and massive, was truly amazing.

"Some Indians worship snakes," Jevy said.

Then what are our missionaries doing? Nate thought. He would ask Rachel about this practice.

The mosquitoes seemed to bother only him. The Indians were immune. Jevy never swatted. Nate slapped his own flesh and scratched until he drew blood. His repellent was in the boat, along with his tent and machete and everything else he owned at the moment, no doubt being examined by the children.

The hike was adventurous for the first half hour, then the heat and the insects made things monotonous. "How far are we going?" Nate asked, not really expecting an answer with any accuracy.

Jevy said something to the point man, who said something in return. "Not far," came the reply. They crossed another trail, then a wider one. There was traffic in the area. Soon they saw the first hut, then smelled smoke.

When they were two hundred yards away, the leader pointed to a shaded area near the river. Nate and Jevy were led to a bench made of hollow cane poles lashed together with string. They were left there with two guards while the others reported to the village.

As time passed, the two guards grew weary and decided to take a nap. They leaned against the trunk of a tree, and were soon asleep.

"I guess we could escape," Nate said.

"To where?"

"Are you hungry?"

"Sort of. Are you?"

"No, I'm stuffed," Nate said. "I ate seven thin cookies nine hours ago. Remind me to slap Welly when I see him."

"I hope he is okay."

"Why shouldn't he be? He's swinging in my hammock, drinking fresh coffee, safe and dry and well fed."

They wouldn't have brought them this far if Rachel wasn't nearby. As Nate rested on the bench and stared at the tops of the huts in the distance, he had many questions about her. He was curious about her appearance—her mother was supposed to have been a beautiful woman. Troy Phelan had a good eye for women. What kind of clothes would she wear? The Ipicas she ministered to were naked. How long since she'd seen civilization? Was he the first American to ever visit the village?

How would she react to his presence? And to the money?

As time dragged along, Nate became more anxious about meeting her.

BOTH OF THE GUARDS were asleep when there was movement from the settlement. Jevy tossed a pebble at them and whistled quietly. They jumped to their feet and resumed their positions.

The weeds along the trail were knee-high, and from the distance they could see a patrol moving their way, along the path. Rachel was with them; she was coming. There was a light yellow shirt in the midst of the brown-skinned chests, and a lighter face under a straw hat. From a hundred yards, Nate could see her.

"We've found our girl," he said.

"Yes, I think we have."

They took their time. Three young men were in front, and three behind. She was slightly taller than the Indians, and carried herself with an easy elegance. She could've been out for a walk among the flowers. There was no hurry.

Nate watched every step. She was very slender, with wide bony shoulders. She began looking in their direction as they grew closer. Nate and Jevy stood to meet her.

The Indians stopped at the edge of the shade, but Rachel kept walking. She removed her hat. Her hair was brown and half-gray, and very short. She stopped a few feet from Jevy and Nate.

"*Boa tarde, senhor,*" she said to Jevy, then looked at Nate. Her eyes were dark blue, almost indigo. No wrinkles, no makeup. She was forty-two years old and aging quite well, with the soft glow of one who knew little stress.

"*Boa tarde.*"

She didn't offer to shake hands, nor did she give her name. The next move belonged to them.

"My name is Nate O'Riley. I'm an attorney from Washington."

"And you?" she said to Jevy.

"I'm Jevy Cardozo, from Corumbá. I'm his guide."

She looked them up and down with a slight grin. The moment was not at all unpleasant for her. She was enjoying the encounter.

"What brings you here?" she asked. It was American English with no accent, no trace of Louisiana or Montana, just the flat, precise, inflectionless English from Sacramento or St. Louis.

"We heard the fishing was good," Nate said.

No response. "He makes bad jokes," Jevy said, apologizing.

"Sorry. I'm looking for Rachel Lane. I have reason to believe you and she are one and the same."

She absorbed this without changing expressions. "Why do you want to find Rachel Lane?"

"Because I'm a lawyer, and my firm has an important legal matter with Rachel Lane."

"What kind of legal matter?"

"I can tell no one but her."

"I'm not Rachel Lane. I'm sorry."

Jevy sighed and Nate's shoulders slumped. She saw every movement, every reaction, every twitch. "Are you hungry?" she asked them.

They both nodded. She called the Indians and gave them instructions. "Jevy," she said, "go with these men into the village. They will feed you, and give you enough food for Mr. O'Riley here."

They sat on the bench, in the darkening shade, watching in silence as the Indians took Jevy to the village. He turned around once, just to make sure Nate was okay.

TWENTY-SEVEN

S HE DIDN'T SEEM as tall away from the Indians. And she had
avoided whatever the women ate that made them thick. Her
legs were thin and long. She wore leather sandals, which seemed
odd in a culture where no one had shoes. Where did she get them?
And where did she get her yellow short-sleeved shirt and khaki
shorts? Oh, the questions he had.

Her clothing was simple and well worn. If she wasn't Rachel
Lane, then surely she knew where Rachel was.

Their knees almost touched. "Rachel Lane ceased to exist many
years ago," she said, gazing at the village in the distance. "I kept the
name Rachel, but dropped the Lane. It must be serious or you
wouldn't be here." She spoke softly and slowly, no syllable missed
and each carefully weighed.

"Troy's dead. He killed himself three weeks ago."

She lowered her head slightly, closed her eyes, and appeared to be
praying. It was a brief prayer, followed by a long pause. Silence
didn't bother her. "Did you know him?" she finally asked.

"I met him once, years ago. Our firm has many lawyers, and I
personally never worked on Troy's business. No, I didn't know him."

"Neither did I. He was my earthly father, and I've spent many hours praying for him, but he was always a stranger."

"When did you last see him?" Nate's words too were softer and slower. She had a soothing effect.

"Many years ago. Before I went to college. . . . How much do you know about me?"

"Not much. You don't leave much of a trail."

"Then how did you find me?"

"Troy helped. He tried to find you before he died, but couldn't. He knew you were a missionary with World Tribes, and that you were in this general part of the world. The rest was up to me."

"How could he have known that?"

"He had an awful lot of money."

"And that's why you're here."

"Yes, that's why I'm here. We need to talk business."

"Troy must've left me something in his will."

"You could say that."

"I don't want to talk business. I want to chat. Do you know how often I hear English?"

"Rarely, I would imagine."

"I go to Corumbá once a year for supplies. I phone the home office, and for about ten minutes I speak English. It's always frightening."

"Why?"

"I'm nervous. My hands shake as I hold the phone. I know the people I'm talking to, but I'm afraid I will use the wrong words. Sometimes I even stutter. Ten minutes a year."

"You're doing a fine job now."

"I'm very nervous."

"Relax. I'm a swell guy."

"But you've found me. I was seeing a patient just an hour ago when the boys came to tell me that an American was here. I ran to my hut and started praying. God gave me strength."

"I come in peace for all mankind."

"You seem like a nice man."

If you only knew, thought Nate. "Thanks. You, uh, said something about seeing a patient."

"Yes."

"I thought you were a missionary."

"I am. I'm also a doctor."

And Nate's specialty was suing doctors. It was neither the time nor the place for a discussion about medical malpractice. "That's not in my research."

"I changed my name after college, before med school and seminary. That's probably where the trail ended."

"Exactly. Why did you change your name?"

"It's complicated, at least it was then. It doesn't seem important now."

A breeze settled in from the river. It was almost five. The clouds over the forest were dark and low. She saw him glance at his watch. "The boys are bringing your tent here. This is a good place to sleep tonight."

"Thanks, I guess. We'll be safe, won't we?"

"Yes. God will protect you. Say your prayers."

At that moment, Nate planned to pray like a preacher. The proximity to the river was of particular concern. He could shut his eyes and see that anaconda slithering up to his tent.

"You do pray, don't you, Mr. O'Riley?"

"Please call me Nate. Yes, I pray."

"Are you Irish?"

"I'm a mutt. More German than anything else. My father had Irish ancestors. Family history has never interested me."

"What church do you attend?"

"Episcopal." Catholic, Lutheran, Episcopal, it didn't matter. Nate hadn't seen the inside of a church since his second wedding.

His spiritual life was a subject he preferred to avoid. Theology was not his long suit, and he didn't want to discuss it with a missionary. She paused, as usual, and he changed directions. "Are these Indians peaceful?"

"For the most part. The Ipicas are not warriors, but they do not trust white people."

"What about you?"

"I've been here eleven years. They have accepted me."

"How long did it take?"

"I was lucky because there was a missionary couple here before me. They had learned the language and translated the New Testament. And I'm a doctor. I made friends fast when I helped the women through childbirth."

"Your Portuguese sounded pretty good."

"I'm fluent. I speak Spanish, Ipica, and Machiguenga."

"What is that?"

"The Machiguenga are natives in the mountains of Peru. I was there for six years. I had just become comfortable with the language when they evacuated me."

"Why?"

"Guerrillas."

As if snakes and alligators and diseases and floods weren't enough.

"They kidnapped two missionaries in a village not far from me. But God saved them. They were released unharmed four years later."

"Any guerrillas around here?"

"No. This is Brazil. The people are very peaceful. There are some drug runners, but nobody comes this deep into the Pantanal."

"Which brings up an interesting point. How far away is the Paraguay River?"

"This time of the year, eight hours."

"Brazilian hours?"

She smiled at this. "You've learned that time is slower here. Eight to ten hours, American time."

"By canoe?"

"That's how we travel. I used to have a boat with a motor. But it was old, and it eventually wore out."

"How long does it take if you have a boat with a motor?"

"Five hours, more or less. It's the flood season, and it's easy to get lost."

"So I've learned."

"The rivers run together. You'll need to take one of the fishermen with you when you leave. There's no way you'll find the Paraguay without a guide."

"And you go once a year?"

"Yes, but I go in the dry season, in August. It's cooler then, not as many mosquitoes."

"You go alone?"

"No. I get Lako, my Indian friend, to travel with me to the Paraguay. It takes about six hours by canoe when the rivers are down. I'll wait for a boat, then catch a ride to Corumbá. I'll stay for a few days, do my business, then catch a boat back."

Nate thought of how few boats he'd seen on the Paraguay. "Just any boat?"

"Usually a cattle boat. The captains are good about taking passengers."

She travels by canoe because her old boat wore out. She bums rides on cattle boats to visit Corumbá, her only contact with civilization. How would the money change her? Nate asked himself. The question seemed impossible to answer.

He would tell her tomorrow, when the day was fresh, when he was rested and fed and they had hours to deal with the issues. Figures appeared at the edge of the settlement—men walking in their direction.

"Here they are," she said. "We eat just before dark, then we go to sleep."

"I guess there's nothing to do afterward."

"Nothing we can discuss," she said quickly, and it was funny.

Jevy appeared with a group of Indians, one of whom handed Rachel a small square basket. She passed it to Nate, who removed a small loaf of hard bread.

"This is manioc," she said. "It's our main food."

And evidently their only food, at least for that meal. Nate was into his second loaf when they were joined by Indians from the first village. They brought the tent, mosquito net, blankets, and bottled water from the boat.

"We're staying here tonight," Nate said to Jevy.

"Says who?"

"It's the best spot," Rachel said. "I would offer you a place in the village, but the leader must first approve a visit by white men."

"That would be me," Nate said.

"Yes."

"And not him?" He nodded at Jevy.

"He went for food, not to sleep. The rules are complicated."

This struck Nate as funny—primitive natives yet to discover clothing but following a complicated system of rules.

"I would like to leave by noon tomorrow," Nate said to her.

"That too will be up to the leader."

"You mean we can't leave when we want?"

"You will leave when he says you can leave. Don't worry."

"Are you and the chief close?"

"We get along."

She sent the Indians back to the village. The sun had disappeared over the mountains. The shadows from the forest were engulfing them.

For a few minutes, Rachel watched as Jevy and Nate struggled with the tent. It looked quite small rolled up in its case, and expanded just a little as they hooked the poles together. Nate wasn't sure it would hold Jevy, let alone the both of them. Fully erected, it was waist-high, pitched sharply from the sides, and painfully small for two grown men.

"I'm going," she announced. "You will be fine here."

"Promise?" Nate said, with sincerity.

"I can have a couple of boys stand watch if you like."

"We'll be fine," Jevy said.

"What time do you folks wake up around here?" Nate asked.

"An hour before sunrise."

"I'm sure we'll be awake," Nate said, glancing at the tent. "Can we meet early? We have a lot to discuss."

"Yes. I'll send some food out at daybreak. Then we'll chat."

"That would be nice."

"Say your prayers, Mr. O'Riley."

"I will."

She stepped into the darkness and was gone. For a moment, Nate could see her silhouette winding along the trail, then nothing. The village was lost in the blackness of the night.

THEY SAT on the bench for hours, waiting for the air to cool, dreading the moment when they would be forced to pack themselves into the tent and sleep back to back, both smelly and sweaty. There was no choice. The tent, flimsy as it was, would protect them from mosquitoes and other insects. It would also keep out things that crawled.

They talked about the village. Jevy told Indian stories, all of which ended in the death of someone. He finally asked, "Did you tell her about the money?"

"No. I'll do that tomorrow."

"You've seen her now. What will she think about the money?"

"I have no idea. She's happy here. It seems cruel to upset her life."

"Then give me the money. It won't upset my life."

They followed the pecking order. Nate crawled into the tent first. He'd spent the previous night watching the sky from the bottom of the boat, so the fatigue hit fast.

When he was snoring, Jevy slowly unzipped the tent door, and nudged here and there until he had a spot. His pal was unconscious.

TWENTY-EIGHT

AFTER NINE HOURS of sleep, the Ipicas arose before dawn to begin their day. The women built small cooking fires outside their huts, then left with the children for the river, to collect water and to bathe. As a rule, they waited until first light to walk the dirt trails. It was prudent to see what lay before them.

In Portuguese, the snake was known as an *urutu*. The Indians called it a *bima*. It was common around the waterways of southern Brazil, and often fatal. The girl's name was Ayesh, age seven, helped into the world by the white missionary. Ayesh was walking in front of her mother instead of behind, as was the custom, and she felt the *bima* squirm under her bare foot.

It struck her below the ankle as she screamed. By the time her father got to her, she was in shock and her right foot had doubled in size. A boy of fifteen, the fastest runner in the tribe, was dispatched to get Rachel.

There were four small Ipica settlements along two rivers that met in a fork very near the spot where Jevy and Nate had stopped. The distance from the fork to the last Ipica hut was no more than five miles. The settlements were distinct and self-contained little tribes, but they were all Ipicas, with the same language, heritage, and customs. They socialized and intermarried.

Ayesh lived in the third settlement from the fork. Rachel was in the second, the largest. The runner found her as she was reading scriptures in the small hut where she'd lived for eleven years. She quickly checked her supplies and filled her small medical bag.

There were four poisonous snakes in their part of the Pantanal, and at various times Rachel had had the antivenin for each. But not this time. The runner told her the snake was a *bima*. Its antivenin was manufactured by a Brazilian company, but she had been unable to find it during her last trip to Corumbá. The pharmacies there had less than half the medicines she needed.

She laced her leather boots and left with her bag. Lako and two other boys from her village joined her as she jogged away, through the tall weeds and into the woods.

According to Rachel's statistics, there were eighty-six adult females, eighty-one adult males, and seventy-two children in the four settlements, a total of 239 Ipicas. When she began working with the Ipicas eleven years earlier, there had been 280. Malaria took the weak ones every few years. An outbreak of cholera killed twenty in one village in 1991. If Rachel hadn't insisted on a quarantine, most of the Ipicas would've been wiped out.

With the diligence of an anthropologist, she kept records of births, deaths, weddings, family trees, illnesses, and treatments. Most of the time she knew who was having an extramarital affair, and with whom. She knew every name in every village. She had baptized Ayesh's parents in the river where they bathed.

Ayesh was small and thin, and she would probably die because there was no medicine. The antivenin was readily available in the States and in the larger cities of Brazil, and not terribly expensive. Her small budget from World Tribes would cover it. Three injections in six hours and death could be prevented. Without it, the child would become violently ill with nausea, then a fever would hit, followed by a coma, then death.

It had been three years since the Ipicas had seen a death by snakebite. And for the first time in two years, Rachel had no antivenin.

Ayesh's parents were Christians, new saints struggling with a new religion. About a third of the Ipicas had been converted. Because of the work of Rachel and her predecessors, half of them could read and write.

She prayed as she trotted behind the boys. She was lean and tough. She walked several miles a day and ate little. The Indians admired her stamina.

JEVY WAS WASHING himself in the river when Nate unzipped the mosquito fly and extricated himself from the tent. He still carried bruises from the plane crash. Sleeping in the boat and on the ground did little to ease the soreness. He stretched his back and legs, aching all over, feeling every one of his forty-eight years. He could see Jevy, waist-deep in water that looked much clearer than the rest of the Pantanal.

I'm lost, Nate whispered to himself. I'm hungry. I have no toilet paper. He gingerly touched his toes as he summed up his sad inventory.

It was an adventure, dammit! It was time for all lawyers to charge into the new year with resolutions to bill more hours, win bigger verdicts, cut more overhead, take home more money. He'd made those vows for years, and now they seemed silly.

With a little luck, he'd sleep in his hammock tonight, swinging in the breeze, sipping coffee. To the best of his recollection, Nate had never before longed for black beans and rice.

Jevy returned as a patrol of Indians arrived from the village. The chief wanted to see them. "He wants to have bread," Jevy said as they walked away.

"Bread's fine. Ask if they have bacon and eggs."

"They eat a lot of monkey."

He didn't appear to be kidding. At the edge of the village, a group of children stood waiting for a look at the strangers. Nate offered them all a frozen smile. He'd never felt so white in his life, and he wanted to be liked. Some naked mothers gawked from the first hut. When he and Jevy entered the wide common area, everyone stopped and stared.

Small fires were burning out; breakfast was over. The smoke hung like fog over the roofs, and made the humid air even stickier. It was a few minutes after seven, and already very hot.

The village architect had done a fine job. Each dwelling was perfectly square with a thatched roof angled steeply, almost to the ground. Some were larger than others, but the design never varied. They circled the settlement in an oval-shaped ring, all facing a large flat area—the town square. In the center were four large structures—two circular and two rectangular—and all had the same thick straw roofs.

The chief was waiting for them. Not surprisingly, his home was the largest hut in the village. And he was the largest Indian of the lot. He was young, and lacked the heavy wrinkles across the forehead and the thick belly the older men carried with pride. He stood and gave Nate a look that would have horrified John Wayne. An older warrior did the interpreting, and within minutes Nate and Jevy were asked to sit near the fire, where the chief's naked wife was preparing breakfast.

When she bent over, her breasts swung about, and poor Nate couldn't help but stare, if only for a long second. There was nothing particularly sexy about the naked woman or her breasts. It was just the fact that she could be so naked and so unconcerned about it.

Where was his camera? The boys around the office would never believe it without proof.

She handed Nate a wooden plate covered with a serving of what appeared to be boiled potatoes. He glanced at Jevy, who gave a quick nod as if he knew everything about Indian cuisine. She served the chief last, and when he began eating with his fingers, so did Nate. It was a cross between a turnip and a redskin potato, with very little taste.

Jevy talked while he ate, and the chief enjoyed the conversation.

After a few sentences, Jevy would translate things into English and pass them along.

The village never flooded. They had been there for more than twenty years. The soil was good. They preferred not to move, but sometimes the soil forced them to. His father had been a chief too. The chief, according to the chief, was the wisest, smartest, and fairest of them all, and he could not engage in extramarital affairs. Most of the other men did, but not the chief.

Nate suspected there was little else to do but fool around.

The chief had never seen the Paraguay River. He preferred hunting over fishing, thus spent more time in the woods than on the rivers. He'd learned basic Portuguese from his father and from the white missionaries.

Nate ate, listened, and watched the village for any sign of Rachel.

She wasn't there, the chief explained. She was in the next village tending to a child who'd been bitten by a snake. He wasn't sure when she would return.

Just wonderful, thought Nate.

"He wants us to stay here tonight, in the village," Jevy said. The wife was refilling their plates.

"Didn't know we were staying," Nate said.

"He says we are."

"Tell him I'll think about it."

"You tell him."

Nate cursed himself for not bringing the SatFone. Josh was surely pacing the floor of his office right now, worried sick. They had not talked in almost a week.

Jevy said something slightly humorous that upon translation became downright funny. The chief roared with laughter, and soon everyone else was laughing too. Including Nate, who laughed at himself for laughing with the Indians.

They declined an invitation to go hunting. A patrol of young men led them back to the first village, to their boat. Jevy wanted to clean the spark plugs again and fiddle with the carburetor. Nate had nothing else to do.

□ □ □ □

LAWYER VALDIR took the early call from Mr. Stafford. The pleasantries took only seconds.

"I haven't heard from Nate O'Riley in days," Stafford said.

"But he has one of those phones," Valdir said, on the defensive, as if it was his duty to protect Mr. O'Riley.

"Yes, he does. That's what worries me. He can call anytime, from anywhere."

"Can he use the phone in bad weather?"

"No. I suppose not."

"We've had many storms down here. It is, after all, the rainy season."

"You haven't heard from your boy?"

"No. They are together. The guide is very good. The boat is very good. I'm sure they are well."

"Then why hasn't he called?"

"I can't answer. But the skies have not been clear. Perhaps he cannot use his phone."

They agreed that Valdir would call at once if something was heard from the boat. Valdir walked to his open window and looked at the busy streets of Corumbá. The Paraguay River was just down the hill. Stories were legion of people who entered the Pantanal and never came back. It was part of the lore, and the lure.

Jevy's father had piloted the rivers for thirty years, and his body was never recovered.

WELLY FOUND the law office an hour later. He had not met Mr. Valdir, but he knew from Jevy that the lawyer was paying for the expedition.

"It's very important," he told the secretary. "It is urgent."

Valdir heard the ruckus and appeared from his office. "Who are you?" he demanded.

"My name is Welly. Jevy hired me as a deckhand on the *Santa Loura*."

"The *Santa Loura!*"

"Yes."

"Where is Jevy?"

"He's still in the Pantanal."

"Where is the boat?"

"It sank."

Valdir realized the boy was tired and frightened. "Sit down," he said, and the secretary ran to get water. "Tell me everything."

Welly clutched the arms of his chair, and spoke rapidly. "They left in the johnboat to find the Indians, Jevy and Mr. O'Riley."

"When?"

"I don't know. A few days ago. I was to stay with the *Santa Loura*. A storm hit, the biggest storm ever. It blew the boat free in the middle of the night, then rolled it over. I was thrown into the water and picked up later by a cattle boat."

"When did you arrive here?"

"Only a half hour ago."

The secretary brought a glass of water. Welly thanked her and asked for coffee. Valdir leaned on her desk and watched the poor kid. He was dirty and smelled like cow manure.

"So the boat is gone?" Valdir said.

"Yes. I'm sorry. There was nothing I could do. I have never seen such a storm."

"Where was Jevy during the storm?"

"Somewhere on the Cabixa River. I fear for him."

Valdir walked to his office, where he closed the door and returned to his window. Mr. Stafford was three thousand miles away. Jevy could survive in a small boat. No sense jumping to conclusions.

He decided not to call for a few days. Give Jevy time, and surely he would return to Corumbá.

THE INDIAN stood in the boat and braced himself by clutching Nate's shoulder. There was no noticeable improvement in the motor's performance. It continued to sputter and miss, and at full throttle had less than half the power it had when they left the *Santa Loura*.

They passed the first settlement, and the river bent and looped almost to the point of going in circles. Then it forked, and the Indian pointed. Twenty minutes later, their little tent came into view. They docked where Jevy had bathed earlier in the day. They broke camp and moved their belongings into the village, where the chief wanted them.

Rachel had not returned.

Because she was not one of them, her hut was not in the oval. It was a hundred feet away, nearer to the edge of the forest, alone. It appeared to be smaller than any of the others, and when Jevy inquired about this, the Indian who'd been assigned to them explained that it was because she had no family. The three of them— Nate, Jevy, and their Indian—spent two hours under a tree at the edge of the village, watching the daily routine while waiting for Rachel.

The Indian had learned Portuguese from the Coopers, the missionary couple who had come before Rachel. And he had a few words of English he intermittently tried on Nate. The Coopers had been the first white people any of the Ipicas had ever seen. Mrs. Cooper died of malaria and Mr. Cooper went back to wherever he came from.

The men were hunting and fishing, he explained to his guests, and the younger ones were no doubt sneaking around seeing their girlfriends. The women had the hard work—cooking, baking, cleaning, watching the children. But labor was at a languid pace. If time moved slower south of the equator, then there was no clock at all among the Ipicas.

The doors to the huts remained open, and children ran from one to the other. Young girls braided their hair in the shade, while their mothers worked over the fires.

Cleanliness was an obsession. The dirt of the common areas was swept with straw brooms. The exteriors of the huts were tidy and neat. The women and children bathed three times a day in the river; twice for the men, and never with the women. Everybody was naked but some things were private.

Late in the afternoon, the men gathered outside the men's house, the larger of the two rectangular buildings in the center. They worked on their hair for a while—cutting and cleaning—then began to wrestle. The matchups were one on one and toe to toe, with the object being to throw the opponent to the ground. It was a rough game, but with strict rules and smiles afterward. The chief settled any disputes. The women watched from their doorways with only a passing interest, as if they were expected to. Little boys imitated their fathers.

And Nate sat on a block of wood, under a tree, watching a drama from another age, and wondering, not for the first time, where he was.

TWENTY-NINE

FEW OF THE INDIANS around Nate knew the girl's name was Ayesh. She was only a child and she lived in another village. They all knew, though, that a girl had been bitten. They gossiped about it throughout the day while they kept their own children closer at hand.

Word came during dinner that the girl had died. A messenger arrived in a rush and delivered the news to the chief, and it swept through the huts in a matter of minutes. Mothers gathered their little ones even closer.

Dinner resumed until there was movement along the main trail. Rachel was returning with Lako and the other men who'd been with her all day. As she entered the village, the eating and the chatting stopped as everyone stood and stared. They lowered their heads as she walked by their huts. She smiled at some, whispered to others, paused long enough to say something to the chief, then continued to her hut, followed by Lako, whose limp was worse.

She passed near the tree where Nate and Jevy and their Indian had spent most of the afternoon, but she didn't see them. She wasn't looking. She was tired and suffering and seemed anxious to get home.

"What do we do now?" Nate asked Jevy, who passed the question along in Portuguese.

"We wait," came the reply.

"Surprise, surprise."

Lako found them as the sun was falling behind the mountains. Jevy and the Indian went to eat leftovers. Nate followed the boy along the trail to Rachel's dwelling. She was standing in the door, drying her face with a hand towel. Her hair was wet and she had changed clothes.

"Good evening, Mr. O'Riley," she said, in the same low, slow tone that betrayed nothing.

"Hello, Rachel. Please call me Nate."

"Sit over there, Nate," she said, pointing to a short square stump remarkably similar to the one he'd been perched upon for the past six hours. It was in front of the hut, near a ring of rocks where she made her fires. He sat, his rear still numb.

"I'm sorry about the little girl," Nate said.

"She is with the Lord."

"Her poor parents aren't."

"No. They are grieving. It's very sad."

She sat in the doorway, arms folded over her knees, eyes lost in the distance. The boy stood guard under a nearby tree, almost unseen in the darkness.

"I would invite you into my home," she said. "But it would not be proper."

"No problem here."

"Only married people can be alone indoors at this time of the day. It's a custom."

"When in Rome, do like the Romans."

"Rome is very far away."

"Everything is very far away."

"Yes it is. Are you hungry?"

"Are you?"

"No. But then I don't eat much."

"I'm fine. We need to talk."

"I'm sorry about today. I'm sure you understand."

"Of course."

"I have some manioc and some juice if you'd like."

"No, really, I'm okay."

"What did you do today?"

"Oh, we met with the chief, had breakfast at his table, hiked back to the first village, got the boat, worked on it, set up our tent behind the chief's hut, then waited for you."

"The chief liked you?"

"Evidently. He wants us to stay."

"What do you think of my people?"

"They're all naked."

"They always have been."

"How long did it take to get accustomed to it?"

"I don't know. A couple of years. It gradually grows on you, like everything else. I was homesick for three years, and there are times now when I would like to drive a car, eat a pizza, and see a good movie. But you adjust."

"I can't begin to imagine."

"It's a matter of calling. I became a Christian when I was fourteen years old, and I knew then that God wanted me to be a missionary. I didn't know exactly where, but I put my faith in Him."

"He picked a helluva spot."

"I enjoy your English, but please don't swear."

"Sorry. Can we talk about Troy?" The shadows were falling fast. They were ten feet apart and could still see each other, but the blackness would soon separate them.

"Suit yourself," she said, with a weary air of resignation.

"Troy had three wives and six children, six that we knew about. You, of course, were a surprise. He didn't like the other six, but evidently was quite fond of you. He left them virtually nothing, just enough to cover their debts. Everything else was given to Rachel Lane, born out of wedlock on November 2, 1954, at Catholic Hospital in New Orleans, to a woman named Evelyn Cunningham, now deceased. That Rachel would be you."

The words fell heavy in the thick air; there were no other sounds. Her silhouette absorbed them, and, as usual, she thought before she spoke. "Troy wasn't fond of me. We hadn't seen each other in twenty years."

"That's not important. He left his fortune to you. No one had a chance to ask why because he jumped out of a window after signing his last testament. I have a copy for you."

"I don't want to see it."

"And I have some other papers which I'd like you to sign, maybe tomorrow, first thing, when we can see. Then I can be on my way."

"What kind of papers?"

"Legal stuff, all for your benefit."

"You're not concerned about my benefit." Her words were much quicker and sharper, and Nate was stung by the rebuke.

"That's not true," he replied weakly.

"Sure it is. You don't know what I want, or need, or like, or dislike. You don't know me, Nate, so how can you know what will or will not benefit me?"

"Okay, you're right. I don't know you, you don't know me. I'm here on behalf of your father's estate. It is still very hard for me to believe that I am actually sitting in the dark outside a hut, in a primitive Indian village, lost in a swamp the size of Colorado, in a third world country I've never seen before, talking to a very lovely missionary who just happens to be the richest woman in the world. Yes, you're right, I don't know what benefits you. But it is very important for you to see these papers, and to sign them."

"I'm not signing anything."

"Oh, come on."

"I have no interest in your papers."

"You haven't seen them yet."

"Tell me about them."

"They're formalities. My firm has to probate your father's estate. All of the heirs named in his will must inform the court, either in person or in writing, that they have been notified of the proceedings, and have been given the opportunity to take part. It's required by the law."

"And if I refuse?"

"Honestly, I haven't thought about that. It's so routine that everybody simply cooperates."

"So I submit myself to the court in . . . ?"

"Virginia. The probate court there takes jurisdiction over you, even though you're absent."

"I'm not sure if I like that idea."

"Fine, then hop in the boat and we'll go to Washington."

"I'm not leaving." And with that a long silence ensued, a pause made even quieter by the darkness that now engulfed them. The boy was perfectly still under the tree. The Indians were settling in their huts, with no noise except for the cry of an infant.

"I'll get us some juice," she almost whispered, then moved into the house. Nate stood and stretched his tender body, and slapped at mosquitoes. His repellent was in his tent.

There was a small light of some sort flickering through the house. Rachel held a clay pot with a flame in the center. "These are leaves from that tree over there," she explained as she sat it on the ground by the door. "We burn them to keep mosquitoes away. Sit here, close to it."

Nate did as he was told. She returned with two cups filled with a liquid he could not see. "It's *macajuno*, similar to orange juice." They sat together on the ground, almost touching, with their backs resting against the hut, the burning pot not far from their feet.

"Speak softly," she said. "Voices carry in the dark, and the Indians are trying to sleep. They are also very curious about us."

"They can't understand anything."

"Yes, but they will listen anyway."

Soap had not touched his body in days, and he was suddenly concerned with his hygiene. He took a small sip, then another.

"Do you have a family?" she asked.

"I've had a couple. Two marriages, two divorces, four children. I now live alone."

"Divorce is so easy, isn't it?"

Nate took a very small sip of the warm liquid. He had thus far managed to avoid the raging diarrhea that struck so many foreigners. Surely the murky liquid was harmless.

Two Americans alone in the wilderness. With so much to talk about, why couldn't they avoid divorce?

"Actually, they were quite painful."

"But we move on. We marry, then divorce. Find someone else, marry, then divorce. Find someone else."

"We?"

"I'm just using the pronoun. Civilized people. Educated, complicated people. The Indians never divorce."

"They haven't seen my first wife either."

"She was unpleasant?"

Nate exhaled and took another drink. Indulge her, he told himself. She's desperate for conversation with one of her own.

"I'm sorry," she said. "I'm not prying. It's not important."

"She was not a bad person, not in the early years. I worked hard, drank even harder. When I wasn't at the office, I was in a bar. She became resentful, then mean, then vicious. Things spiraled out of control and we grew to hate each other."

The little confessional was over in a flash, and it was enough for both of them. His marital debris seemed so irrelevant then and there.

"You've never married?" he asked.

"No." She took a sip. She was left-handed, and when she raised the cup her elbow touched Nate's. "Paul never married, you know."

"Paul who?"

"The Apostle Paul."

"Oh, that Paul."

"Do you read the Bible?"

"No."

"I thought I was in love once, in college. I wanted to marry him, but the Lord led me away."

"Why?"

"Because the Lord wanted me here. The boy I loved was a good Christian, but he was weak physically. He would have never survived on the mission field."

"How long will you stay here?"

"I don't plan to leave."

"So the Indians will bury you?"

"I suppose. It's not something I worry about."

"Do most World Tribes missionaries die in the field?"

"No. Most retire and go home. But then, they have families to bury them."

"You'd have lots of family and friends if you went home now. You'd be quite famous."

"That's another good reason to stay here. This is home. I don't want the money."

"Don't be foolish."

"I'm not foolish. Money means nothing to me. That should be obvious."

"You don't even know how much it is."

"I haven't asked. I went about my work today with no thought of the money. I'll do the same tomorrow, and the next day."

"It's eleven billion, give or take."

"Is that supposed to impress me?"

"It got my attention."

"But you worship money, Nate. You're part of a culture where everything is measured by money. It's a religion."

"True. But sex is pretty important too."

"Okay, money and sex. What else?"

"Fame. Everybody wants to be a celebrity."

"It's a sad culture. People live in a frenzy. They work all the time to make money to buy things to impress other people. They're measured by what they own."

"Am I included?"

"Are you?"

"I suppose."

"Then you're living without God. You're a very lonely person, Nate, I can sense it. You don't know God."

He squirmed and considered a quick defense, but the truth disarmed him. He had no weapons, no punches, no foundation to stand on. "I believe in God," he said, truthfully but weakly.

"It's easy to say that," she said, her words still slow and soft. "And I don't doubt you. But saying is one thing, living is another matter. That crippled boy under the tree over there is Lako. He's seventeen, small for his age, and always sick. His mother told me he was born early. Lako is the first to catch every disease that comes our way. I doubt if he'll live to be thirty. Lako doesn't care. Lako became a Christian several years ago, and he has the sweetest spirit of anyone here. He talks to God all day long; in fact he's probably praying right now. He has no worries, no fears. If he has a problem, he goes straight to God and leaves it there."

Nate looked at the darkness under the tree where Lako was praying, but saw nothing.

She continued, "That little Indian has nothing on this earth, but he's storing riches in heaven. He knows that when he dies he'll spend eternity in heaven with his creator. Lako is a wealthy boy."

"What about Troy?"

"I doubt if Troy believed in Christ when he died. If not, then he's burning in hell right now."

"You don't believe that."

"Hell is a very real place, Nate. Read the Bible. Right now Troy would give his eleven billion for a drink of cold water."

Nate was ill-equipped to argue theology with a missionary, and he knew it. He said nothing for a while, and she took the cue. Minutes passed as the last infant fell asleep in the village. The night was perfectly black and still, no moon or stars, the only light coming from the thin yellow flame near their feet.

Very gently, she touched him. She patted him three times on his arm, and said, "I'm sorry. I shouldn't have said that you are lonely. How would I know?"

"It's okay."

She kept her fingers on his arm, as if desperate to touch something.

"You are a good person, aren't you, Nate?"

"No, I am actually not a good person. I do lots of bad things. I am weak, and fragile, and I don't want to talk about it. I didn't come here to find God. Finding you was hard enough. I'm required by law to give you these papers."

"I'm not signing the papers and I don't want the money."

"Come on—"

"Please don't beg. My decision is final. Let's not talk about the money."

"But the money is the only reason I'm here."

She removed her fingers, but managed to lean an inch or two closer so that their knees were touching. "I'm sorry you came. You've wasted a trip."

Another gap in the conversation. He needed to relieve himself, but the thought of stepping three feet in any direction was horrifying.

Lako said something and startled Nate. He was less than ten feet away, still unseen.

"He needs to go to his hut," she said, rising to her feet. "Follow him."

Nate unfolded himself and slowly stood, joints popping and muscles reluctantly stretching. "I would like to leave tomorrow."

"Good. I'll speak to the chief."

"It won't be a problem, will it?"

"Probably not."

"I need thirty minutes of your time, to at least go over the papers and show you a copy of the will."

"We can talk. Good night."

He practically breathed down the back of Lako's neck as they shuffled along the short trail and into the village.

"Over here," Jevy whispered in the dark. He had somehow managed to secure the use of two hammocks on the small porch of the men's building. Nate asked how. Jevy promised to explain in the morning.

Lako vanished in the night.

THIRTY

F. PARR WYCLIFF was in his courtroom, running late with a docket of dull motion hearings. Josh waited in the Judge's office with the video. He paced the floor of the cluttered room, gripping his cell phone, his mind in another hemisphere. There was still no word from Nate.

Valdir's assurances seemed well rehearsed—the Pantanal is a big place, the guide is very good, the boat is large, the Indians move about, the Indians do not wish to be found, everything is fine. He would call when he heard from Nate.

Josh had considered the idea of a rescue. But getting to Corumbá seemed enough of a challenge; penetrating the Pantanal to find a missing lawyer seemed impossible. Still, he could go there and sit with Valdir until they heard something.

He was working twelve hours a day, six days a week, and the Phelan matter was about to explode. Josh barely had time for lunch, let alone a trip to Brazil.

He tried Valdir on his cell phone, but the line was busy.

Wycliff entered the office, apologizing and removing his robe at the same time. He wanted to impress a powerful lawyer like Stafford with the importance of his docket.

It was just the two of them. They watched the first part of the video without comment. It began with old Troy sitting in his wheelchair, Josh adjusting the microphone in front of him, and the three psychiatrists with their pages of questions. The exam lasted twenty-one minutes, and ended with the unanimous opinions that Mr. Phelan knew exactly what he was doing. Wycliff couldn't suppress a grin.

The room cleared. The camera directly across from Troy was kept on. He whipped out the holographic will, and signed it four minutes after the mental exam had ended.

"This is where he jumps," Josh said

The camera didn't move. It caught Troy as he suddenly pushed back from the table and stood. He disappeared off-screen as Josh and Snead and Tip Durban watched in disbelief for a second, then bolted after the old man. The footage was quite dramatic.

Five and a half minutes elapse, the camera records nothing but empty chairs and voices. Then poor Snead takes the seat where Troy sat. He's visibly shaken and on the verge of tears, but manages to tell the camera what he just witnessed. Josh and Tip Durban do the same thing.

Thirty-nine minutes of video.

"How are they going to unravel that?" Wycliff asked when it was over. It was a question with no answer. Two of the heirs—Rex and Libbigail—had already filed petitions to contest the will. Their lawyers—Hark Gettys and Wally Bright respectively—had managed to attract significant attention and get themselves interviewed and photographed by the press.

The other heirs would quickly follow suit. Josh had spoken with most of their lawyers, and the scramble for the courthouse was in process.

"Every discredited shrink in the country wants a piece of this," Josh said. "There will be lots of opinions."

"Does the suicide worry you?"

"Sure it does. But he planned everything so carefully, even his death. He knew precisely how and when he wanted to die."

"What about the other will? The thick one he signed first."

"He didn't sign it."

"But I saw him. It's on the video."

"No. He scrawled the name Mickey Mouse."

Wycliff was taking notes on a legal pad, and his hand stopped in mid-sentence. "Mickey Mouse?" he repeated.

"Here's where we are, Judge. From 1982 until 1996, I prepared eleven wills for Mr. Phelan. Some were thick, others were thin, and they disposed of his fortune in more ways than you can imagine. The law says that with each new will, the old one has to be destroyed. So I would bring the new will to his office, we'd spend two hours nitpicking our way through it, then he'd sign it. I kept the wills in my office, and I always brought the last one along. Once he signed the new one, we—Mr. Phelan and I—would feed the old one through a shredder he kept near his desk. It was a ceremony that he enjoyed immensely. He'd be happy for a few months, then one of his kids would make him mad, and he'd start talking about changing his will.

"If the heirs can prove that he lacked sufficient mental capacity when he executed the handwritten will, then there is no other will. They were all destroyed."

"In which case he died without a will," Wycliff added.

"Yes, and, as you well know, under Virginia law his estate is then divided among his children."

"Seven children. Eleven billion dollars."

"Seven that we know about. Eleven billion seems to be fairly accurate. Wouldn't you attack the will?"

A big nasty will contest was exactly what Wycliff wanted. And he knew that the lawyers, including Josh Stafford, would get even richer from the war.

But the battle needed two sides, and so far only one had surfaced. Someone had to defend Mr. Phelan's last testament.

"Any word from Rachel Lane?" he asked.

"No, but we're looking."

"Where is she?"

"We think she's a missionary somewhere in South America. But we haven't found her. We have people down there." Josh realized he was using the word "people" quite loosely.

Wycliff was gazing at the ceiling, deep in thought. "Why would he give eleven billion to an illegitimate daughter who is a missionary?"

"I can't answer that, Judge. He surprised me so many times that I became jaded."

"Sounds a little crazy, doesn't it?"

"It's strange."

"Did you know about her?"

"No."

"Could there be other heirs?"

"Anything is possible."

"Do you think he was unbalanced?"

"No. Weird, eccentric, whimsical, mean as hell. But he knew what he was doing."

"Find the girl, Josh."

"We're trying."

THE MEETING involved only the chief and Rachel. From where Nate sat, on the porch under his hammock, he could see their faces and hear their voices. The chief was bothered by something in the clouds. He would talk, then listen to Rachel, then raise his eyes slowly upward as if anticipating death from the skies. It was obvious to Nate that the chief not only listened to Rachel but also sought her advice.

Around them, the morning meal was winding down as the Ipicas prepared for another day. The hunters gathered in small groups at the men's house to sharpen their arrows and string their bows. The fishermen laid out their nets and lines. The young women began the day-long task of keeping the dirt properly swept around their huts. Their mothers were leaving for the gardens and fields near the forest.

"He thinks it's going to storm," Rachel explained when the meeting was over. "He says you can go, but he will not send a guide. It's too dangerous."

"Can we make it without a guide?" Nate asked.

"Yes," Jevy said, and Nate shot him a look that conveyed many thoughts.

"It would not be wise," she said. "The rivers run together. It's easy to get lost. Even the Ipicas have lost fishermen during the rainy season."

"When might the storm be over?" Nate asked.

"We'll have to wait and see."

Nate breathed deeply as his shoulders sagged. He was sore and tired, covered with mosquito bites, hungry, sick of his little adventure, and worried that Josh was worried. His mission so far had been a failure. He wasn't homesick because there was nothing at home. But he wanted to see Corumbá again, with its cozy little cafés and nice hotels and lazy streets. He wanted another opportunity to be alone, clean and sober and unafraid of drinking himself to death.

"I'm sorry," she said.

"I really need to get back. There are people at the office waiting to hear from me. This has already taken much longer than expected."

She listened but she really didn't care. A few worried people in a law office in D.C. didn't concern her that much.

"Can we talk?" he asked.

"I have to go the next village for the funeral of the little girl. Why don't you go with me? We will have plenty of time to talk."

Lako led the way, his right foot twisted in, so that with each step he dipped to the left, then jerked himself to the right. It was painful to watch. Rachel followed him, then Nate, laden with a cloth bag she'd brought. Jevy stayed well behind them, afraid he might overhear their conversation.

Beyond the oval ring of huts, they passed small square patches of farmland, now abandoned and overrun with scrub brush. "The Ipicas grow their food on small plots which they carve out of the jungle," she explained. Nate was close behind her, trying to keep up. She took long strides with her wiry legs. A two-mile hike through the woods was child's play. "They are hard on the soil, and after a few years it stops producing. They abandon it, nature reclaims it, and they dig farther into the jungle. In the long run, the soil returns to normal and no harm is done. Land means everything to the Indians. It is their life. Most of it has been taken away by the civilized folks."

"Sounds familiar."

"Yes, it does. We decimate their population with bloodshed and disease, and take away their land. Then we put them on reservations and can't understand why they're not happy about it."

She said hello to two naked little ladies tilling soil near the trail. "The women get the hard work," Nate observed.

"Yes. But the work is easy compared to childbirth."

"I'd rather watch them work."

The air was humid, but free of the smoke that hung eternally over the village. When they entered the woods, Nate was already sweating.

"So tell me about yourself, Nate," she said over her shoulder. "Where were you born?"

"This could take a while."

"Just hit the high points."

"There are more low ones."

"Come on, Nate. You wanted to talk, let's talk. The hike takes half an hour."

"I was born in Baltimore, oldest of two sons, parents divorced when I was fifteen, high school at St. Paul, college at Hopkins, law school at Georgetown, then I never left D.C."

"Was it a happy childhood?"

"I suppose. Lots of sports. My father worked for National Brewery for thirty years, and he always had tickets to the Colts and

Orioles. Baltimore is a great city. Are we going to talk about your childhood?"

"If you like. It wasn't very happy."

What a surprise, thought Nate. This poor woman has never had a chance at happiness.

"Did you want to be a lawyer when you grew up?"

"Of course not. No kid in his right mind wants to be a lawyer. I was going to play for the Colts or the Orioles, maybe both."

"Did you go to church?"

"Sure. Every Christmas and Easter."

The trail almost disappeared and they were wading through stiff weeds. Nate walked while watching her boots, and when he couldn't see them, he said, "This snake that killed the girl, what kind is it?"

"It's called a *bima*, but don't worry."

"Why shouldn't I worry?"

"Because you're wearing boots. It's a small snake that bites below the ankle."

"The big one will find me."

"Relax."

"What about Lako up there? He's never worn shoes."

"Yes, but he sees everything."

"I take it the *bima* is quite deadly."

"It can be, but there is an antivenin. I've actually had it here before, and if I'd had it yesterday, the little girl wouldn't have died."

"Then if you had lots of money you could buy lots of antivenin. You could stock your shelves with all the medicines you need. You could buy a nice little outboard to take you to Corumbá and back. You could build a clinic and a church and a school, and spread the Gospel all over the Pantanal."

She stopped and turned abruptly. They were face to face. "I've done nothing to earn the money, and I didn't know the man who made it. Please don't mention it again." Her words were firm, but her face gave no hint of frustration.

"Give it away. Give it all to charity."

"It's not mine to give."

"It'll be squandered. Millions will go to the lawyers, and what's left will be divided among your siblings. And, believe me, you don't want that. You have no idea of the misery and heartache these people will cause if they get the money. What they don't waste they'll pass down to their kids, and the Phelan money will pollute the next generation."

She took his wrist and squeezed it. Very slowly she said, "I don't care. I'll pray for them."

Then she turned and started walking again. Lako was far ahead. Jevy could barely be seen behind them. They hiked in silence through a field near a stream, then entered a patch of tall thick trees. The limbs and branches were woven together to form a dark canopy. The air was suddenly cool.

"Let's take a break," she said. The stream curved through the woods and the trail crossed it in a bed of blue and orange rocks. She knelt by the water and splashed her face.

"You can drink this," she said. "It comes from the mountains."

Nate squatted near her and felt the water. It was cold and clear.

"This is my favorite spot," she said. "I come here almost every day to bathe, to pray, to meditate."

"It's hard to believe we're in the Pantanal. It's much too cool."

"We're on the very edge of it. The mountains of Bolivia are not far away. The Pantanal begins somewhere near here and stretches east forever."

"I know. We flew over it trying to find you."

"Oh you did?"

"Yes, it was a short flight, but I had a good view of the Pantanal."

"And you didn't find me?"

"No. We flew into a storm and had to make an emergency landing. I got lucky and walked away. I'll never get near another small airplane."

"There's no place to land around here."

They took off their socks and boots and dipped their feet into the stream. They sat on the rocks and listened as the water trickled by. They were alone; neither Lako nor Jevy were within eyesight.

"When I was a little girl in Montana, we lived in a small town where my father, my adoptive father, was a minister. Not far from the edge of town was a little creek, about the size of this. And there was a place, under some tall trees, similar to these, where I would go and put my feet in the water and sit for hours."

"Were you hiding?"

"Sometimes."

"Are you hiding now?"

"No."

"I think you are."

"No, you are wrong. I have perfect peace, Nate. I surrendered my will to Christ many years ago, and I follow wherever He leads. You think I'm lonely—you're wrong. He is with me every step of the way. He knows my thoughts, my needs, and He takes away my fears and worries. I am completely and perfectly at peace in this world."

"I've never heard that before."

"You said last night that you are weak and fragile. What does that mean?"

Confession was good for the soul, Sergio had told him during therapy. If she wanted to know, then he would try and shock her with the truth.

"I'm an alcoholic," he said, almost proudly, the way he'd been trained to admit it during rehab. "I've hit the bottom four times in the past ten years, and I came out of detox to make this trip. I cannot say for sure that I will never drink again. I've kicked cocaine three times, and I think, though I'm not certain, that I will never touch the stuff again. I filed for bankruptcy four months ago, while in rehab. I'm currently under indictment for income tax evasion, and stand a fifty-fifty chance of going to jail and losing my license to practice law. You know about the two divorces. Both women dislike me, and they've poisoned my children. I've done a fine job of wrecking my life."

There was no noticeable pleasure or relief in laying himself bare. She took it without flinching. "Anything else?" she asked.

"Oh yes. I've tried to kill myself at least twice—twice that I can recall. Once last August that landed me in rehab. Then just a few days ago in Corumbá. I think it was Christmas night."

"In Corumbá?"

"Yes, in my hotel room. I almost drank myself to death with cheap vodka."

"You poor man."

"I'm sick, okay. I have a disease. I've admitted it many times to many counselors."

"Have you ever confessed it to God?"

"I'm sure He knows."

"I'm sure He does. But He won't help unless you ask. He is omnipotent, but you have to go to Him, in prayer, in the spirit of forgiveness."

"What happens?"

"Your sins will be forgiven. Your slate will be wiped clean. Your addictions will be taken away. The Lord will forgive all of your transgressions, and you will become a new believer in Christ."

"What about the IRS?"

"That won't go away, but you'll have the strength to deal with it. Through prayer you can overcome any adversity."

Nate had been preached at before. He had surrendered to Higher Powers so many times he could almost deliver the sermons. He had been counseled by ministers and therapists and gurus and shrinks of every stripe and variety. Once, during a three-year stretch of sobriety, he actually worked as a counselor for AA, teaching the twelve-point recovery plan to other alcoholics in the basement of an old church in Alexandria. Then he crashed.

Why shouldn't she try to save him? Wasn't it her calling in life to convert the lost?

"I don't know how to pray," he said.

She took his hand and squeezed it firmly. "Close your eyes, Nate. Repeat after me: Dear God, Forgive me of my sins, and help me to forgive those who have sinned against me." Nate mumbled the words and squeezed her hand even harder. It sounded vaguely similar to the Lord's Prayer. "Give me strength to overcome temptations, and addictions, and the trials ahead." Nate kept mumbling, kept repeating her words, but the little ritual was confusing. Prayer was easy for Rachel because she did so much of it. For him, it was a strange rite.

"Amen," she said. They opened their eyes but kept their hands together. They listened to the water as it rushed gently over the rocks. There was an odd sensation as his burdens seemed to be lifted; his shoulders felt lighter, his head clearer, his soul was less troubled. But Nate carried so much baggage he wasn't certain which loads had been taken away and which remained.

He was still frightened by the real world. It was easy to be brave deep in the Pantanal where the temptations were few, but he knew what awaited him at home.

"Your sins are forgiven, Nate," she said.

"Which ones? There are so many."

"All of them."

"It's too easy. There's a lot of wreckage back there."

"We'll pray again tonight."

"It will take more for me than most folks."

"Trust me, Nate. And trust God. He's seen worse."

"I trust you. It's God who's got me worried."

She squeezed his hand even tighter, and for a long still moment they watched the water bubble around them. Finally, she said, "We need to go." But they didn't move.

"I've been thinking about this burial, this little girl," Nate said.

"What about it?"

"Will we see her body?"

"I suppose. It will be hard to miss."

"Then I'd rather not. Jevy and I will go back to the village and wait."

"Are you sure, Nate? We could talk for hours."

"I don't want to see a dead child."

"Very well. I understand."

He helped her to her feet, though she certainly didn't need assistance. They held hands until she reached for her boots. As usual, Lako materialized from nowhere, and they were off, soon lost in the dark woods.

He found Jevy asleep under a tree. They picked their way along the trail, watching for snakes with every step, and slowly returned to the village.

THIRTY-ONE

THE CHIEF wasn't much of a weatherman. The storm never materialized. It rained twice during the day as Nate and Jevy fought the tedium by napping in their borrowed hammocks. The showers were brief, and after each the sun returned to bake the dampened soil and raise the humidity. Even in the shade, moving only when necessary, the two men sweltered in the heat.

They watched the Indians whenever there was activity, but the work and play ebbed and flowed with the heat. When the sun was out in full force the Ipicas retreated to their huts or to the shade trees behind them. During the brief showers the children played in the rain. When the sun was blocked by clouds, the women ventured out to do their chores and go to the river.

After a week in the Pantanal, Nate was numbed by the listless pace of life. Each day appeared to be an exact copy of the one before. Nothing had changed in centuries.

Rachel returned in mid-afternoon. She and Lako went straight to the chief and reported on events in the other village. She spoke to Nate and Jevy. She was tired and wanted a quick nap before they discussed business.

What's another hour to be killed? thought Nate. He watched her walk away. She was lean and tough and could probably run marathons.

"What are you looking at?" Jevy asked with a grin.

"Nothing."

"How old is she?"

"Forty-two."

"How old are you?"

"Forty-eight."

"Has she been married?"

"No."

"Do you think she's ever been with a man?"

"Why don't you ask her?"

"Do you?"

"I really don't care."

They fell asleep again, sleeping because there was nothing else to do. In a couple of hours the wrestling would start, then dinner, then darkness. Nate dreamed of the *Santa Loura*, a humble vessel at best, but with each passing hour the boat grew finer. In his dreams it was fast becoming a sleek, elegant yacht.

When the men began to gather to fix their hair and prepare for their games, Nate and Jevy eased away. One of the larger Ipicas yelled at them, and with teeth flashing issued what seemed to be an invitation to come wrestle. Nate scooted away even faster. He had a sudden image of himself getting flung about the village by some squatty little warrior, genitals flying everywhere. Jevy wanted no part of the action either. Rachel rescued them.

She and Nate left the huts and walked toward the river, to their old spot on the narrow bench under the trees. They sat close, their knees touching again.

"You were wise not to go," she said. Her voice was tired. The nap had failed to revive her.

"Why?"

"Every village has a doctor. He's called a *shalyun*, and he cooks herbs and roots for his remedies. He also calls forth spirits to help with all sorts of problems."

"Ah, the old medicine man."

"Something like that. More of a witch doctor. There are lots of spirits in the Indian world, and the *shalyun* supposedly directs their traffic. Anyway, the *shalyun* are my natural enemies. I am a threat to their religion. They are always on the attack. They persecute the Christian believers. They prey on new converts. They want me to leave and so they are always lobbying the chiefs to run me off. It's a daily struggle. In the last village down the river, I had a small school where I taught reading and writing. It was for the believers, but it was also open to anyone. A year ago we had a bout of malaria and three people died. The local *shalyun* convinced the chief down there that the disease was a punishment on the village because of my school. It's now closed."

Nate just listened. Her courage, already admirable, was reaching new heights. The heat and languid pace of life had lured him into the belief that all was at peace among the Ipicas. No visitor would suspect a war was raging over souls.

"The parents of Ayesh, the girl who died, are Christians, and very strong in their faith. The *shalyun* spread the word that he could've saved the girl, but the parents didn't call on him. They, of course, wanted me to treat her. The *bima* snake has been around forever, and there are home remedies that the *shalyun* brew up. I've never seen one work. After she died yesterday, and after I left, the *shalyun* called some spirits forth and held a ceremony in the center of the village. He blamed me for her death. And he blamed God."

Her words were pouring forth, faster than normal, as if she wanted to hurry and use her English one more time.

"During the burial today, the *shalyun* and a few troublemakers began chanting and dancing nearby. The poor parents were completely overcome with grief and humiliation. I couldn't finish the service." Her voice cracked, just slightly, and she bit her lip.

Nate patted her arm. "It's okay. It's over."

Crying was not something she could do in front of the Indians.

She had to be strong and stoic, filled with faith and courage under all circumstances. But she could cry with Nate, and he would understand. He expected it.

She wiped her eyes and slowly collected her emotions. "I'm sorry," she said.

"It's okay," Nate said again, anxious to help. The tears of a woman melted the facade of coolness, whether in a bar or sitting by a river.

There was hollering in the village. The wrestling had started. Nate had a quick thought about Jevy. Surely he had not succumbed to the temptation of playing with the boys.

"I think you should go now," she said abruptly, breaking the silence. Her emotions were under control, her voice was back to normal.

"What?"

"Yes, now. Very soon."

"I'm anxious to go, but what's the rush? It'll be dark in three hours."

"There is reason to worry."

"I'm listening."

"I think I saw a case of malaria in the other village today. Mosquitoes carry it and it spreads quickly."

Nate began scratching and was ready to hop in the boat, then he remembered his pills. "I'm safe. I'm taking chloro-something."

"Chloroquine?"

"That's it."

"When did you start?"

"Two days before I left the States."

"Where are the pills now?"

"I left them on the big boat."

She shook her head with disapproval. "You're supposed to take them before, during, and after the trip." Her tone was medically authoritative, as if death could be imminent.

"And what about Jevy?" she asked. "Is he taking the pills?"

"He was in the army. I'm sure he's okay."

"I'm not going to argue, Nate. I've already spoken to the chief. He sent two fishermen out this morning before sunrise. The flooded waters are tricky for the first two hours, then the navigation becomes familiar. He will provide three guides in two canoes, and I'll send Lako to handle the language. Once you're on the Xeco River, it's a straight shot to the Paraguay."

"How far away is that?"

"The Xeco is about four hours away. The Paraguay, six. And you're going with the current."

"Whatever. You seem to have everything planned."

"Trust me, Nate. I've had malaria twice, and you don't want it. The second time almost killed me."

It had never occurred to Nate that she might die. The Phelan estate would be chaotic enough with Rachel hiding in the jungles and rejecting the paperwork. If she died, it would take years to settle things.

And he admired her greatly. She was everything he wasn't—strong and brave, grounded in faith, happy with simplicity, certain of her place in the world and the hereafter. "Don't die, Rachel," he said.

"Death is not something I fear. For a Christian, death is a reward. But do pray for me, Nate."

"I'm going to pray more, I promise."

"You're a good man. You have a good heart and a good mind. You just need some help."

"I know. I'm not very strong."

He had the papers in a folded envelope in his pocket. He pulled them out. "Can we at least discuss these?"

"Yes, but only as a favor to you. I figure you've come this far, the least I can do is have our little law chat."

"Thank you." He handed her the first sheet, a copy of Troy's one-page will. She read it slowly, struggling with parts of the handwriting. When she finished, she asked, "Is this a legal will?"

"So far."

"But it's so primitive."

"Handwritten wills are valid. Sorry, it's the law."

She read it again. Nate noticed the shadows falling along the tree line. He had become afraid of the dark, both on land and on water. He was anxious to leave.

"Troy didn't care for his other offspring, did he?" she said with amusement.

"You wouldn't either. But then I doubt if he was much of a father."

"I remember the day my mother told me about him. I was seventeen. It was late summer. My father had just died of cancer, and life was pretty bleak. Troy had somehow found me and was bugging my mother to visit. She told me the truth about my biological parents, and it meant nothing to me. I didn't care about those people. I'd never known them, and had no desire to meet them. I found out later that my birth mother killed herself. How do you figure that, Nate? Both of my real parents killed themselves. Is there something in my genes?"

"No. You're much stronger than they were."

"I welcome death."

"Don't say that. When did you meet Troy?"

"A year went by. He and my mother became phone pals. She became convinced his motives were good, and so one day he came to our house. We had cake and tea, then he left. He sent money for college. He began pressuring me to take a job with one of his companies. He started acting like a father, and I grew to dislike him. Then my mother died, and the world caved in around me. I changed my name and went to med school. I prayed for Troy over the years, the same way I pray for all the lost people I know. I assumed he had forgotten about me."

"Evidently not," Nate said. A black mosquito landed on his thigh, and he slapped with enough violence to crack lumber. If it carried malaria, the insect would spread it no further. A red outline of a handprint appeared on his flesh.

He gave her the waiver and the acknowledgment. She read them carefully and said, "I'm not signing anything. I don't want the money."

"Just keep them, okay. Pray over them."

"Are you making fun of me?"

"No. I just don't know what to do next."

"I can't help you. But I will ask one favor."

"Sure. Anything."

"Don't tell anyone where I am. I beg you, Nate. Please protect my privacy."

"I promise. But you have to be realistic."

"What do you mean?"

"The story is irresistible. If you take the money, then you're probably the richest woman in the world. If you decline it, then the story is even more compelling."

"Who cares?"

"Bless your heart. You're protected from the media. We have nonstop news now, twenty-four hours of endless coverage of everything. Hours and hours of news programs, news magazines, talking heads, late-breaking stories. It's all junk. No story is too small to be tracked down and sensationalized."

"But how can they find me?"

"That's a good question. We got lucky because Troy had picked up your trail. To our knowledge, though, he told no one."

"Then I'm safe, right? You can't tell. The lawyers in your firm can't tell."

"That's very true."

"And you were lost when you arrived here, right?"

"Very lost."

"You have to protect me, Nate. This is my home. These are my people. I don't want to run again."

HUMBLE MISSIONARY IN JUNGLE SAYS NO TO ELEVEN-BILLION-DOLLAR FORTUNE

What a headline. The vultures would invade the Pantanal with helicopters and amphibious landing craft to get the story. Nate felt sorry for her.

"I'll do what I can," he said.

"Do I have your word?"

"Yes, I promise."

The send-off party was led by the chief himself, followed by his wife, then a dozen men, then Jevy followed by at least ten more men. They snaked along the trail, headed for the river. "It's time to go," she said.

"I guess so. You're sure we'll be safe in the dark."

"Yes. The chief is sending his best fishermen. God will protect you. Say your prayers."

"I will."

"I'll pray for you every day, Nate. You're a good person with a good heart. You're worth saving."

"Thank you. You wanna get married?"

"I can't."

"Sure you can. I'll take care of the money, you take care of the Indians. We'll get a bigger hut and throw away our clothes."

They both laughed, and they were still smiling when the chief got to them. Nate stood to say hello or good-bye or something, and for a second his vision was gone. A surge of dizziness rolled from his chest through his head. He caught himself, cleared his vision, and glanced at Rachel to see if she had noticed.

She had not. His eyelids began to ache. The joints at his elbows were throbbing.

There was a flourish of grunts in Ipica, and everyone stepped to the river. Food was placed in Jevy's boat and in the two narrow canoes the guides and Lako would use. Nate thanked Rachel, who in turn thanked the chief, and when all the right farewells were finished it was time to go. Standing ankle-deep in water, Nate hugged her gently, patting her on the back and saying, "Thanks."

"Thanks for what?"

"Oh, I don't know. Thanks for creating a fortune in legal fees."

She smiled and said, "I like you, Nate, but I couldn't care less about the money and the lawyers."

"I like you too."

"Please don't come back."

"Don't worry."

Everyone was waiting. The fishermen were already on the river. Jevy had his paddle, anxious to shove off.

Nate took a step into the boat, and said, "We could honeymoon in Corumbá."

"Good-bye, Nate. Just tell your people you never found me."

"I will. So long." He pushed away, and swung himself into the boat, where he sat down hard, his head spinning again. As they drifted away, he waved at Rachel and the Indians, but the figures were blurred together.

Pushed by the current, the canoes glided over the water, the Indians paddling in perfect tandem. They wasted no effort and no time. They were in a hurry. The motor started on the third pull, and they soon caught the canoes. When Jevy throttled down, the motor sputtered but did not quit. At the first turn in the river, Nate glanced over his shoulder. Rachel and the Indians hadn't moved.

He was sweating. With clouds shielding the sun, and with a nice breeze in his face, Nate realized that he was sweating. His arms and legs were wet. He rubbed his neck and forehead and looked at the dampness on his fingers. Instead of praying as he had promised, he mumbled, "Oh shit. I'm sick."

The fever was low, but coming fast. The breeze chilled him. He huddled on his seat and looked for something else to wear. Jevy noticed him, and after a few minutes said, "Nate, are you okay?"

He shook his head no, and pain shot from his eyes to his spine. He wiped drainage from his nose.

After two bends in the river, the trees grew thin and the ground was lower. The river widened, then spilled into a flooded lake with three decaying trees in the center of it. Nate knew they had not passed the trees on the way in. They were taking a different route out. Without the current, the canoes slowed a little but still cut through the water with amazing quickness. The guides did not study the lake. They knew exactly where they were going.

"Jevy, I think I have malaria," Nate said. His voice was hoarse; his throat already sore.

"How do you know?" Jevy lowered the throttle for a second.

"Rachel warned me. She saw it in the other village yesterday. That's why we left when we did."

"Do you have a fever?"

"Yes, and I'm having trouble seeing things."

Jevy stopped the boat and yelled at the Indians, who were almost out of sight. He moved empty gas tanks and the remnants of their supplies, then quickly unrolled the tent. "You will get chills," he said as he worked. The boat rocked back and forth as he moved around.

"Have you had malaria?"

"No. But most of my friends have died from it."

"What!"

"Bad joke. It doesn't kill many, but you will be very sick."

Moving gently, keeping his head as still as possible, Nate crawled behind his seat and lay in the center of the boat. A bedroll was his pillow. Jevy spread the lightweight tent over him and anchored it with two empty gas tanks.

The Indians were beside them, curious about what was happening. Lako inquired in Portuguese. Nate heard the word malaria spoken by Jevy, and it caused mumblings in Ipica. Then they were off.

The boat seemed faster. Maybe it was because Nate was lying on the bottom of it, feeling it slice through the water. An occasional branch or limb that Jevy didn't see jolted Nate, but he didn't care. His head ached and throbbed like no hangover he'd ever experienced. His muscles and joints hurt too much to move. And he was growing colder. The chills were starting.

There was a low rumble in the distance. Nate thought it might be thunder. Wonderful, he thought. That's precisely what we need now.

THE RAINS stayed away. The river turned once to the west, and Jevy saw the orange and yellow remnants of a sunset. Then it turned back to the east, to the approaching darkness across the Pantanal. Twice the canoes slowed as the Ipicas conferred about which fork to take. Jevy kept their boat a hundred feet or so behind, but as darkness settled in he followed closer. He couldn't see Nate buried under the tent, but he knew his friend was suffering. Jevy actually once knew a man who died from malaria.

Two hours into the journey, the guides led them through a bewildering series of narrow streams and quiet lagoons, and when they emerged into a broader river the canoes slowed for a moment. The Indians needed a rest. Lako called to Jevy and explained that they were now safe, that they had just gone through the difficult part and the rest should be easy. The Xeco was about two hours away, and it led straight to the Paraguay.

Can we make it alone? Jevy asked. No, came the reply. There were still forks to deal with, plus the Indians knew a spot on the Xeco that would not be flooded. There they would sleep.

How is the American? Lako asked. Not well, Jevy replied.

The American heard their voices, and he knew the boat was not moving. The fever burned him from head to toe. His flesh and clothes were soaked, and the aluminum under him was wet as well. His eyes were swollen shut, his mouth so dry it hurt to open it. He heard Jevy asking him something in English, but he could not answer. Consciousness came and went.

In the darkness, the canoes moved more slowly. Jevy trailed closer, at times using his flashlight to help the guides study the forks and tributaries. At half-throttle, his unsteady outboard settled into a constant whine. They stopped just once, to eat a loaf of bread and drink juice, and to relieve themselves. They latched the three craft together and floated for ten minutes.

Lako was concerned about the American. What shall I tell the missionary about him? he asked Jevy. Tell her he has malaria.

Lightning in the distance ended their brief dinner and rest. The Indians set off again, paddling as hard as ever. They had not seen solid ground in hours. There was no place to land and ride out a storm.

The motor finally quit. Jevy switched to his last full tank, and started it again. At half-throttle, he had enough fuel for about six hours, long enough to find the Paraguay. There would be traffic there, and houses, and at some point, the *Santa Loura*. He knew the exact spot where the Xeco emptied into the Paraguay. Going downriver, they should find Welly by dawn.

The lightning followed, but did not catch them. Each flash made the guides work harder. But they began to tire. At one point, Lako grabbed a side of the johnboat, another Ipica held the other, Jevy held the flashlight above his head, and they plowed forward like a barge.

The trees and brush grew thicker and the river widened. There was solid ground on both sides. The Indians were chattering more, and when they entered the Xeco the paddling stopped. They were exhausted and ready to stop. It's three hours past their bedtime, Jevy thought. They found their spot and landed.

Lako explained that he had been the missionary's assistant for many years. He'd seen lots of malaria; he'd even had it himself three times. He eased the tent off Nate's head and chest, and touched his forehead. A very high fever, he told Jevy, who was holding the flashlight, standing in mud, and anxious to get back in the boat.

There's nothing you can do, he said as he completed his diagnosis. The fever will go away, then there will be another attack in forty-eight hours. He was disturbed by the swollen eyes, something he'd never seen before with malaria.

The oldest guide began talking to Lako and pointing to the dark river. The translation to Jevy was to keep it in the center, ignore the small divides, especially the ones to the left, and in two hours he should find the Paraguay. Jevy thanked them profusely, and took off.

The fever didn't die. An hour later, Jevy checked Nate and his face was still burning. He was curled into a fetal position, semiconscious and mumbling incoherently. Jevy forced water into his mouth, then poured the rest over his face.

The Xeco was wide and easy to navigate. They passed a house, the first they'd seen in a month, it seemed. Like a lighthouse beckoning a wayward ship, the moon broke through the clouds and lit the waters in front of them.

"Can you hear me, Nate?" Jevy said, not loud enough to be heard. "Our luck is changing."

He followed the moon to the Paraguay.

THIRTY-TWO

THE BOAT was a *chalana*, a floating shoe box, thirty feet long, eight feet wide, flat-bottomed, and used to haul cargo through the Pantanal. Jevy had captained dozens of them. He saw the light coming around a bend, and when he heard the knock of the diesel, he knew precisely what kind of boat it was.

And he knew the captain, who was sleeping on his bunk when the deckhand stopped the *chalana*. It was almost 3 A.M. Jevy tied his johnboat to the bow and hopped on board. They fed him two bananas while he gave them a quick summary of what he was doing. The deckhand brought sweet coffee. They were headed north to Porto Indio, to the army base there to trade with the soldiers. They could spare five gallons of gas. Jevy promised to pay them back in Corumbá. No problem. Everybody helps on the river.

More coffee, and some sugared wafers. Then he asked about the *Santa Loura*, and Welly. "It's at the mouth of the Cabixa," Jevy told them, "docked where the old pier used to be," he said.

They shook their heads. "It wasn't there," the captain said. The deckhand agreed. They knew the *Santa Loura*, and they had not seen it. It would have been impossible to miss.

"It has to be there," Jevy said.

"No. We passed the Cabixa at noon yesterday. There was no sign of the *Santa Loura*."

Perhaps Welly had taken it a few miles into the Cabixa to look for them. He had to be worried sick. Jevy would forgive him for moving the *Santa Loura*, but not before a tongue lashing.

The boat would be there, he was certain. He sipped more coffee and told them about Nate and the malaria. There were fresh rumors in Corumbá about waves of the disease sweeping through the Pantanal. Jevy had heard these all of his life.

They filled a tank from a barrel on board the *chalana*. As a general rule, river traffic during the rainy season was three times faster downstream than up. A johnboat with a good motor should reach the Cabixa in four hours, the trading post in ten, Corumbá in eighteen. The *Santa Loura*, if and when they found it, would take longer, but at least they would have hammocks and food.

Jevy's plan was to stop and rest briefly on the *Santa Loura*. He wanted to get Nate into a bed, and he would use the SatFone to call Corumbá and talk to Valdir. Valdir in turn could find a good doctor who would know what to do when they reached home.

The captain gave him another box of wafers and a paper cup of coffee. Jevy promised to find them in Corumbá next week. He thanked them and unhitched his boat. Nate was alive, but motionless. The fever had not broken.

The coffee quickened Jevy's pulse and kept him awake. He played with the throttle, raising it until the engine began to sputter, then backing down before it died. As the darkness faded, a heavy mist fell upon the river.

He arrived at the mouth of the Cabixa an hour after dawn. The *Santa Loura* was not there. Jevy docked at the old pier and went to find the owner of the only nearby house. He was in his stable, milking a cow. He remembered Jevy, and told the story of the storm that took away the boat. The worst storm ever. It happened in the middle of the night, and he didn't see much. The wind was so fierce that he, his wife, and his child hid under a bed.

"Where did it sink?" Jevy asked.

"I don't know."

"What about the boy?"

"Welly? I don't know."

"Haven't you talked to anyone else? Has anyone seen the boy?"

No one. He had not spoken with anyone off the river since Welly disappeared in the storm. He was very sad about everything, and for good measure offered the opinion that Welly was probably dead.

Nate was not. The fever dipped significantly, and when he awoke he was cold and thirsty. He opened his eyes with his fingers, and saw only the water around him, the brush on the bank, and the farmhouse.

"Jevy," he said, his throat raw, his voice weak. He sat up and worked on his eyes for a few minutes. Nothing focused. Jevy did not answer. Every part of his body ached—muscles, joints, the blood pumping through his brain. There was a hot rash on his neck and chest, and he scratched it until the skin broke. He was sickened by his own odor.

The farmer and his wife followed Jevy back to the boat. They didn't have a drop of gasoline, and this irritated their visitor.

"How are you, Nate?" he asked, stepping into the boat.

"I'm dying." He exhaled the words.

Jevy felt his forehead, then gently touched the rash. "Your fever's down."

"Where are we?"

"We're at the Cabixa. Welly is not here. The boat sank in a storm."

"Our luck continues," Nate said, then grimaced as pain shot through his head. "Where is Welly?"

"I don't know. Can you make it to Corumbá?"

"I'd rather just go ahead and die."

"Lie down, Nate."

They left the bank with the farmer and his wife standing ankle-deep in mud, waving but getting ignored.

Nate sat for a while. The wind felt good against his face. Before long, though, he was cold again. A chill shuttered through his chest, and he lowered himself gently under the tent. He tried to pray for Welly, but thoughts lasted only for seconds. He simply couldn't believe he'd caught malaria.

HARK PLANNED the brunch in great detail. It was in a private dining room of the Hay-Adams Hotel. There were oysters and eggs, caviar and salmon, champagne and mimosas. By eleven they were all there, dressed casually, and laying into the mimosas.

He had assured them the meeting was of the utmost importance. It had to be kept confidential. He'd found the one witness who could win the case for them.

Only the lawyers for the Phelan children were invited. The Phelan wives had not yet contested the will, and there seemed little enthusiasm on their part for getting involved. Their legal position was very weak. Judge Wycliff had hinted off the record to one of their lawyers that he would not look favorably upon frivolous suits by the ex-wives.

Frivolous or not, the six children had wasted no time contesting the will. All six had rushed into the fray, all with the same basic claim—that Troy Phelan lacked mental capacity when he signed his last testament.

A maximum of two lawyers per heir were allowed at the meeting, and preferably one, if possible. Hark was alone, representing Rex. Wally Bright was alone, representing Libbigail. Yancy was the only lawyer Ramble knew. Grit was there for Mary Ross. Madam Langhorne, the former professor of law, was there for Geena and Cody. Troy Junior had hired and fired three firms since his father's death. His latest lawyers were from a firm of four hundred. Their names were Hemba and Hamilton, and they introduced themselves to the loose-knit confederation.

Hark closed the door and addressed the group. He gave a short biography of Malcolm Snead, a man he'd been meeting with almost daily. "He was with Mr. Phelan for thirty years," he said gravely.

"Maybe he helped him write his last will. Maybe he is prepared to say the old man was completely nuts at the time."

The lawyers were surprised by the news. Hark watched their happy faces for a moment, then said, "Or, maybe he is prepared to say he knew nothing of the handwritten will and that Mr. Phelan was perfectly rational and lucid the day he died."

"How much does he want?" asked Wally Bright, cutting to the chase.

"Five million dollars. Ten percent now, the rest upon settlement."

Snead's fee did not faze the lawyers. There was so much at stake. In fact, his greed seemed rather modest.

"Our clients, of course, do not have the money," Hark said. "So if we want to purchase his testimony, then it's up to us. For about eighty-five thousand per heir, we can sign a contract with Mr. Snead. I'm convinced he will deliver testimony that will either win the case or force a settlement."

The range of wealth in the room was broad. Wally Bright's office account was overdrawn. He owed back taxes. At the other end of the spectrum, the firm where Hemba and Hamilton worked had partners earning more than a million bucks a year.

"Are you suggesting we pay a lying witness?" Hamilton asked.

"We don't know if he's lying," Hark responded. He could anticipate every question. "No one knows. He was alone with Mr. Phelan. There are no witnesses. The truth will be whatever Mr. Snead wants it to be."

"This sounds shady," Hemba added.

"You have a better idea?" Grit growled. He was into his fourth mimosa.

Hemba and Hamilton were big-firm lawyers, unaccustomed to the dirt and grime from the streets. Not that they or their ilk were beyond corruption, but their clients were rich corporations that used lobbyists for legal bribery to land fat government contracts and hid money in Swiss accounts for foreign despots, all with the help of their trusty lawyers. But because they were big-firm lawyers they quite naturally looked down upon the type of unethical behavior being suggested by Hark, and condoned by Grit and Bright and the other ham-and-eggers.

"I'm not sure our client will agree to this," Hamilton said.

"Your client will jump at it," Hark said. It was almost humorous to drape ethics over TJ Phelan. "We know him better than you. The question is whether you're willing to do it."

"Are you suggesting we, the lawyers, front the initial five hundred thousand?" Hemba asked, his tone one of contempt.

"Exactly," Hark said.

"Then our firm would never go along with such a scheme."

"Then your firm is about to be replaced," Grit chimed in. "Keep in mind, you're the fourth bunch in a month."

In fact, Troy Junior had already threatened to fire them. They grew quiet and listened. Hark had the floor.

"To avoid the embarrassment of asking each of us to cough up the cash, I have found a bank willing to loan five hundred thousand dollars for a year. All we need is six signatures on the loan. I've already signed."

"I'll sign the damned thing," Bright said in a burst of machismo. He was fearless because he had nothing to lose.

"Let me get this straight," Yancy said. "We pay Snead the money first, then he talks. Right?"

"Right."

"Shouldn't we hear his version first?"

"His version needs some work. That's the beauty of the deal. Once we pay him, he's ours. We get to shape his testimony, to structure it to suit ourselves. Keep in mind, there are no other witnesses, maybe with the exception of a secretary."

"How much does she cost?" asked Grit.

"She's free. She's included in Snead's package."

How many times in a career would you get the chance to rake off a percentage of the country's tenth largest fortune? The lawyers did the math. A little risk here, a gold mine later.

Madam Langhorne surprised them by saying, "I'll recommend to my firm that we take the deal. But this has to be a graveyard secret."

"Graveyard," repeated Yancy. "We could all be disbarred, probably indicted. Suborning perjury is a felony."

"You're missing the point," Grit said. "There can be no perjury. The truth is defined by Snead and Snead alone. If he says he helped write the will, and at the time the old man was nuts, then who in the world can dispute it? It's a brilliant deal. I'll sign."

"That makes four of us," Hark said.

"I'll sign," Yancy said.

Hemba and Hamilton were squirming. "We'll have to discuss it with our firm," Hamilton said.

"Do we have to remind you boys that all of this is confidential?" Bright said. It was comical, the street fighter from night school chiding the law review editors on ethics.

"No," Hemba said. "You don't have to remind us."

Hark would call Rex, tell him about the deal, and Rex would then call his brother TJ and inform him that his new lawyers were screwing up the deal. Hemba and Hamilton would be history within forty-eight hours.

"Move quickly," Hark warned them. "Mr. Snead claims to be broke, and is perfectly willing to cut a deal with the other side."

"Speaking of which," Langhorne said, "do we know any more about who's on the other side? We're all contesting the will. Someone has to be its proponent. Where is Rachel Lane?"

"Evidently she's hiding," Hark said. "Josh has assured me that they know where she is, that they are in contact with her, and that she will hire lawyers to protect her interests."

"For eleven billion, I would hope so," added Grit.

They pondered the eleven billion for a moment, each dividing it by various magnitudes of the number six, then applying their own personal percentages. Five million for Snead seemed such a reasonable sum.

□ □ □ □

JEVY AND NATE limped to the trading post early in the afternoon. The outboard was missing badly and low on gas. Fernando, the owner of the store, was in a hammock on the porch, trying to avoid the scorching sun. He was an old man, a rugged veteran of the river who'd known Jevy's father.

Both men helped Nate from the boat. He was burning with fever again. His legs were numb and weak, and the three of them inched carefully along the narrow pier and up the steps to the porch. When they folded him into the hammock, Jevy delivered a quick review of the past week. Fernando missed nothing on the river.

"The *Santa Loura* sank," he said. "There was a big storm."

"Have you seen Welly?" Jevy asked.

"Yes. He was pulled from the river by a cattle boat. They stopped here. He told me the story. I'm sure he's in Corumbá."

Jevy was relieved to hear that Welly was alive. The loss of the boat, however, was tragic news. The *Santa Loura* was one of the finer boats in the Pantanal. It went down under his watch.

Fernando was studying Nate as they talked. Nate could barely hear their words. He certainly couldn't understand them. Not that he cared.

"This is not malaria," Fernando said, touching the rash on Nate's neck. Jevy moved to the hammock and looked at his friend. His hair was matted and wet, his eyes still swollen shut.

"What is it?" he asked.

"Malaria doesn't produce a rash like this. Dengue does."

"Dengue fever?"

"Yes. It's similar to malaria—fever and chills, sore muscles and joints, spread by mosquitoes. But the rash means it's dengue."

"My father had it once. He was a very sick man."

"You need to get him to Corumbá, as quickly as possible."

"Can I borrow your motor?"

Fernando's boat was docked under the rickety building. His outboard wasn't as rusty as Jevy's, and it had five more horsepower. They scurried around, swapping motors and filling tanks, and after an hour in the hammock, comatose, poor Nate was shuffled back down the pier and laid into the boat under the tent. He was too sick to realize what was happening.

It was almost two-thirty. Corumbá was nine to ten hours away. Jevy left Valdir's phone number with Fernando. On rare occasions a boat on the Paraguay would have a radio. If Fernando happened to encounter one, Jevy wanted him to contact Valdir with the news.

He sped away at full throttle, quite proud to once again have a boat that sliced through the water with speed. The wake boiled behind him.

Dengue fever could be fatal. His father had been deathly ill for a week, with blinding headaches and fevers. His eyes hurt so badly that his mother kept him in a dark room for days. He was a tough river man, accustomed to injuries and pain, and when Jevy heard him moaning like a child he knew his father was dying. The doctor visited every other day, and finally the fever broke.

He could see Nate's feet from under the tent, nothing else. Surely he wouldn't die.

THIRTY-THREE

H E WOKE ONCE, but couldn't see. He woke again and it
was dark. He tried to say something to Jevy about water, just
a small drink, and maybe a bite of bread. But his voice was gone.
Speaking required effort and movement, especially when trying to
yell over the howl of the engine. His joints pulled him tightly into a
knot. He was welded to the aluminum shell of the boat.

Rachel lay beside him under the smelly tent, her knees also
pulled close and just touching his, same as when they sat together
on the ground in front of her hut, and later on the bench under the
tree by the river. A cautious little contact from a woman starved for
the innocent feeling of flesh. She had lived among the Ipicas for
eleven years, and their nakedness kept a distance between themselves and any civilized person. A simple hug was complicated.
Where do you hold? Where do you pat? How long do you squeeze?
Surely she'd never touched any of the males.

He wanted to kiss her, if only on the cheek, because she had
obviously gone years without such affection. "When was your last
kiss, Rachel?" he wanted to ask her. "You've been in love. How
physical was it?"

But he kept his questions to himself, and instead they talked about people they didn't know. She'd had a piano teacher whose breath was so bad the ivory keys turned yellow. He'd had a lacrosse coach who was paralyzed from the waist down because he cracked his spine in a lacrosse game. A girl in her church got pregnant, and her father condemned her from the pulpit. She killed herself a week later. He'd lost a brother to leukemia.

He rubbed her knees and she seemed to like it. But he would go no further. It wouldn't pay to get fresh with a missionary.

She was there to keep him from dying. She'd fought malaria twice herself. The fevers rise and fall, the chills hit like ice in the belly, then fade away. The nausea comes in waves. Then there is nothing for hours. She patted his arm and promised he was not going to die. She tells everybody this, he thought. Death would be welcome.

The touching stopped. He opened his eyes and reached for Rachel, but she was gone.

JEVY HEARD the delirium twice. Each time he stopped the boat and pulled the tent off Nate. He forced water into his mouth, and poured it gently through his sweating hair.

"We're almost there," he said over and over. "Almost there."

The first lights of Corumbá brought tears to his eyes. He had seen them many times when returning from excursions into the northern Pantanal, but they had never been so welcome. They flickered on the hill in the distance. He counted them until they blurred together.

It was almost 11 P.M. when he jumped into the shallow water and pulled his rig onto the broken concrete. The boat dock was deserted. He ran up the hill to a pay phone.

VALDIR WAS WATCHING television in his pajamas, smoking his last cigarette of the night and ignoring his cranky wife, when the phone rang. He answered it without getting up, then jumped to his feet.

"What is it?" she asked, as he ran to the bedroom.

"Jevy's back," he answered over his shoulder.

"Who's Jevy?"

Passing by her on the way out, he said, "I'm going to the river." She couldn't have cared less.

Driving across the city, he called a doctor friend, who had just gone to bed, and cajoled him into meeting them at the hospital.

Jevy was pacing along the dock. The American was sitting on a rock, his head resting on his knees. Without a word, they gently shuffled him into the backseat, and took off, gravel flying behind them.

Valdir had so many questions he didn't know where to start. The harsh words could wait. "When did he get sick?" he asked in Portuguese. Jevy sat next to him, rubbing his eyes, trying to stay awake. His last sleep had been with the Indians. "I don't know," he said. "The days all run together. It's dengue fever. The rash comes on the fourth or fifth day, and I think he's had it for two days. I don't know."

They were racing through downtown, ignoring lights and signs. The sidewalk cafés were closing. There was little traffic.

"Did you find the woman?"

"We did."

"Where?"

"She's close to the mountains. I think she's in Bolivia. A day south of Porto Indio."

"Was she on the map?"

"No."

"Then how did you find her?"

No Brazilian could ever admit to being lost, especially a seasoned guide like Jevy. It would hurt his self-esteem, and perhaps his business. "We were in a flooded region where maps mean nothing. I found a fisherman who helped us. How's Welly?"

"Welly's fine. The boat's gone." Valdir was much more concerned about the boat than about its deckhand.

"I've never seen such storms. We've been hit with three of them."

"What did the woman say?"

"I don't know. I didn't really talk to her."

"Was she surprised to see you?"

"She didn't seem to be. She was pretty cool. I think she liked our friend back there."

"How did their meeting go?"

"Ask him."

Nate was curled tightly in the backseat, hearing nothing. And Jevy was supposed to know nothing, so Valdir didn't press. The lawyers could talk later, as soon as Nate was able.

A wheelchair was waiting at the curb when they arrived at the hospital. They poured Nate into it, and followed the orderly along the sidewalk. The air was warm and sticky, still very hot. On the front steps, a dozen maids and assistants in white uniforms smoked cigarettes and chatted quietly. The hospital had no air conditioning.

The doctor friend was brusque and all business. The paperwork would be done in the morning. They pushed Nate through the empty lobby, along a series of hallways and into a small exam room where a sleepy nurse took him. With Jevy and Valdir watching in a corner, the doctor and nurse stripped the patient bare. The nurse washed him with alcohol and white cloths. The doctor studied the rash, which began at his chin and stopped at his waist. He was covered with mosquito bites, many of which he'd scratched into little red sores. They checked his temperature, blood pressure, heart rate.

"Looks like dengue fever," the doctor said after ten minutes. He then rattled off a list of details for the nurse, who hardly listened because she'd done it before. She began washing Nate's hair.

Nate mumbled something, but it had nothing to do with anyone present. His eyes were still swollen shut; he hadn't shaved in a week. He would've been at home in a gutter outside a bar.

"The fever is high," the doctor said. "He's delirious. We'll start an IV with antibiotics and painkillers, lots of water, maybe a little food later."

The nurse placed a heavy gauze bandage over Nate's eyes, then strapped it down with tape from ear to ear. She found a vein and started the IV. She pulled a yellow gown from a drawer and dressed him.

The doctor checked his temperature again. "It should begin falling soon," he told the nurse. "If not, call me at home." He glanced at his watch.

"Thanks," Valdir said.

"I'll see him early in the morning," the doctor said, and left them there.

Jevy lived on the edge of town, where the houses were small, the streets unpaved. He fell asleep twice as Valdir drove him home.

MRS. STAFFORD was shopping for antiques in London. The phone rang a dozen times before Josh grabbed it. The digital gave the time as 2:20 A.M.

"This is Valdir," the voice announced.

"Oh yes, Valdir." Josh rubbed his hair and blinked his eyes. "This better be good."

"Your boy is back."

"Thank God."

"He's very sick, though."

"What! What's the matter with him?"

"He has dengue fever, similar to malaria. Mosquitoes carry it. It is not uncommon here."

"I thought he had shots for everything." Josh was on his feet, bent at the waist, pulling his hair now.

"There is no shot for dengue."

"He's not going to die, is he?"

"Oh no. He's in the hospital. I have a good friend who is a doctor, and he's taking care of him. He says your boy will be fine."

"When can I talk to him?"

"Maybe tomorrow. He has a high fever and he's unconscious."

"Did he find the woman?"

"Yes."

Atta boy, thought Josh. He exhaled in relief and sat on the bed. So she's really out there. "Give me his room number."

"Well, they don't have phones in the rooms."

"It's a private room, isn't it? Come on, Valdir, money is no problem here. Tell me he's being taken care of."

"He is in good hands. But the hospital is a little different from yours."

"Should I come down there?"

"If you wish. It's not necessary. You can't change the hospital. He has a good doctor."

"How long will he be there?"

"A few days. We should know more in the morning."

"Call me early, Valdir. I mean it. I have to talk to him as soon as possible."

"Yes, I will call early."

Josh went to the kitchen for ice water. Then he paced around his den. At three, he gave up, made a pot of strong coffee, and went to his office in the basement.

BECAUSE HE WAS a rich American, they cut no corners. Nate got pumped into his veins the best drugs available from the pharmacy. The fever dipped a little, the sweating stopped. The pain vanished, washed away by a tide of the finest American-made chemicals. He was snoring heavily as the nurse and an orderly rolled him to his room, two hours after his arrival.

He would share the room for the night with five others. Mercifully, he was blindfolded and comatose. He couldn't see the open sores, the uncontrolled shaking of the old man next to him, the lifeless shriveled creature across the room. He couldn't smell the waste.

THIRTY-FOUR

THOUGH HE HELD no assets in his own name, and had been on the financial ropes for most of his adult life, Rex Phelan had a talent for numbers. It was one of the very few things he inherited from his father. He was the only Phelan heir with both the aptitude and the stamina to read all six of the petitions contesting Troy's will. When he finished, he realized that six law firms were basically duplicating each other's work. In fact, some of the legalese sounded as if it had been borrowed from the last petition, or the next one.

Six firms fighting the same fight, and each wanting an exorbitant piece of the pie. It was time for a little familial harmony. He decided to begin with his brother TJ, who was the easiest target because his lawyers were clinging to their ethics.

The two brothers agreed to meet in secret; their wives hated each other and discord could be avoided if the women simply didn't know. Rex told Troy Junior on the phone that it was time to bury the hatchet. Economics demanded it.

They met for breakfast in a suburban pancake house, and after a few minutes of waffles and football talk the edge was off. Rex got down to business by telling the Snead story. "This is enormous," he gushed. "It could literally make or break our case." He layered the story, slowing building to the promissory note the lawyers wanted to sign, all lawyers except for Troy Junior's. "Your attorneys are screwing up the deal," he said grimly, eyes darting around as if spies were grazing at the egg and bacon bar.

"Son of a bitch wants five million?" Troy Junior said, still in disbelief over Snead.

"It's a bargain. Look, he's willing to say he was the only person with Dad when he wrote the will. Whatever it takes to strike it down. He only wants half a million now. We can screw him out of the rest of it later."

This appealed to Troy Junior. And changing law firms was certainly nothing new to him. If he'd been candid, he would have admitted that Hemba and Hamilton's firm was intimidating. Four hundred lawyers. Marble foyers. Art on the wall. Somebody was paying for their good taste.

Rex switched gears. "Have you read the six petitions?" he asked.

Troy Junior chomped a strawberry and shook his head no. He hadn't even read the one filed on his behalf. Hemba and Hamilton had discussed it with him, and he'd signed it, but it was thick and Biff had been waiting in the car.

"Well I've read them, slowly and carefully, and they're all the same. We have six law firms doing the same work, all attacking the same will. It's absurd."

"I've been thinking about that," Troy Junior added helpfully.

"And all six expect to get rich when we settle. How much are your boys getting?"

"How much is Hark Gettys getting?"

"Twenty-five percent."

"Mine wanted thirty. We agreed on twenty." There was a quick flash of pride because Troy Junior had outnegotiated Rex.

"Let's play with the numbers," Rex continued. "Hypothetically, let's say we hire Snead, he says all the right things, we got our shrinks, the mess gets stirred up, and the estate wants to settle. Let's say each heir gets, I don't know, say twenty million. That's forty at this table. Five goes to Hark. Four goes to your boys. That's nine, so we get thirty-one."

"I'll take it."

"Me too. But if we take your boys out of the picture, and join up, then Hark will cut his fee. We don't need all these lawyers, TJ. They're just riding each other's backs and waiting to pounce on our money."

"I hate Hark Gettys."

"Fine. Let me deal with him. I'm not asking you to be friends."

"Why don't we fire Hark and stick with my guys?"

"Because Hark found Snead. Because Hark found the bank that'll loan the money to buy Snead. Because Hark is willing to sign the papers and your boys are too ethical. This is a nasty business, TJ. Hark understands it."

"He strikes me as being a crooked bastard."

"Yes! And he's our crook. If we join forces, his take goes from twenty-five to twenty. If we can bring in Mary Ross, then he'll cut it to seventeen-five. Libbigail, down to fifteen."

"We'll never get Libbigail."

"There's always a chance. If the three of us are on board, she might listen."

"What about that thug she's married to?" Troy Junior actually asked the question with complete sincerity. He was talking to his brother, who was married to a stripper.

"We'll take 'em one at a time. Let's cut our deal, then we go see Mary Ross. Her lawyer is that Grit guy, and he doesn't strike me as being too sharp."

"There's no sense fighting," Troy Junior said sadly.

"It'll cost us a bloody fortune. It's time for a truce."

"Mom will be proud."

THE HIGH GROUND on the Xeco had been used by the Indians for decades. It was a camp for fishermen who sometimes stayed the night, and it was a stopping place for river traffic. Rachel and Lako, and another tribesman named Ten, huddled under a lean-to with a straw roof and waited for the storm to pass. The roof leaked and the wind blew the rain sideways at their faces. The canoe was at their feet, dragged from the Xeco after battling the storm for a horrifying hour. Rachel's clothing was soaked, but at least the rainwater was warm. The Indians wore no clothing, except for a string around their waists and a leather covering over their privates.

She once had a wooden boat with an old motor. It had belonged to the Coopers, her predecessors. When there was gasoline, she used it on the rivers between the four Ipica settlements. And it would take her to Corumbá in two very long days, four on the return.

The motor had finally quit, and there was no money for a new one. Each year when she submitted her modest budget to World Tribes, she prayerfully requested a new outboard, or at least a good used one. She had found one in Corumbá for three hundred dollars. But budgets were tight around the world. Her allotments went for medical supplies and Bible literature. Keep praying, she was told. Maybe next year.

She accepted this without question. If the Lord meant for her to have a new outboard, then she would have one. The questions of if and when were left for Him. They were not for her to worry about.

Without a boat, she traveled between the villages on foot, almost always with Lako limping at her side. And once each August she convinced the chief to loan her a canoe and a guide for the journey to the Paraguay. There, she would wait for a cattle boat or a *chalana* headed south. Two years before, she had waited for three days, sleeping in the stable of a small *fazenda* on the river. In three days she went from a stranger to a friend to a missionary as the farmer and his wife became Christians under her teachings and prayer.

She would stay with them tomorrow, and wait for a boat to Corumbá.

The wind howled through the lean-to. She held Lako's hand and they prayed, not for their safety, but for the health of their friend Nate.

□ □ □ □

BREAKFAST was served to Mr. Stafford at his desk—cereal and fruit. He refused to leave the office, and when he declared that he would in fact hole up there all day, both of his secretaries scurried to rearrange no less than six meetings. A bagel at ten, at the desk. He called Valdir and was told that he was out of the office, in a meeting somewhere across town. Valdir had a cell phone. Why hadn't he called?

An associate delivered a two-page summary of dengue, taken from the Internet. The associate said he was needed in court, and asked if Mr. Stafford had any more medical work for him. Mr. Stafford did not see the humor.

Josh read the summary with his bagel. It was in all-caps, double-spaced with one-inch margins, about a page and a half long. A Stafford Memo. Dengue fever is a viral infection common throughout the tropical regions of the world. It is spread by a mosquito known as the Aedes, which prefers to bite during the day. The first sign is tiredness, followed quickly by a severe headache behind the eyes, then a mild fever that soon turns into an intense one with sweating and nausea and vomiting. As the fever rises, the muscles in the calves and back begin to ache. The fever is also known as "breakbone fever" because of the brutal muscle and joint pains. A rash appears after all other symptoms are present. The fever may break for a day or so, but it usually returns with increased intensity. After about a week, the infection wanes and the danger is gone. There is no cure and no vaccine. It takes a month of rest and liquids to return to normal.

And that's a mild case. Dengue can progress into dengue hemorrhagic fever or dengue shock syndrome, both of which are sometimes fatal, especially in children.

Josh was prepared to send Mr. Phelan's jet to Corumbá to collect Nate. On board would be a doctor and a nurse, and anything else that might be needed.

"It's Mr. Valdir," a secretary said through the intercom. No other calls were being taken.

He was at the hospital. "I've just checked on Mr. O'Riley," he said slowly, precisely. "He is okay. But he is not very conscious."

"Can he talk?" Josh asked.

"No. Not now. They are giving him drugs for his pain."

"Does he have a good doctor?"

"The best. A friend of mine. The doctor's with him now."

"Ask him when Mr. O'Riley will be able to fly home. I will send a private jet and a doctor to Corumbá."

There was a conversation in the background. "Not soon," Valdir reported. "He will need rest when he leaves the hospital."

"When will he leave the hospital?"

Another conversation. "He can't say right now."

Josh shook his head and flung the remnants of his bagel into the wastebasket. "Did you say anything to Mr. O'Riley?" he growled at Valdir.

"No. I think he's asleep."

"Listen, Mr. Valdir, it is very important that I talk to him as soon as possible, okay?"

"I understand this. But you must be patient."

"I'm not a patient man."

"I understand this. But you must try."

"Call me this afternoon."

Josh slammed the phone down and began pacing. It had been an unwise decision to send Nate, fragile and unstable as he was, into the dangers of the tropics. Convenience had been the reason. Send him away for a couple of weeks more, keep him busy elsewhere while the firm sorts out his mess. There were four lesser partners in his firm besides Nate, four Josh had handpicked and hired and mentored and listened to on some matters of management. Tip was one, and he was the sole voice of support for Nate. The other three wanted him gone.

Nate's secretary had been reassigned. A rising associate had been borrowing his office lately, and was said to have found a home.

If dengue fever didn't get poor Nate, the IRS was waiting.

□ □ □ □

THE IV BAG emptied silently around the middle of the day, though no one bothered to check it. Several hours later Nate woke up. His head was light, and at peace, with no fever. He was stiff but not sweating. He felt the heavy gauze over his eyes, felt the tape holding it there, and after some thought decided to have a look. His left arm held the IV, so he began picking at the tape with the fingers of his right hand. He was aware of voices in another room, and steps on a hard floor. People were busy down the hall. Closer, someone was moaning in a low, steady, painful voice.

He slowly worked the tape from his skin and hair, and cursed the person who'd stuck it there. He laid the bandage to one side; it hung over his left ear. His first image was peeling paint, a dull shade of faded yellow on the wall just above him. The lights were off, rays of sun drifted in from a window. The paint on the ceiling was cracked too, large black gaps shrouded with cobwebs and dust. A rickety fan dropped from the center and wobbled as it spun.

Two feet caught his attention, two old, gnarled, scarred feet layered with wounds and calluses from toes to soles, sticking in the air, and when he lifted his head slightly he saw that they belonged to a shriveled little man whose bed almost touched his. He appeared dead.

The moaning came from the wall near the window. This poor guy was just as small and just as shriveled. He sat in the middle of his bed, arms and legs folded and tucked into a ball, and suffered his affliction in a trance.

The smell was of old urine, human waste, and heavy antiseptic all mixed into one thick odor. Nurses laughed down the hall. The paint was peeling on every wall. There were five beds besides Nate's, all of the rollaway variety, parked here and there with little effort at order.

His third roommate was by the door. He was naked except for a wet diaper, and his body was covered with open red sores. He too appeared dead, and Nate certainly hoped he was. For his own good.

There were no buttons to push, no emergency cord or intercom, no way to summon help except for yelling, and this might wake the dead. These creatures might arise and want to visit with him.

He wanted to run, to swing his feet off the bed, onto the floor, rip the IV from his arm, and sprint for freedom. He would take his chances on the street. Surely there couldn't be as much disease out there. Any place was better than this leper's ward.

But his feet were like bricks. Nate tried mightily to lift them, one at a time, but they barely moved.

Nate sunk his head to his pillow, closed his eyes, and thought about crying. I am in a hospital in a third world country, he said over and over. I left Walnut Hill, a thousand bucks a day, pushbutton everything, carpet, showers, therapists at my beck and call.

The man with the sores grunted, and Nate sank even lower. Then he carefully took the gauze and placed it over his eyes, and he taped it just like before, only tighter this time.

THIRTY-FIVE

SNEAD ARRIVED for the meeting with a contract of his own, one he had prepared without the aid of a lawyer. Hark read it, and had to admit that it was not a bad job of drafting. It was titled Contract for Expert Witness Services. Experts give opinions. Snead would deal primarily with the facts, but Hark didn't care what the contract said. He signed it, and handed over a certified check for half a million. Snead took it delicately, examined every word, then folded it and tucked it away in his coat pocket. "Now where do we start?" he said with a smile.

There was so much to cover. The other Phelan lawyers wanted to be present. Hark had time only for a primer. "In general terms," he said, "what was the old man's frame of mind the morning he died?"

Snead squirmed and twisted and frowned as if in deep thought. He really wanted to say the right things. He felt as though he had four-point-five million riding on him now. "He was out of his mind," he said, the words hanging in the air while he waited for approval.

Hark nodded. So far so good. "Was this unusual?"

"No. In his last days he was hardly rational."

"How much time did you spend with him?"

"Off and on, twenty-four hours a day."

"Where did you sleep?"

"My room was down the hall, but he had a buzzer for me. I was on call around the clock. He would sometimes get up in the middle of the night and want juice or a pill. He simply pushed a button, the buzzer rang me, and I fetched whatever he wanted."

"Who else lived with him?"

"No one."

"Who else did he spend time with?"

"Perhaps young Nicolette, the secretary. He fancied her."

"Did he have sex with her?"

"Would it help our case?"

"Yes."

"Then they were screwing like rabbits."

Hark couldn't help but smile. The allegation that Troy was chasing his last secretary would surprise no one.

It hadn't taken long for them to find the same sheet to sing from. "Look, Mr. Snead, this is what we want. We need the quirks, the little oddities, the glaring lapses, the strange things he said and did that when taken as a whole will convince anyone he was not of sound mind. You have time. Sit down and begin writing. Put the pieces together. Have a chat with Nicolette, make sure they were having sex, listen to what she says."

"She'll say anything we need."

"Good. Then rehearse, and make sure there are no gaps that other lawyers can find. Your stories must hold together."

"There's no one to contradict them."

"No one? No limo driver or maid or ex-lover or maybe another secretary?"

"He had all those, sure. But no one lived on the fourteenth floor but Mr. Phelan and myself. He was a very lonely man. And quite crazy."

"Then how did he perform so well for the three psychiatrists?"

Snead thought about this for a moment. Fiction failed him. "What would you guess?" he asked.

"I would guess that Mr. Phelan knew the examination would be difficult because he knew he was slipping, and so he asked you to prepare lists of anticipated questions, and that you and Mr. Phelan spent that morning reviewing such simple matters as the day's date, he couldn't keep it straight, and the names of children, names he'd virtually forgotten, where they went to college, whom they were married to, etcetera, then you covered questions about his health. I would guess that after you had drilled him on these basics, you spent at least two hours prompting him on his holdings, the structure of The Phelan Group, the companies he owned, the acquisitions he'd made, the closing prices of certain stocks. He relied on you more and more for financial news, and so this came easy for you. It was tedious for the old man, but you were determined to keep him sharp just before you wheeled him in for the exam. Does this sound familiar?"

Snead liked it immensely. He was awed by the lawyer's gift of creating lies on the spot. "Yes, yes, that's it! That's how Mr. Phelan snowed the psychiatrists."

"Then work on it, Mr. Snead. The more you work on your stories, the better witness you'll be. The lawyers on the other side will come after you. They will attack your testimony and call you a liar, so you must be ready. Write everything down, so you'll always have a record of your stories."

"I like that idea."

"Dates, times, places, incidents, oddities. Everything, Mr. Snead. Same for Nicolette. Make her write it down."

"She doesn't write well."

"Help her. It's up to you, Mr. Snead. You want the rest of the money, then earn it."

"How much time do I have?"

"We, the other lawyers and myself, would like to video you in a few days. We'll hear your stories, pepper you with questions, then watch your performance. I'm sure we'll want to change some things. We'll coach you along, maybe do more videos. When things are perfect, then you'll be ready for your deposition."

Snead left in a hurry. He wanted to put the money in the bank, and buy a new car. Nicolette needed one too.

A NIGHT ORDERLY on his rounds noticed the empty bag. The handprinted instructions on the back of it said that the fluids should not be interrupted. He took it to the pharmacy, where a part-time student nurse remixed the chemicals and gave the bag back to the orderly. There were rumors around the hospital about the rich American patient.

In his sleep, Nate was refortified with drugs he didn't need.

When Jevy found him before breakfast, he was half-awake, eyes still covered because he preferred the darkness. "Welly's here," Jevy whispered.

The nurse on duty helped Jevy roll the bed from the room, down the hall, and into a small courtyard where there was sunshine. The nurse turned a crank and half the bed inclined. She removed the gauze and tape, and Nate never flinched. He slowly opened his eyes and tried to focus. Jevy, just inches away, said, "The swelling is down."

"Hello, Nate," Welly said. He was hovering on the other side. The nurse left them.

"Hello, Welly," Nate said, his words deep, slow, thick. He was groggy, but happy. How well he knew the feeling of being stoned.

Jevy patted his forehead and announced, "The fever is gone too." The Brazilians smiled at each other, relieved that they had not killed the American during their excursion into the Pantanal.

"What happened to you?" Nate asked Welly, trying to clip his words and not sound like a drunk. Jevy passed along the question in Portuguese. Welly was instantly animated, and began his long narrative about the storm and the sinking of the *Santa Loura*. Jevy stopped him every thirty seconds for the translation. Nate listened while trying to keep his eyes open, but he floated in and out of the scene.

Valdir found them there. He greeted Nate warmly, delighted that their guest was sitting up in bed and looking better. He whipped out a cell phone, and as he punched numbers he said, "You must talk to Mr. Stafford. He is quite anxious."

"I'm not sure I . . . ." Nate's words trailed off as he drifted.

"Here, sit up, it's Mr. Stafford," Valdir said, handing him the phone and puffing up his pillow. Nate took the phone and said, "Hello."

"Nate!" came the reply. "Is that you!"

"Josh."

"Nate, tell me you're not going to die. Please tell me."

"I'm not sure," Nate said. Valdir gently pushed the phone closer to Nate's head, and helped him hold it in place. "Speak louder," he whispered. Jevy and Welly stepped back.

"Nate, did you find Rachel Lane?" Josh yelled into the phone.

Nate rallied for a second. He frowned hard, trying to concentrate. "No," he said.

"What!"

"Her name's not Rachel Lane."

"What the hell is it?"

Nate thought hard for a second, then fatigue hit him. He slumped a bit, still trying to remember her name. Maybe she never told him her last name. "I don't know," he mumbled, his lips barely moving. Valdir pressed the phone harder.

"Nate, talk to me! Did you find the right woman?"

"Oh yes. Everything's okay down here, Josh. Relax."

"What about the woman?"

"She's lovely."

Josh hesitated for a second, but he couldn't waste any time. "That's nice, Nate. Did she sign the papers?"

"I can't think of her name."

"Did she sign the papers?"

There was a long pause as Nate's chin dropped to his chest and he appeared to be napping. Valdir nudged his arm and tried to move his head with the phone. "I really liked her," Nate suddenly babbled. "A lot."

"You're stoned, aren't you, Nate? They've got you on painkillers, right?"

"Yep."

"Look, Nate, call me when your head is clear, okay?"

"I don't have a phone."

"Then use Valdir's. Please call me, Nate."

His head nodded and his eyes closed. "I asked her to marry me," he said into the phone, then his chin fell for the last time.

Valdir took the phone and walked to a corner. He tried to describe Nate's condition.

"Do I need to come down there?" Josh yelled for the third or fourth time.

"That is not necessary. Please be patient."

"I'm tired of you telling me to be patient."

"I understand."

"Get him well, Valdir."

"He is fine."

"No he's not. Call me later."

TIP DURBAN found Josh standing in the window of his office, staring at the cluster of buildings that composed his view. Tip closed the door, took a seat, and asked, "What did he say?"

Josh kept staring out the window. "He said he found her, that she's lovely, and that he asked her to marry him." There was no trace of humor in his voice.

Tip found it humorous nonetheless. When it came to women, Nate culled little, especially between divorces. "How is he?"

"Feeling no pain, pumped full of painkillers, semiconscious. Valdir said the fever is gone and he looks much better."

"So he's not going to die?"

"It appears not."

Durban began chuckling. "That's our boy Nate. Never met a skirt he didn't like."

When Josh turned around he looked quite amused. "It's beautiful," he said. "Nate's bankrupt. She's only forty-two, probably hasn't seen a white man in years."

"Nate wouldn't care if she was as ugly as sin. She happens to be the richest woman in the world."

"I'm not surprised, now that I think about it. I thought I was doing him a favor sending him off on an adventure. It never occurred to me he would try to seduce a missionary."

"You think he hit on her?"

"Who knows what they did in the jungle."

"I doubt it," Tip added on second thought. "We know Nate, but we don't know her. It takes two."

Josh sat on the edge of his desk, still amused, grinning at the floor. "You're right. I'm not sure she would go for Nate. There's a lot of baggage."

"Did she sign the papers?"

"We didn't get that far. I'm sure she did or he wouldn't have left her."

"When is he coming home?"

"As soon as he can travel."

"Don't be so sure. For eleven billion, I might stick around for a while."

THIRTY-SIX

T HE DOCTOR found his patient snoring in the shade of the courtyard, still sitting up in bed, mouth open, gauze removed, head fallen to one side. His friend from the river was napping on the ground nearby. He studied the IV bag and stopped the flow. He touched Nate's forehead and felt no fever.

"Senhor O'Riley," he said loudly as he tapped the patient's shoulder. Jevy jumped to his feet. The doctor did not speak English.

He wanted Nate to return to his room, but when this was translated by Jevy it was not well received. Nate pleaded with Jevy and Jevy begged the doctor. Jevy had seen the other patients, the open sores, the seizures and dying men just down the hall, and he promised the doctor he would sit right there in the shade with his friend until dark. The doctor relented. He really didn't care.

Across the courtyard was a small separate ward with thick black bars sunk in cement. Patients wandered out from time to time to gawk through the bars into the courtyard. They could not escape. A screamer appeared late in the morning, and took offense at the presence of Nate and Jevy across the way. He had brown spotted skin and red patchy hair, and looked as crazy as he was. He clasped two bars, stuck his face between them, and began yelling. His voice was shrill and echoed around the courtyard and down the halls.

"What's he saying?" Nate asked. The lunatic's yelling startled him, and helped clear his head.

"I can't understand a word. He's insane."

"They have me in the same hospital with the crazy people?"

"Yes. Sorry. It's a small town."

The yelling intensified. A nurse from the safe side appeared and shouted for him to be quiet. He lashed back at her with language that made her run away. Then he refocused on Nate and Jevy. He squeezed the bars until his knuckles were white, and began hopping as he screamed.

"Poor guy," Nate said.

The screaming turned to wailing, and after a few minutes of nonstop racket a male nurse appeared behind the man and attempted to lead him away. He didn't want to go, and a short scuffle ensued. With witnesses, the nurse was firm but cautious. The man's hands, however, were glued around the bars and could not be removed. The wailing turned to shrieking as the nurse tugged from behind.

Finally, the nurse gave up and disappeared. The screamer pulled down his pants and began peeing through the bars, laughing loudly as he aimed in the general direction of Nate and Jevy, who were out of range. While his hands were off the bars, the nurse suddenly attacked from the rear, grabbing him in a full nelson and dragging him away. Once he was out of sight, the yelling ceased immediately.

When the daily drama was over and the courtyard was once again quiet, Nate said, "Jevy, get me out of here."

"What do you mean?"

"Get me out of here. I feel fine. The fever is gone, my strength is returning. Let's go."

"We can't leave until the doctor releases you. And you have that," he added, pointing to the IV in Nate's left forearm.

"This is nothing," Nate said as he quickly slid the needle from his arm and yanked the IV free. "Find me some clothes, Jevy. I'm checking out."

"You don't know dengue. My father had it."

"It's over. I can feel it."

"No, it's not. The fever will return, and it will be worse. Much worse."

"I don't believe that. Take me to a hotel, Jevy, please. I'll be fine there. I'll pay you to stay with me, and if the fever returns you can feed me pills. Please, Jevy."

Jevy was standing at the foot of the bed. He glanced around as if someone might understand their English. "I don't know," he said, waivering. It was not such a bad idea.

"I'll pay you two hundred dollars to get me some clothes and take me to a hotel. And I'll pay you fifty dollars a day to guard me until I'm okay."

"It's not about money, Nate. I'm your friend."

"And I'm your friend, Jevy. And friends help friends. I can't go back to that room. You saw those poor sick people in there. They're all rotting and dying and pissing all over themselves. It smells like human waste. The nurses don't care. The doctors don't check on you. The insane asylum is just over there. Please, Jevy, get me out of here. I'll pay you good money."

"Your money went down with the *Santa Loura*."

That stopped him cold. Nate had not even thought about the *Santa Loura*, and his belongings—his clothes, money, passport, and briefcase with all the gadgets and papers Josh had sent. There had been few lucid moments since leaving Rachel, just a few clear intervals during which he had thought about living and dying. Never about tangible things or assets. "I can get plenty of money, Jevy. I'll wire it in from the States. Please help me."

Jevy knew that dengue was rarely fatal. Nate's bout with it appeared to be under control, though the fever would surely return. No one could blame him for wanting to escape the hospital. "Okay," he said, glancing around again. No one was near them. "I'll return in a few minutes."

Nate closed his eyes and contemplated his lack of a passport. And he had no cash, not a dime. No clothes, no toothbrush. No SatFone, cell phone, no calling cards. And matters weren't much better at home. From the ruins of his personal bankruptcy, he could expect to keep his leased car, his clothing and modest furniture, and the money put away in his IRA. Nothing else. The lease on his small condo in Georgetown had been surrendered during rehab. There was no place to go when he returned. No family to speak of. His two older kids were distant and unconcerned. The two middle schoolers from the second marriage had been taken far away by their mother. He hadn't seen them in six months, and had scarcely thought about them at Christmas.

On his fortieth birthday, Nate had won a $10 million verdict against a doctor who failed to diagnose cancer. It was the largest verdict of his career, and when the appeals were finished two years later the firm collected over $4 million in fees. Nate's bonus that year had been $1.5 million. He was a millionaire for a few months, until he bought the new house. There were furs and diamonds, cars and trips, some shaky investments. Then he started seeing a college girl who loved cocaine, and the wall cracked. He crashed hard and spent two months locked away. His second wife left with the money, then came back briefly without it.

He'd been a millionaire, and now he imagined how he looked from the roof of the courtyard—sick, alone, broke, under indictment, afraid of the return home, and terrified of the temptations there.

His quest to find Rachel had kept him focused. There was excitement in the hunt. Now that it was over, and he was flat on his back again, he thought of Sergio and rehab and addictions and all the trouble waiting for him. Darkness was looming again.

He couldn't spend the rest of his life riding *chalanas* up and down the Paraguay with Jevy and Welly, far removed from booze and drugs and women, oblivious to his legal troubles. He had to go back. He had to face the music one more time.

A piercing squawk jolted him from his daydreams. The red-headed screamer was back.

JEVY ROLLED the bed under a veranda, then down a hallway headed toward the front of the hospital. He stopped by a janitor's closet, and helped the patient out of bed. Nate was weak and shaky, but determined to escape. Inside the closet, he ripped off the gown and put on a pair of baggy soccer shorts, a red tee shirt, the obligatory rubber sandals, a denim cap, and a pair of plastic sunshades. Though he looked the part, he did not feel the least bit Brazilian. Jevy had spent little on his outfit. He was adjusting the cap when he fainted.

Jevy heard him hit the door. He quickly opened it, and found Nate slumped in a pile with buckets and mops rattling around. He clutched him under the arms and dragged him back to the bed. He rolled him into it and covered him with the sheet.

Nate opened his eyes and said, "What happened?"

"You fainted," came the reply. The bed was moving; Jevy was behind him. They passed two nurses who didn't seem to notice them. "This is a bad idea," Jevy said.

"Just keep going."

They parked near the lobby. Nate crawled out of bed, felt faint again, and began walking. Jevy placed a heavy arm around his shoulder and steadied him by clutching his bicep. "Take it easy," Jevy kept saying. "Nice and slow."

No stares from the admissions clerks, nor the sick people trying to get in. No odd looks from the nurses and orderlies smoking on the front steps. The sun hit Nate hard and he leaned on Jevy. They crossed the street to where Jevy's massive Ford was parked.

They narrowly avoided death at the first intersection. "Could you please drive slower," Nate snapped. He was sweating and his stomach was rolling.

"Sorry," Jevy said, and the truck slowed considerably.

With charm and the promise of future payment, Jevy cajoled a double room out of the young girl at the front desk of the Palace Hotel. "My friend is sick," he whispered to her, nodding at Nate, who certainly appeared ill. Jevy didn't want the pretty lady to get the wrong idea. They had no bags.

In the room, Nate collapsed on the bed. The little escape had tired him immensely. Jevy found the rerun of a soccer game on TV, but after five minutes was bored. He left to continue his flirting.

Nate tried twice to get an international operator. He had a vague recollection of hearing Josh's voice on the phone, and he suspected that a follow-up was needed. On the second attempt, he got an earful of Portuguese. When she tried English, he thought he caught the words "calling card." He hung up and went to sleep.

The doctor called Valdir. Valdir found Jevy's truck parked on the street outside the Palace Hotel, and he found Jevy in the pool sipping a beer.

Valdir squatted at the edge of the pool. "Where is Mr. O'Riley?" he asked. His irritation was obvious.

"Upstairs in his room," Jevy answered, then took another sip.

"Why is he here?"

"Because he wanted to leave the hospital. Do you blame him?"

Valdir's only surgery had been in Campo Grande, four hours away. No one with money would ever voluntarily submit themselves to the hospital in Corumbá. "How is he?"

"I think he's fine."

"Stay with him."

"I don't work for you anymore, Mr. Valdir."

"Yes, but there is the matter of the boat."

"I can't raise it. I didn't sink it. A storm did. What do you want me to do?"

"I want you to watch Mr. O'Riley."

"He needs money. Can you wire it in for him?"

"I suppose."

"And he needs a passport. He lost everything."

"Just watch him. I'll take care of the details."

□ □ □ □

THE FEVER returned quietly during the night, warming his face as he slept, taking its time as it built momentum for the havoc to come. Its calling card was a row of tiny pellets of sweat lined perfectly above the eyebrows, then sweat in the hair that rested on the pillow. It simmered while he slept, stewing, preparing to erupt. It sent tremors, little waves of chills, through his body, but he was fatigued and there were the remnants of so many chemicals that he kept sleeping. It built pressure behind his eyes, so that when he did open them he would want to scream. It drained the fluids from his mouth.

Nate finally groaned. He felt the vicious pounding of a jackhammer between his temples. When he opened his eyes, death awaited him. He was in a pool of sweat, his face on fire, his knees and elbows bending in pain. "Jevy," he whispered. "Jevy!"

Jevy hit the switch for the table lamp between them, and Nate groaned even louder. "Turn that off!" he said. Jevy ran to the bathroom and found a less direct source of light. For the ordeal, he had purchased bottled water, ice, aspirin, over-the-counter pain medications, and a thermometer. He thought he was prepared.

An hour passed and Jevy counted every minute of it. The fever climbed to 102; the chills came in waves so violent that the small bed rattled and shook on the floor. When Nate wasn't shaking, Jevy stuffed pills in his mouth and poured down water. He soaked his face with wet towels. Nate suffered in silence, bravely gritting his teeth so that the pain was quiet. He was determined to suffer through the fevers in the relative luxury of the small hotel room. Every time he wanted to scream, he remembered the cracked plaster and smells of the hospital.

At 4 A.M., the fever climbed to 103, and Nate began to drift away. His knees almost touched his chin. His arms were wrapped around his calves. He held himself tightly. Then a chill would hit and untangle him as his body shuddered.

The last temperature reading was 105, and Jevy knew at some point his friend would go into shock. He finally panicked, not from the temperature, but from the sight of sweat dripping from the bedsheets onto the floor. His friend had suffered enough. There were better drugs at the hospital.

He found a janitor asleep on the third floor, and together they dragged Nate to the elevator, through the empty lobby, and to his truck. He called Valdir at 6 A.M., waking him.

When Valdir finished cursing Jevy, he agreed to call the doctor.

THIRTY-SEVEN

THE TREATMENT was phoned in from the doctor's bed. Fill the IV bag with lots of goodies, poke the needle in his arm, try to find a better room. The rooms were full, so they simply left him in the hall of the men's ward, near a messy desk they called the nurses' station. At least they couldn't ignore him. Jevy was asked to leave. There was nothing he could do but wait.

At one point in the morning, during a lull in other activities, an orderly appeared with a pair of scissors. He cut off the new gym shorts and the new red tee shirt, and replaced them with another yellow gown. In the process Nate lay naked on the bed for five full minutes, in plain view of everyone passing by. No one noticed; Nate certainly didn't care. The sheets were changed because they were soaked. The rags that had been the shorts and shirt were thrown away, and once again Nate O'Riley had no clothes.

If he shook too much or moaned too loud, the nearest doctor or nurse or orderly would gently open the IV. And when he was snoring too loud, someone would close it a little.

A cancer death created an opening. Nate was rolled into the nearest room where he was parked between a worker who'd just

lost a foot and a man dying from kidney failure. The doctor saw
him twice during the day. The fever wavered between 102 and 104.
Valdir stopped by late in the afternoon for a chat but Nate was not
awake. He reported the day's events to Mr. Stafford, who was not
pleased.

"The doctor says this is normal," Valdir said, speaking into his
cell phone in the hallway. "Mr. O'Riley will be fine."

"Don't let him die, Valdir," Josh growled from America.

Money was being wired. They were working on the passport.

ONCE AGAIN the IV bag dripped itself empty, and no one noticed. Hours passed and the drugs gradually wore off. It was pitch
dark, the middle of the night, and there was no movement from the
other three beds when Nate finally shook off the cobwebs of his
coma and showed signs of life. He could barely see his roommates.
The door was open and there was a faint light down the hallway.
No voices, no feet shuffling by.

He touched his gown—drenched from the sweat—and realized
he was again naked underneath. He rubbed his swollen eyes and
tried to straighten his cramped legs. His forehead was very hot. He
was thirsty and could not remember his last meal. He tried not to
move for fear of waking those around him. Surely a nurse would
stop by soon.

The sheets were wet, so when the chills began again there was no
way to get warm. He shook and vibrated, rubbing his arms and
legs, his teeth clapping together. After the chills stopped, he tried to
sleep and managed a few naps as the night wore on, but when it was
darkest the fever rose again. His temples pounded so hard that Nate
began to cry. He wrapped the pillow around his head and squeezed
as hard as he could.

In the darkness of the room, a silhouette entered and moved from
bed to bed, finally stopping beside Nate's. She watched him floun-
der and fight under the sheets, his low moans muffled by the pillow.
She touched him gently on the arm. "Nate," she whispered.

Under normal circumstances, he would have been startled. But hallucinating had become a common symptom. He lowered the pillow to his chest and tried to focus on the figure.

"It's Rachel," she whispered.

"Rachel?" he whispered, his breathing labored. He tried to sit up, then tried to open his eyes with his fingers. "Rachel?"

"I'm here, Nate. God sent me to protect you."

He reached for her face and she took his hand. She kissed his palm. "You are not going to die, Nate," she said. "God has plans for you."

He could say nothing. Slowly his eyes adjusted and he could see her. "It's you," he said. Or was it another dream?

He reclined again, resting his head on the pillow, relaxing as his muscles unclenched themselves and his joints became loose. He closed his eyes, but still held her hand. The pounding behind his eyes faded. The heat left his forehead and face. The fever had sapped his strength, and he drifted away again, into a deep sleep induced not by chemicals but by sheer exhaustion.

He dreamed of angels—white-robed young maidens floating in the clouds above him, there to protect him, humming hymns he'd never heard but that somehow seemed familiar.

HE LEFT THE HOSPITAL at noon the next day, armed with his doctor's orders and accompanied by Jevy and Valdir. There was no trace of fever, no rash, just a little soreness in the joints and muscles. He insisted on leaving, and the doctor readily concurred. The doctor was happy to be rid of him.

The first stop was a restaurant where he consumed a large bowl of rice and a plate of boiled potatoes. He avoided the steaks and chops. Jevy did not. They were both still hungry from their adventure. Valdir sipped coffee, smoked his cigarettes, and watched them eat.

No one had seen Rachel come and go at the hospital. Nate had whispered the secret to Jevy, who had inquired of the nurses and maids. After lunch, Jevy left them and began roaming downtown on foot, searching for her. He went to the river where he talked to deckhands on the last cattle boat. She had not traveled with them. The fishermen hadn't seen her. No one seemed to know anything about the arrival of a white woman from the Pantanal.

In Valdir's office, alone, Nate dialed the number of the Stafford Law Firm, a number he had trouble remembering. They pulled Josh out of a meeting. "Talk to me, Nate," he said. "How are you?"

"The fever is gone," he said, rocking in Valdir's easy chair. "I feel fine. A little sore and tired, but I feel good."

"You sound great. I want you home."

"Give me a couple of days."

"I'm sending a jet down, Nate. It will leave tonight."

"No. Don't do that, Josh. That's not a good idea. I'll get there whenever I want."

"Okay. Tell me about the woman, Nate."

"We found her. She is the illegitimate daughter of Troy Phelan, and she has no interest in the money."

"So how did you talk her into taking it?"

"Josh, you don't talk this woman into anything. I tried, got nowhere, so I stopped."

"Come on, Nate. Nobody walks away from this kind of money. Surely you talked some sense into her."

"Not even close, Josh. She is the happiest person I've ever met, perfectly content to spend the rest of her life working among her people. It's where God wants her to be."

"She signed the papers though?"

"Nope."

There was a long pause as Josh absorbed it. "You must be kidding," he finally said, barely audible in Brazil.

"Nope. Sorry, boss. I tried my best to convince her to at least sign the papers, but she wouldn't budge. She'll never sign them."

"Did she read the will?"

"Yes."

"And you told her it was eleven billion dollars?"

"Yep. She lives alone in a hut with a thatched roof, no plumbing, no electricity, simple food and clothes, no phones or faxes, and no concern about the things she's missing. She's in the Stone Age, Josh, right where she wants to be, and money would change that."

"It's incomprehensible."

"I thought so too, and I was there."

"Is she bright?"

"She's a doctor, Josh, an M.D. And she has a degree from a seminary. She speaks five languages."

"A doctor?"

"Yeah, but we didn't talk about medical practice litigation."

"You said she was lovely."

"I did?"

"Yeah, on the phone two days ago. I think you were stoned."

"I was, and she is."

"So you liked her?"

"We became friends." It would serve no purpose to tell Josh that she was in Corumbá. Nate hoped to find her quickly, and, while in civilization, try to discuss Troy's estate.

"It was quite an adventure," Nate said. "To say the least."

"I've lost sleep worrying about you."

"Relax. I'm still in one piece."

"I wired five thousand dollars. Valdir has it."

"Thanks, boss."

"Call me tomorrow."

Valdir invited him to dinner, but he declined. He collected the money and left on foot, loose again on the streets of Corumbá. His first stop was a clothing store where he bought underwear, safari shorts, plain white tee shirts, and hiking boots. By the time he hauled his new wardrobe four blocks to the Palace Hotel, Nate was exhausted. He slept for two hours.

JEVY FOUND no trace of Rachel. He watched the crowds on the busy streets. He talked to the river people he knew so well, and heard nothing about her arrival. He walked through the lobbies of the downtown hotels and flirted with the receptionists. No one had seen an American woman of forty-two traveling alone.

As the afternoon wore on, Jevy doubted his friend's story. Dengue makes you see things, makes you hear voices, makes you believe in ghosts, especially in the night. But he kept searching.

Nate roamed too, after his nap and another meal. He walked slowly, pacing himself, trying to keep in the shade and always with a bottle of water in hand. He rested on the bluff above the river, the majesty of the Pantanal spread before him for hundreds of miles.

Fatigue hit him hard, and he limped back to the hotel for another rest. He slept again, and when he awoke Jevy was tapping on the door. They had promised to meet for dinner at seven. It was after eight, and when Jevy entered the room he immediately began looking for empty bottles. There were none.

They ate roasted chicken at a sidewalk café. The night was alive with music and foot traffic. Couples with small children bought ice cream and drifted back home. Teenagers moved in packs with no apparent destination. The bars spilled outdoors, to the edges of the streets. Young men and women moved from one bar to the next. The streets were warm and safe; no one seemed concerned about getting shot or mugged.

At a nearby table, a man drank a cold Brahma beer from a brown bottle, and Nate watched every sip.

After dessert, they said good-bye and promised to meet early for another day of searching. Jevy went one direction, Nate another. He was rested, and tired of beds.

Two blocks away from the river, and the streets were quieter. The shops were closed; the homes were dark; traffic was lighter. Ahead, he saw the lights of a small chapel. That, he said almost aloud, is where she'll be.

The front door was wide open, so from the sidewalk Nate could see rows of wooden pews, the empty pulpit, the mural of Christ on the cross, and the backs of a handful of worshipers leaning forward in prayer and meditation. The organ music was low and soft, and it pulled him in. He stopped in the door and counted five people scattered among the pews, no two sitting together, no one with even the slightest resemblance to Rachel. Under the mural, the organ bench was empty. The music came from a speaker.

He could wait. He had the time; she might appear. He shuffled along the back row and sat alone. He studied the crucifixion, the nails through His hands, the sword in His side, the agony in His face. Did they really kill Him in such a dreadful manner? Along the way, at some point in his miserable secular life, Nate had read or heard the basic stories of Christ: the virgin birth, thus Christmas; the walking on the water; maybe another miracle or two; was he swallowed by the whale or was that someone else? And then the betrayal by Judas; the trial before Pilate; the crucifixion, thus Easter, and, finally, the ascension into heaven.

Yes, Nate knew the basics. Perhaps his mother had told him. Neither of his wives had been churchgoers, though number two was Catholic and they did midnight mass at Christmas every other year.

Three more stragglers came from the street. A young man with a guitar appeared from a side door and went to the pulpit. It was exactly nine-thirty. He strummed a few chords and began singing, his face glowing with words of faith and praise. A tiny little woman one pew up clapped her hands and sang along.

Maybe the music would draw Rachel. She had to crave real worship in a church with wooden floors and stained glass, with fully clothed people reading Bibles in a modern language. Surely she visited the churches when she was in Corumbá.

When the song was finished, the young man read some scripture and began teaching. His Portuguese was the slowest Nate had encountered so far in his little adventure. Nate was mesmerized by the soft, slurring sounds, and the unhurried cadence. Though he understood not a word, he tried to repeat the sentences. Then his thoughts drifted.

His body had purged the fevers and chemicals. He was well fed, alert, rested. He was his old self again, and that suddenly depressed

him. The present was back, hand in hand with the future. The
burdens he'd left with Rachel had found him again, found him then
and there in the chapel. He needed her to sit with him, to hold his
hand and help him pray.

He hated his weaknesses. He named them one by one, and was
saddened by the list. The demons were waiting at home—the good
friends and the bad friends, the haunts and habits, the pressures he
couldn't stand anymore. Life could not be lived with the likes of
Sergio at a thousand bucks a day. And life could not be lived free on
the streets.

The young man was praying, his eyes clenched tightly, his arms
waving gently upward. Nate closed his eyes too, and called God's
name. God was waiting.

With both hands, he clenched the back of the pew in front of
him. He repeated the list, mumbling softly every weakness and flaw
and affliction and evil that plagued him. He confessed them all. In
one long glorious acknowledgment of failure, he laid himself bare
before God. He held nothing back. He unloaded enough burdens
to crush any three men, and when he finally finished Nate had tears
in his eyes. "I'm sorry," he whispered to God. "Please help me."

As quickly as the fever had left his body, he felt the baggage leave
his soul. With one gentle brush of the hand, his slate had been
wiped clean. He breathed a massive sigh of relief, but his pulse was
racing.

He heard the guitar again. He opened his eyes and wiped his
cheeks. Instead of seeing the young man in the pulpit, Nate saw the
face of Christ, in agony and pain, dying on the cross. Dying for
him.

A voice was calling Nate, a voice from within, a voice leading
him down the aisle. But the invitation was confusing. He felt many
conflicting emotions. His eyes were suddenly dry.

Why am I crying in a small hot chapel, listening to music I don't
understand, in a town I'll never see again? The questions poured
forth, the answers elusive.

It was one thing for God to forgive his astounding array of iniquities, and Nate certainly felt as though his burdens were lighter. But it was a far more difficult step to expect himself to become a follower.

As he listened to the music, he became bewildered. God couldn't be calling him. He was Nate O'Riley—boozer, addict, lover of women, absent father, miserable husband, greedy lawyer, swindler of tax money. The sad list went on and on.

He was dizzy. The music stopped and the young man prepared for another song. Nate hurriedly left the chapel. As he turned a corner, he glanced back, hoping to see Rachel, but also to make sure God hadn't sent someone to follow him.

He needed someone to talk to. He knew she was in Corumbá, and he vowed to find her.

THIRTY-EIGHT

T HE *DESPACHANTE* is an integral part of Brazilian life. No business, bank, law firm, medical group, or person with money can operate without the services of a *despachante*. He is a facilitator extraordinaire. In a country where the bureaucracy is sprawling and antiquated, the *despachante* is the guy who knows the city clerks, the courthouse crowd, the bureaucrats, the customs agents. He knows the system and how to grease it. No official paper or document is obtained in Brazil without waiting in long lines, and the *despachante* is the guy who'll stand there for you. For a small fee, he'll wait eight hours to renew your auto inspection, then affix it to your windshield while you're busy at the office. He'll do your voting, banking, packaging, mailing—the list has no end.

No bureaucratic obstacle is too intimidating.

Firms of *despachantes* display their names in windows just like lawyers and doctors. They're in the yellow pages. The job requires no formal training. All one needs is a quick tongue, patience, and a lot of brass.

Valdir's *despachante* in Corumbá knew another one in São Paulo, a powerful one with high contacts, and for a fee of two thousand dollars a new passport would be delivered.

JEVY SPENT the next few mornings at the river, helping a friend repair a *chalana*. He watched everything and heard the gossip. Not a word about the woman. By noon on Friday, he was convinced she had not arrived in Corumbá, at least not in the past two weeks. Jevy knew all the fishermen, captains, and deckhands. And they loved to talk. If an American woman who lived with the Indians suddenly arrived in town, they would know it.

Nate searched until the end of the week. He walked the streets, watched the crowds, checked out hotel lobbies and sidewalk cafés, looked at the faces, and saw no one even remotely resembling Rachel.

At one on his last day, he stopped at Valdir's office and collected his passport. They said good-bye like old friends, and promised to see each other soon. Both knew it would never happen. At two, Jevy drove him to the airport. They sat in the departure lounge for half an hour, watching as the only plane was unloaded, then prepped for reboarding. Jevy wanted to spend time in the United States, and needed Nate's help. "I'll need a job," he said. Nate listened with sympathy, not certain if he himself was still employed.

"I'll see what I can do."

They talked about Colorado and the West and places Nate had never been. Jevy was in love with the mountains, and after two weeks in the Pantanal Nate understood this. When it was time to go, they embraced warmly and said farewell. Nate walked across the hot pavement to the plane, carrying his entire wardrobe in a small gym bag.

The turbo-prop with twenty seats landed twice before it reached Campo Grande. There, the passengers boarded a jet for São Paulo. The lady in the seat next to him ordered a beer from the drink cart. Nate studied the can less than ten inches away. Not anymore, he told himself. He closed his eyes and asked God to give him strength. He ordered coffee.

The flight to Dulles left at midnight. It would arrive in D.C. at nine the next morning. His search for Rachel had taken him out of the country for almost three weeks.

He wasn't sure where his car was. He had no place to live, and no means to get one. But he couldn't worry. Josh would take care of the details.

THE PLANE dropped through the clouds at nine thousand feet. Nate was awake, sipping coffee, dreading the streets of home. The streets were cold and white. The earth was blanketed by a heavy snow. It was lovely for a few minutes as they approached Dulles, then Nate remembered how much he hated the winter. He wore a thin pair of trousers, no socks, cheap sneakers, and a fake Polo shirt he'd paid six dollars for in the São Paulo airport. He had no coat.

He would sleep somewhere that night, probably in a hotel, unsupervised in D.C. for the first time since August 4, the night he'd staggered into a suburban motel room. It had happened at the bottom of a long, pathetic crash. He'd worked hard to forget it.

But that was the old Nate, and now there was a new one. He was forty-eight years old, thirteen months away from fifty, and ready for a different life. God had fortified him, and strengthened his resolve. He had thirty years left. They wouldn't be spent clutching empty bottles. Nor would they be spent on the run.

Snowplows raced about as they taxied to the terminal. The runways were wet and flurries were still falling. When Nate stepped off the plane into the tunnel, winter hit him and he thought of the humid streets of Corumbá. Josh was waiting at the baggage claim, and of course he had an extra overcoat.

"You look awful," were his first words.

"Thanks." Nate grabbed the coat and put it on.

"You're skinny as a rail."

"You wanna lose fifteen pounds, find the right mosquito."

They moved with a mob toward the exits, bodies jostling and bumping, a shove here, a push there, the throng squeezing tighter to fit through doors. Welcome home, he said to himself.

"You're traveling light," Josh said, pointing at his gym bag.

"My worldly possessions."

With no socks or gloves, Nate was freezing on the curb by the time Josh found him with the car. The snowstorm had hit during the night, and had attained the status of a blizzard. Against the buildings the drifts had reached two feet.

"It was ninety-three yesterday in Corumbá," Nate said as they left the airport.

"Don't tell me you miss it."

"I do. Suddenly, I do."

"Look, Gayle is in London. I thought you could stay at our place for a couple of days."

Josh's house could sleep fifteen. "Sure, thanks. Where's my car?"

"In my garage."

Of course it was. It was a leased Jaguar, and it no doubt had been properly serviced, washed, and waxed, and the monthly payments were current. "Thanks, Josh."

"I put your furnishings in a mini-storage. Your clothes and personal effects are packed in the car."

"Thanks." Nate was not at all surprised.

"How do you feel?"

"I'm fine."

"Look, Nate, I've read about dengue fever. It takes a month to fully recover. Level with me."

A month. It was the opening jab in the fight over Nate's future with the firm. Take another month, old boy. Maybe you're too ill to work. Nate could write the script.

But there would be no fight.

"I'm a little weak, that's all. I'm sleeping a lot, drinking a lot of liquids."

"What kind of liquids?"

"Get right to the point, don't you?"

"I always do."

"I'm clean, Josh. Relax. No stumbles."

Josh had heard that many times. The exchange had been a bit

sharper than both men wanted, so they rode in silence for a while. The traffic was slow.

The Potomac was half-frozen with large chunks of ice floating slowly toward Georgetown. Stalled in traffic on the Chain Bridge, Nate announced, matter-of-factly, "I'm not going back to the office, Josh. Those days are over."

There was no visible reaction from Josh. He could've been disappointed because an old friend and fine litigator was calling it quits. He could've been delighted because a major headache was quietly leaving the firm. He could've been indifferent because Nate's exit was probably inevitable. The tax evasion mess would ultimately cost him his license anyway.

So he simply asked, "Why?"

"Lots of reasons, Josh. Let's just say I'm tired."

"Most litigators burn out after twenty years."

"So I've heard."

Enough of the retirement talk. Nate's mind was made up, and Josh didn't want to change it. The Super Bowl was two weeks away, and the Redskins were not in it. They seized the topic of football, as men usually do when they have to keep the conversation going in the midst of weightier matters.

Even under a heavy layer of snow, the streets looked mean to Nate.

THE STAFFORDS owned a large house in Wesley Heights, in Northwest D.C. They also had a cottage on the Chesapeake and a cabin in Maine. The four kids were grown and scattered. Mrs. Stafford preferred to travel while her husband preferred to work.

Nate retrieved some warm clothes from the trunk of his car, then enjoyed a hot shower in the guest quarters. The water pressure was weaker in Brazil. The shower in his hotel room was never hot, and never cold. The bars of soap were smaller. He compared the things around him. He was amused at the thought of the shower on the *Santa Loura*, a cord above the toilet that, when pulled, delivered lukewarm river water from a shower head. He was tougher than he thought; the adventure had taught him that much.

He shaved and then worked on his teeth, going about his habits with great deliberation. In many ways, it was nice to be home.

Josh's office in his basement was larger than the one downtown, and just as cluttered. They met there for coffee. It was time to debrief. Nate began with the ill-fated effort to find Rachel by air, the crash landing, the dead cow, the three little boys, the bleakness of Christmas in the Pantanal. With great detail, he recounted the story of his ride on the horse, and the encounter in the swamp with the curious alligator. Then the rescue by helicopter. He said nothing about the binge on Christmas night; it would serve no purpose and he was terribly ashamed of it. He described Jevy, Welly, the *Santa Loura,* and the trip north. When he and Jevy were lost in the johnboat, he remembered being frightened but too busy to be consumed with fear. Now, in the safety of civilization, their wanderings seemed terrifying.

Josh was astounded by the adventure. He wanted to apologize for sending Nate into such a treacherous place, but the excursion had obviously been exciting. The alligators grew as the narrative continued. The lone anaconda, sunning by the river, was joined by another that swam near their boat.

Nate described the Indians, their nakedness and bland food and languid lives, the chief and his refusal to let them leave.

And Rachel. At that point in the debriefing, Josh took his legal pad and began writing notes. Nate portrayed her in great detail, from her soft slow voice to her sandals and hiking boots. Her hut and medicine bag, Lako and his limp, and the way the Indians looked at her when she walked by. He told the story of the child who died from the snakebite. He relayed what little of her history she'd given him.

With the precision of a courtroom veteran, Nate covered everything about Rachel that he'd gathered on his visit. He used her exact words when talking about the money and the paperwork. He remembered her comment about how primitive Troy's handwritten will looked.

Nate recounted what little he remembered of their retreat from the Pantanal. And he downplayed the horror of dengue fever. He had survived, and that in itself surprised him.

A maid brought soup and hot tea for lunch. "Here's where we are," Josh said after a few spoonfuls. "If she rejects the gift under Troy's will, then the money remains in his estate. If, however, the will is found to be invalid for any reason, then there is no will."

"How can the will be invalid? They had psychiatrists talking to him minutes before he jumped."

"Now there are more psychiatrists, well paid and with different opinions. It'll get messy. All of his prior wills were shredded. If it's one day found that he died with no valid will, then his children, all seven of them, will share equally in his estate. Since Rachel doesn't want a share, then hers will be divided by the other six."

"Those fools will get a billion dollars each."

"Something like that."

"What are the chances of striking down his will?"

"Not good. I'd rather have our case than theirs, but things can change."

Nate walked around the room, nibbling on a saltine, weighing the issues. "Why fight for the validity of the will if Rachel declines everything?"

"Three reasons," Josh said quickly. As usual, he had analyzed everything from all possible angles. There was a master plan, and it would be revealed to Nate piece by piece. "First, and most important, my client prepared a valid will. It gave away his assets exactly as he wanted. I, as his lawyer, have no choice but to fight to protect the integrity of the will. Second, I know how Mr. Phelan felt about his children. He was horrified that they would somehow get their hands on his money. I share his feelings about them, and I shudder to think what would happen if they got a billion each. Third, there's always a chance Rachel will change her mind."

"Don't count on it."

"Look, Nate, she's only human. She has those papers with her. She'll wait a few days and start to think about them. Maybe thoughts of wealth have never entered her mind, but at some point she has to think of all the good things she could do with the money. Did you explain trusts and charitable foundations to her?"

"I barely know what those are myself, Josh. I was a litigator, remember?"

"We're gonna fight to protect Mr. Phelan's will, Nate. Problem is, the biggest seat at the table is empty. Rachel needs representation."

"No she doesn't. She's oblivious."

"The litigation can't proceed until she has a lawyer."

Nate was no match for the master strategist. The black hole opened from nowhere, and he was already falling into it. He closed his eyes and said, "You must be kidding."

"No. And we can't delay much longer. Troy died a month ago. Judge Wycliff is desperate to know the whereabouts of Rachel Lane. Six lawsuits have been filed contesting the will, and there's a lot of pressure behind them. Everything gets reported in the papers. If we give any hint that Rachel plans to decline the bequest, then we lose control. The Phelan heirs and their lawyers go crazy. The Judge suddenly loses interest in upholding Troy's last testament."

"So I'm her lawyer?"

"There's no way around it, Nate. If you're quitting, that's fine, but you have to take one last case. Just sit at the table and protect her interests. We'll do the heavy lifting."

"But there's a conflict. I'm a partner in your firm."

"It's a minor conflict because our interests are the same. We—the estate and Rachel—have the same goal of protecting the will. We sit at the same table. And technically, we can claim you left the firm last August."

"There's a lot of truth in that."

Both acknowledged the sad truth. Josh sipped his tea, his eyes never leaving Nate. "At some point we go to Wycliff and tell him that you found Rachel, that she plans to make no appearance at this time, that she's not sure what to do, but that she wants you to protect her interests."

"Then we'll be lying to the Judge."

"It's a small lie, Nate, and he'll thank us for it later. He's anxious to start proceedings, but he can't until he hears from Rachel. If you're her lawyer, the war begins. I'll do the lying."

"So I'm a one-man office working on my last case."

"Right."

"I'm leaving town, Josh. I'm not staying." Nate said this, then he laughed. "Where would I stay?"

"Where are you going?"

"I don't know. I haven't thought that far ahead."

"I have an idea."

"I'm sure you do."

"Take my cottage on Chesapeake Bay. We don't use it in the wintertime. It's at St. Michaels, two hours away. You can drive in when you're needed, and stay here. Again, Nate, we'll do the work."

Nate studied the bookshelves for a while. Twenty-four hours earlier he'd been eating a sandwich on a park bench, in Corumbá, watching the pedestrians and waiting for Rachel to appear. He had vowed to never again voluntarily step into a courtroom.

But he grudgingly admitted that the plan had its strong points. He certainly couldn't imagine a better client. The case would never go to trial. And with the money at stake he could at least earn a living for a few months.

Josh finished his soup and moved to the next item on the list. "I propose a fee of ten thousand dollars a month."

"That's generous, Josh."

"I think we can squeeze it from the old man's estate. With no overhead, it'll get you back on your feet."

"Until . . ."

"Right, until we settle with the IRS."

"Any word from the Judge?"

"I call him occasionally. We had lunch last week."

"So he's your buddy?"

"We've known each other for a long time. Forget jail, Nate. The government will settle for a big fine and a five-year suspension of your law license."

"They can have my law license."

"Not yet. We need it for one more case."

"How long will the government wait?"

"A year. It's not a priority."

"Thanks, Josh." Nate was tired again. The all-night flight, the ravages of the jungle, the mental jousting with Josh. He wanted a warm soft bed in a dark room.

THIRTY-NINE

AT SIX SUNDAY MORNING, Nate finished another hot shower, his third in twenty-four hours, and began making plans for a quick departure. One night in the city, and he was anxious to leave. The cottage on the bay was calling him. D.C. had been his home for twenty-six years, and since the decision to leave had been made, he was eager to move on.

With no address, moving was easy. He found Josh in the basement, at his desk, on the phone with a client in Thailand. As Nate listened to one-half of the conversation about natural gas deposits, he was quite happy to be leaving the practice of law. Josh was twelve years older, a very rich man, and his idea of fun was to be at his desk at six-thirty on a Sunday morning. Don't let it happen to me, Nate said to himself, but he knew it wouldn't. If he went back to the office, he would return to the grind. Four rehabs meant a fifth was somewhere down the road. He wasn't as strong as Josh. He'd be dead in ten years.

There was an element of excitement in walking away. Suing doctors was a nasty business, one he could do without. Nor would he miss the stress of a high-powered office. He'd had his career, his triumphs. Success had brought him nothing but misery; he couldn't handle it. Success had thrown him in the gutter.

Now that the horror of jail had been removed, he could enjoy a new life.

He left with a trunkload of clothes, leaving the rest in a box in Josh's garage. The snow had stopped, but the plows were still catching up. The streets were slick, and after two blocks it occurred to Nate that he had not held the wheel of a car in over five months. There was no traffic, though, and he crept along Wisconsin into Chevy Chase, then onto the Beltway where the ice and snow had been cleared.

Alone, in his own fine car, he began to feel like an American again. He thought of Jevy in his loud, dangerous Ford truck, and wondered how long he would last on the Beltway. And he thought of Welly, a kid so poor his family owned no car. Nate planned to write letters in the days to come, and he would send one to his buddies in Corumbá.

The phone caught his attention. He picked it up; it appeared to be working. Of course Josh had made sure the bills were paid. He called Sergio at home, and they talked for twenty minutes. He got scolded for not calling sooner. Sergio had been worried. He explained the situation with telephone service in the Pantanal. Things were going in a different direction, there were some unknowns, but his adventure was continuing. He was leaving the profession and avoiding jail.

Sergio never asked about sobriety. Nate certainly sounded clean and strong. He gave him the number at the cottage, and they promised to have lunch soon.

He called his oldest son at Northwestern, in Evanston, and left a message on the recorder. Where would a twenty-three-year-old grad student be at 7 A.M. on a Sunday morning? Not at early mass. Nate didn't want to know. Whatever his son was doing, he would never screw up as badly as his father. His daughter was twenty-one, an on-again off-again student at Pitt. Their last conversation had been about tuition, a day before Nate checked into the motel room with a bottle of rum and a sack full of pills.

He couldn't find her phone number.

Their mother had remarried twice since leaving Nate. She was an unpleasant person whom he called only when absolutely necessary. He would wait a couple of days, then ask her for their daughter's phone number.

He was determined to make the painful trip west, to Oregon, to at least see his two youngest children. Their mother had remarried too, remarkably to another lawyer, but one who evidently lived a clean life. He would ask them for forgiveness, and try to establish the frail beginnings of a relationship. He wasn't sure how to do this, but he vowed to try.

In Annapolis, he stopped at a café and had breakfast. He listened to the weather predictions from a group of rowdy regulars in a booth, and he mindlessly scanned the *Post*. From the headlines and late-breaking stories, Nate saw nothing that interested him in the least. The news never changed: trouble in the Middle East, trouble in Ireland; scandals in Congress; the markets were up then down; an oil spill; another AIDS drug; guerrillas killing peasants in Latin America; turmoil in Russia.

His clothes hung loose on him, so he ate three eggs with bacon and biscuits. A shaky consensus emerged from the booth that more snow was on the way.

He crossed the Chesapeake on the Bay Bridge. The highways on the eastern shore had not been plowed well. The Jaguar skidded twice, and he slowed down. The car was a year old, and he couldn't remember when the lease expired. His secretary had handled the paperwork. He'd picked the color. He decided to get rid of it as soon as possible and find an old four-wheel drive. The fancy lawyer's car had once seemed so important. Now he had no need for it.

At Easton, he turned onto State Route 33, a road with two inches of loose snow still resting on the blacktop. Nate followed the tracks of other vehicles, and soon passed through sleepy little settlements with harbors filled with sailboats. The shores of the Chesapeake were covered with heavy snow; its waters were deep blue.

St. Michaels had a population of thirteen hundred. Route 33 became Main Street for a few blocks as it ran through the town. There were shops and stores on both sides, old buildings side by side, all well preserved and ready for the postcard.

Nate had heard of St. Michaels all his life. There was a maritime museum, an oyster festival, an active harbor, dozens of quaint little bed-and-breakfasts which attracted city folks for long weekends. He passed the post office and a small church, where the Rector was shoveling snow from the front steps.

The cottage was on Green Street, two blocks off Main, facing north with a view of the harbor. It was Victorian, with twin gables, and a long front porch that wrapped around to the sides. Painted slate blue, with white and yellow trim, the house had snow drifts almost to the front door. The front lawn was small, the driveway under two feet of snow. Nate parked at the curb and fought his way to the porch. He flipped on lights inside as he walked to the rear. In a closet by the back door, he found a plastic shovel.

He spent a wonderful hour cleaning the porch, clearing the drive and sidewalk, working his way back to his car.

Not surprisingly, the house was richly decorated with period pieces, and it was tidy and organized. Josh said a maid came every Wednesday to dust and clean. Mrs. Stafford stayed there for two weeks in the spring and one in the fall. Josh had slept there three nights in the past eighteen months. There were four bedrooms and four baths. Some cottage.

But there was no coffee to be found, and this presented the first emergency of the day. Nate locked the doors and headed for town. The sidewalks were clear and wet from melting snow. According to the thermometer in the window of the barbershop, the temperature was thirty-five degrees. The shops and stores were closed. Nate studied their windows as he ambled along. Ahead, the church bells began.

ACCORDING to the bulletin handed to Nate by the elderly usher, the Rector was Father Phil Lancaster, a short, wiry little man with thick horn-rimmed glasses and curly hair that was red and gray. He could've been thirty-five or fifty. His flock for the eleven o'clock service was old and thin, no doubt hampered by the weather. Nate counted twenty-one people in the small sanctuary, and that included Phil and the organist. There were many gray heads.

It was a handsome church, with a vaulted ceiling, pews and floors of dark wood, four windows of stained glass. When the lone usher took his seat in the back pew, Phil rose in his black robe and welcomed them to Trinity Church, where everyone was at home. His voice was high and nasal, and he needed no microphone. In his prayer he thanked God for snow and winter, for the seasons given as reminders that He was always in control.

They struggled through the hymns and prayers. When Father Phil preached he noticed Nate, the sole visitor, sitting in the next to last row. They exchanged smiles, and for one scary moment Nate was afraid he was about to be introduced to the small crowd.

His sermon was on the subject of enthusiasm, an odd choice given the average age of his congregation. Nate struggled hard to pay attention, but began to drift. His thoughts returned to the little chapel in Corumbá, with the front doors open, the windows up, the heat drifting through, the dying Christ suffering on the cross, the young man with the guitar.

Careful not to offend Phil, he managed to keep his eyes fixed on the globe of a dim light on the wall behind and above the pulpit. Given the thickness of the preacher's eyeglasses, he figured his disinterest would go unnoticed.

Sitting in the warm little church, finally safe from the uncertainties of his great adventure, safe from fevers and storms, safe from the dangers of D.C., safe from his addictions, safe from spiritual extinction, Nate realized that for the first time in memory he was at peace. He feared nothing. God was pulling him in some direction. He wasn't certain where, but he wasn't afraid either. Be patient, he told himself.

Then he whispered a prayer. He thanked God for sparing his life, and he prayed for Rachel, because he knew she was praying for him.

The serenity made him smile. When the prayer was over, he opened his eyes and saw that Phil was smiling at him.

After the benediction, they filed past Phil at the front door, each complimenting him on the sermon and mentioning some brief bit of church news. The line moved slowly; it was a ritual. "How's your aunt?" Phil asked one of his flock, then listened carefully as the aunt's latest affliction was described. "How's that hip?" he asked another. "How was Germany?" He clutched their hands and bent forward to hear every word. He knew what was on their minds.

Nate waited patiently at the end of the line. There was no hurry. He had nothing else to do. "Welcome," Father Phil said as he grabbed Nate by the hand and arm. "Welcome to Trinity." He squeezed so tightly Nate wondered if he were the first guest in years.

"I'm Nate O'Riley," he said, then added, "From Washington," as if that would help define him.

"So nice to have you with us this morning," Phil said, his big eyes dancing behind the glasses. Up close, the wrinkles revealed that he was at least fifty. His head had more gray curls than red.

"I'm staying in the Stafford cottage for a few days," Nate said.

"Yes, yes, a lovely home. When did you arrive?"

"This morning."

"Are you alone?"

"Yes."

"Well, then you must join us for lunch."

The aggressive hospitality made Nate laugh. "Well, uh, thanks, but—"

Phil was all smiles too. "No, I insist. My wife makes a lamb stew every time it snows. It's on the stove now. We have so few guests in the wintertime. Please, the parsonage is just behind the church."

Nate was in the hands of a man who'd shared his Sunday table with hundreds. "Really, I was just stopping by, and I—"

"It's our pleasure," Phil said, already tugging at Nate's arm and leading him back toward the pulpit. "What do you do in Washington?"

"I'm a lawyer," Nate said. A complete answer would get complicated.

"What brings you here?"

"It's a long story."

"Oh wonderful! Laura and I love stories. Let's have a long lunch and tell stories. We'll have a grand time." His enthusiasm was irresistible. Poor guy was starved for fresh conversation. Why not? thought Nate. There was no food in the cottage. All stores appeared to be closed.

They passed the pulpit and went through a door leading to the rear of the church. Laura was turning off lights. "This is Mr. O'Riley, from Washington," Phil said loudly to his wife. "He's agreed to join us for lunch."

Laura smiled and shook Nate's hand. She had short gray hair and looked at least ten years older than her husband. If a sudden guest at the table surprised her, it wasn't evident. Nate got the impression it happened all the time. "Please call me Nate," he said.

"Nate it is," Phil announced, peeling off his robe.

The parsonage was adjacent to the church lot, facing a side street. They carefully stepped through the snow. "How was my sermon?" Phil asked her as they stepped onto the porch.

"Excellent, dear," she said without a trace of enthusiasm. Nate listened and smiled, certain that every Sunday for years Phil had asked the same question, at the same place and time, and received the same answer.

Any hesitation about staying for lunch vanished when he stepped into the house. The rich, heavy aroma of the lamb stew wafted through the den. Phil poked at the orange coals in the fireplace while Laura prepared the meal.

In the narrow dining room between the kitchen and the den, a table had been set for four. Nate was pleased that he had accepted their invitation, not that he'd had the chance to decline it.

"We're so glad you're here," Phil said as they took their seats. "I had a hunch we might have a guest today."

"Whose place is that?" Nate asked, nodding to the empty setting.

"We always set four places on Sunday," Laura said, and let the explanation go at that. They held hands as Phil thanked God again for the snow and the seasons, and for the food. He concluded with, "And keep us ever mindful of the needs and wants of others." Those words triggered something in Nate's memory. He'd heard them before, many, many years before.

As the food was passed around, there was the usual talk about the morning. They averaged forty at the eleven o'clock service. The snow had indeed kept people away. And there was a flu bug on the peninsula. Nate complimented them on the simple beauty of the sanctuary. They had been in St. Michaels for six years. Not long into the lunch, Laura said, "You have a nice tan for January. You didn't get that in Washington?"

"No. I just returned from Brazil." They both stopped eating and leaned closer. The adventure was on again. Nate took a large spoonful of stew, which was thick and delicious, then began the story.

"Please eat," Laura said every five minutes or so. Nate took a bite, chewed slowly, then proceeded. He referred to Rachel only as "the daughter of a client." The storms grew fiercer, the snakes longer, the boat smaller, the Indians less friendly. Phil's eyes danced with amazement as Nate went from chapter to chapter.

It was the second time Nate had told the story since his return. Other than a slight exaggeration here and there, he kept to the facts. And it amazed even him. It was a remarkable story to tell, and his hosts got a long, rich version of it. They wedged in questions whenever they could.

When Laura cleared the table and served brownies for dessert, Nate and Jevy had just arrived at the first Ipica settlement.

"Was she surprised to see you?" Phil asked when Nate described the scene with the band of Indians leading the woman out of the village to meet them.

"Not really," Nate said. "She seemed to know we were coming."

Nate did his best to describe the Indians and their Stone Age culture, but words failed to deliver the right images. He ate two brownies, clearing his plate with large bites during brief gaps in the narrative.

They pushed their plates away and had coffee. Sunday lunch for Phil and Laura was more about conversation than eating. Nate wondered who'd been the last guest lucky enough to be invited in for stories and food.

It was hard to downplay the horrors of dengue, but Nate tried gamely. A couple of days in the hospital, some medication, and he was back on his feet. When he finished, the questions began. Phil wanted to know everything about the missionary—her denomination, her faith, her work with the Indians. Laura's sister had lived in China for fifteen years, working in a church hospital, and this became the source of more stories.

It was almost three o'clock when Nate made it to the door. His hosts would have gladly sat at the table or in the den and talked until dark, but Nate needed a walk. He thanked them for their hospitality, and when he left them waving on the porch he felt as though he'd known them for years.

It took an hour to walk St. Michaels. The streets were narrow and lined with homes a hundred years old. Nothing was out of place, no stray dogs, vacant lots, abandoned buildings. Even the snow was neat—carefully shoveled so that the streets and sidewalks were clear and no neighbor was offended. Nate stopped at the pier and admired the sailboats. He had never set foot on one.

He decided he wouldn't leave St. Michaels until he was forced. He would live in the cottage, and remain there until Josh politely evicted him. He would save his money, and when the Phelan matter was over he would find some way to hang on.

Near the harbor he stumbled on to a small grocery about to close for the day. He bought coffee, canned soup, saltines, and oatmeal for breakfast. There was a display of bottled beer by the counter. He smiled at it, happy those days were behind him.

FORTY

GRIT GOT HIMSELF fired by fax and by e-mail, a first for his office. Mary Ross did it to him, early Monday morning, after a tense weekend with her brothers.

Grit did not exit gracefully. He faxed her back and submitted a bill for his services to date—148 hours at $600 per, for a total of $88,800. His hourly billings were to be applied against his percentage upon settlement or other favorable outcome. Grit didn't want $600 an hour. Grit wanted a piece of the pie, a healthy fraction of his client's cut, the 25 percent he'd negotiated. Grit wanted millions, and as he sat in his locked office, staring at the fax, he found it impossible to believe that his fortune had slipped away. He truly believed that after a few months of hardball litigation, the Phelan estate would settle with the children. Throw twenty million at each of the six, watch them attack it like hungry dogs, and there wouldn't be the slightest dent in the Phelan fortune. Twenty million to his client was five million to him, and Grit, alone, had to confess that he'd already thought of several ways to spend it.

He called Hark's office to curse him, but was told Mr. Gettys was too busy at the moment.

Mr. Gettys now had three of the four heirs from the first family. His percentage had dropped from twenty-five to twenty, and now to seventeen-five. But his upside potential was enormous.

Mr. Gettys walked into his conference room a few minutes after ten and greeted the remaining Phelan lawyers, gathered there for an important meeting. He cheerfully said, "I have an announcement. Mr. Grit is no longer involved in this case. His ex-client, Mary Ross Phelan Jackman, has asked me to represent her, and, after much consideration, I have agreed to do so."

His words hit like small bombs around the conference table. Yancy stroked his scraggly beard and wondered what method of coercion had been used to pry the woman away from Grit's tentacles. He felt somewhat safe, though. Ramble's mother had used every means possible to lure the kid to another lawyer. But the kid hated his mother.

Madam Langhorne was surprised, especially since Hark had just added Troy Junior as a client. But after the brief shock, she felt secure. Her client, Geena Phelan Strong, detested her older half-brothers and -sisters. Surely she wouldn't throw in with their lawyer. Nonetheless, a power lunch was needed. She would call Geena and Cody when the meeting was over. They'd dine at the Promenade near the Capitol, and maybe catch a glimpse of a powerful subcommittee vice chairman.

The back of Wally Bright's neck turned scarlet with the news. Hark was raiding clients, chasing ambulances. Only Libbigail remained from the first family, and Wally Bright would kill Hark if he tried to steal her. "Stay away from my client, okay?" he said loudly and bitterly, and the entire room froze.

"Relax."

"Relax, my ass. How can we relax when you're stealing clients?"

"I didn't steal Mrs. Jackman. She called me. I didn't call her."

"We know the game you're playing, Hark. We're not stupid." Wally said this while looking at his fellow lawyers. They certainly didn't consider themselves to be stupid, but they weren't so sure about Wally. Truth was, no one could trust anyone. There was simply too much money at stake to assume that the lawyer next to you would not pull out a knife.

They led Snead in, and this changed the focus of the discussion. Hark introduced him to the group. Poor Snead looked like a man facing a firing squad. He sat at the end of the table, with two video cameras aimed at him. "This is just a rehearsal," Hark assured him. "Relax." The lawyers pulled out legal pads covered with questions, and they inched closer to Snead.

Hark walked behind him, patted him on the shoulder, and said, "Now, when you give your deposition, Mr. Snead, the lawyers for the other side will be allowed to interrogate you first. So for the next hour or so, you are to assume that we are the enemy. Okay?"

It certainly wasn't okay with Snead, but he'd taken their money. He had to play along.

Hark picked up his legal pad and began asking questions, simple things about his birth, background, family, school, easy stuff that Snead handled well and relaxed with. Then the early years with Mr. Phelan, and a thousand questions that seemed completely irrelevant.

After a bathroom break, Madam Langhorne took the baton and grilled Snead about the Phelan families, the wives, the kids, the divorces, and mistresses. Snead thought it was a lot of unnecessary dirt, but the lawyers seemed to enjoy it.

"Did you know about Rachel Lane?" Langhorne asked.

Snead pondered this for a moment, then said, "I haven't thought about that." In other words, help me with the answer. "What would you guess?" he asked Mr. Gettys.

Hark was quick with the fiction. "I would guess that you knew everything about Mr. Phelan, especially his women and their offspring. Nothing escaped you. The old man confided everything in you, including the existence of his illegitimate daughter. She was ten or eleven when you went to work for Mr. Phelan. He tried to reach out to her over the years but she would have nothing to do with him. I would guess that this hurt him deeply, that he was a man who got whatever he wanted, and when Rachel spurned him his pain turned to anger. I would guess that he disliked her immensely. Thus, for him to leave her everything was an act of sheer insanity."

Once again, Snead marveled at Hark's ability to spin tales so quickly. The other lawyers were impressed too. "What do you think?" Hark asked them.

They nodded their approvals. "Better get him all the background on Rachel Lane," Bright said.

Snead then repeated for the cameras the same story Hark had just told, and in doing so showed a passable skill at expanding on a theme. When he finished, the lawyers couldn't suppress their pleasure. The worm would say anything. And there was no one to contradict it.

When Snead was asked a question that needed assistance, he responded by saying, "Well, I haven't thought about that." The lawyers would then reach out to help. Hark, who seemed to anticipate Snead's weaknesses, usually had a quick narrative at hand. Often, though, the other lawyers chimed in with their little plots, all anxious to display their skills at lying.

Layer upon layer was fabricated, and fine-tuned, carefully molded to ensure that Mr. Phelan was out of his mind the morning he scrawled his last testament. Snead was coached by the lawyers, and he proved quite easy to lead. In fact, he was so coachable the lawyers worried that he might say too much. His credibility could not be damaged. There could be no holes in his testimony.

For three hours they built his story, then for two hours they tried to tear it down with relentless cross-examination. They didn't feed him lunch. They sneered at him and called him a liar. At one point Langhorne had him near tears. When he was exhausted and ready to collapse, they sent him home with the pack of videos and instructions to study them over and over.

He wasn't ready to testify, they told him. His stories weren't airtight. Poor Snead drove home in his new Range Rover, tired and bewildered, but also determined to practice his lies until the lawyers applauded him.

□ □ □ □

JUDGE WYCLIFF enjoyed the quiet little lunches in his office. As usual, Josh picked up sandwiches from a Greek deli near Dupont Circle. He unpacked them, along with iced tea and pickles, on the small table in a corner. They huddled over their food, at first talking about how busy they were, then quickly getting around to the Phelan estate. Something was up, or Josh wouldn't have called.

"We found Rachel Lane," he said.

"Wonderful. Where?" The relief in Wycliff's face was obvious.

"She made us promise not to tell. At least not now."

"Is she in the country?" The Judge forgot about his corned beef on kaiser.

"No. She's in a very remote spot in the world, and quite content to stay there."

"How did you find her?"

"Her lawyer found her."

"Who's her lawyer?"

"A guy who used to work in my firm. Name's Nate O'Riley, a former partner. Left us back in August."

Wycliff narrowed his eyes and considered this. "What a coincidence. She hires a former partner of the law firm her father used."

"There's no coincidence. As the attorney for the estate, I had to find her. I sent Nate O'Riley. He found her, she hired him. It's really pretty simple."

"When does she make her appearance?"

"I doubt if she'll do it in person."

"What about the acknowledgment and waiver?"

"They're coming. She's very deliberate, and, frankly, I'm not sure what her plans are."

"We have a will contest, Josh. The war has already erupted. Things can't wait. This court must have jurisdiction over her."

"Judge, she has legal representation. Her interests will be protected. Let's fight. We'll start discovery, and see what the other side has."

"Can I talk to her?"

"It's impossible."

"Come on, Josh."

"I swear. Look, she's a missionary in a very remote place, in a different hemisphere. That's all I can tell you."

"I want to see Mr. O'Riley."

"When?"

Wycliff walked to his desk and grabbed the nearest appointment book. He was so busy. Life was regulated by a docket calendar, a trial calendar, a motion calendar. His secretary kept an office calendar. "How about this Wednesday?"

"Fine. For lunch? Just the three of us, off the record."

"Sure."

LAWYER O'RILEY had planned to read and write throughout the morning. His plans were diverted, though, with a phone call from the Rector. "Are you busy?" Father Phil asked, his strong voice resonating over the phone.

"Well, no, not really," Nate said. He was sitting in a deep leather chair, under a quilt, beside the fire, sipping coffee and reading Mark Twain.

"Are you sure?"

"Of course I'm sure."

"Well, I'm at the church, working in the basement, doing some remodeling, and I need a hand. I thought you might be bored, you know, since there's not much to do here in St. Michaels, at least not in the winter. It's supposed to snow again today."

The lamb stew crossed Nate's mind. There was plenty of it left over. "I'll be there in ten minutes."

The basement was directly under the sanctuary. Nate heard hammering as he carefully descended the shaky steps. It was an open room, long and wide with a low ceiling. A remodeling project had been under way for a long time, with no end in sight. The general plan appeared to be a series of small rooms against the outer walls, with an open space in the center. Phil stood between two sawhorses, tape measure in hand, sawdust on his shoulders. He wore a flannel shirt, jeans, boots, and would've easily passed for a carpenter.

"Thanks for coming," he said with a big smile.

"You're welcome. I was bored," Nate said.

"I'm hanging wallboard," he said, waving his arm at the construction. "It's easier if there are two people. Mr. Fuqua used to help, but he's eighty now and his back is not what it used to be."

"What are you building?"

"Six classrooms for Bible study. This center area will be a fellowship hall. I started two years ago. Our budget doesn't allow much in the way of new projects, so I'm doing it myself. Keeps me in shape."

Father Phil hadn't been in shape in years. "Point me in the right direction," Nate said. "And remember I'm a lawyer."

"Not a lot of honest work, huh?"

"No."

They each took an end of a sheet of wallboard and wrestled it across the floor to the current classroom in progress. The sheet was four feet by six, and as they lifted it into place Nate realized that it was indeed a job for two people. Phil grunted and frowned and bit his tongue, and when the piece fit the puzzle, he said, "Now just hold it right there." Nate pressed the board against the two by four studs while Phil quickly tacked it into place with sheetrock nails. Once secure, he drove six more nails into the studs, and admired his handiwork. Then he produced a tape and began to measure the next open space.

"Where did you learn to be a carpenter?" Nate asked as he watched with interest.

"It's in my blood. Joseph was a carpenter."

"Who's he?"

"The father of Jesus."

"Oh, that Joseph."

"Do you read the Bible, Nate?"

"Not much."

"You should."

"I'd like to start."

"I can help you, if you want."

"Thanks."

Phil scribbled dimensions on the wallboard they had just installed. He measured carefully, then remeasured. Before long, Nate realized why the project was taking so long. Phil took his time and believed in a vigorous regimen of coffee breaks.

After an hour, they walked up the stairs to the main floor, to the Rector's office, which was ten degrees warmer than the basement. Phil had a pot of strong coffee on a small burner. He poured two cups and began scanning the rows of books on the shelves. "Here's a wonderful daily devotional guide, one of my favorites," he said, gently removing the book, wiping it as if it were covered in dust, then handing it to Nate. It was a hardback with the dust jacket intact. Phil was particular about his books.

He selected another, and handed it to Nate. "This is a Bible study for busy people. It's very good."

"What makes you think I'm busy?"

"You're a lawyer in Washington, aren't you?"

"Technically, but those days are about to be over."

Phil tapped his fingertips together, and looked at Nate as only a minister can. His eyes said, "Keep going. Tell me more. I'm here to help."

So Nate unloaded some of his troubles, past and present, with emphasis on the pending showdown with the IRS and the imminent loss of his law license. He would avoid jail, but be required to pay a fine he couldn't afford.

Nonetheless, he wasn't unhappy about the future. In fact, he was relieved to be leaving the profession.

"What will you do?" Phil asked.

"I have no idea."

"Do you trust God?"

"Yes, I think so."

"Then relax. He'll show you the way."

THEY TALKED long enough to stretch the morning to the lunch hour, then walked next door and feasted once again on the lamb stew. Laura joined them late. She taught kindergarten and only had thirty minutes for lunch.

Around two, they made it back to the basement, where they reluctantly resumed their labor. Watching Phil work, Nate became convinced that the project would not be finished in his lifetime. Joseph may have been a fine carpenter, but Father Phil belonged in the pulpit. Every open space on the wall had to be measured, remeasured, pondered over, looked at from various angles, then measured again. The sheet of wallboard destined to fill the open space went through the same procedures. Finally, after enough pencil markings to confuse an architect, Phil, with great trepidation, took the electric saw and cut the wallboard. They carried the sheet to the open space, tacked it, then secured it. The fit was always perfect, and with each one Phil seemed genuinely relieved.

Two classrooms appeared to be finished and ready for paint. Late in the afternoon, Nate decided that tomorrow he would become a painter.

FORTY-ONE

TWO DAYS of pleasant labor yielded little progress in the chilly basement of Trinity Church. But much coffee was consumed, the lamb stew was finally finished, some paint and wallboard fell into place, and a friendship was built.

Nate was scraping paint from his fingernails Tuesday night when the phone rang. It was Josh, calling him back to the real world. "Judge Wycliff wants to see you tomorrow," he said. "I tried to call earlier."

"What does he want?" Nate asked, his voice flat with dread.

"I'm sure he'll have questions about your new client."

"I'm really busy, Josh. I'm into remodeling, painting, and sheet-rock, stuff like that."

"Oh really."

"Yeah, I'm doing the basement of a church. Time is of the essence."

"Didn't know you had such talents."

"Do I have to come, Josh?"

"I think so, pal. You agreed to take this case. I've already told the Judge. You're needed, old boy."

"When and where?"

"Come to my office at eleven. We'll ride over together."

"I don't want to see the office, Josh. It's all bad memories. I'll just meet you at the courthouse."

"Fine. Be there at noon. Judge Wycliff's office."

Nate put a log on the fire and watched the snow flurries float across the porch. He could put on a suit and tie and carry a briefcase around. He could look and talk the part. He could say "Your Honor" and "May it please the court," and he could yell objections and grill witnesses. He could do all the things a million others did, but he no longer considered himself a lawyer. Those days were gone, thank God.

He could do it once more, but only once. He tried to convince himself it was for his client, for Rachel, but he knew she didn't care.

He still hadn't written her, though he'd planned the letter many times. The one to Jevy had required two hours of hard work, for a page and a half.

After three days in the snow, he missed the humid streets of Corumbá, with the lazy pedestrian traffic, the outdoor cafés, the pace of life that said everything could wait until tomorrow. It was snowing harder by the minute. Maybe it's another blizzard, he thought, and the roads will be closed, and I won't have to go after all.

MORE SANDWICHES from the Greek deli, more pickles and tea. Josh prepared the table as they waited for Judge Wycliff. "Here's the court file," he said, handing a bulky red binder to Nate. "And here's your response," he said, handing over a manila file. "You need to read and sign this as soon as possible."

"Has the estate filed an answer?" Nate asked.

"Tomorrow. The answer of Rachel Lane is in there, already prepared, just waiting for your signature."

"There's something wrong here, Josh. I'm filing an answer to a will contest on behalf of a client who doesn't know it."

"Send her a copy."

"To where?"

"To her only known address, that of World Tribes Missions in Houston, Texas. It's all in the file."

Nate shook his head in frustration at Josh's preparations. He felt like a pawn on a gameboard. The Answer of the Proponent, Rachel Lane, was four pages long and denied, both generally and specifically, the allegations set forth in the six petitions challenging the will. Nate read the six petitions while Josh worked his cell phone.

When all the rash allegations and legalese were pared down, it was a simple case: Did Troy Phelan know what he was doing when he wrote his last testament? The trial would be a circus though, with the lawyers trotting in psychiatrists of every sort and species. Employees, ex-employees, old girlfriends, janitors, maids, chauffeurs, pilots, bodyguards, doctors, prostitutes, anybody who'd spent five minutes with the old man would be hauled in to testify.

Nate didn't have the stomach for it. The file grew heavier as he read. It would fill a room when the war was finally over.

Judge Wycliff made his usual fussy entrance at twelve-thirty, apologizing for being so busy while yanking off his robe. "You're Nate O'Riley," he said, thrusting forth a hand.

"Yes, Judge, a pleasure to meet you."

Josh managed to disengage himself from the cell phone. They squeezed around the small table and began eating. "Josh tells me you found the richest woman in the world," Wycliff said, smacking his food.

"Yes, I did. About two weeks ago."

"And you can't tell me where she is?"

"She begged me not to. I promised."

"Will she appear and testify at the appropriate time?"

"She won't have to," Josh explained. Of course he had a brief, a Stafford Memo, in his file on the issue of her presence during the lawsuit. "If she knows nothing about Mr. Phelan's mental capacity, she can't be a witness."

"But she's a party," Wycliff said.

"Yes she is. But her presence can be excused. We can litigate without her."

"Excused by whom?"

"You, Your Honor."

"I plan to file a motion at the appropriate time," Nate said, "asking the court to allow the trial to be held without her presence." Josh smiled across the table. Atta boy, Nate.

"I guess we'll worry about it later," Wycliff said. "I'm more concerned about discovery. Needless to say, the contestants are quite anxious to move ahead."

"The estate will file its answer tomorrow," Josh said. "We're ready for battle."

"What about the proponent?"

"I'm still working on her answer," Nate said somberly, as if he'd labored days on it. "But I can file it tomorrow."

"Are you ready for discovery?"

"Yes sir."

"When can we expect the waiver and acknowledgment from your client?"

"I'm not sure."

"Technically, I don't have jurisdiction over her until I receive them."

"Yes, I understand. I'm sure they'll be here soon. Her mail service is very slow."

Josh smiled at his protégé.

"You actually found her, showed her a copy of the will, explained the waiver and acknowledgment, and agreed to represent her?"

"Yes sir," Nate said, but only because he had to.

"Will you put that in an affidavit for the file?"

"That's a bit unusual, isn't it?" Josh asked.

"Maybe, but if we start discovery without her waiver and acknowledgment, I want some record in the file showing that she has been contacted and knows what we're doing."

"Good idea, Judge," Josh said, as if the idea had been his to start with. "Nate will sign it."

Nate nodded and took a large bite of his sandwich, hoping they would let him eat without being forced to tell more lies.

"Was she close to Troy?" Wycliff asked.

Nate chewed as long as he could before answering. "We're off the record here, aren't we?"

"Of course. This is just gossip."

Yes, and gossip can win and lose lawsuits. "I don't think they were that close. She hadn't seen him in years."

"How did she react when she read the will?"

Wycliff's tone was indeed gossipy and chatty, and Nate knew the Judge wanted all the details. "She was surprised, to say the least," he said dryly.

"I'll bet. Did she ask how much?"

"Eventually, yes. I think she was overwhelmed, as anyone would be."

"Is she married?"

"No."

Josh realized the questions about Rachel could go on for a while. And the questions were dangerous. Wycliff could not know, at least not at that point, that Rachel had no interest in the money. If he kept digging, and if Nate kept telling the truth, something would slip. "You know, Judge," he said, gently steering the conversation in another direction, "this is not a complicated case. Discovery shouldn't take forever. They're anxious. We're anxious. There's a pile of money sitting on the table and everybody wants it. Why can't we fast-track discovery and set a trial date?"

Speeding litigation along in a probate matter was unheard of. Estate lawyers were paid by the hour. Why hurry?

"That's interesting," Wycliff said. "What do you have in mind?"

"Have a discovery conference as soon as possible. Get all the lawyers in one room, make each produce a list of potential trial witnesses and documents. Designate thirty days for all depositions, and set a trial date ninety days away."

"That's awfully fast."

"We do it in federal court all the time. It works. The boys on the other side will jump at it because their clients are all broke."

"What about you, Mr. O'Riley? Is your client anxious to get the money?"

"Wouldn't you be anxious, Judge?" Nate asked.

And they all laughed.

WHEN GRIT finally penetrated Hark's line of phone defenses, his first words were, "I'm thinking about going to the Judge."

Hark pressed the record button on his phone, and said, "Good afternoon to you, Grit."

"I might tell the Judge the truth, that Snead has sold his testimony for five million dollars, and nothing he says is the truth."

Hark laughed just loud enough for Grit to hear. "You can't do that, Grit."

"Of course I can."

"You're not very bright, are you. Listen to me, Grit, and listen good. First, you signed the note along with the rest of us, so you're implicated in any wrongdoing you allege. Second, and most important, you know about Snead because you were involved in the case as an attorney for Mary Ross. That's a confidential relationship. If you divulge any information learned as her attorney, then you breach the confidentiality. If you do something stupid, she will file a complaint with the bar, and I'll hound your ass into disbarment. I'll take your license, Grit, do you understand that?"

"You're scum, Gettys. You stole my client."

"If your client was happy, then why was she looking for another lawyer?"

"I'm not finished with you."

"Don't do anything stupid."

Grit slammed the phone down. Hark enjoyed the moment, then went back to work.

□ □ □ □

NATE DROVE ALONE into the city, over the Potomac River, past the Lincoln Memorial, moving with the traffic, in no hurry. Flurries hit his windshield, but the heavier snow had not materialized. At a red light on Pennsylvania, he looked in his rearview mirror and saw the building, clustered among a dozen others, where he had spent most of the past twenty-three years. His office window was six floors up. He could barely see it.

On M Street into Georgetown, he began to see the hangouts—the old bars and joints where he'd passed long dark hours with people he couldn't remember anymore. He could, however, remember the names of the bartenders. Every pub had a story. In the drinking days, a hard day at the office or in the courtroom had to be softened with a few hours of alcohol. He couldn't go home without it. He turned north on Wisconsin and saw a bar where he'd once fought a college boy, a kid drunker than himself. A sleazy co-ed had prompted the dispute. The bartender sent them outside for the fisticuffs. Nate had worn a Band-Aid into court the next morning.

And there was a small café where he'd bought enough cocaine to almost kill himself. The narcs raided it when he was in recovery. Two stockbroker buddies went to jail.

He'd spent his glory days on those streets, while his wives were waiting and his kids were growing up without him. He was ashamed of the misery he'd caused. As he left Georgetown, he vowed never to return.

At the Stafford home, he loaded his car again with more clothes and personal items, then left in a hurry.

In his pocket was a check for ten thousand dollars, the first month's retainer. The IRS wanted sixty thousand in back taxes. The fine would be at least that much too. He owed his second wife about thirty thousand in past-due child support, monthly obligations racked up while he recovered with Sergio.

His bankruptcy did not discharge these debts. He conceded that his financial future was indeed bleak. The younger children cost him three thousand a month each in support. The two older ones were almost as expensive with tuition and room and board. He could live off the Phelan money for a few months, but the way Josh and Wycliff were talking the trial would be held sooner rather than later. When the estate was finally closed, Nate would go before a federal judge, plead guilty to tax evasion, and surrender his license.

Father Phil was teaching him not to worry about the future. God would take care of His own.

Once again, Nate wondered if God was getting more than He bargained for.

SINCE HE WAS incapable of writing on anything but a legal pad, with its wide lines and broad margins, Nate took one and tried to begin a letter to Rachel. He had the address of World Tribes in Houston. He would mark the envelope "Personal and Confidential," address it to Rachel Lane, and attach an explanatory note: To Whom It May Concern.

Someone at World Tribes knew who and where she was. Perhaps someone knew Troy was her father. Maybe this someone put two and two together, and now knew that their Rachel was the beneficiary.

Nate was also assuming Rachel would contact World Tribes, if she had not already done so. She'd been in Corumbá when she'd come to the hospital. It was reasonable to believe she'd called Houston and told someone about his visit.

She had mentioned her annual budget with World Tribes. There had to be a method of corresponding by mail. If his letter got in the right hands in Houston, then maybe it would find the right place in Corumbá.

He wrote the date, then "Dear Rachel:"

An hour passed while he watched the fire and tried to think of words that would sound intelligent. Finally, he opened the letter with a paragraph about snow. Did she miss it from her childhood? What was it like in Montana? There was a foot on the ground outside his window.

He was compelled to confess that he was acting as her lawyer, and once he fell into the rhythm of legalese, the letter took off. He explained as simply as he could what was happening with the lawsuit.

He told her about Father Phil, and the church and its basement. He was studying the Bible and enjoying it. He was praying for her.

When he finished, the letter was three pages long, and Nate was quite proud of himself. He reread it twice, and declared it to be worthy of sending. If it somehow made it to her hut, he knew that she would read it again and again, and give not the slightest thought to any shortcomings in style.

Nate longed to see her again.

FORTY-TWO

ONE REASON for the sluggish progress of the church's basement was Father Phil's penchant for sleeping late. Laura said she left home each weekday morning at eight, for kindergarten, and more often than not the Rector was still buried under the blankets. He was a night owl, he said in self-defense, and he loved to watch old black-and-white movies after midnight.

So when he called at seven-thirty Friday morning, Nate was somewhat surprised. "Have you seen the *Post?*" he asked.

"I don't read newspapers," Nate replied. He had broken the habit during rehab. Phil, on the other hand, read five a day. They were a good source of material for his sermons.

"Perhaps you should," he said.

"Why?"

"There's a story about you."

Nate put on his boots and trudged two blocks to a coffee shop on Main Street. There was a nice story on the front page of Metro about the finding of the lost heir of Troy Phelan. Papers had been filed late the day before in the Circuit Court of Fairfax County in which she, acting through her attorney, a Mr. Nate O'Riley, disputed the allegations of those contesting her late father's will. Since there wasn't much to say about her, the story dwelt on her attorney. According to his affidavit, also filed in court, he had tracked down Rachel Lane, showed her a copy of the handwritten will, discussed the various legal issues with her, and had somehow managed to become her lawyer. There was no indication of exactly where Ms. Lane was.

Mr. O'Riley was a former partner in the Stafford Law Firm; had once been a prominent trial lawyer; had left the firm in August; filed for bankruptcy in October; been indicted in November; and a final disposition of his tax evasion charges was still pending. The IRS claimed he beat them out of sixty thousand dollars. For good measure, the reporter mentioned the useless fact that he had been divorced twice. To complete the humiliation, a bad photo ran with the story, one of Nate with a drink in his hand at a D.C. bar function several years earlier. He studied the grainy image of himself, eyes glowing, cheeks darkened with alcohol, goofy smile as if he were mixing and mingling with people he enjoyed. It was embarrassing, but it was another life.

Of course no story could be complete without a quick recital of the messy statistics of Troy's life and death—three wives, seven known children, eleven billion or so in assets, his last flight from fourteen floors up.

Mr. O'Riley could not be found for comment. Mr. Stafford had nothing to say. The lawyers for the Phelan heirs had evidently said so much already that they were not asked to comment again.

Nate folded the paper and returned to the cottage. It was eight-thirty. He had an hour and a half before construction commenced in the basement.

The bloodhounds now knew his name, but finding his scent would be difficult. Josh had arranged for his mail to be routed to a post office box in D.C. He had a new office phone number, one for Nathan F. O'Riley, Attorney-at-Law. The calls were answered by a secretary in Josh's office who filed away the messages.

In St. Michaels, only the Rector and his wife knew who he was.

Rumor had it that he was a wealthy lawyer from Baltimore writing a book.

Hiding was addictive. Maybe that was why Rachel did it.

COPIES of Rachel Lane's response were mailed to all the Phelan lawyers, who, as a group, were electrified by the news. She was indeed alive, and willing to fight, though her choice of lawyer was somewhat puzzling. O'Riley's reputation was accurate—an efficient litigator with flashes of brilliance who couldn't handle the pressure. But the Phelan lawyers, along with Judge Wycliff, suspected Josh Stafford was calling the shots. He'd rescued O'Riley from rehab, cleaned him up, put the file in his hands, and pointed him toward the courthouse.

The Phelan lawyers met Friday morning at Ms. Langhorne's place, a modern building packed among many on Pennsylvania Avenue, in the business district. Her firm was a wanna-be—with forty lawyers it wasn't big enough to attract blue-chip clients, but the leadership was very ambitious. The furnishings were showy and pretentious, the trappings of a bunch of lawyers desperate for the big time.

They had decided to meet once a week, each Friday at eight, for no more than two hours, to discuss the Phelan litigation and plot strategy. The idea had been Langhorne's. She had realized that she would have to be the peacemaker. The boys were busy strutting and fighting. And there was too much money to be lost in a trial where the contestants, all on one side of the room, were knifing each other in the back.

It appeared, at least to her, that the raiding was over. Her clients, Geena and Cody, were sticking. Yancy seemed to have Ramble adequately collared. Wally Bright was practically living with Libbigail and Spike. Hark had the other three—Troy Junior, Rex, and Mary Ross—and seemed content with his harvest. The dust was settling around the heirs. Relationships were becoming familiar. The issues had been defined. The lawyers knew they had better work as a team or lose the case.

Number one was Snead. They had spent hours watching the videos of his first effort, and each had prepared lengthy notes of ways to improve his performance. The fabricating was shameless. Yancy, in years past an aspiring screenwriter, had actually written a fifty-page script for Snead, filled with enough bald allegations to make poor Troy appear thoroughly brainless.

Number two was Nicolette, the secretary. They would hammer her in a few days on video, and there were certain things she needed to say. Bright had the idea that perhaps the old man had had a stroke during sex with her just hours before he faced the three psychiatrists, and this was something both Nicolette and Snead could testify to. A stroke would mean diminished mental capacity. It was a decent idea, generally well received, and it prompted a lengthy discussion about the autopsy. They had not yet seen a copy of it. Poor guy was splattered on the bricks, with terrible trauma to his head, as one would expect. Could the autopsy reveal a stroke?

Number three was their own experts. Grit's shrink had made a hasty exit with the attorney, so they were down to four, one per firm. Four was not an unmanageable number at trial, in fact, four could be persuasive, especially if they all reached the same conclusions but by different routes. They agreed that they should also rehearse the testimony of their psychiatrists, grilling them and trying to make them crack under pressure.

Number four was other witnesses. They had to find others who were around the old man in his last days. Snead could help them there.

The last item of business was the appearance of Rachel Lane and her lawyer. "There is nothing in the file signed by this woman," Hark said. "She's a recluse. No one knows where she is, except for her lawyer and he's not telling. It took a month to find her. She has signed nothing. Technically the court does not have jurisdiction. It's obvious to me that this woman is reluctant to come forward."

"So are some lottery winners," Bright inserted. "They want to keep it quiet, otherwise every bum in the neighborhood's beating on the door."

"What if she doesn't want the money?" Hark asked, and the room was stunned.

"That's crazy," Bright said on instinct, his words trailing away as he considered the impossible.

While they were scratching their heads, Hark pushed forward. "It's just a thought, but one we should consider. Under Virginia law, a bequest in a will can be renounced. The gift remains in the estate, subject to the remainder provisions. If this will is struck down, and if there are no other wills, then the seven children of Troy Phelan take all. Since Rachel Lane wants nothing, then our clients divide the estate."

Dizzying calculations raced through their heads. Eleven billion, less estate taxes, divided by six. Then apply the appropriate percentages, and serious wealth was possible. Fees of seven figures became fees of eight figures.

"That's a bit far-fetched," Langhorne said slowly, her brain still burning with the math.

"I'm not so sure," Hark said. It was obvious he knew more than the rest. "A waiver is a very simple document to execute. Are we expected to believe Mr. O'Riley traveled to Brazil, found Rachel Lane, told her about Troy, got himself hired, but did not get a simple signature on a short document that would give the court jurisdiction? Something's going on here."

Yancy was the first to say, "Brazil?"

"Yes. He just returned from Brazil."

"How do you know this?"

Hark slowly reached into a file and removed some papers. "I have a very good investigator," he said, and the room was silent. "Yesterday, after I received her answer and O'Riley's affidavit, same as you, I called the investigator. In three hours, he learned the following: On December twenty-second, Nate O'Riley left Dulles on Varig Flight 882 nonstop to São Paulo. From there he flew Varig Flight 146 to Campo Grande, and then he took an Air Pantanal commuter to a small city called Corumbá, arriving on the twenty-third. He stayed almost three weeks and then he returned to Dulles."

"Maybe it was a vacation," Bright mumbled. He was as amazed as the rest of them.

"Maybe, but I doubt it. Mr. O'Riley spent last fall in rehab, not for the first time. He was in the tank when Troy jumped. He was released on the twenty-second, same day he left for Brazil. His trip had only one purpose, and that was to find Rachel Lane."

"How do you know all this?" Yancy had to ask.

"It's not that difficult, really. Especially the flight information. Any good hacker can get it."

"How did you know he was in rehab?"

"Spies."

There was a long silence as they digested this. They simultaneously despised Hark and admired him. He seemed to always have information they didn't, yet he was on their side now. They were a team.

"It's just leverage," he said. "We go full speed ahead with discovery. We attack the will with a vengeance. We say nothing about the court's lack of jurisdiction over Rachel Lane. If she doesn't show either in person or by waiver, then it's an excellent indication that she doesn't want the money."

"I'll never believe that," Bright said.

"That's because you're a lawyer."

"What are you?"

"The same, just not as greedy. Believe it or not, Wally, there are people in this world who are not motivated by money."

"There are about twenty of them," Yancy said. "And they're all my clients."

A little laughter broke the tension.

Before adjourning, they once again forced each other to agree that everything they said was confidential. Each meant it, but no one completely trusted the other. The news about Brazil was especially delicate.

FORTY-THREE

T HE ENVELOPE was brown and slightly larger than legal-sized. Beside the World Tribes address in Houston were the words, in bold black print: For Rachel Lane, Missionary in South America, Personal and Confidential.

It was received by the mail clerk, examined for a few moments, then sent upstairs to a supervisor. Its journey continued throughout the morning until it landed, still unopened, on the desk of Neva Collier, Coordinator of South American Missions. She gaped at it in disbelief—no one knew Rachel Lane was a World Tribes missionary. No one but her.

Evidently, those who'd passed it along did not make the connection between the name on the envelope and the name in the recent news. It was Monday morning, the offices were slow and quiet.

Neva locked her door. Inside was a letter, addressed: "To Whom It May Concern," and a smaller, sealed envelope. She read the letter aloud, astounded by the fact that someone knew even the partial identity of Rachel Lane.

To Whom It May Concern:

Enclosed is a letter to Rachel Lane, one of your missionaries in Brazil. Please forward it to her, unopened.

I met Rachel about two weeks ago. I found her in the Pantanal, living among the Ipicas, where, as you know, she has been for eleven years now. The purpose of my visit was a pending legal matter.

For your information, she is doing well. I promised Rachel that I would not, under any circumstances, tell anyone of her location. She does not wish to be disturbed with any more legal matters, and I agreed to her request.

She does need money for a new boat and motor, and also additional funds for medicines. I will gladly forward a check to your organization for these expenses; just give me directions.

I plan to write Rachel again, though I have no idea how she gets her mail. Could you please drop me a line and let me know this letter was received and that her letter was forwarded to her? Thanks.

It was signed Nate O'Riley. At the bottom of the letter was a phone number in St. Michaels, Maryland, and an address at a law firm in Washington.

Corresponding with Rachel was a very simple matter. Twice a year, on March 1 and on August 1, World Tribes sent packages to the post office in Corumbá. Included were medical supplies, Christian literature, and anything else that she might need or want. The post office agreed to hold the August packages for thirty days, and if they went unclaimed they were to be returned to Houston. This had never happened. In August of every year, Rachel made her annual trek to Corumbá, at which time she called the home office and practiced her English for ten minutes. She collected her packages and returned to the Ipicas. In March, after the rainy season, the packages were sent upriver on a *chalana* and dropped off at a *fazenda* near the mouth of the Xeco River. Lako would retrieve them eventually. The March packages were always smaller than the August ones.

In eleven years, Rachel had never received a personal letter, at least not through World Tribes.

Neva copied the phone number and address on a notepad, then hid the letter in a drawer. She would send it in a month or so, along with the usual supplies for March.

THEY WORKED for almost an hour cutting two by fours for the next little classroom. The floor was covered with sawdust. Phil had some in his hair. The screech of the saw still rang in their ears. It was time for coffee. They sat on the floor, their backs to the wall, near a portable heater. Phil poured strong latte from a thermos.

"You missed a great sermon yesterday," he said with a grin.

"Where?"

"What do you mean, where? Here of course."

"What was the subject?"

"Adultery."

"For it or against it?"

"Against it, as always."

"I wouldn't think that'd be much of a problem with your congregation."

"I give the sermon once a year."

"Same sermon?"

"Yes, but always fresh."

"When was the last time one of your members had a problem with adultery?"

"Couple of years ago. One of our younger members thought her husband had another woman in Baltimore. He traveled there once a week on business, and she noticed that he returned home a different person. He had more energy, more enthusiasm for life. This would last for two or three days, then he was his usual cranky self again. She became convinced he had fallen in love."

"Cut to the chase."

"He was seeing a chiropractor."

Phil laughed loudly through his nose, a strange cackle that was infectious and usually funnier than the punch line. When the humor passed, they sipped in unison. Then Phil asked, "In your other life, Nate, did you ever have a problem with adultery?"

"None whatsoever. It wasn't a problem, it was a way of life. I chased anything that walked. Every semiattractive woman was nothing but a potential quickie. I was married, but I never thought that I was committing adultery. It wasn't sin; it was a game. I was a sick puppy, Phil."

"I shouldn't have asked."

"No, confession is good for the soul. I'm ashamed of the person I used to be. The women, booze, drugs, bars, fights, divorces, neglected children—I was a mess. I wish I had those days back. But it's important now to remember how far I've come."

"You have many good years left, Nate."

"I hope so. I'm just not sure what to do."

"Be patient. God will lead you."

"Of course, at the rate we're going, I could have a very long career right here."

Phil smiled but didn't erupt with a cackle. "Study your Bible, Nate, and pray. God needs people like you."

"I suppose."

"Trust me. It took me ten years to find God's will. I ran for a while, then I stopped and listened. Slowly, he led me into the ministry."

"How old were you?"

"I was thirty-six when I entered the seminary."

"Were you the oldest one?"

"No. It's not uncommon to see people in their forties in seminary. Happens all the time."

"How long does it take?"

"Four years."

"That's worse than law school."

"It wasn't bad at all. In fact, it was quite enjoyable."

"Can't say that for law school."

They worked for another hour, then it was time for lunch. The snow had finally melted, all of it, and there was a crab house down the road in Tilghman that Phil enjoyed. Nate was anxious to buy lunch.

"Nice car," Phil said as he belted himself in. Sawdust shook from his shoulder onto the spotless leather seat of the Jaguar. Nate couldn't have cared less.

"It's a lawyer's car, leased of course because I couldn't afford to pay cash for it. Eight hundred bucks a month."

"Sorry."

"I'd love to unload it and get me a nice little Blazer or something."

Route 33 narrowed as they left town, and they were soon winding along the bay.

HE WAS IN BED when the phone rang, but not asleep. Sleep was an hour away. It was only ten, but his body was still accustomed to the routine of Walnut Hill, his trip south notwithstanding. And at times he felt some residual fatigue from the dengue.

It was difficult to believe that for most of his professional life he often worked until nine or ten at night, then had dinner in a bar and drinks until one. He grew weary just thinking about it.

Since the phone seldom rang, he grabbed it quickly, certain it was trouble. A female voice said, "Nate O'Riley, please."

"This is Nate O'Riley."

"Good evening, sir. My name is Neva Collier, and I received a letter from you for our friend in Brazil."

The covers flew off as Nate jumped from the bed. "Yes! You got my letter?"

"We did. I read it this morning, and I will send Rachel's letter to her."

"Wonderful. How does she get mail?"

"I send it to Corumbá, at certain times of the year."

"Thank you. I'd like to write her again."

"That's fine, but please don't put her name on the envelopes."

It occurred to Nate that it was nine o'clock in Houston. She was calling from home, and this seemed more than odd. The voice was pleasant enough, but tentative.

"Is something wrong?" he asked.

"No, except that no one here knows who she is. No one but me. Now with your involvement, there are two people in the world who know where she is and who she is."

"She swore me to secrecy."

"Was she difficult to find?"

"You could say that. I wouldn't worry about others finding her."

"But how did you do it?"

"Her father did it. You know about Troy Phelan?"

"Yes. I'm clipping news stories."

"Before he left this world, he tracked her to the Pantanal. I have no idea how he did it."

"He had the means."

"Yes he did. We knew generally where she was, and I went down there, hired a guide, got lost, and found her. Do you know her well?"

"I'm not sure anyone knows Rachel well. I speak to her once a year in August, from Corumbá. She tried a furlough five years ago, and I had lunch with her one day. But no, I don't know her that well."

"Have you heard from her recently?"

"No."

Rachel had been in Corumbá two weeks earlier. He knew this for a fact because she had come to the hospital. She had spoken to him, touched him, and then vanished along with his fevers. But she hadn't called the home office? How strange.

"She is doing well," he said. "Very much at home with her people."

"Why did you track her down?"

"Someone had to. Do you understand what her father did?"

"I'm trying to."

"Someone had to notify Rachel, and it had to be a lawyer. I just

357

happened to be the only one in our firm with nothing better to do."

"And now you're representing her?"

"You are paying attention, aren't you?"

"We may have more than a passing interest. She is one of us, and she is, shall we say, out of the loop."

"That would be an understatement."

"What does she plan to do about her father's estate?"

Nate rubbed his eyes and paused to slow the conversation. The nice lady on the other end was stepping over the line. He doubted if she realized it. "I don't want to be rude, Ms. Collier, but I can't discuss with you things Rachel and I talked about pertaining to her father's estate."

"Of course not. I wasn't trying to pry. It's just that I'm not sure what World Tribes should do at this point."

"Nothing. You have no involvement unless Rachel asks you to step in."

"I see. So I'll just follow events in the newspapers."

"I'm sure the proceedings will be well documented."

"You mentioned certain things she needs down there."

Nate told her the story of the little girl who died because Rachel had no antivenin. "She can't find enough medical supplies in Corumbá. I'd love to send her whatever she needs."

"Thank you. Send the money to my attention at World Tribes, and I'll make sure she gets the supplies. We have four thousand Rachels around the world, and our budgets get stretched."

"Are the others as remarkable as Rachel?"

"Yes. They are chosen by God."

They agreed to keep in touch. Nate could send all the letters he wanted. Neva would ship them to Corumbá. If either one heard from Rachel, he or she would call the other.

Back in bed, Nate replayed the phone call. The things that weren't said were amazing. Rachel had just learned from him that her father had died and left her one of the world's great fortunes.

358

She then sneaked into Corumbá because she knew from Lako that Nate was very ill. And then she left, without calling anyone at World Tribes to discuss the money.

When he left her on the riverbank, he was convinced that she had no interest in the money. Now he was convinced even more.

FORTY-FOUR

THE DEPOSITION DERBY began on Monday, February 17, in a long bare room in the Fairfax County Courthouse. It was a witness room, but Judge Wycliff had pulled strings and reserved it for the last two weeks of the month. At least fifteen people were scheduled to be deposed, and the lawyers had been unable to agree on places and times. Wycliff had intervened. The depositions would be taken in an orderly fashion, one after the other, hour after hour, day after day, until finished. Such a marathon was rare, but then, so were the stakes. The lawyers had shown an amazing ability to clear their calendars for the discovery phase of the Phelan matter. Trials had been postponed; other depositions wiggled out of; important deadlines delayed yet again; briefs shoved off on other partners; vacations happily put off until summer. Associates were sent to handle lesser chores. Nothing was as important as the Phelan mess.

For Nate, the prospect of spending two weeks in a room crowded with lawyers, grilling witnesses, was a misery just short of hell itself.

If his client didn't want the money, why should he care who got it?

His attitude changed somewhat when he met the Phelan heirs.

The first deponent was Mr. Troy Phelan, Jr. The court reporter swore him to honesty, but with his shifty eyes and reddened cheeks, he lost credibility within seconds of being seated at the head of the table. A video camera at the other end zoomed in on his face.

Josh's staff had prepared hundreds of questions for Nate to hammer him with. The work and research had been done by a half-dozen associates, people Nate would never meet. But he could've handled it himself, off the cuff, with no preparation whatsoever. It was just a deposition, a fishing trip, and Nate had been there a thousand times.

Nate introduced himself to Troy Junior, who gave him a nervous smile, much like the inmate looking at the executioner. "This is not going to be painful, is it?" he seemed to ask.

"Are you currently under the influence of any illegal drugs, prescription drugs, or alcohol?" Nate began pleasantly, and this rankled the Phelan lawyers on the other side of the table. Only Hark understood. He had taken almost as many depositions as Nate O'Riley.

The smile vanished. "I am not," Troy Junior snapped. His head was pounding from a hangover, but he was currently sober.

"And you understand that you have just sworn to tell the truth?"

"Yes."

"Do you understand what perjury is?"

"I certainly do."

"Which one is your lawyer?" Nate asked, waving at the crowd opposite.

"Hark Gettys."

The arrogance of Mr. O'Riley rankled the attorneys again, this time Hark included. Nate hadn't bothered to learn which lawyers were attached to which client. His disdain for the entire group was offensive.

Within the first two minutes, Nate had established a nasty tone for the day. There was little doubt that he distrusted Troy Junior immensely, and perhaps the guy was under the influence. It was an old trick.

"How many wives have you had?"

"How many have you had?" Junior shot back, then looked at his lawyer for approval. Hark was studying a sheet of paper.

Nate kept his cool. Who knew what the Phelan lawyers had been saying behind his back? He did not care.

"Let me explain something to you, Mr. Phelan," Nate said without the slightest irritation. "I will go over this very slowly, so listen carefully. I am the lawyer, you are the witness. Do you follow me so far?"

Troy Junior slowly nodded.

"I ask the questions, you give the answers. Do you understand that?"

The witness nodded again.

"You don't ask questions, and I don't give answers. Understand?"

"Yep."

"Now, I don't think you'll have trouble with the answers if you'll pay attention to the questions. Okay?"

Junior nodded again.

"Are you still confused?"

"Nope."

"Good. If you get confused again, please feel free to consult with your attorney. Am I getting through?"

"I understand."

"Wonderful. Let's try it again. How many wives have you had?"

"Two."

An hour later they finished with his marriages, his children, his divorce. Junior was sweating and wondering how long his deposition would last. The Phelan lawyers were staring blankly at sheets of paper and asking themselves the same thing. Nate, however, had yet to look at the pages of questions prepared for him. He could peel the skin off any witness simply by staring at his eyes and using one question to lead to another. No detail was too small for him to investigate. Where was your first wife's high school, college, first job? Was it her first marriage? Give us her employment history. Let's talk about the divorce. How much was your child support? Did you pay all of it?

For the most part it was useless testimony, evoked not for the sake of information, but rather to annoy the witness and put him on notice that the skeletons could be summoned from the closet. He filed the lawsuit. He had to suffer the scrutiny.

His employment history took them to the brink of lunch. He stumbled badly when Nate grilled him about his various jobs for his father's companies. There were dozens of witnesses who could be called to rebut his version of how useful he'd been. With each job, Nate asked for the names of all his co-workers and supervisors. The trap was laid. Hark saw it coming and called time-out. He stepped into the hall with his client and lectured him about telling the truth.

The afternoon session was brutal. Nate asked about the five million dollars he'd received on his twenty-first birthday, and the entire wall of Phelan lawyers seemed to stiffen.

"That was a long time ago," Troy Junior said with an air of resignation. After four hours with Nate O'Riley, he knew the next round would be painful.

"Well, let's try to remember," Nate said with a smile. He showed no signs of fatigue. In fact, he'd been there so many times he actually seemed anxious to grind through the details.

His acting was superb. He hated being there and tormenting people he hoped he'd never see again. The more questions Nate asked, the more determined he was to start a new career.

"How was the money given to you?" he asked.

"It was initially placed in an account in a bank."

"You had access to the account?"

"Yes."

"Did anyone else have access to the account?"

"No. Just me."

"How did you get money out of the account?"

"By writing checks."

And write them he did. His first purchase had been a brand-new Maserati, dark blue. They talked about the damned car for fifteen minutes.

Troy Junior never returned to college after receiving the money, not that any of the schools he'd attended were anxious to have him back. He simply partied, though this came not in the form of a confession. Nate hammered him about his employment from ages twenty-one to thirty, and slowly extricated enough facts to reveal that Troy Junior did not work at all for those nine years. He played golf and rugby, traded cars with gusto, spent a year in the Bahamas and a year in Vail, lived with an amazing assortment of women before finally marrying number one at the age of twenty-nine, and indulged himself in grand style until the money ran out.

Then the prodigal son crawled to his father and asked for a job.

As the afternoon wore on, Nate began to envision the havoc this witness would sow upon himself and those around him if he got his sticky fingers on the Phelan fortune. He would kill himself with the money.

At 4 P.M., Troy Junior asked to be excused for the day. Nate refused. During the break that followed, a note was sent to Judge Wycliff down the hall. While they waited, Nate looked at Josh's questions for the first time.

The return message instructed that the proceedings keep going.

A week after Troy's suicide, Josh had hired a security firm to conduct an investigation into the Phelan heirs. The probe was more financial than personal. Nate skimmed the highlights while the witness smoked in the hall.

"What kind of car are you driving now?" Nate asked when they resumed. The exam took yet another direction.

"A Porsche."

"When did you buy it?"

"I've had it awhile."

"Try to answer the question. When did you buy it?"

"Couple of months ago."

"Before or after your father's death?"

"I'm not real sure. Before, I think."

Nate lifted a sheet of paper. "What day did your father die?"

"Lemme see. It was a Monday, uh, December the ninth, I think."

"Did you buy the Porsche before or after December the ninth?"

"Like I said, I think it was before."

"Nope, wrong again. On Tuesday, December tenth, did you go to Irving Motors in Arlington and purchase a black Porsche Carrera Turbo 911 for ninety thousand dollars, give or take?" Nate asked the question while reading from the sheet of paper.

Troy Junior squirmed and fidgeted yet again. He looked at Hark, who shrugged as if to say, "Answer the question. He's got the paperwork."

"Yes, I did."

"Did you buy any other cars that day?"

"Yes."

"How many?"

"A total of two."

"Two Porsches?"

"Yes."

"For a total of nearly one hundred and eighty thousand dollars?"

"Something like that."

"How did you pay for them?"

"I haven't."

"So the cars were gifts from Irving Motors?"

"Not exactly. I bought them on credit."

"You qualified for credit?"

"Yes, at Irving Motors anyway."

"Do they want their money?"

"Yes, you could say that."

Nate picked up more papers. "In fact, they've filed suit to recover either the money or the cars, haven't they?"

"Yes."

"Did you drive the Porsche to the deposition today?"

"Yes. It's in the parking lot."

"Let me get this straight. On December tenth, the day after your father died, you went to Irving Motors and bought two expensive cars, on some type of credit, and now, two months later, you haven't paid a dime and are being sued. Correct?"

The witness nodded.

"This is not the only lawsuit, is it?"

"No," Troy Junior said in defeat. Nate almost felt sorry for him. A rental company was suing for nonpayment on a furniture lease. American Express wanted over fifteen thousand. A bank sued Troy Junior a week after the reading of his father's will. Junior had fast-talked it into a loan of twenty-five thousand dollars, secured by nothing but his name. Nate had copies of all the litigation, and they trudged through the details of each lawsuit.

At five, another argument occurred. Another note was sent to Wycliff. The Judge appeared himself and asked about their progress. "When do you think you'll finish with this witness?" he asked Nate.

"There's no end in sight," Nate said, staring at Junior, who was in a trance and praying for liquor.

"Then work until six," Wycliff said.

"Can we start at eight in the morning?" Nate asked, as if they were going to the beach.

"Eight-thirty," His Honor decreed, then left.

For the last hour, Nate peppered Junior with random questions on many subjects. The deponent had no clue where his interrogator was going, and Junior was being led by a master. Just as they settled on one topic and he began to feel comfortable, Nate changed course and hit him with something new.

How much money did he spend from December 9 to December 27, the day the will was read? What did he buy his wife for Christmas, and how did he pay for the gifts? What did he buy for his children? Back to the five million, did he put any of the money in stocks or bonds? How much money did Biff earn last year? Why did her first husband get custody of her kids? How many lawyers had he hired and fired since his father died? And on and on.

At precisely six, Hark stood and announced the deposition was being adjourned. Ten minutes later, Troy Junior was in a bar in a hotel lobby two miles away.

Nate slept in the Stafford guest room. Mrs. Stafford was somewhere in the house, but he never saw her. Josh was in New York on business.

THE SECOND DAY of questioning started on time. The cast was the same, though the lawyers were dressed much more casually. Junior wore a red cotton sweater.

Nate recognized the face of a drunk—the red eyes, the puffy flesh around them, the pink cheeks and nose, the sweat above the brows. The face had been his for years. Treating the hangover was as much a part of the morning as the shower and the dental floss. Take some pills, drink lots of water and strong coffee. If you're gonna be stupid you gotta be tough.

"You realize that you're still under oath, Mr. Phelan?" he began.

"I do."

"Are you under the influence of any drugs or alcohol?"

"No sir, I am not."

"Good. Let's go back to December the ninth, the day your father died. Where were you when he was examined by the three psychiatrists?"

"I was in his building, in a conference room with my family."

"And you watched the entire examination, didn't you?"

"I did."

"There were two color monitors in the room, right? Each twenty-six inches wide?"

"If you say so. I didn't measure them."

"But you could certainly see them, couldn't you?"

"Yes."

"Your view was unobstructed?"

"I had a clear view, yes."

"And you had a clear reason to watch your father closely?"

"I did."

"Did you have any trouble hearing him?"

"No."

The lawyers knew where Nate was going. It was an unpleasant aspect of their case, but one that could not be avoided. Each of the six heirs would be led down this path.

"So you watched and heard the entire exam?"

"I did."

"You missed nothing?"

"I missed nothing."

"Of the three psychiatrists, Dr. Zadel had been hired by your family, correct?"

"That's correct."

"Who found him?"

"The lawyers."

"You trusted your lawyers to hire the psychiatrist?"

"Yes."

For ten minutes, Nate quizzed him on exactly how they came to select Dr. Zadel for such a crucial exam, and in the process got what he wanted. Zadel was hired because he had excellent credentials, came highly recommended, and was very experienced.

"Were you pleased with the way he handled the exam?" Nate asked.

"I suppose."

"Was there something you didn't like about Dr. Zadel's performance?"

"Not that I recall."

The trip to the edge of the cliff continued as Troy Junior admitted that he was pleased with the exam, pleased with Zadel, happy with the conclusions reached by all three doctors, and left the building with no doubt that his father knew what he was doing.

"After the exam, when did you first doubt your father's mental stability?" Nate asked.

"When he jumped."

"On December the ninth?"

"Right."

"So you had doubts immediately."

"Yes."

"What did Dr. Zadel say to you when you expressed these doubts?"

"I didn't talk to Dr. Zadel."

"You didn't?"

"No."

"From December ninth to December twenty-seventh, the day the will was read in court, how many times did you talk to Dr. Zadel?"

"I don't remember any."

"Did you see him at all?"

"No."

"Did you call his office?"

"No."

"Have you seen him since December the ninth?"

"No."

Having walked him to the edge, it was time for the shove. "Why did you fire Dr. Zadel?"

Junior had been prepped to some degree. "You'll have to ask my lawyer that," he said, and hoped Nate would just go away for a while.

"I'm not deposing your lawyer, Mr. Phelan. I'm asking you why Dr. Zadel was fired."

"You'll have to ask the lawyers. It's part of our legal strategy."

"Did the lawyers discuss it with you before Dr. Zadel was fired?"

"I'm not sure. I really can't remember."

"Are you pleased that Dr. Zadel no longer works for you?"

"Of course I am."

"Why?"

"Because he was wrong. Look, my father was a master con man, okay. He bluffed his way through the exam, same way he did all of his life, then jumped out of the window. He snowed Zadel and the other shrinks. They fell for his act. He was obviously off his rocker."

"Because he jumped?"

"Yes, because he jumped, because he gave his money to some unknown heir, because he made no effort to shield his fortune from estate taxes, because he'd been crazy as hell for some time. Why do you think we had the exam to begin with? If he hadn't been nuts, would we have needed three shrinks to check him out before he signed his will?"

"But the three shrinks said he was okay."

"Yeah, and they were dead wrong. He jumped. Sane people don't fly out of windows."

"What if your father had signed the thick will and not the handwritten one? And then he jumped? Would he be crazy?"

"We wouldn't be here."

It was the only time during the two-day ordeal that Troy Junior fought to a draw. Nate knew to move on, then to come back later.

"Let's talk about Rooster Inns," he announced, and Junior's shoulders fell three inches. It was just another one of his bankrupt ventures, nothing more or less. But Nate had to have every little detail. One bankruptcy led to another. Each failure prompted questions about other doomed enterprises.

Junior's had been a sad life. Though it was hard to be sympathetic, Nate realized that the poor guy had never had a father. He had longed for Troy's approval, and never received it. Josh had told him that Troy had taken great delight when his children's ventures collapsed.

The lawyer freed the witness at five-thirty, day two. Rex was next. He'd waited in the hall throughout the day, and was highly agitated at being put off again.

Josh had returned from New York. Nate joined him for an early dinner.

FORTY-FIVE

REX PHELAN had spent most of the previous day on the cell phone in the hallway while his brother was roughed up by Nate O'Riley. Rex had been in enough lawsuits to know that litigation meant waiting: waiting for lawyers, judges, witnesses, experts, trial dates, and appeals courts, waiting in hallways for your turn to give testimony. When he raised his right hand and swore to tell the truth, he already despised Nate.

Both Hark and Troy Junior had warned him of what was to come. The lawyer could get under your skin and fester there like a boil.

Again, Nate started with inflammatory questions, and within ten minutes the room was tense. For three years, Rex had been the target of an FBI investigation. A bank had failed in 1990; Rex had been an investor and director. Depositors lost money. Borrowers lost their loans. Litigation had been raging for years with no end in sight. The president of the bank was in jail, and those close to the epicenter thought Rex would be next. There was enough dirt to keep Nate going for hours.

For fun, he continually reminded Rex that he was under oath.

There was also a very good chance the FBI would see his deposition.

It was mid-afternoon before Nate worked his way to the strip bars. Rex owned six of them—held in his wife's name—in the Fort Lauderdale area. He'd bought them from a man killed in a gunfight. They were simply irresistible as subjects of conversation. Nate took them one by one—Lady Luck, Lolita's, Club Tiffany, et cetera—and asked a hundred questions. He asked about the girls, the strippers, where they came from, how much they earned, did they use drugs, what drugs, did they touch the customers, and on and on. He asked question after question about the economics of the skin business. After three hours of carefully painting a portrait of the sleaziest business in the world, Nate asked, "Didn't your current wife work in one of the clubs?"

The answer was yes, but Rex couldn't just blurt it out. His throat and neck flashed red and for a moment he appeared ready to lunge across the table.

"She was a bookkeeper," he said with a clenched jaw.

"She ever do any dancing, on the tables?"

Another pause, as Rex squeezed the table with his fingers. "She certainly did not." It was a lie, and everyone in the room knew it.

Nate flipped through some papers searching for the truth. They watched him carefully, half-expecting him to pull out a photo of Amber in a G-string and kinky heels.

They adjourned at six again, with the promise of more tomorrow. When the video camera was off and the court reporter was busy putting away her equipment, Rex stopped at the door, pointed at Nate, and said, "No more questions about my wife, okay?"

"That's impossible, Rex. All assets are in her name." Nate waved some papers at him, as if he had all their records. Hark shoved his client through the door.

Nate sat alone for an hour, skimming notes, flipping pages, wishing he were in St. Michaels sitting on the porch of the cottage with a view of the bay. He needed to call Phil.

This is your last case, he kept telling himself. And you're doing it for Rachel.

By noon of the second day, the Phelan lawyers were openly discussing whether Rex's deposition would take three days or four. He had over seven million dollars in liens and judgments filed against him, yet the creditors couldn't execute because all assets were in the name of his wife, Amber, the ex-stripper. Nate took each judgment, laid it on the table, examined it from every conceivable angle and direction, then placed it back in the file where it might stay and it might not. The tedium was unnerving everyone but Nate, who somehow kept an earnest demeanor as he plodded ahead.

For the afternoon session he selected the topic of Troy's leap and the events leading up to it. He followed the same line he'd used on Junior, and it was obvious Hark had prepped Rex. His answers to the questions about Dr. Zadel were rehearsed, but adequate. Rex hung with the party line—the three psychiatrists were simply wrong because Troy jumped minutes later.

More familiar territory was covered when Nate grilled him about his dismal employment career with The Phelan Group. Then they spent two painful hours wasting the five million Rex had received as his inheritance.

At five-thirty, Nate abruptly said he was finished, and walked out of the room.

Two witnesses in four days. Two men laid bare on video, and it wasn't a pretty sight. The Phelan lawyers went to their separate cars and drove away. Perhaps the worst was behind them, perhaps not.

Their clients had been spoiled as children, ignored by their father, cast into the world with fat checking accounts at an age when they were ill-equipped to handle money, and expected to prosper. They had made bad choices, but all blame ultimately went back to Troy. That was the considered judgment of the Phelan lawyers.

Libbigail was led in early Friday morning and placed in the seat of honor. Her hair was of a style quite similar to a crew cut, with the sides peeled to the skin and an inch of gray on top. Cheap jewelry hung from her neck and wrists so that when she raised her hand to be sworn there was a racket at her elbow.

She looked at Nate in horror. Her brothers had told her the worst.

But it was Friday, and Nate wanted out of the city more than he wanted food when he was hungry. He smiled at her and began with easy background questions. Kids, jobs, marriages. For thirty minutes, all was pleasant. Then he began to probe into her past. At one point, he asked, "How many times have you been through rehab for drugs and alcohol?"

The question shocked her, so Nate said, "I've done it four times myself, so don't be ashamed." His candor disarmed her.

"I really can't remember," she said. "But I've been clean for six years."

"Wonderful," said Nate. One addict to another. "Good for you."

From that point on, the two talked about things as if they were alone. Nate had to pry, and he apologized for doing so. He asked about the five million, and with no small amount of humor she told tales of good drugs and bad men. Unlike her brothers, Libbigail had found stability. His name was Spike, the ex-biker who'd also been detoxed into submission. They lived in a small house in the suburbs of Baltimore.

"What would you do if you got one sixth of your father's estate?" Nate asked.

"Buy lots of things," she said. "Same as you. Same as anybody else. But I would be smart with the money this time. Real smart."

"What's the first thing you'd buy?"

"The biggest Harley in the world, for Spike. Then a nicer house, not a mansion though." Her eyes danced as she spent the money.

Her deposition lasted less than two hours. Her sister, Mary Ross Phelan Jackman, followed her, and likewise looked at Nate as if he had fangs. Of the five adult Phelan heirs, Mary Ross was the only one still married to her first spouse, though he had a prior wife. He was an orthopedist. She was dressed tastefully, with nice jewelry.

The early questions revealed the standard prolonged college experience, but without arrests, addictions, or expulsions. She'd taken her money and lived in Tuscany for three years, then Nice for two. At twenty-eight, she married the doctor, had two girls, one now seven, the other five. It was unclear how much of the five million was left. The doctor handled their investments, so Nate figured they were practically broke. Wealthy, but heavily in debt. Josh's background on Mary Ross showed a massive home with imported cars stacked in the driveway, a condo in Florida, and an estimated income by the doc of $750,000 a year. He was paying $20,000 a month to a bank, his part of the residual damage from a failed partnership that tried to corner the car wash business in northern Virginia.

The doctor also had an apartment in Alexandria where he kept a mistress. Mary Ross and her husband were rarely seen together. Nate decided not to discuss these matters. He was suddenly in a hurry, but careful not to show it.

Ramble slouched into the room after the lunch break, his lawyer Yancy leading and pointing and fussing over him, obviously terrified now that his client was expected to carry on an intelligent conversation. The kid's hair was bright red now, and it sort of matched his zits. No portion of his face had gone unmutilated— rings and studs littered and scarred his features. The collar of his black leather jacket was turned up, James Dean style, so that it touched the earrings dangling from his lobes.

After a few questions, it was obvious the kid was as stupid as he looked. Since he had not yet had the opportunity to squander his money, Nate left him alone. They established that he seldom went to school, lived alone in the basement, had never held a job for which he was paid, liked to play the guitar, and planned to be a serious rock star real soon. His new band was aptly called the Demon Monkeys, but he wasn't sure they would record under that name. He played no sports, had never seen the inside of a church, spoke to his mother as little as possible, and preferred to watch MTV whenever he was awake and not playing his music.

It would take a billion dollars in therapy to straighten out this poor kid, Nate thought. He finished with him in less than an hour.

Geena was the last witness of the week. Four days after her father's death, she and her husband Cody had signed a contract to purchase a home for $3.8 million. When Nate assaulted her with this information right after she was sworn, she began to stutter and stammer and look at her lawyer, Ms. Langhorne, who was equally surprised. Her client had not told her about the contract.

"How did you plan to pay for the home?" Nate asked.

The answer was obvious but she couldn't confess it. "We have money," she said defensively, and this opened a door that Nate went barging through.

"Let's talk about your money," he said with a smile. "You're thirty years old. Nine years ago you received five million dollars, didn't you?"

"I did."

"How much of it is left?"

She struggled with the answer for a long time. The answer was not so simple. Cody had made a lot of money. They had invested some, spent a lot, it was all co-mingled, so you couldn't just look at their balance sheet and say there was X amount left from the five million. Nate gave her the rope, and she slowly hung herself.

"How much money do you and your husband have today in your checking accounts?" he asked.

"I'd have to look."

"Guess, please. Just give me an estimate."

"Sixty thousand dollars."

"How much real estate do you own?"

"Just our home."

"What is the value of your home?"

"I'd have to get it appraised."

"Guess, please. Just a ballpark figure."

"Three hundred thousand."

"And how much is your mortgage?"

"Two hundred thousand."

"What is the approximate value of your portfolio?"

She scribbled some notes and closed her eyes. "Approximately two hundred thousand dollars."

"Any other significant assets?"

"Not really."

Nate did his own calculations. "So in nine years, your five million dollars has been reduced to something in the range of three hundred to four hundred thousand dollars. Am I correct?"

"Surely not. I mean, it seems so low."

"So tell us again how you were going to pay for this new home?"

"Through Cody's work."

"What about your dead father's estate? Ever think about that?"

"Maybe a little."

"Now you've been sued by the seller of the house, haven't you?"

"Yes, and we've countersued. There are a lot of issues."

She was shifty and dishonest, glib and quick with the half-truth. Nate thought she might be the most dangerous Phelan yet. They walked through Cody's ventures, and it was quickly apparent where the money had gone. He'd lost a million gambling on copper futures in 1992. He'd put half a million into "Snow-Packed Chickens," and lost it all. An indoor worm farm in Georgia took six hundred thousand dollars when a heat wave cooked the bait.

They were two immature kids living a pampered life with someone else's money, and dreaming of the big score.

Near the end of her deposition, with Nate still feeding her all the rope she wanted, she testified with a straight face that her involvement in the will contest had nothing to do with money. She loved her father deeply, and he loved her, and if he'd had his right mind he would have taken care of his children in his will. To give it all to a stranger was strong evidence of his illness. She was there fighting to protect the reputation of her father.

It was a well-rehearsed little oration, and it convinced no one.

Nate let it slide. It was five o'clock, Friday afternoon, and he was tired of fighting.

As he left the city and fought the heavy traffic on Interstate 95 to Baltimore, his thoughts were on the Phelan heirs. He had pried into their lives, to the point of embarrassment. He felt sympathy for them, for the way they were raised, for the values they were never taught, for their hollow lives revolving around nothing but money.

But Nate was convinced that Troy knew exactly what he was doing when he scrawled his testament. Serious money in the hands of his children would cause unmitigated chaos and untold misery. He left his fortune to Rachel, who had no interest in it. He excluded the others, whose lives were consumed by it.

Nate was determined to uphold the validity of Troy's last testament. But he was also very much aware that the final distribution of the estate would not be determined by anyone in the northern hemisphere.

It was late when he arrived in St. Michaels, and as he passed Trinity Church he wanted to stop, go inside, kneel and pray, and ask God to forgive him for the sins of the week. Confession and a hot bath were needed after five days of depositions.

FORTY-SIX

AS A HARRIED big-city professional, Nate had never been introduced to the ritual of sitting. Phil, on the other hand, was an accomplished practitioner. When a parishioner was ill, he was expected to visit and sit with the family. If there was a death, he would sit with the widow. If a neighbor stopped by, regardless of the time, he and Laura would sit and chat. Sometimes they practiced the art by themselves, on the porch, in the swing, alone. Two elderly gentlemen in his congregation expected Phil to stop by once a week and simply sit for an hour while they dozed by the fire. Conversation was nice, but not required. It was perfectly fine to just sit and enjoy the stillness.

But Nate caught on quickly. He sat with Phil on the front steps of the Stafford cottage, both men wearing heavy sweaters and gloves, and sipping hot cocoa Nate had prepared in the microwave. They gazed at the bay before them, at the harbor and the choppy waters beyond. Conversation crept up occasionally, but there was a lot of silence. Phil knew his friend had suffered a bad week. By now, Nate had told him most of the details of the Phelan mess. Theirs was a confidential relationship.

"I'm planning a road trip," Nate announced quietly. "Wanna come?"

"To where?"

"I need to see my kids. I have two younger ones, Austin and Angela, in Salem, Oregon. I'll probably go there first. My older son is a grad student at Northwestern in Evanston, and I have a daughter in Pittsburgh. It'll be a nice little tour."

"How long?"

"There's no rush. A couple of weeks. I'm driving."

"When did you see them last?"

"It's been over a year since I've seen Daniel and Kaitlin, the two from my first marriage. I took the two younger ones to an Orioles game last July. I got drunk and didn't remember driving back to Arlington."

"Do you miss them?"

"Sure, I guess. Truth is, I never spent much time with them. I know so little about them."

"You were working hard."

"I was, and I was drinking even harder. I was never at home. On those rare occasions when I could take off, I would go to Vegas with the boys, or golfing or deep-sea fishing in the Bahamas. I never took the kids."

"You can't change that."

"No, I can't. Why don't you come with me? We could talk for hours."

"Thanks, but I can't leave. I've finally built some momentum in the basement. I'd hate to lose it."

Nate had seen the basement earlier in the day. There was evidence of momentum.

Phil's only child was a twenty-something drifter who'd flunked out of college and fled to the West Coast. Laura had let it slip that they had no idea where the kid was. He hadn't called home in over a year.

"Do you expect the trip to be successful?" Phil asked.

"I'm not sure what to expect. I want to hug my kids and apologize for being such a lousy father, but I'm not sure how that's supposed to help them now."

"I wouldn't do that. They know you've been a lousy father. Flogging yourself won't help. But it's important to be there, to take the first step in building new relationships."

"I was such a miserable failure for my kids."

"You can't beat yourself up, Nate. You're allowed to forget the past. God certainly has. Paul murdered Christians before he became one, and he didn't flail himself for what he'd been before. Everything is forgiven. Show your kids what you are now."

A small fishing boat backed away from the harbor, and turned into the bay. It was the only blip on their screen, and they watched with rapt attention. Nate thought of Jevy and Welly, back on the river now, guiding a *chalana* loaded with produce and wares, the steady knock of the diesel pushing them deep into the Pantanal. Jevy would have the wheel, Welly would be strumming his guitar. All the world was at peace.

Later, long after Phil had gone home, Nate huddled by the fire and began another letter to Rachel. It was his third. He dated it, Saturday, February 22. "Dear Rachel," he began. "I have just spent a very unpleasant week with your brothers and sisters."

He talked about them, beginning with Troy Junior and ending three pages later with Ramble. He was honest about their shortcomings and the damage they would inflict on themselves and others if they got the money. And he was sympathetic too.

He was sending a check to World Tribes for five thousand dollars for a boat, a motor, and medical supplies. There was plenty more if she needed. The interest on her fortune was about two million dollars a day, he informed her, so a lot of good things could be done with the money.

HARK GETTYS and his conspirators at law blundered badly when they terminated the services of Drs. Flowe, Zadel, and Theishen. The lawyers had rebuked the doctors, and offended them, and caused irreparable damage.

The new batch of psychiatrists had the benefit of Snead's newly fabricated testimony upon which to create their opinions. Flowe, Zadel, and Theishen did not. When Nate deposed them Monday, he followed the same script with all three. He began with Zadel, and showed him the video of the examination of Mr. Phelan. He asked him if he had any reason to alter his opinions. Zadel, as expected, said no. The video happened before the suicide. The eight-page affidavit was prepared just hours afterward, at the insistence of Hark and the other Phelan lawyers. Zadel was asked by Nate to read the affidavit to the court reporter.

"Do you have any reason to change any of the opinions set out in that affidavit?" Nate asked.

"I do not," Zadel said, looking at Hark.

"Today is February twenty-fourth, more than two months after your examination of Mr. Phelan. Is it your opinion today that he had sufficient mental capacity to execute a valid will?"

"It is," Zadel answered, smiling at Hark.

Flowe and Theishen smiled too, each genuinely happy to turn the screws on the lawyers who'd hired them and fired them. Nate showed each of them the video, asked them the same questions, and received the same answers. Each read his affidavit into the record. They adjourned at four, Monday afternoon.

At eight-thirty sharp, Tuesday morning, Snead was escorted into the room and placed in the chair of honor. He wore a dark suit with a bow tie which gave him a brainy aura that was undeserved. The lawyers had carefully selected his wardrobe. They'd been molding and programming Snead for weeks, and the poor man doubted if he could utter a spontaneous or honest word. Every syllable had to be right. He had to project an air of confidence, yet avoid even the slightest hint of arrogance. He and he alone defined reality, and it was crucial that his stories were believable.

Josh had known Snead for many years. He was a servant whom Mr. Phelan often talked of getting rid of. Of the eleven wills Josh had prepared for Troy Phelan, only one mentioned the name of

Malcolm Snead. A gift of a million dollars had been designated for him, a gift revoked months later with yet another will. Mr. Phelan had removed Snead's name precisely because Snead had inquired as to how much he might expect to receive.

Snead had been too preoccupied with the money to suit his master. His name on the witness list for the contestants meant only one thing—money. He was being paid to testify, and Josh knew it. Two weeks of simple surveillance had discovered a new Range Rover, a newly leased condo in a building where the prices started at eighteen hundred dollars a month, and a trip to Rome, first class.

Snead faced the video camera and was somewhat comfortable. He felt as though he'd been looking at one for a year. He'd spent all of Saturday and half of Sunday in Hark's office, getting himself grilled again. He'd watched the videos of himself for hours. He'd written dozens of pages of fiction on the final days of Troy Phelan. He'd rehearsed with Nicolette the bimbo.

Snead was ready. The lawyers had anticipated questions about the money. If asked whether he was being paid to testify, Snead was trained to lie. It was that simple. There was no way around it. Snead had to lie about the half a million bucks already in hand, and he had to lie about the promise of $4.5 million upon settlement or other favorable outcome. He had to lie about the existence of the contract between himself and the lawyers. Since he was lying about Mr. Phelan he could certainly lie about the money.

Nate introduced himself and then asked, quite loudly, "Mr. Snead, how much are you being paid to testify in this case?"

Snead's lawyers thought the question would be, "Are you being paid?" not, "How much?" Snead's rehearsed answer was a simple "No, I certainly am not!" But to the question still ringing around the room he had no quick response. Hesitation sank him. He seemed to gasp as he looked wildly at Hark, whose spine had become rigid and his stare frozen like a deer's.

Snead had been warned that Mr. O'Riley had done his homework and seemed to know everything before he asked the questions. In the long painful seconds that followed, Mr. O'Riley frowned at him, cocked his head sideways, and lifted some papers.

"Come on, Mr. Snead, I know you're being paid. How much?"

Snead cracked his knuckles hard enough to break them. Beads of sweat popped out in the creases of his forehead. "Well, I, uh, I'm not—"

"Come on, Mr. Snead. Did you or did you not purchase a new Range Rover last month?"

"Well, yes, as a matter of—"

"And you leased a two-bedroom condo at Palm Court?"

"Yes I did."

"And you just returned from ten days in Rome, didn't you?"

"I did."

He knew everything! The Phelan lawyers shrank in their seats, each cowering lower, ducking their heads so the ricocheting bullets wouldn't strike them.

"So how much are you being paid?" Nate asked angrily. "Keep in mind you're under oath!"

"Five hundred thousand dollars," Snead blurted out. Nate stared at him in disbelief, his jaw dropping slowly. Even the court reporter froze.

A couple of the Phelan lawyers managed to exhale, slightly. As horrible as the moment was, it could certainly have been bloodier. What if Snead had panicked even more and confessed to the entire five million?

But it was a very small comfort. At the moment, the news that they had paid a witness a half a million dollars seemed fatal to their cause.

Nate shuffled papers as if he needed some document. The words still echoed through all the ears in the room.

"I take it you have already received this money?" Nate asked.

Unsure whether he was supposed to lie or go straight, Snead simply said, "Yes."

On a hunch, Nate asked, "Half a million now, how much later?"

Anxious to begin the lying, Snead answered, "Nothing." It was a casual denial, one that appeared believable. The other two Phelan lawyers were able to breathe.

"Are you sure about that?" Nate asked. He was fishing. He could ask Snead if he'd been convicted of grave-robbing if he wanted to.

It was a game of high-stakes chicken, and Snead held firm. "Of course I'm sure," he said with enough indignance to seem plausible.

"Who paid you this money?"

"The lawyers for the Phelan heirs."

"Who signed the check?"

"It came from a bank, certified."

"Did you insist they pay you for your testimony?"

"I guess you could say that."

"Did you go to them, or did they come to you?"

"I went to them."

"Why did you go to them?"

Finally, they seemed to be approaching familiar territory. There was a general relaxing on the Phelan side of the table. The lawyers began to scribble notes.

Snead crossed his legs under the table and frowned intelligently at the camera. "Because I was with Mr. Phelan before he died, and I knew the poor man was out of his mind."

"How long had he been out of his mind?"

"All day."

"When he woke up, he was crazy?"

"When I fed him breakfast, he did not know my name."

"What did he call you?"

"Nothing, he just grunted at me."

Nate leaned on his elbows and ignored the paperwork around him. This was a jousting match, and he actually enjoyed it. He knew where he was going, but poor Snead did not.

"Did you see him jump?"

"Yes."

"And fall?"

"Yes."

"And hit the ground?"

"Yes."

"Were you standing near him when he was examined by the three psychiatrists?"

"Yes."

"And this was about two-thirty in the afternoon, right?"

"Yes, as I recall."

"And he'd been crazy all day, right?"

"I'm afraid so, yes."

"How long did you work for Mr. Phelan?"

"Thirty years."

"And you knew everything about him, right?"

"As much as one person can know about another."

"So you knew his lawyer, Mr. Stafford?"

"Yes, I'd met him many times."

"Did Mr. Phelan trust Mr. Stafford?"

"I suppose."

"I thought you knew everything."

"I'm sure he trusted Mr. Stafford."

"Was Mr. Stafford sitting by his side during the mental examination?"

"He was."

"What was Mr. Phelan's mental state during the exam, in your opinion?"

"He was unsound, uncertain of where he was and what he was doing."

"You're sure about this?"

"I am."

"Who did you tell?"

"It wasn't my job to tell."

"Why not?"

"I would've been fired. Part of my job was to keep my mouth shut. It's called discretion."

"You knew Mr. Phelan was going to sign a will dividing his vast fortune. At the same time he was of unsound mind, yet you didn't tell his lawyer, a man he trusted?"

"It wasn't my job."

"Mr. Phelan would've fired you?"

"Immediately."

"Then what about after he jumped? Who did you tell then?"

"No one."

"Why not?"

Snead took a breath and recrossed his legs. He was rallying nicely, he thought. "It was a matter of privacy," he said gravely. "I considered my relationship with Mr. Phelan to be confidential."

"Until now. Until they offered you half a million bucks, right?"

Snead could think of no quick reply, and Nate didn't offer much of a chance. "You're selling not only your testimony but also your confidential relationship with Mr. Phelan, right, Mr. Snead?"

"I'm trying to undo an injustice."

"How noble. Would you be undoing it if they weren't paying you?"

Snead managed to utter a shaky "Yes," and Nate erupted in laughter. He laughed loud and long and did so while looking at the solemn and partially hidden faces of the Phelan lawyers. He laughed directly at Snead. He stood and walked along his end of the table, chuckling to himself. "What a trial," he said, then sat down again.

He glanced at some notes, then continued, "Mr. Phelan died on December the ninth. His will was read on December the twenty-seventh. During the interval, did you tell anyone that he was of unsound mind when he signed his will?"

"No."

"Of course not. You waited until after the will was read, then, realizing you had been cut out, decided to go to the lawyers and strike a deal, didn't you, Mr. Snead?"

The witness answered, "No," but Nate ignored him.

"Was Mr. Phelan mentally ill?"

"I'm not an expert in that field."

"You said he was out of his mind. Was this a permanent condition?"

"It came and went."

"How long had it been coming and going?"

"For years."

"How many years?"

"Ten maybe. It's just a guess."

"In the last fourteen years of his life, Mr. Phelan executed eleven wills, one of which left you a million dollars. Did you ever think of telling anyone then that he was of unsound mind?"

"It wasn't my job to tell."

"Did he ever see a psychiatrist?"

"Not to my knowledge."

"Did he ever see any mental health professional?"

"Not to my knowledge."

"Did you ever suggest to him that he seek professional help?"

"It wasn't my job to suggest such things."

"If you'd found him lying on the floor having a seizure would you have suggested to someone that perhaps he needed help?"

"Of course I would have."

"If you'd found him coughing blood, would you have told some-one?"

"Yes."

Nate had a memo two inches thick with summaries of Mr. Phelan's holdings. He flipped to a page at random and asked Snead if he knew anything about Xion Drilling. Snead struggled mightily to remember, but his mind had been so overloaded with new data that it failed him. Delstar Communications? Again, Snead grimaced but could not make the connection.

The fifth company Nate mentioned rang a bell. Snead proudly informed the lawyer that he knew the company. Mr. Phelan had owned it for quite some time. Nate had questions about sales, prod-ucts, holdings, earnings, an endless list of financial statistics. Snead answered nothing right.

"How much did you know about Mr. Phelan's holdings?" Nate asked repeatedly. Then he asked questions about the structure of The Phelan Group. Snead had memorized the basics, but the smaller details escaped him. He could name no mid-level manager. He did not know the name of the company's accountants.

Nate hammered him relentlessly about the things he didn't know. Late in the afternoon, with Snead weary and punch-drunk, Nate, in the midst of the millionth question about financials, asked, with no warning, "Did you sign a contract with the lawyers when you took the half a million?"

A simple "No" would have sufficed, but Snead was caught off guard. He hesitated, looked at Hark then looked at Nate, who was again shuffling through papers as if he had a copy of the contract. Snead hadn't lied in two hours, and wasn't quick.

"Uh, of course not," he stuttered, and convinced no one.

Nate saw the untruth, and let it go. There were other ways to obtain a copy of the contract.

THE PHELAN LAWYERS met in a dark bar to lick their wounds. Snead's dismal performance seemed even worse after two rounds of stiff drinks. He could be propped up some for trial, but the fact that he'd been paid so much would forever taint his testimony.

How did O'Riley know? He was so certain Snead had been paid.

"It was Grit," Hark said. Grit, they all repeated to themselves. Surely Grit hadn't gone to the other side.

"That's what you get for stealing his client," Wally Bright said after a long silence.

"Shut up," Ms. Langhorne said.

Hark was too tired to fight. He finished his drink and ordered another. In the flood of testimony, the other Phelan lawyers had forgotten about Rachel. There was still no official record of her in the court file.

FORTY-SEVEN

THE DEPOSITION of Nicolette the secretary lasted eight minutes. She gave her name, address, and brief employment history, and the Phelan lawyers on the other side settled into their chairs to await the details of her sexual escapades with Mr. Phelan. She was twenty-three, with few qualifications beyond a slender body, nice chest, and a pretty face with sandy blond hair. They couldn't wait to hear her spend a few hours talking about sex.

Getting right to the point, Nate asked, "Did you ever have sex with Mr. Phelan?"

She tried to appear embarrassed by the question, but said yes anyway.

"How many times?"

"I didn't count them."

"For how long?"

"Usually ten minutes."

"No, I mean for how long a period of time. Starting in what month and ending when?"

"Oh, I only worked there five months."

"Roughly twenty weeks. On the average, how many times each week did you have sex with Mr. Phelan?"

"Two times I guess."

"So about forty times?"

"I guess. That sounds like a lot, doesn't it?"

"Not to me. Did Mr. Phelan take his clothes off when you guys did it?"

"Sure. We both did."

"So he was completely naked?"

"Yes."

"Did he have any visible birthmarks on his body?"

When witnesses concoct lies, they often miss the obvious. So do their lawyers. They become so consumed with their fiction that they overlook a fact or two. Hark and the guys had access to the Phelan wives—Lillian, Janie, Tira—any one of whom could have told them that Troy had a round purple birthmark the size of a silver dollar at the very top of his right leg, near the hip, just below the waist.

"Not that I recall," Nicolette answered.

The answer surprised Nate, and then it didn't. He could've easily believed that Troy was doing his secretary, something he'd done for decades. And he could just as easily have believed Nicolette was lying.

"No visible birthmarks?" Nate asked again.

"None."

The Phelan lawyers were stricken with fear. Could another star witness be melting before their eyes?

"No further questions," Nate said, and left the room to refill his coffee.

Nicolette looked at the lawyers. They were staring at the table, wondering exactly where the birthmark was.

After she left, Nate slid an autopsy photo across the table to his bewildered enemies. He didn't say a word, didn't need to. Old Troy was on the slab, nothing but withered and battered flesh with the birthmark staring out from the photo.

□ □ □ □

THEY SPENT the rest of Wednesday and all day Thursday with the four new psychiatrists who'd been hired to say that the three old ones really didn't know what they were doing. Their testimony was predictable and repetitive—people with sound minds do not jump out of windows.

As a group they were less distinguished than Flowe, Zadel, and Theishen. A couple were retired and picked up a few retainers here and there as professional testifiers. One taught at a crowded community college. One eked out a living in a small office in the suburbs.

But they weren't paid to be impressive; rather, their purpose was simply to muddy the water. Troy Phelan was known to be erratic and eccentric. Four experts said he didn't have the mental capacity to execute a will. Three said he did. Keep the issues dense and tangled and hope those supporting the will would one day grow weary and settle. If not, it would be up to a jury of laymen to sift through the medical jargon and make sense of the conflicting opinions.

The new experts were paid well to stick to their convictions, and Nate didn't try to change them. He had deposed enough doctors to know not to argue medicine with them. Instead, he dwelt on their credentials and experience. He made them watch the video and criticize the first three psychiatrists.

When they adjourned Thursday afternoon, fifteen depositions had been completed. Another round was scheduled for late March. Wycliff was planning a trial for the middle of July. The same witnesses would testify again, but in open court with spectators watching and jurors weighing every word.

NATE FLED THE CITY. He went west through Virginia, then south through the Shenandoah Valley. His mind was numb from nine days of hardball probing into the intimate lives of others. At some undefined point in his life, pushed by his work and his addictions, he had lost his decency and shame. He had learned to lie, cheat, deceive, hide, badger, and attack innocent witnesses without the slightest twinge of guilt.

But in the quiet of his car and the darkness of the night, Nate was ashamed. He had pity for the Phelan children. He felt sorry for Snead, a sad little man just trying to survive. He wished he hadn't attacked the new experts with such vigor.

His shame was back, and Nate was pleased. He was proud of himself for feeling so ashamed. He was human after all.

At midnight, he stopped at a cheap motel near Knoxville. There was heavy snow in the Midwest, in Kansas and Iowa. Lying in bed with his atlas, he mapped a trail through the Southwest.

He slept the second night in Shawnee, Oklahoma; the third in Kingman, Arizona; the fourth in Redding, California.

THE KIDS from his second marriage were Austin and Angela, twelve and eleven respectively, seventh and sixth grades. He'd last seen them in July, three weeks before the last crash, when he took them to an Orioles game. The pleasant outing later turned into another ugly scene. Nate had drunk six beers at the game—the kids counted because their mother told them to—and he drove the two hours from Baltimore to Arlington under the influence.

At the time, they were moving to Oregon with their mother, Christi, and her second husband, Theo. The game was to be Nate's last visit with them for some time, and instead of dwelling on good-byes Nate got plastered. He fought with his ex-wife in the driveway while the children watched, all too familiar with the scene. Theo had threatened him with a broom handle. Nate woke up in his car, parked in the handicapped zone of a McDonald's, an empty six-pack on the seat.

When they met fourteen years earlier, Christi was the headmistress of a private school in Potomac. She was on a jury. Nate was one of the lawyers. She wore a short black skirt on the second day of the trial, and the litigation practically stopped. Their first date was a week later. For three years Nate stayed clean, long enough to get remarried and have the two kids. When the dam started cracking, Christi was scared and wanted to run. When it burst, she fled with the children and didn't return for a year. The marriage endured ten chaotic years.

She was working at a school in Salem. Theo was with a small law firm there. Nate had always believed that he ran them out of Washington. He couldn't blame them for fleeing to the other coast.

He called the school from his car near Medford, four hours away, and was put on hold for five minutes; time, he was certain, for her to lock her door and collect her thoughts. "Hello," she finally said.

"Christi, it's me, Nate," he said, feeling silly identifying his voice to a woman he'd lived with for ten years.

"Where are you?" she asked, as if an attack were imminent.

"Near Medford."

"In Oregon?"

"Yes. I'd like to see the kids."

"Well, when?"

"Tonight, tomorrow, I'm in no hurry. I've been on the road for a few days, just seeing the country. I have no itinerary."

"Well, sure, Nate. I guess we can work something out. But the kids are very busy, you know, school, ballet, soccer."

"How are they?"

"They're doing very well. Thanks for asking."

"And you? How's life treating you?"

"I'm fine. We love Oregon."

"I'm doing well too. Thanks for asking. I'm clean and sober, Christi, really. I've finally kicked the booze and drugs for good. Looks like I'll be leaving the practice of law, but I'm doing really well."

She'd heard it before. "That's good, Nate." Her words were cautious. She was planning two sentences in advance.

They agreed to have dinner the following night, enough time for her to prepare the kids and fix up the house and allow Theo to decide what his role should be. Enough time to rehearse and plan exits.

"I won't get in the way," Nate promised, before hanging up.

THEO DECIDED to work late and skip the reunion. Nate hugged Angela tightly. Austin just shook hands. The one thing he vowed not to do was gush about how much they'd grown. Christi loitered in her bedroom for an hour as the father was reintroduced to his children.

Nor would he bury them with apologies about things he couldn't change. They sat on the floor of the den and talked about school, and ballet, and soccer. Salem was a pretty town, much smaller than D.C., and the kids had adjusted well, with lots of friends, a good school, nice teachers.

Dinner was spaghetti and salad, and it lasted for one hour. Nate told tales from the jungles of Brazil as he took them on his journey to find the missing client. Evidently, Christi had not seen the right newspapers. She knew nothing of the Phelan matter.

At seven sharp, he said he had to go. They had homework, and school came early. "I have a soccer game tomorrow, Dad," Austin said, and Nate's heart almost stopped. He couldn't remember the last time he'd been called Dad.

"It's at the school," Angela said. "Could you come?"

The little ex-family shared an awkward moment as each of them glanced at the other. Nate had no idea what to say.

Christi settled the issue by saying, "I'll be there. We could talk."

"Of course I'll be there," he said. The children hugged him as he left. Driving away, Nate suspected Christi wanted to see him two days in a row to examine his eyes. She knew the signs.

Nate stayed in Salem for three days. He watched the soccer game and was overcome with pride in his son. He got himself invited back to dinner, but agreed to come only if Theo would join them. He had lunch with Angela and her friends at school.

After three days, it was time to leave. The kids needed their normal routines back, without the complications Nate brought. Christi was tired of pretending nothing had ever happened between them. And Nate was getting attached to his children. He promised to call and e-mail and see them soon.

He left Salem with a broken heart. How low could a man sink to lose such a wonderful family? He remembered almost nothing of his kids when they were smaller—no school plays, Halloween costumes, Christmas mornings, trips to the mall. Now they were practically grown, and another man was raising them.

He turned east, and drifted with the traffic.

WHILE NATE was meandering through Montana, thinking of Rachel, Hark Gettys filed a motion to dismiss her answer to the will contest. His reasons were clear and obvious, and he supported his attack with a twenty-page brief he'd worked on for a month. It was March 7, almost three months after the death of Mr. Phelan, not quite two months after the entry of Nate O'Riley into the matter, nearly three weeks into discovery, four months before the trial, and the court still did not have jurisdiction over Rachel Lane. But for the allegations of her attorney, there'd been no sign of her. No document in the official court file had her signature on it.

Hark referred to her as the "phantom party." He and the other contestants were litigating against a shadow. The woman stood to inherit eleven billion dollars. The least she could do was sign a waiver and follow the law. If she'd gone to the trouble to hire a lawyer, she could certainly subject herself to the jurisdiction of the court.

The passage of time was benefiting the heirs greatly, though it was hard for them to be patient while dreaming of such wealth. Each week that passed with no word from Rachel was further proof that she had no interest in the proceedings. At the Friday morning meetings, the Phelan lawyers reviewed discovery, talked about their clients, and plotted trial strategy. But they spent most of their time speculating why Rachel had not made an official appearance. They were enthralled with the ridiculous notion that she might not want the money. It was absurd, yet it somehow managed to surface every Friday morning.

The weeks were turning into months. The lottery winner was not claiming her prize.

There was another significant reason for putting pressure on the defenders of Troy's testament. His name was Snead. Hark, Yancy, Bright, and Langhorne had watched their star witness's deposition until it was memorized, and they were not confident of his ability to sway jurors. Nate O'Riley had made a fool out of him, and that was only in a deposition. Imagine how sharp the daggers would be at trial, in front of a jury made up primarily of middle-class folks struggling to pay their monthly bills. Snead pocketed a half a million to tell his story. It would be a hard sell.

The problem with Snead was obvious. He was lying, and liars eventually get caught in court. After Snead stumbled so badly in the deposition, the lawyers were terrified of presenting him to a jury. Another lie or two exposed to the world, and their case was down the toilet.

The birthmark had rendered Nicolette completely useless as a witness.

Their own clients were not particularly sympathetic. With the exception of Ramble, who was the scariest of all, each had been handed five million dollars with which to get a start. None of the jurors would earn that much in a lifetime. Troy's children could whine about being raised by an absent father, but half the jurors would be from broken homes.

The battle of the shrinks would be hard to call, but it was the segment of the trial that worried them the most. Nate O'Riley had been shredding doctors in courtrooms for more than twenty years. Their four substitutes could not withstand his brutal cross-examinations.

To avoid a trial, they had to settle. To settle, they had to find a weakness. Rachel Lane's apparent lack of interest was more than sufficient, and certainly their best shot.

□ □ □ □

JOSH REVIEWED the Motion to Dismiss with admiration. He loved the legal maneuvering, the ploys and tactics, and when someone, even an opponent, got it right, he silently applauded. Everything about Hark's move was perfect—the timing, the rationale, the superbly argued brief.

The contestants had a weak case, but their problems were small compared to Nate's. Nate had no client. He and Josh had managed to keep this quiet for two months, but the ruse had run its course.

FORTY-EIGHT

DANIEL, his oldest child, insisted on meeting him in a pub. Nate found the place after dark, two blocks off the campus, on a street lined with bars and clubs. The music, the flashing beer signs, the co-eds yelling across the street—it was all too familiar. It was Georgetown just a few months ago, and none of it appealed to him. A year earlier he would've been yelling back, chasing them from one bar to the other, believing he was still twenty and able to go all night.

Daniel was waiting in a cramped booth, along with a girl. Both were smoking. Each had two longneck bottles sitting on the table in front of them. Father and son shook hands because anything more affectionate would make the son feel uncomfortable.

"This is Stef," Daniel said, introducing the girl. "She's a model," he added quickly, proving to his old man that he was chasing a high caliber of woman.

For some reason, Nate had hoped they could spend a few hours alone. It was not going to happen.

The first thing he noticed about Stef was her gray lipstick, applied heavily to the thick and pouty lips, lips that scarcely cracked when she gave him the obligatory half-smile. She was certainly plain and gaunt enough to be a model. Her arms were as skinny as broom handles. Though Nate couldn't see them, he knew her bony legs ran to her armpits, and without a doubt there were at least two tattoos burned into the flesh around her ankles.

Nate disliked her immediately, and got the impression the feeling was mutual. No telling what Daniel had told her.

Daniel had finished college at Grinnell a year earlier, then spent the summer in India. Nate had not seen him in thirteen months. He had not gone to his commencement, had not sent a card or a gift, had not bothered to call with congratulations. There was enough tension at the table without the mannequin puffing smoke and looking at Nate with a completely blank stare.

"You wanna beer?" Daniel asked when a waiter got close. It was a cruel question, a quick little shot designed to inflict pain.

"No, just water," Nate said. Daniel yelled at the waiter, then said, "Still on the wagon, huh?"

"Always," Nate said with a smile, trying to deflect the arrows.

"Have you fallen off since last summer?"

"No. Let's talk about something else."

"Dan tells me you've been through rehab," Stef said, smoke drifting from her nostrils. Nate was surprised she was able to start and finish a sentence. Her words were slow, her voice as hollow as her eye sockets.

"I have, several times. What else has he told you?"

"I've done rehab," she said. "But only once." She seemed proud of her accomplishment, yet saddened by her lack of experience. The two beer bottles in front of her were empty.

"That's nice," Nate said, dismissing her. He couldn't pretend to like her, and in a month or two she'd have another serious love.

"How's school?" he asked Daniel.

"What school?"

"Grad school."

"I dropped out." His words were edgy and strained. There was pressure behind them. Nate was involved in the dropping out; he just wasn't exactly sure how and why. His water arrived. "Have you guys eaten?" he asked.

Stef avoided food and Daniel wasn't hungry. Nate was starving but didn't want to eat alone. He glanced around the pub. Pot was being smoked somewhere in another corner. It was a rowdy little dump, the kind of place he'd loved in a not too distant life.

Daniel lit another cigarette, a Camel with no filter, the worst cancer sticks on the market, and he blasted a cloud of thick smoke at the cheap beer chandelier hanging above them. He was angry and tense.

The girl was there for two reasons. She would prevent harsh words and maybe a fight. Nate suspected his son was broke, that he wanted to lash out at his father for his lack of support, but that he was afraid to do so because the old man was fragile and had been prone to crack and go off the deep end. Stef would throttle his anger and his language.

The second reason was to make the meeting as brief as possible. It took about fifteen minutes to figure this out.

"How's your mother?" he asked.

Daniel attempted to smile. "She's fine. I saw her Christmas. You were gone."

"I was in Brazil."

A co-ed in tight jeans walked by. Stef inspected her from top to bottom, her eyes finally showing some life. The girl was even skinnier than Stef. How did emaciation become so cool?

"What's in Brazil?" Daniel asked.

"A client." Nate was tired of the stories from his adventure.

"Mom says you're in some kind of trouble with the IRS."

"I'm sure that pleases your mother."

"I guess. She didn't seem bothered by it. You going to jail?"

"No. Could we talk about something else?"

"That's the problem, Dad. There is nothing else, nothing but the past and we can't go there."

Stef, the referee, rolled her eyes at Daniel, as if to say, "That's enough."

"Why did you drop out of school?" Nate asked, anxious to get it over with.

"Several reasons. It got boring."

"He ran out of money," Stef said, helpfully. She gave Nate her best blank look.

"Is that true?" Nate asked.

"That's one reason."

Nate's first instinct was to pull out his checkbook and solve the kid's problems. That's what he'd always done. Parenting for him had been one long shopping trip. If you can't be there, send money. But Daniel was now twenty-three, a college grad, hanging around with the likes of Ms. Bulimia over there, and it was time for him to sink or swim on his own.

And the checkbook wasn't what it used to be.

"It's good for you," Nate said. "Work for a while. It'll make you appreciate school."

Stef disagreed. She had two friends who'd dropped out and pretty much fallen off the face of the earth. As she prattled on, Daniel withdrew to his corner of the booth. He drained his third bottle. Nate had all sorts of lectures about alcohol, but he knew how phony they'd sound.

After four beers, Stef was bombed and Nate had nothing else to say. He scribbled his phone number in St. Michaels on a napkin and gave it to Daniel. "This is where I'll be for the next couple of months. Call me if you need me."

"See you, Pop," Daniel said.

"Take care."

Nate stepped into the frigid air and walked toward Lake Michigan.

TWO DAYS LATER he was in Pittsburgh for his third and final reunion, one that did not occur. He'd spoken twice to Kaitlin, his daughter from marriage number one, and the details were clear. She was to meet him for dinner at 7:30 P.M., in front of the restaurant in the lobby of his hotel. Her apartment was twenty minutes away. She paged him at 8:30 with the news that a friend had been involved in an auto accident, and that she was at the hospital where things looked bad.

Nate suggested they have lunch the following day. Kaitlin said that wouldn't work because the friend had a head injury, was on life support, and she planned to stay with her there until she was stable. With his daughter in full retreat, Nate asked where the hospital was located. At first she didn't know, then she wasn't sure, then upon further thought a visit was not a good idea because she couldn't leave the bedside.

He ate in his room, at a small table next to the window, with a view of downtown. He picked at his food and thought of all the possible reasons his daughter didn't want to see him. A ring in her nose? A tattoo on her forehead? Had she joined a cult and shaved her head? Had she gained a hundred pounds or lost fifty? Was she pregnant?

He tried to blame her so he wouldn't be forced to face the obvious. Did she hate him that much?

In the loneliness of the hotel room, in a city where he knew no one, it was easy to pity himself, to suffer once again through the mistakes of his past.

He grabbed the phone and got busy. He called Father Phil to check on things in St. Michaels. Phil had been bothered by the flu, and since it was chilly in the church basement Laura wouldn't let him work there. How wonderful, thought Nate. Though many uncertainties lay in his path, the one constant, at least for the near future, would be the promise of steady work in the basement of Trinity Church.

He called Sergio for their weekly pep session. The demons were well in hand, and he felt surprisingly under control. His hotel room had a mini-bar, and he had not been near it.

He called Salem and had a pleasant chat with Angela and Austin. Odd how the younger kids wanted to talk while the older ones did not.

He called Josh, who was in his basement office, thinking about the Phelan mess. "You need to come home, Nate," he said. "I have a plan."

FORTY-NINE

NATE WASN'T INVITED to the first round of peace talks. There were a couple of reasons for his absence. First, Josh arranged the summit, so it was therefore held on his turf. Nate had thus far avoided his old office and wanted this to continue. Second, the Phelan lawyers viewed Josh and Nate as allies, and rightfully so. Josh wanted the role of peacemaker, the intermediary. To gain trust from one side, he had to ignore the other, if only for a short while. His plan was to meet with Hark et al., then with Nate, then back and forth for a few days if necessary until a deal was struck.

After a lengthy session of pleasantries and chitchat, Josh asked for their attention. They had lots of territory to cover. The Phelan lawyers were anxious to get started.

A settlement can happen in seconds, during a recess in a heated trial when a witness stumbles, or when a new CEO wants to start fresh and unload nagging litigation. And a settlement can take months, as the lawsuit inches toward a trial date. As a whole, the Phelan lawyers dreamed of a quickie, and the meeting in Josh's suite was the first step. They truly believed they were about to become millionaires.

Josh began by diplomatically offering his opinion that their case was rather flimsy. He knew nothing about his client's plans to whip out a holographic will and create chaos, but it was a valid will nonetheless. He had spent two hours with Mr. Phelan the previous day finishing the other new will, and he was prepared to testify that he knew exactly what he was doing. He would also testify, if necessary, that Snead was nowhere in the picture when they met.

The three psychiatrists who examined Mr. Phelan had been carefully chosen by Phelan's children and ex-wives, and their lawyers, and had impeccable credentials. The four now on retainer were flaky. Their résumés were thin. The battle of the experts would be won by the original three, in his opinion.

Wally Bright had on his best suit, which wasn't saying much. He took this criticism with a clenched jaw, bottom lip between his teeth so he wouldn't say something stupid, and he took useless notes on a legal pad because that's what everybody else was doing. It was not his nature to sit back and accept such disparagement, even from a renowned lawyer like Josh Stafford. But he would do anything for the money. The month before, February, his little office generated twenty-six hundred dollars in fees, and consumed the usual four thousand in overhead. Wally took home nothing. Of course, most of his time had been spent on the Phelan matter.

Josh skated onto thin ice when he summarized the testimony of their clients. "I've watched the videos of their depositions," he said sadly. "Frankly, with the exception of Mary Ross, I think they will make terrible witnesses at trial."

Their lawyers took this in stride. This was a settlement conference, not a trial.

He didn't dwell on the heirs. The less said the better. Their lawyers knew they would get butchered before the jury.

"That brings us to Snead," he said. "I've watched his deposition too, and, frankly, if you call him as a witness at trial it will be a terrible mistake. In my opinion, in fact, it will border on legal malpractice."

Bright, Hark, Langhorne, and Yancy huddled even closer over

their legal pads. Snead was a dirty word among them. They'd fought over who was to blame for botching it so badly. They'd lost sleep fretting over the man. They were half a million down, and as a witness he was worthless.

"I've known Snead for almost twenty years," Josh said, then spent fifteen minutes effectively portraying him as a butler of marginal talents, a gofer who was not always reliable, a servant Mr. Phelan often talked of firing. They believed every word of it.

So much for Snead. Josh managed to gut their star witness without even mentioning the fact that he'd been bribed with five hundred thousand dollars to tell his story.

And so much for Nicolette too. She was lying along with her buddy Snead.

They had been unable to locate other witnesses. There were some disgruntled employees, but they wanted no part of a trial. Their testimony was tainted anyway. There were two rivals from the business world who'd been wiped out trying to compete with Troy. But they knew nothing about his mental capacity.

Their case was not very strong, Josh concluded. But everything's risky with a jury.

He talked about Rachel Lane as if he'd known her for years. Not too many specifics, but enough generalizations to convey the impression that Josh knew her well. She was a lovely lady who lived a very simple life, in another country, and was not the type of person who understood litigation. She ran from controversy. She despised confrontation. And she'd been closer to old Troy than most people knew.

Hark wanted to ask if Josh had ever met her. Ever seen her? Ever heard her name before he read the will? But it was neither the time nor the place for discord. Money was about to be laid upon the table, and Hark's percentage was seventeen point five.

Ms. Langhorne had researched the town of Corumbá, and was wondering again what an American woman, age forty-two, could possibly be doing in such a place. She and Hark, behind the backs of Bright and Yancy, had quietly become confidants. They had talked at length about leaking the whereabouts of Rachel Lane to certain reporters. The press would certainly find her down there, in Corumbá. They'd smoke her out, and in the process the world would learn what she planned to do with the money. If, as they hoped and dreamed, she didn't want it, then their clients could press for all the money.

It was a risk, and they were still talking about it.

"What does Rachel Lane plan to do with all this money?" Yancy asked.

"I'm not sure," Josh said, as if he and Rachel discussed it every day. "She'll probably keep a little, and give most of it to charity. In my opinion, that's why Troy did what he did. He figured that if your clients got the money, it wouldn't last ninety days. By leaving it to Rachel, he knew it would be passed on to those in need."

There was a long pause in the conversation when Josh finished with this. Dreams slowly crumbled. Rachel Lane indeed existed, and she was not going to decline the money.

"Why hasn't she made an appearance?" Hark finally asked.

"Well, you have to know this woman to answer that question. Money means nothing to her. She did not expect to be named in her father's will. Then, suddenly, she finds out that she has inherited billions. She's still in shock."

Another long pause as the Phelan lawyers doodled on their pads. "We are prepared to litigate to the Supreme Court, if necessary," Langhorne said. "Does she realize this could take years?"

"She does," Josh replied. "And that's one reason she would like to explore settlement possibilities."

Now they were making progress.

"Where do we start?" asked Wally Bright.

It was a difficult question. On one side of the table was a pot of gold worth eleven billion or so. Estate taxes would take more than half, leaving five to play with. On the other side were the Phelan heirs, all of whom were broke with the exception of Ramble. Who would throw out the first figure? How much would it be? Ten million per heir? Or a hundred?

Josh had it planned. "Let's start with the will," he said. "Assuming it's held to be valid, it contains clear language terminating any gift to any heir who challenges it. That would apply to your clients. Therefore, you start from a position of zero. Then, the will gives to each of your clients a sum of money equal to their debts as of the day of Mr. Phelan's death." Josh lifted another sheet of paper and studied it for a second. "According to what we've learned so far, Ramble Phelan has no debts, yet. Geena Phelan Strong had debts of four hundred twenty thousand on December ninth. Libbigail and Spike had debts of around eighty thousand. Mary Ross and her doctor husband had debts of nine hundred thousand. Troy Junior had discharged most of his in one bankruptcy or another, but still owed a hundred and thirty thousand. Rex, as we know, wins the prize. He and his lovely wife Amber owed, on December ninth, a total of seven point six million dollars. Any problem with these numbers?"

No. The numbers were accurate. It was the next number that concerned them.

"Nate O'Riley has been in contact with his client. To settle this matter, she will offer each of the six heirs ten million dollars."

The lawyers had never calculated and scribbled so fast. Hark had three clients; 17.5 percent gave him a fee of $5.25 million. Geena and Cody had agreed on a 20 percent cut for Langhorne, so her little firm would collect $2 million. Same for Yancy, subject to court approval because Ramble was still a minor. And Wally Bright, a street hustler who scratched out a living by advertising quickie divorces on bus benches, would collect half of the $10 million under his unconscionable contract with Libbigail and Spike.

Wally reacted first. Though his heart was frozen and his esophagus clamped shut, he managed to say, with some measure of brass, "No way my client will settle for less than fifty million."

The others shook their heads too. They frowned and tried to appear disgusted with the paltry sum being offered, while in fact they were already spending the money.

Wally Bright couldn't write fifty million and get the zeros in the correct places. But he managed to throw the figure out like a Vegas high-roller.

They had agreed before the meeting that if money was discussed, they would go no lower than fifty million per heir. This sounded fine, before the meeting. Now, the ten million on the table looked awfully good.

"That's about one percent of the estate," Hark said.

"You can look at it that way," Josh said. "In fact, there are many ways to look at it. But I prefer to start at zero, which is where you are now, and work up, rather than look at the entire estate and work down."

But Josh also wanted their trust. They kicked the numbers around for a while, then he said, "No, personally, if I represented one of the heirs, I wouldn't take ten million."

They froze and listened intently.

"She is not a greedy woman. I think Nate O'Riley could convince her to settle at twenty million per heir."

The fees doubled—over ten million for Hark. Four million for Langhorne and Yancy. Poor Wally, at ten now, was suddenly struck with diarrhea and asked to leave the meeting.

NATE WAS HAPPY and busy painting door trim when his cell phone buzzed. Josh made him keep the damned thing within reach.

"If it's for me, take a number," Father Phil said. He was measuring a complicated corner for the next piece of wallboard.

It was Josh. "It couldn't have gone better," he announced. "I stopped at twenty million, they want fifty."

"Fifty?" Nate said in disbelief.

"Yeah, but they're already spending the money. I'll bet at least two of them are at the Mercedes dealer right now."

"Who'll spend it faster? Lawyers or clients?"

"I'd bet on the lawyers. Look, I just talked to Wycliff. The meeting is for Wednesday at three, in his office. We should wrap it up by then."

"I can't wait," Nate said, and folded the phone. Time for a

coffee break. They sat on the floor, backs to a wall, and sipped warm latte.

"They wanted fifty?" Phil asked. By now, he knew the details. Alone in the basement, the two had kept few secrets as they drifted through their labors. Conversation was more important than progress. Phil was clergy. Nate was a lawyer. Everything said was covered by some manner of confidential privilege.

"It's a nice starting place," Nate said. "But they'll take a lot less."

"You expect it to be settled?"

"Sure. We'll meet on Wednesday with the Judge. He'll apply more pressure. By then the lawyers and their clients will be counting the money."

"So when do you leave?"

"Friday, I guess. You wanna come?"

"I can't afford it."

"Sure you can. My client will foot the bill. You can be my spiritual adviser for the trip. Money is no object."

"It wouldn't be right."

"Come on, Phil. I'll show you the Pantanal. You can meet my pals Jevy and Welly. We'll go for a boat ride."

"You haven't made it sound very appealing."

"It's not dangerous. There's quite a tourist business in the Pantanal. It's a great ecological preserve. Seriously, Phil, if you're interested I can make it happen."

"I don't have a passport," he said and sipped his coffee. "Plus I have so much work to do here."

Nate would be gone for a week, and he somehow liked the fact that the basement would look the same when he returned.

"Mrs. Sinclair is expected to die any day now," Phil said quietly. "I can't be gone."

The church had been waiting for Mrs. Sinclair to die for at least a month. Phil was fearful about a trip to Baltimore. Nate knew he would never leave the country.

"So you're gonna see her again," Phil said.

"Yes, I am."

"Are you excited?"

"I don't know. I look forward to seeing her, but I'm not sure she wants to see me. She's very happy and wants no part of this world. She will resent more of the legal stuff."

"Then why do it?"

"Because there's nothing to lose. If she rejects the money again, we're in the same position as now. The other side gets everything."

"And that's a disaster."

"Yes. It would be difficult to find a group of people less equipped to handle serious money than the Phelan heirs. They'll kill themselves with it."

"Can't you explain this to Rachel?"

"I tried. She has no interest in hearing it."

"So she's not going to change her mind?"

"No. Never."

"And the trip down is a waste of time?"

"I'm afraid so. But at least we'll try."

FIFTY

WITH THE EXCEPTION of Ramble, all of the Phelan heirs insisted on being either in the courthouse or within a rock's throw during the meeting. Each had a cell phone, as did each lawyer inside Wycliff's office.

Much sleep had been lost by the clients and their lawyers.

How often does one become an instant millionaire? At least twice for the Phelan heirs, and they vowed to themselves that they would be much wiser this time around. They would never get another chance.

They walked the hallways of the courthouse, waiting. They smoked outside by the front doors. They kept warm in their cars in the parking lot, fidgeting. They checked their watches, tried to read newspapers, chatted nervously when they bumped into each other.

Nate and Josh sat on one side of the room. Josh of course wore an expensive dark suit. Nate wore a denim shirt with specks of white paint on the collar. No tie. Jeans and hiking boots rounded out his ensemble.

Wycliff first addressed the Phelan lawyers across the room. He informed them that he was not inclined to dismiss the answer of

Rachel Lane, at least not at that time. There was too much at stake to cut her from the proceedings. Mr. O'Riley was doing a fine job of representing her interests; therefore the lawsuit would proceed as scheduled.

The purpose of the meeting was to explore settlement, something every judge wanted for every case. Wycliff was still enthralled with the vision of a long, nasty, high-profile trial, but he could never admit it. It was his duty to push, prod, and cajole the parties into a settlement.

Prodding and cajoling would not be necessary.

His Honor had reviewed all the pleadings and documents, and he'd watched every minute of every deposition. He recapped the evidence as he viewed things, and offered the grave conclusion to Hark, Bright, Langhorne, and Yancy that, in his learned opinion, they didn't have much of a case.

They took it well. It came as no surprise. Money was on the table and they were anxious to get to it. Insult us all you want, they said to themselves, but let's hurry along to the money.

On the other hand, Wycliff was saying, you never know what a jury will do. He spoke as if he empaneled juries every week, which he did not. And the lawyers knew it.

He asked Josh to recap the initial settlement conference of Monday, two days earlier. "I want to know exactly where we are," he said.

Josh was brief. The bottom line was simple. The heirs wanted fifty million dollars each. Rachel, the sole major beneficiary, was offering twenty million only to settle, without admitting the other side had a valid case.

"That's a substantial gap," Wycliff observed.

Nate was bored but tried to appear sharp. These were high-powered settlement negotiations involving one of the greatest self-made fortunes in the world. Josh had scolded him for his appearance. He didn't care. He kept himself interested by watching the faces of the lawyers across the room. They were an edgy bunch, not anxious or worried, but animated and desperate to learn how much they would be getting. Their eyes were keen and quick; their hand movements impulsive.

How much fun it would be to abruptly stand, announce Rachel wasn't offering a dime to settle, and storm out of the room. They would sit in shock for a few seconds, then they would chase him like hungry dogs.

When Josh finished, Hark spoke for the group. He had notes and he'd spent time on his remarks. He got their attention by admitting that the development of their case had not followed the course they'd wanted. Their clients were not good witnesses. The current psychiatrists were not as solid as the first three. Snead was not reliable. He admitted all this, and his sincerity was admirable.

Instead of arguing legal theories, Hark dwelt on people. He talked about their clients, the Phelan children, and he admitted that on the surface they were not a sympathetic bunch. But once you got past the surface, and you got to know them the way their lawyers had, you realized they simply never had a chance. As children they were rich and spoiled, raised in privilege by nannies who came and went, thoroughly ignored by their father, who was either in Asia buying factories or living at the office with his latest secretary. Hark did not intend to disparage the dead, but Mr. Phelan was what he was. Their mothers were an odd collection, but they too had endured the hell of life with Troy.

The Phelan children had not been raised in normal families. They had not been taught the lessons most children learn from their parents. Their father was a great businessman whose approval they craved but never received. Their mothers busied themselves with clubs and causes and the art of shopping. Their father's idea of providing his children with a proper start in life was simply to give each five million dollars when he or she turned twenty-one. This was much too late, and it was much too early. The money couldn't provide the wisdom, guidance, and love they needed as children. And they had clearly proved that they weren't ready for the responsibilities of new wealth.

The gifts had been disastrous, yet they had also brought maturity.

Now, with the benefit of the years, the Phelan children looked back at their mistakes. They were embarrassed by how foolish they'd been with the money. Imagine waking up one day like the prodigal son, as Rex had once done at the age of thirty-two—divorced, broke, and standing before a judge who was about to jail him for nonpayment of child support. Imagine sitting in jail for eleven days while your brother, also broke and divorced, tried to convince your mother to bail you out. Rex said he spent his time behind bars trying to recount where the money had gone.

Life has been hard for the Phelan children. Many of their wounds were self-inflicted, but many had been inevitable because of their father.

The final act of neglect by their father had been his handwritten will. They would never understand the malice of the man who'd spurned them as children, chastised them as adults, and erased them as heirs.

Hark concluded by saying, "They are Phelans, Troy's own flesh and blood, for better or for worse, and they certainly deserve a fair portion of their father's estate."

When Hark finished he sat down, and the room was silent. It was a heart-felt plea, and Nate and Josh, even Wycliff, were moved by it. It would never play to a jury because he couldn't admit in open court that his clients had no case. But for the moment and the setting, Hark's little oration was just perfect.

Nate supposedly held the money, at least that was his part of the game. He could haggle and squeeze, bluff and dicker for an hour and trim a few million from the fortune. But he was simply in no mood to do so. If Hark could shoot straight, so could he. It was all a ruse anyway.

"What's your bottom line?" he asked Hark, their eyes locking like radar.

"I'm not sure we have a bottom line. I think fifty million per heir is reasonable. I know it sounds like a lot, and it is, but look at the size of the estate. After taxes, we're still only talking about five percent of the money."

"Five percent is not very much," Nate said, then let the words hang between them. Hark was watching him, but the others were not. They were hunched over their legal pads, pens ready for the next round of calculations.

"It really isn't," Hark said.

"My client will agree to fifty million," Nate said. At the moment, his client was probably teaching Bible songs to small children under the shade of a tree by the river.

Wally Bright had just earned a fee of twenty-five million dollars, and his first impulse was to bolt across the room and kiss Nate's feet. But instead he frowned with intelligence and made careful notes, notes he couldn't read.

Josh knew it was coming, of course, his bean counters had done the math, but Wycliff did not. A settlement had just occurred, no trial would be held. He had to appear pleased. "Well, then," he said, "do we have a settlement?"

Out of nothing but sheer habit, the Phelan lawyers engaged in one last huddle. They grouped around Hark and tried to whisper, but words failed them.

"It's a deal," Hark announced, twenty-six million dollars richer.

Josh just happened to have the rough draft of a settlement agreement. They began filling in the blanks, when suddenly the Phelan lawyers remembered their clients. They asked to be excused, then ran into the hallway, cell phones appearing from every pocket. Troy Junior and Rex were waiting by a soft drink machine on the first floor. Geena and Cody were reading newspapers in an empty courtroom. Spike and Libbigail were sitting in their old pickup down the street. Mary Ross was in her Cadillac in the parking lot. Ramble was at home in the basement, door locked, headphones on, in another world.

The settlement would not be complete until signed and approved by Rachel Lane. The Phelan lawyers wanted it to be strictly confidential. Wycliff agreed to seal the court file. After an hour the agreement was complete. It was signed by each of the Phelan heirs and their lawyers. It was signed by Nate.

Only one signature was left. Nate informed them that it would take him a few days to get it.

If they only knew, he thought as he left the courthouse.

FRIDAY AFTERNOON, Nate and the Rector left St. Michaels in the lawyer's leased car. The Rector drove so he could get used to it. Nate napped in the passenger's seat. As they crossed the Bay Bridge, Nate woke up and read the final settlement agreement to Phil, who wanted all the details.

The Phelan Group Gulfstream IV was waiting at the Baltimore-Washington airport. It was sleek and shiny, big enough to haul twenty people anywhere in the world. Phil wanted a better look, so they asked the pilots for a tour. No problem. Whatever Mr. O'Riley wanted. The cabin was all leather and wood, with sofas, recliners, a conference table, several television screens. Nate would've been happy to travel like a normal person, but Josh had insisted.

He watched Phil drive away, then reboarded the plane. In nine hours he would be in Corumbá.

The trust agreement was deliberately thin, in as few words as possible, and with words as short and as plain as the drafters of such impossible instruments could invent. Josh had made them rewrite it numerous times. If Rachel had the slightest inclination to sign it, then it was imperative she be able to grasp its meaning. Nate would be there to do the explaining, but he knew she had little patience with such matters.

The assets she received under her father's last will and testament would be placed in a trust, named the Rachel Trust, for lack of anything more creative. The principal would remain intact for ten years, with only the interest and earnings available for charitable giving. After ten years, 5 percent of the principal per year, in addition to the interest and earnings, could be spent at the discretion of the trustees. The annual disbursements were to be used for a variety of charitable purposes, with emphasis on the mission work of World Tribes. But the language was so loose that the trustees could use the money for almost any benevolent cause. The original trustee was Neva Collier, at World Tribes, and she had the authority to appoint up to a dozen other trustees to help with the work. The trustees would govern themselves and report to Rachel, if she wanted.

If Rachel so desired, she would never see or touch the money. The trust would be set up with the assistance of attorneys chosen by World Tribes.

It was such a simple solution.

It would take only a signature, one quick Rachel Lane or whatever her last name was. One signature on the trust, one on the settlement agreement, and the Phelan estate could be closed in due course with no more fireworks. Nate could move on, face his troubles, take his medicine, and begin rebuilding his life. He was anxious to get started.

If she refused to sign the trust and the settlement, then Nate needed her signature on a document of renunciation. She could decline the gift, but she had to notify the court.

A renunciation would render Troy's testament worthless. It would be valid, but not operable. The assets would have no place to go, so the effect would be the same as if he'd died with no will. The law would divide the estate into six shares, one for each of his heirs.

How would she react? He wanted to think she would be delighted to see him, but he wasn't convinced of that. He remembered her waving to his boat as he left, just before the dengue hit. She was standing among her people, waving him away, saying good-bye forever. She did not want to be bothered with the things of the world.

FIFTY-ONE

VALDIR WAS WAITING at the Corumbá airport when the Gulfstream taxied to the small terminal. It was 1 A.M.; the airport was deserted, only a handful of small planes were at the far end of the tarmac. Nate glanced at them, and wondered if Milton's had ever returned from the Pantanal.

They greeted each other like old friends. Valdir was impressed with how healthy Nate looked. When they last saw each other, Nate was reeling from dengue fever and looked like a skeleton.

They drove away in Valdir's Fiat, windows down, the warm muggy air blowing in Nate's face. The pilots would follow in a taxi. The dusty streets were empty. No one moved about. Downtown, they stopped in front of the Palace Hotel. Valdir handed him a key. "Room two-twelve," he said. "I'll see you at six."

Nate slept four hours, and was waiting on the sidewalk when the morning sun peeked between the buildings. The sky was clear, and that was one of the first things he took note of. The rainy season had ended a month earlier. Cooler weather was approaching, though in Corumbá the daytime high seldom dipped below seventy-five degrees.

In his heavy satchel he had the paperwork, a camera, a new SatFone, a new cell phone, a pager, a quart of the strongest insect repellent known to modern chemistry, a small gift for Rachel, and two changes of clothes. All limbs were covered; thick khakis over the legs, long sleeves over the arms. He might get uncomfortable and sweat a little, but no insect would penetrate his armor.

At 6 A.M. sharp Valdir arrived, and they sped away to the airport. The town was slowly coming to life.

Valdir had rented the helicopter from a company in Campo Grande for a thousand dollars an hour. It could hold four passengers, came with two pilots, and had a range of three hundred miles.

Valdir and the pilots had studied Jevy's maps of the Xeco River and the tributaries that filled it. With the floods down, the Pantanal was much easier to navigate, both on water and from the air. Rivers were in their banks. Lakes were back within their shores. *Fazendas* were above water and could be found on aerial maps.

As Nate loaded his satchel into the helicopter, he tried not to think of his last flight over the Pantanal. Odds were in his favor. No way he would crash on successive flights.

Valdir preferred to stay behind, close to a phone. He did not enjoy flying, especially in a helicopter, especially over the Pantanal. The sky was calm and cloudless when they lifted off. Nate wore a seat belt, shoulder harness, and helmet. They followed the Paraguay out of Corumbá. Fishermen waved at them. Small boys knee-deep in river water stopped and stared upward. They flew over a *chalana* loaded with bananas, headed north, in their direction. Then another rickety *chalana* headed south.

Nate adjusted to the racket and vibration of the aircraft. He listened with his earphones as the pilots chatted back and forth in Portuguese. He remembered the *Santa Loura*, and his hangover the last time he'd left Corumbá headed north.

They climbed to two thousand feet and leveled off. Thirty minutes into the flight, Nate saw Fernando's trading post at the edge of the river.

He was amazed at the difference in the Pantanal from one season to the next. It was still an endless variety of swamps, lagoons, and rivers spinning wildly in all directions, but it was much greener now that the floods had receded.

They stayed above the Paraguay. The skies remained clear and blue under Nate's watchful eyes. He recalled the crash in Milton's plane on Christmas Eve. The storm had boiled over the mountains in an instant.

Dropping to a thousand feet as they circled, the pilots began pointing as if they'd found their target. Nate heard the word Xeco, and saw a tributary enter the Paraguay. He, of course, remembered nothing about the Xeco River. During his first encounter with it, he'd been curled under a tent at the bottom of the boat, wanting to die. They turned west and left the main river, twisting with the Xeco, heading for the mountains of Bolivia. The pilots became more occupied with things below. They were searching for a blue and yellow *chalana*.

On the ground, Jevy heard the distant thumping of the chopper. He quickly lit an orange flare and sent it flying. Welly did the same. The flares burned bright and left a trail of blue and silver smoke. Within minutes, the chopper came into view. It circled slowly.

Jevy and Welly had used machetes to cut a clearing in a patch of dense shrub, fifty yards from the edge of the river. The ground had been under water just a month earlier. The chopper rocked and swayed and slowly lowered itself to the ground.

After the blades stopped, Nate jumped out and hugged his old pals. He hadn't seen them in more than two months, and the fact that he was even there was a surprise to all three.

Time was precious. Nate feared storms, darkness, floods, and mosquitoes, and he wanted to move as quickly as possible. They walked to the *chalana* at the river. Next to it was a long, clean johnboat, which appeared to be waiting for its maiden voyage. Attached to it was a brand-new outboard, all compliments of the Phelan estate. Nate and Jevy quickly loaded themselves into it, said good-bye to Welly and the pilots, and sped off.

The settlements were two hours away, Jevy explained, yelling over the motor. He and Welly had arrived yesterday afternoon with the *chalana*. The river had become too small even for it, so they had docked it near land flat enough to handle the helicopter. Then they had ventured on with the johnboat, eventually going near the first settlement. He had recognized the approach, but turned around before the Indians heard them.

Two hours, maybe three. Nate hoped it wouldn't be five. He would not, under any circumstances, sleep on the ground, or in a tent, or a hammock. No skin would be exposed to the dangers of the jungle. The horrors of dengue were too fresh.

If they were unable to find Rachel, then he would return to Corumbá in the chopper, have a nice dinner with Valdir, sleep in a bed, then try again tomorrow. The estate could buy the damned helicopter if necessary.

But Jevy seemed confident, which was not unusual. They slashed through the water, the bow bouncing as the powerful motor sped them along. How nice to have an outboard that whined in one long, efficient, uninterrupted roar. They were invincible.

Nate was mesmerized once again with the Pantanal; the alligators thrashing in the shallow waters as they flew by, the birds dipping low over the river, the magnificent isolation of the place. They were in too deep to see *fazendas*. They were searching for people who'd been there for centuries.

Twenty-four hours earlier he'd been sitting on the porch of the cottage, under a quilt, sipping coffee, watching the boats drift into the bay, waiting for Father Phil to call and say he was headed for the basement. It took an hour in the boat to fully adjust to where he was.

The river did not look familiar. The last time they had found the Ipicas they were very lost, and scared, wet, hungry, and relying on the guidance of a young fisherman. The waters were up, the landmarks hidden from them.

Nate watched the sky as if he expected bombs to fall. The first sign of a dark cloud, and he would bolt.

Then a bend in the river looked vaguely familiar, maybe they were close. Would she greet him with a smile, and a hug, and want to sit in the shade and chat in English? Any chance she'd missed him, or even thought about him? Had she received the letters? It was mid-March, her packages were supposed to be there. Did she have her new boat by now, and all the new medicines?

Or would she run? Would she huddle with the chief and ask him to protect her, to get rid of the American for the last time? Would Nate even get the chance to see her?

He would be firm, much tougher than last time. It wasn't his fault Troy had made such a ridiculous will, nor could he help the fact that she was his illegitimate daughter. She couldn't change things either, and it was not asking too much for a little cooperation. Either agree to the trust, or sign the renunciation. He would not leave without her signature.

She could turn her back on the world, but she would always be the daughter of Troy Phelan. That in itself required some small measure of cooperation. Nate practiced his arguments out loud. Jevy couldn't hear him.

He would tell her about her siblings. He would paint a dreadful picture of what would happen if they received the entire fortune. He would list the worthwhile causes she could advance if she simply signed the trust. He practiced and practiced.

The trees on both sides grew thicker and leaned over the river where they touched. Nate recognized the tunnel. "Up there," Jevy said, pointing ahead to the right, to the spot where they had first seen the children swimming in the river. He throttled down, and they eased by the first settlement without seeing a single Indian. When the huts were out of sight, the river forked and the streams became smaller.

It was familiar territory. They zigzagged deeper into the woods, the river looping almost in circles, the mountains occasionally visible through clearings. At the second settlement, they stopped near the large tree where they'd slept the first night, back in January. They stepped ashore in the same spot where Rachel had stood when she'd waved good-bye, just as the dengue was calling. The bench was there, its cane poles lashed tightly together.

Nate was watching the village while Jevy was tying off the boat. A young Indian ran along the trail toward them. Their outboard had been heard.

He spoke no Portuguese, but through grunts and hand signals conveyed the message that they were to stay there, by the river, until further orders. If he recognized them, he didn't show it. He appeared scared.

And so they took their places on the bench and waited. It was almost 11 A.M. There was a lot to talk about. Jevy'd been busy on the rivers, running *chalanas* with goods and supplies into the Pantanal. He occasionally captained a tourist boat, where the money was better.

They talked about Nate's last visit, how they'd raced in from the Pantanal with Fernando's borrowed motor, the horrors of the hospital, their efforts to find Rachel in Corumbá.

"I tell you," Jevy said, "I have listened much on the river, and the lady did not come. She was not in the hospital. You were dreaming, my friend."

Nate wasn't about to argue. He wasn't sure himself.

The man who owned the *Santa Loura* had been slandering Jevy around town. It sank on his watch, but everyone knew the storm did it. The man was a fool anyway.

As Nate expected, the conversation soon swung around to Jevy's future in the States. Jevy had applied for a visa, but needed a sponsor and a job. Nate bobbed and weaved, and slid enough punches to keep his friend confused. He couldn't muster the courage to tell him that he too would soon be looking for work.

"I'll see what I can do," he said.

Jevy had a cousin in Colorado who was also looking for a job.

A mosquito circled Nate's hand. His first impulse was to crush it with a violent slap, but instead he watched to gauge the effectiveness of his super-repellent. When it tired of surveying its target, it made a sudden nosedive toward the back of his right hand. But two inches away, it suddenly stopped, pulled away, and vanished. Nate smiled. His ears, neck, and face were lathered with the oil.

The second attack of dengue usually causes hemorrhaging. It's much worse than the first, and often fatal. Nate O'Riley would not be a victim.

They faced the village as they talked, and Nate watched every move. He expected to see Rachel stride elegantly between the huts and along the path to greet them. By now, she knew the white man was back.

But did she know it was Nate? What if the Ipica had not recognized them, and Rachel was terrified that someone else had found her?

Then they saw the chief slowly walking toward them. He carried a long ceremonial spear and was followed by an Ipica Nate recognized. They stopped at the edge of the trail, a good fifty feet from the bench. They were not smiling; in fact, the chief looked particularly unpleasant. In Portuguese, he asked, "What do you want?"

"Tell him we want to see the missionary," Nate said, and Jevy translated it.

"Why?" came the reply.

Jevy explained that the American had traveled a great distance to be there, and that it was very important to see the woman. The chief again asked, "Why?"

Because they have things to discuss, big things that neither Jevy nor the chief would understand. It was very important or else the American wouldn't be there.

Nate remembered the chief as a loud character with a quick smile, a big laugh, and a trigger temper. Now his face had little expression. From fifty feet his eyes looked hard. He had once insisted they sit by his fire and share his breakfast. Now he stood as far away as possible. Something was wrong. Something had changed.

He told them to wait, then left again, slowly making his way back to the village. Half an hour passed. By now Rachel knew who they were, the chief would have told her. And she was not coming to meet them.

A cloud passed in front of the sun, and Nate watched it closely. It was puffy and white, not the least bit threatening, but it scared him nonetheless. Any thunder in the distance, and he'd be ready to move. They ate some wafers and cheese while sitting in the boat.

The chief whistled for them and interrupted their snack. He was alone, coming from the village. They met halfway, and followed him for a hundred feet, then changed directions and moved behind the huts on another trail. Nate could see the common area of the village. It was deserted, not a single Ipica wandering about. No children playing. No young ladies raking the dirt around the dwellings. No women cooking and cleaning. Not a sound. The only movement was the drifting smoke of their fires.

Then he saw faces in the windows, little heads peeking through doors. They were being watched. The chief kept them away from the huts as if they were carrying diseases. He turned onto another trail, one that led through the woods for a few moments. When they emerged into a clearing, they were across from Rachel's hut.

There was no sign of her. The chief led them past the front door, and to the side, where, under the thick shade trees, they saw the graves.

FIFTY-TWO

THE MATCHING white crosses were made of wood and had been carefully cut and polished by the Indians, then lashed together with string. They were small, less than a foot tall, and stuck into the fresh dirt at the far end of both graves. There was no writing on them, nothing to indicate who had died, or when.

It was dark under the trees. Nate put his satchel on the ground between the graves, and sat on it. The chief began talking softly and quickly.

"The woman is on the left. Lako is on the right. They died on the same day, about two weeks ago," Jevy translated. More words from the chief, then, "Malaria has killed ten people since we left," Jevy said.

The chief delivered a long narrative without stopping for any translating. Nate heard the words, yet heard nothing. He looked at the mound of dirt to the left, a neat pile of black soil laid in a perfect little rectangle, carefully bordered by shaved limbs four inches round. Buried there was Rachel Lane, the bravest person he'd ever known because she had absolutely no fear of death. She welcomed it. She was at peace, her soul finally with the Lord, her body forever lying among the people she loved.

And Lako was with her, his heavenly body cured of defects and afflictions.

The shock came and went. Her death was tragic, but then it wasn't. She wasn't a young mother and wife who left a family behind. She didn't have a wide circle of friends who'd rush to mourn her passing. Only a handful of people in her native land would ever know she was gone. She was an oddity among the people who'd buried her.

He knew her well enough to know she wouldn't want anyone grieving. She wouldn't approve of tears, and Nate had none to give her. For a few moments he stared at her grave in disbelief, but reality soon set in. This was not an old friend with whom he'd shared many moments. He'd barely known her. His motives in finding her had been purely selfish. He had invaded her privacy, and she had asked him not to return.

But his heart ached anyway. He'd thought about her every day since he'd left the Pantanal. He'd dreamed of her, felt her touch, heard her voice, remembered her wisdom. She had taught him to pray, and given him hope. She was the first person in decades to see anything good in him.

He had never met anyone like Rachel Lane, and he missed her greatly.

The chief was quiet. "He says we can't stay very long," Jevy said.

"Why not?" Nate asked, still staring at her grave.

"The spirits are blaming us for the malaria. It arrived when we came the first time. They are not happy to see us."

"Tell him his spirits are a bunch of clowns."

"He has something to show you."

Slowly, Nate stood and faced the chief. They walked through the door of her hut, bending at the knees to get through. The floor was dirt. There were two rooms. The front room had furniture too primitive to believe, a chair made of cane pole and lashings, a sofa with stumps for legs and straw for cushions. The back room was a bedroom and a kitchen. She slept in a hammock like the Indians. Under the hammock, on a small table, was a plastic box that once held medical supplies. The chief pointed to the box and began speaking.

"There are things in there for you to see," Jevy translated.

"For me?"

"Yes. She knew she was dying. She asked the chief to guard her hut. If an American came, then show him the box."

Nate was afraid to touch it. The chief picked it up and gave it to him. He backed out of the room and sat on the sofa. The chief and Jevy stepped outside.

His letters never made it, at least they were not in the box. There was a Brazilian identification badge, one required of every non-Indian in the country. There were three letters from World Tribes. Nate didn't read them because at the bottom of the box he saw her will.

It was in a white, legal-sized envelope and had a Brazilian name engraved for the return address. On it, she had neatly printed the words: Last Testament of Rachel Lane Porter.

Nate stared at it in disbelief. His hands shook as he carefully opened it. Folded inside were two sheets of white letter-sized paper, stapled together. On the first sheet, in large letters across the top she had printed, again, Last Testament of Rachel Lane Porter.

It read:

I, Rachel Lane Porter, child of God, resident of His world, citizen of the United States, and being of sound mind, do hereby make this as my last testament.

1. I have no prior testaments to revoke. This is my first and last. Every word is written by my hand. This is intended to be a holographic will.

2. I have in my possession a copy of the last testament of my father, Troy Phelan, dated December 9, 1996, in which he

gives me the bulk of his estate. I am attempting to pattern this will after his.

3. I do not reject or decline that portion of his estate due me. Nor do I wish to receive it. Whatever his gift is to me, I want it placed in a trust.

4. The earnings from the trust are to be used for the following purposes: a) to continue the work of World Tribes missionaries around the world, b) to spread the Gospel of Christ, c) to protect the rights of indigenous peoples in Brazil and South America, d) to feed the hungry, heal the sick, shelter the homeless, and save the children.

5. I appoint my friend Nate O'Riley to manage the trust, and I grant him broad discretionary powers in its administration. I also appoint him as executor of this testament.

Signed, the sixth day of January 1997, at Corumbá, Brazil.

RACHEL LANE PORTER

He read it again, and again. The second sheet was typed and in Portuguese. It would have to wait for a moment.

He studied the dirt between his feet. The air was sticky and perfectly still. The world was silent, not a sound from the village. The Ipicas were still hiding from the white man and his plagues.

Do you sweep dirt? To make it neat and clean? What happens when it rains and the straw roof leaks? Does it puddle and turn to mud? On the wall facing him were handmade shelves filled with books—Bibles, devotionals, studies in theology. The shelves were slightly uneven, tilting an inch or two to the right.

This was her home for eleven years.

He read it again. January 6 was the day he walked out of the hospital in Corumbá. She wasn't a dream. She'd touched him and told him he wouldn't die. Then she had written her will.

The straw rustled under him as he moved. He was in a trance when Jevy poked his head through the door and said, "The chief wants us to leave."

"Read this," Nate said, handing him the two sheets of paper with the second one on top. Jevy stepped forward to catch the light from the door. He read slowly, then said, "Two people here. The first is a lawyer, who says that he saw Rachel Lane Porter sign her testament in his office, in Corumbá. She was mentally okay. And she knew what she was doing. His signature is officially marked by a, what do you say—"

"A notary."

"Yes, a notary. The second, here on the bottom, is the lawyer's secretary, who, it looks like, says the same things. And the notary certifies her signature too. What does this mean?"

"I'll explain later."

They stepped into the sunlight. The chief had his arms folded over his chest—his patience was almost gone. Nate removed his camera from the satchel and began taking pictures of the hut and the graves. He made Jevy hold her will while squatting by her grave. Then Nate held it as Jevy took photos. The chief would not agree to have his picture taken with Nate. He kept as much distance as possible. He grunted, and Jevy was afraid he might erupt.

They found the trail and headed for the woods, again staying away from the village. As the trees grew thicker, Nate stopped and turned for one last look at her hut. He wanted to take it with him, to lift it somehow and transport it to the States, to preserve it as a monument so that the millions of people she would touch could have a place to visit and say thanks. And her grave too. She deserved a shrine.

That's the last thing she would want. Jevy and the chief were out of sight, so Nate hurried ahead.

They made it to the river without infecting anyone. The chief grunted something at Jevy as they got in the boat. "He says for us not to come back," Jevy said.

"Tell him he has nothing to worry about."

Jevy said nothing, but instead started the engine and backed away from the bank.

The chief was already walking away, toward his village. Nate wondered if he missed Rachel. She'd been there for eleven years. She seemed to have considerable influence over him, but she had not been able to convert him. Did he mourn her passing, or was he relieved that his gods and his spirits now had free rein? What would happen to the Ipicas who had become Christians, now that she was gone?

He remembered the *shalyuns*, the witch doctors in the villages who hounded Rachel. They were celebrating her death. And assailing her converts. She had fought a good fight, now she was resting in peace.

Jevy stopped the motor and guided the boat with a paddle. The current was slow, the water smooth. Nate carefully opened the SatFone and arranged it on a bench. The sky was clear, the signal strong, and within two minutes he had Josh's secretary scurrying to find her boss.

"Tell me she signed that damned trust, Nate," were his first words. He was yelling into the phone.

"You don't have to yell, Josh. I can hear you."

"Sorry. Tell me she signed it."

"She signed a trust, but not ours. She's dead, Josh."

"No!"

"Yes. She died two weeks ago. Malaria. She left a holographic will, just like her father."

"Do you have it!?"

"Yes. It's safe. Everything goes into a trust. I'm the trustee and executor."

"Is it valid?"

"I think so. It's written entirely in her hand, signed, dated, witnessed by a lawyer in Corumbá and his secretary."

"Sounds valid to me."

"What happens now?" Nate asked. He could see Josh standing behind his desk, eyes closed in concentration, one hand holding the phone, the other patting his hair. He could almost hear him plotting over the phone.

"Nothing happens. His will is valid. Its bequests are carried out."

"But she's dead."

"His estate is transferred to hers. Happens all the time in car wrecks when one spouse dies one day, then the other dies the next. The bequests go from estate to estate."

"What about the other heirs?"

"The settlement stands. They get their money, or what's left of it after the lawyers take their cuts. The heirs are the happiest people on the face of the earth, with the possible exception of their lawyers. There's nothing for them to attack. You have two valid wills. Looks like you've just become a career trustee."

"I have broad discretionary powers."

"You have a lot more than that. Read it to me."

Nate found it deep in his satchel, and read it, very slowly, word for word.

"Hurry home," Josh said.

Jevy absorbed every word too, though he appeared to be watching the river. When Nate hung up and put the phone away, Jevy asked, "The money is yours?"

"No. The money goes into a trust."

"What is a trust?"

"Think of it as a big bank account. It sits in the bank, protected, earning interest. The trustee decides where the interest goes."

Jevy still wasn't convinced. He had many questions, and Nate sensed his confusion. It was not the time for a primer on the Anglo version of wills, estates, and trusts.

"Let's go," Nate said.

The motor started again, and they flew across the water, roaring around curves, a wide wake spraying behind them.

THEY FOUND the *chalana* late in the afternoon. Welly was fishing. The pilots were playing cards on the back of the boat. Nate called Josh again, and told him to retrieve the jet from Corumbá. He wouldn't be needing it. He would take his time coming home.

Josh objected, but that was all he could do. The Phelan mess had been settled. There was no real rush.

Nate told the pilots to contact Valdir when they returned, then sent them on their way.

The crew of the *chalana* watched the chopper disappear like an insect, then cast off. Jevy was at the wheel. Welly sat below, at the front of the boat, his feet dangling inches above the water. Nate found a bunk and tried to nap. But the diesel was next door. Its steady knock prevented sleep.

The vessel was a third the size of the *Santa Loura*, even the bunks were shorter. Nate lay on his side and watched the riverbanks go by.

Somehow she'd known he wasn't a drunk anymore, that his addictions were gone, that the demons who'd controlled his life had been forever locked away. She had seen something good in him. Somehow she knew he was searching. She'd found his calling for him. God told her.

Jevy woke him after dark. "We have a moon," he said. They sat on the front of the boat, Welly at the wheel just behind them, following the light of a full moon as the Xeco snaked its way toward the Paraguay.

"The boat is slow," Jevy said. "Two days to Corumbá."

Nate smiled. He didn't care if it took a month.

AUTHOR'S NOTE

The Pantanal region of Brazil, in the states of Mato Grosso and Mato Grosso do Sul, is a land of great natural beauty and a fascinating place to visit. I hope I haven't portrayed it as one big swamp, fraught with danger. It is not. It's an ecological gem that attracts many tourists, most of whom survive. I've been there twice, and look forward to going back.

Carl King, my friend and a Baptist missionary in Campo Grande, took me deep into the Pantanal. I'm not sure how much of his information was accurate, but we had a wonderful time for four days counting alligators, photographing wildlife, looking for anacondas, eating black beans and rice, telling stories, all from a boat that somehow grew smaller. Many thanks to Carl for the adventure.

Thanks also to Rick Carter, Gene McDade, Penny Pynkala, Jonathan Hamilton, Fernando Catta-Preta, Bruce Sanford, Marc Smirnoff, and Estelle Laurence. And thanks, as always, to David Gernert for poring over the manuscript and making the book better.